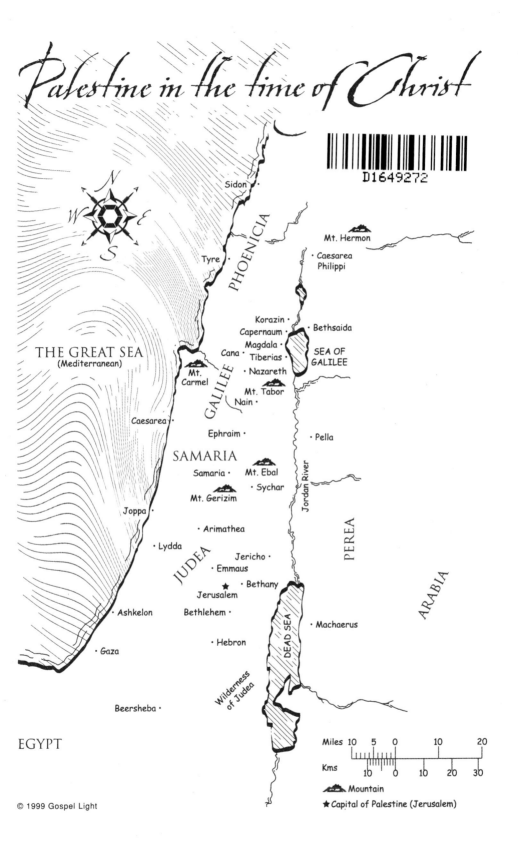

Palestine in the time of Christ

D1649272

N W E S

Sidon

Mt. Hermon

Tyre

PHOENICIA

· Caesarea Philippi

THE GREAT SEA
(Mediterranean)

Korazin ·
Capernaum ·
Magdala ·
Cana · Tiberias ·
· Nazareth

· Bethsaida

SEA OF GALILEE

Mt. Carmel

GALILEE

Mt. Tabor
Nain ·

Caesarea ·

Ephraim ·

· Pella

SAMARIA

Samaria ·   Mt. Ebal
· Sychar
Mt. Gerizim

Jordan River

PEREA

Joppa ·

· Arimathea

· Lydda

JUDEA

Jericho ·
· Emmaus
★ · Bethany
Jerusalem

Bethlehem ·

ARABIA

· Ashkelon

· Hebron

DEAD SEA

· Machaerus

· Gaza

Wilderness of Judea

Beersheba ·

EGYPT

Miles 10 5 0   10   20

Kms   10   0   10   20   30

🔺 Mountain

★ Capital of Palestine (Jerusalem)

Dr. Elmer Towns's vivid description of the Gospel accounts makes you feel like you are actually there alongside the Lord Jesus Himself. Highly recommended.

BILL BRIGHT
FOUNDER AND PRESIDENT, CAMPUS CRUSADE FOR CHRIST INTERNATIONAL
ORLANDO, FLORIDA

We believe this historical novel on the life of Jesus has the potential of leading many people to Him. The author's easy-to-read style makes this book ideal as a family devotional. We heartily endorse *The Son*.

DAVID AND GRACE CHO
SENIOR PASTORS, YOIDO FULL GOSPEL CHURCH
SEOUL, KOREA

Every married couple has a responsibility to communicate the story of the Savior to their kids and grandkids. *The Son* is a warm, human, "this-is-real" way to share this rich treasure with your family.

JACK AND ANNA HAYFORD
SENIOR PASTORS, THE CHURCH ON THE WAY
VAN NUYS, CALIFORNIA

The Son is an approach to the gospel that carries me and my wife, Anne, back to the days when we first shared the greatest story ever told with our daughter Jennifer in the early days of our ministry. How precious are these immortal stories of our Lord as He dwelt among humankind! Elmer Towns's narrative is easy to read and faithful to the details of Scripture. Excellent family reading!

D. JAMES KENNEDY

SENIOR MINISTER, CORAL RIDGE PRESBYTERIAN CHURCH
FORT LAUDERDALE, FLORIDA

A unique and fascinating presentation of the life of our Lord by a man who can always be counted on to be faithful to the Scriptures, *The Son* makes for enjoyable reading of the greatest story ever told!

TIM LA HAYE

COAUTHOR, *LEFT BEHIND* AND *SOUL HARVEST*
RANCHO MIRAGE, CALIFORNIA

The life and times of the most important figure in all of history have been beautifully rendered in this compelling masterwork. Elmer Towns has realized the life of Christ as a grand adventure that amuses and entertains even as it uplifts and inspires. *The Son* is a book for the ages.

ROBERT H. SCHULLER

FOUNDING PASTOR, CRYSTAL CATHEDRAL MINISTRIES
GARDEN GROVE, CALIFORNIA

THE SON

HE WAS SENT TO SAVE THE WORLD

The SON

a novel

E. L. TOWNS

Regal

A Division of Gospel Light
Ventura, California, U.S.A.

Published by Regal Books
A Division of Gospel Light
Ventura, California, U.S.A.
Printed in U.S.A.

Regal Books is a ministry of Gospel Light, an evangelical Christian publisher dedicated to serving the local church. We believe God's vision for Gospel Light is to provide church leaders with biblical, user-friendly materials that will help them evangelize, disciple and minister to children, youth and families.

It is our prayer that this Regal book will help you discover biblical truth for your own life and help you meet the needs of others. May God richly bless you.

For a free catalog of resources from Regal Books and Gospel Light please call your Christian supplier, or contact us at 1-800-4-GOSPEL.

Cover Design by Kevin Keller
Interior Design by Robert Williams
Edited by David Webb

LIBRARY OF CONGRESS CATALOGING-IN-PUBLICATION DATA
Towns, Elmer L.
    The Son: stories / told by Elmer L. Towns.
        p.   cm.
    ISBN 0-8307-2428-1 (trade)
    1. Jesus Christ—Fiction. 2. Bible. N.T.—History of Biblical events—Fiction.
    3. Christian fiction, American. I. Title.
    PS3570.09334J47   1999   99-31673
    813'.54—dc21   CIP

1 2 3 4 5 6 7 8 9 10 11 12 13 14 15 / 09 07 06 05 04 03 02 01 00 99

Rights for publishing this book in other languages are contracted by Gospel Literature International (GLINT). GLINT also provides technical help for the adaptation, translation and publishing of Bible study resources and books in scores of languages worldwide. For further information, write to GLINT at P.O. Box 4060, Ontario, CA 91761-1003, U.S.A. You may also send E-mail to Glintint@aol.com, or visit their web site at www.glint.org.

CONTENTS

In the beginning was the Word.

AND THE WORD WAS WITH GOD, AND THE WORD
WAS GOD. ALL THINGS WERE MADE THROUGH
HIM, AND WITHOUT HIM NOTHING WAS MADE
THAT WAS MADE. IN HIM WAS LIFE, AND THE LIFE
WAS THE LIGHT OF MEN.

AND THE WORD BECAME FLESH AND DWELT
AMONG US, AND WE BEHELD HIS GLORY,
THE GLORY AS OF THE ONLY BEGOTTEN OF THE
FATHER, FULL OF GRACE AND TRUTH.

HE WAS IN THE WORLD, AND THE WORLD WAS
MADE THROUGH HIM, BUT THE WORLD DID NOT
KNOW HIM. HE CAME TO HIS OWN, AND HIS OWN
DID NOT RECEIVE HIM.

chapter one

THE FIRST WORD FROM HEAVEN IN FOUR HUNDRED YEARS

LUKE 1:5-22

The old man looked wistfully to the distant red mountains. There was a glow in his tired eyes, reflecting the setting sun. The tight, leathery skin stretched over his frail bones told that he was past sixty years of age. He looked for Messiah to come each day—the one who would deliver his people from the oppression of Rome. But the Messiah had not come, and things were getting worse, rather than better.

"Come inside to eat." His elderly wife stood at the door of their home in Abia, a community that was home to the Temple priests who served in nearby Jerusalem.

"I'm not hungry . . . ." He let the words trail off.

"Not hungry?" the wife echoed. "Is it because of joy . . . or sadness?"

Zechariah didn't answer; he just smiled.

Tomorrow would be Zechariah's last day of Temple duty. He was retiring and it was with regret that he would no longer serve in the Temple. Tomorrow, when he entered the Holy Room to burn the incense and offer the evening prayers, it would be his first—and last—time to intercede for his nation. Out of ten thousand priests, he had finally been chosen to pray for all Israel.

Tomorrow Zechariah would have the honor that all priests sought. Priestly duties were assigned by lottery, and a priest could have the privilege of burning incense in the Holy Place only once in his lifetime—sometimes never. If the selection had not been made for tomorrow, Zechariah would have ended his service . . . unfulfilled.

"Eat so you'll be strong," his wife Elizabeth scolded him. "And don't frown," she added. "You'll do fine."

Zechariah was not worried about praying. He planned to just open his heart to God. His prayer would be spontaneous; he would not read a prayer.

"I'm concerned about the younger priests," he told his wife. "They do not love people, they love power. They love their finely embroidered robes . . . ." Again Zechariah let his words trail into nothing. He had complained to his wife many times that the young priests did not bring the same dedication to the Temple that he had as a young man some thirty years earlier.

"The young priests don't look for Messiah," Zechariah echoed a criticism he'd pronounced often. "They have lost their faith."

"And why not?" Elizabeth believed in God. She had not lost her faith, but she looked at things more realistically than her husband. After all, it had been four hundred years since God's prophets had spoken, centuries since a legitimate miracle from God. "What is there to have faith in?" she demanded.

"Hush!" Zechariah protested, as any stern Jewish husband would rebuke a doubting wife.

But Elizabeth went on. "These phony zealots do phony miracles."

"The day of miracles has passed," Zechariah told his wife. "We must have faith in the Word of God—not look for miracles."

"I do. I *do*," Elizabeth declared. "But where *is* God? We are ruled by cruel Romans, not a Son of David. We pay taxes to Caesar, not to Jehovah!"

"Hush."

"If the Almighty One loves his people," Elizabeth said, "why doesn't he send Messiah to drive the Romans into the sea?"

"Let's eat."

Excitement swept Zechariah and Elizabeth along the path on their short walk to Jerusalem the next day. Friends and family accompanied them, making a special journey to honor Zechariah because it was his last day in the priesthood . . . and he was chosen to say the evening prayers. They broke out into a psalm when they saw Jerusalem,

"Open to me the gates of righteousness;
    I will go into them,
and I will praise the Lord:
    This gate of the Lord,
into which the righteous shall enter . . ."

Zechariah tenderly put his arm around Elizabeth to help her up a step on the steep path. "I am sorry we have no son," he said.

She knew he continually fretted because they had no children. She consoled him. "You've been more to me than children."

"Yes . . . ," Zechariah mused on his wife's words. "But if I had a son, I'd have taught him to be a good priest. I'd make sure he was sincere. My son would have faith in God." He lowered his voice; he didn't want family members to hear his criticism. "My son wouldn't be corrupt like these young priests."

In front of them was the Temple. They entered the Gate Beautiful, and Zechariah reached out to rub the gold on the gate one last time in his official role as a priest. Inside he glimpsed the twelve golden stairs and on a platform the Levitical choir, singing as angels:

"I was glad when they said unto me,
   Let us go into the house of the Lord."

Behind the choir were twelve more golden stairs. Priests in white robes— the robes they wore when sacrificing the offerings—were going about their duties. Clusters of people milled about, beginning to fill the large court-yards of the Temple.

Zechariah looked up to the pinnacle, where a white-robed priest waited with trumpet in hand. When the sun descended to the perfect spot in the sky—halfway between full noon and the horizon—at that moment the trum-pet would be sounded, and everyone in the Temple would gather to the mas-sive stairs for the evening prayers. Zechariah would then begin his climb up the golden stairs. It was the moment for which he was born.

The priest in the pinnacle measured the falling shadow on the sundial, and when it was the tenth hour, or four o'clock in the afternoon, he put the silver trumpet to his lips and sounded the call for prayers. When the last note finished, the Levitical choir began to sing:

"One thing have I desired of the Lord,
   That will I seek after;
That I may dwell in the house of the Lord

All the days of my life.
To behold the beauty of the Lord,
    And to enquire in His Temple."

Old Zechariah began to climb the long, golden stairs toward the Holy Room. Slowly he ascended, inwardly singing with the choir.

A little boy pointed at Zechariah. "Mommy, that old man walks funny." Everyone in the Temple courtyard watched as he labored painfully with each step. An old archpriest held his breath.

"Mommy, where's the old man going?" the squeaky voice of the boy was heard by all in the crowd. They, too, were holding their breath.

Some worshipers turned to glare at the little boy, others smiled. The mother put a finger to her mouth, then bent to whisper in her son's ear, "Sh-h-h," the embarrassed mother tried to quiet her son. Zechariah had made it to the top of the stairs. "He's going into the Holy Room to pray for us."

Zechariah was stoop-shouldered and thin, the intercessory robe too large for his frame. Elizabeth was afraid he might stumble on the drooping folds. The noise of his sandals dragging on the stone floor was intensified by the silence of the crowd. The prayer shawl draped over his head hid his shaggy, gray hair.

Silently, supportive eyes watched him disappear between the tall, heavy curtains. Zechariah was now in the presence of God.

Zechariah stood before the Lord.

He bowed his head in deep gratitude for the opportunity to finally enter the Holy Room. *I'm going to pray for myself, before I pray for Israel,* he thought.

Zechariah lifted his aged hands high into the air. Trembling hands, wrinkled hands. Then with a loud voice he prayed from the top of his head and from the bottom of his heart.

"Lord . . . give me a son."

He didn't mean to ask for a child—at least not first. He just blurted out the words without thinking. It was a prayer he had uttered many times, ever since he had become a priest. He yearned for a son to carry on the family tradition. When Zechariah was young he believed God would answer him, but now he was old—too old to have children. Elizabeth, his wife, was barren. No son had been born, and now it was too late. He had often thought, *Maybe if I had prayed for a son in the Holy Room, just maybe . . . .*

"Give me a son," he again said aloud to the Lord.

Zechariah shivered suddenly. Not a shiver of age, not a shiver from a cold breeze. It was a kind of shiver he had never before experienced. Zechariah sensed that someone was in the room with him.

No one must enter the Holy Room! he reasoned to himself. He shuffled his feet to turn around. There before him was a beautiful young man, standing across the room next to an incense altar. Something about the young man frightened Zechariah.

"Fear not," the young man said.

"Who are you?" Zechariah's voice quavered. "What are you doing here?"

"I am Gabriel."

Not knowing what to say to that, the elderly priest kept quiet. He recognized the name Gabriel as belonging to an angel of the Lord, but he wasn't sure who this fellow was.

"I am sent from God with a message," the young man paused. "God wants you to know your prayers have been heard."

Zechariah didn't know what to think. The young man had startled him. The message startled him more.

"Your wife will become pregnant and deliver a son."

"No!" the old priest protested. "My wife and I are too old for children."

Zechariah accepted that Gabriel was from God, that he was God's messenger. True, he had never seen an angel, but Zechariah knew this encounter was supernatural, if only because it was so terrifying. God wanted to tell him something in this holy place. He knew now why God had chosen him on the last day of his priesthood to appear before him.

"Your son will be special," Gabriel continued. "He will announce the Deliverer of Israel."

"The Messiah is coming?" Zechariah's eyes lit up as he whispered reverently the name *Messiah*.

"Your son will not be Messiah," the angel explained, "but your son will prepare the people for his coming. Your son will be great in the sight of the Lord. When he preaches, many will turn away from unrighteousness and return to God.

"Your son will never drink wine, he will not cut his hair. He will be a Nazirite—one who is separated to the Lord from birth."

"But I'm too old," Zechariah protested again. "Miracles don't happen today."

Gabriel paid no attention to Zechariah's denials.

"Your son will have the name John," the angel instructed.

"How can I believe in miracles?" the feeble old priest shook his head in unbelief.

"I am Gabriel," the angel replied. "I stand in the presence of God. He has heard your prayers and sent me to deliver this good news to you."

"Can you prove this?" Zechariah sputtered. "How will I know?"

"You, Zechariah, will be unable to speak until the child is born," Gabriel pronounced. "Because you did not believe the words of God, your speech will be taken from you." Gabriel pointed with an outstretched finger to Zechariah's mouth, and it happened.

"Ugh . . . ugh . . . ugh . . . ." Nothing came out of Zechariah's mouth, only gruntings and gurglings. Bowing his head, tears welled in Zechariah's eyes. Now he believed God, but it was too late. Zechariah didn't want to talk to Gabriel any longer. He wanted to tell God he was sorry. As he bowed his head in prayer, tears squeezed their way out of his tightly shut eyes.

Forgive me . . . forgive me, Zechariah prayed silently, unable to form the words. No sound was heard in the Holy Room, but God heard his heart. *Forgive me.*

Then the old man crumpled to the cold stone floor.

"Maybe he died in there," the little boy blurted out to his mother. "Why doesn't he come out?"

The mother smiled and patted her son on the head. She glanced up at the late afternoon sun setting in the west. The mountain haze had turned the sun into a pale red wafer, telling her the priest had been in the Holy Place much longer than was usual.

He is taking a long time, she thought.

"Ahh, he doesn't know what to do," a young priest impatiently whispered to his friend. "The old man has forgotten what to pray."

The crowd of worshipers was becoming restless. The priests knew they couldn't enter the Holy Room, but they had to do something. The sun was setting, and the blessing hadn't been given.

"You can't leave until you receive the benediction," a priest spoke to quiet the crowd. "Wait. Be patient . . . he will come out soon."

The curtains rippled. The crowd could see that the old priest was feeling about, looking for the break between the two large curtains so he could exit.

"He's finally coming out!" the critical young priest raised his voice.

Zechariah stepped out onto the top of the stairs, blinking his eyes at the brightness of the setting sun. Shielding his eyes with the back of his hand, he stumbled down the stairs . . . slowly . . . unsteadily. The crowd could tell something had happened in the Holy Room.

"Give the benediction!" the younger cleric called in a loud, agitated voice, revealing his impatience.

"Give the benediction," another demanded.

Zechariah shook his head from side to side and pointed to his mouth. The people didn't understand.

"Give the benediction!" the crowd repeated.

"Ugh . . . ugh . . . ugh . . . ." were the only sounds he could make.

The aged archpriest, sensing trouble, stepped beside his old friend, steadying Zechariah with one hand. Then, lifting his other hand, he said to the people, "The Lord bless you and keep you. The Lord make His face to shine upon you. The Lord lift up His countenance upon you and give you peace."

So it was, as soon as the days of his service were completed, [Zechariah] departed to his own house. Now after those days his wife Elizabeth conceived.

LUKE 1 : 2 3 , 2 4

chapter two

DREAMING GREAT DREAMS IN AN UNLIKELY TOWN

LUKE 1:26-38

Mary was small and petite, a pretty young woman nearly always adorned with a smile. But today she wore a worried look as she walked toward the synagogue at the center of Nazareth. A warm spring had come to the hill country of Galilee, and the sun was grinning, but Mary was concerned. Joseph was posting banns for their marriage this morning.

"Suppose the elders say no?" Mary asked her mother.

"They will approve," she assured her anxious daughter. Mary's mother had talked to the wives of the elders to make sure there would be no such surprises.

A black lock of hair fell from the kerchief around Mary's head and curled about her perpetually pink cheeks. Now in her mid-teens, Mary was no longer a child. She was a woman with youthful charm. Her roseate lips were as alluring as her appealing grin. When she dropped her bashful eyes, a smile blushed her cheeks.

Mary and her mother climbed the outside stairs to the synagogue loft where the women and children sat. They positioned themselves where they could see the elders' response when Joseph approached them. Mary nervously leaned forward and sat with one foot under her to get just a little higher. She didn't want to miss anything.

"They *must* give approval to Joseph," Mary whispered to her mother. "I have prayed they'll say yes."

Her mother smiled, but she knew that sometimes prayers were not enough. She had talked to the wives of the elders to make sure they knew how proper young Mary and Joseph had been in their relationship. It wasn't enough to be obedient Hebrew young people to get the elders' approval; they had to be discreet and wise—no hint of youthful indiscretions. Mary's mother had seen to that. She had been present every time they talked, or they had talked in public places—and even then, very carefully.

The people in the community agreed that Mary was the most godly young woman in the synagogue. The town matchmaker said of her, "She's as good as she is beautiful." When Mary had caught Joseph's eye, the old grandmothers approved. They knew Joseph was a fine catch for her, and a godly young man too.

Joseph rose from his seat in the synagogue—in the back because he was an unmarried male—and walked toward the elders, his face flushed with embarrassment. He shouldn't have been self-conscious; everyone in the synagogue knew what he would request. Nazareth was a small village, where everyone knew everyone and every home was touched by all the others. Joseph handed the parchment to the ruling elder. He didn't even read it. He simply turned to the others and nodded.

Mary watched without blinking from the balcony. The elders, arranged like pale clay dolls in a row, were ready to make the announcement. Betrothal was a solemn business, breakable only by a formal divorce and then only if adultery had been committed. Normally, the old men frowned when young men asked permission to marry. But for Joseph, their wrinkled, old eyes twinkled, their gray beards nodding up and down in approval. One elder even broke into a youthful grin. Joseph was the pride of the community.

The elderly man who had grinned looked up at where Mary sat and smiled. She had been given the man of her dreams. Joseph was the man of any girl's dreams.

When the approving eyes of the elder met hers, Mary blushed, embarrassment momentarily displacing her joy.

After dinner, Mary rushed to the fig tree to pray. As she came near the tree, she could no longer feel her feet touch the ground, as though she were running on the scarlet clouds painting the sunset. Mary loved God. And she loved to talk with God.

Her dark hair, habitually combed, was covered with her father's prayer shawl, the tassels of the shawl bouncing as she ran. Mary had seen her father retreat to the fig tree many times. It was a traditional place to meditate upon God, to pray. Her father was proud of his fig tree. "Where every man can unite with God," he would say, grinning at his children. "Sitting under the fig tree is like being in my 'holy of holies.'"

Spring had arrived in the highlands of Galilee. Most of the days were warm, but still there were chilly nights and some freezing rain up on the mountains. On this evening, the raw wind whipped off the precipice of the hill overlooking Nazareth. Mary's face was stung by the breeze as she reached the tree. *Under the fig tree, I will be out of the wind,* Mary said to herself.

Mary knelt under the familiar branches of the fig tree to pray for future happiness, just as she had seen her father do on many occasions. As a little girl she had spied on him. She would watch in awe as her father spread his massive hands to heaven. Now she, too, lifted her hands.

O Lord God, may your kingdom come in our village . . . in our family . . . in my life . . . .

Mary paused to think about what it would be like to live in the perfect kingdom of God—a kingdom without Roman soldiers, with King David ruling over the land. She continued praying.

May Your kingdom come in my marriage . . . .

Then she stopped praying. Mary often had trouble keeping her thoughts focused when she prayed.

Mary had dreams, and her thoughts now drifted in that direction. She wanted her marriage to be the best of marriages. She wanted to be a perfect wife, a perfect mother, a perfect woman of God. Now that she was promised to Joseph, she couldn't be happier. Yet she had fears. She had seen other couples begin life together in marital bliss, only to later argue and bicker and ridicule one another in public. *We will not argue,* she told herself. *We will be forever in love.*

But might we . . . ? Doubts nagged at Mary.

No! I will make my marriage perfect, she resolved.

Smiling, she parted the fig branches with her hands to search the sky. She was looking for a star in the blue, early evening sky. The pink fringe on the clouds reflected the last rays of the sun nestling just below the horizon behind her. Distractions were always a problem for Mary. When she began praying, her mind wandered to other thoughts—usually thoughts about God or thoughts about Joseph.

She began to count the stars aloud, "One . . . two . . . ." Then she thought, *God says that the stars are like angels*. Mary again was distracted. *There must be* thousands *of stars*, she thought. As daylight undressed into darkness, more stars appeared.

Suddenly, a shiver. Her body quivered as she felt the presence of somebody else near the tree. Pivoting, she saw a stranger in the twilight.

"Greetings," said the pleasant young man, standing there, smiling. "You who are highly favored, the Lord is with you."

Mary gasped. "Who are you?"

"Gabriel," the young man answered politely. "My name is Gabriel."

"What do you want . . . ?" Mary let the question trail off into nothing. She recognized Gabriel as the name of an angel in the Scriptures, but she was troubled by his greeting. His words, his manner were much too formal for addressing a poor girl from a lowly village like Nazareth.

"Do not be afraid," he said. "I have a message for you. The Lord has seen your heart." The young man stopped to let Mary think about what he had just said. Then he continued, "You have found favor with God."

"What does God want of me?"

"You are to have a child," Gabriel said to young Mary. "Your son shall be conceived in your womb, and when he is born, you shall give him the name Jesus."

Mary's heart leaped at the thought of a son. She had often hoped for a son and had considered many names, but never the Greek name Jesus. In Hebrew, the language of her people, the name translated to Joshua, meaning "Jehovah saves." A little boy named Jesus would call to mind Joshua, the great leader who had conquered the Promised Land and defeated Israel's enemies.

Gabriel interrupted her thoughts. "He will be called the Son of the Highest, and the Lord God of heaven shall give to your son the throne of his father, David. And his kingdom shall never end."

The Deliverer? Mary thought. *My son will be the Messiah?*

The coming of the Messiah, the Anointed One of Israel, had been foretold by the prophets for hundreds of years. According to the prophecies, Mary was from the right family, descended from David. So was Joseph. They had King David's blood flowing in their veins. Her son could defeat the Romans just as the boy David had defeated Goliath, the Philistine giant.

Mary was delighted! God had chosen her to be the mother of the Deliverer. Her son, the Son of David, would deliver her people from Rome.

But this must wait, Mary thought.

She said to the angel, "I am not yet married to Joseph."

"Joseph is not to be the father," the angel told Mary.

"How can this happen since I am a virgin? How can I have a child?"

"The Holy Spirit shall come upon you," Gabriel said to her, "and the power of the Highest shall overshadow you, and the holy child born to you shall be called the Son of God."

Mary's thoughts tumbled one over another. What Gabriel was saying didn't make sense. How could she have a child without a father? What would people think? She would be ridiculed, perhaps even stoned. And what of Joseph? What about her dreams of life with him, of having his children? She had been happy with the prospect of being a carpenter's wife, especially this carpenter. Whenever she thought of Joseph, she blushed though no eyes were there to see her cheeks.

Yet a voice inside her cried for obedience to God. She had heard the angel; she recognized the Lord's messenger. But if she said yes to God . . . .

She wanted more time to think about it. She walked on the rim of two worlds, but it was the splintered edge of opposing worlds. To bear the Messiah would almost certainly mean forsaking her dreams of marriage.

Love must choose and not look back. Part of her would die no matter what she chose, but either death would be a gentle death, because she had deep love for both alternatives. With the innocence of early morning, she faced the simplicity of yes . . . or no.

Mary thought of the prayer she had made before Gabriel's appearance. She had prayed for God's kingdom to come in the earth, to manifest itself in her life.

As though he could read her thoughts, the angel Gabriel reassured young Mary. "Your cousin Elizabeth is too old to have children," he said to her. "She was said to be barren, but she has conceived and will have a son."

Gabriel paused. "With God nothing is impossible."

Mary struggled briefly, but she knew what she must do. Regardless of the loss of her reputation, of the man she loved, of perhaps her own life, she would choose now what she had always chosen—to do God's will. She bowed her head, not to the angel, but to God.

"Behold, Lord," she submitted, "I will be your handmaiden. Do to me what you have promised."

With that prayer, Mary yielded the whole of her heart to God. She was not going to be concerned about public ridicule, with what her parents might think, or even with what Joseph might do. If God wanted her to be the mother of David's Son who would deliver Israel, she was willing. She would name her boy Jesus.

When Mary opened her eyes, Gabriel was not there. Quickly she stepped out from beneath the canopy of the tree, parting the leaves, but she did not see him leaving down the path. She quickly ran to the other side of the fig tree, but he was nowhere to be seen.

As she returned to the house, Mary gazed at the stars in heaven. Again, she thought about the angels who were called the stars of God. She knew the angels were messengers of God.

"Lord," she whispered under her breath, "I will be your handmaiden!"

> *"Behold, the virgin shall be with child, and bear a Son, and they shall call His name Immanuel," which is translated, "God with us."*
>
> MATTHEW 1:23

chapter three

THE BABE LEAPED IN HER WOMB

LUKE 1:39-56

Mary walked up the rough-hewn path toward the village high above her. She was sixty miles from home, entering the village Abia, near Jerusalem, where lived the priests who served in the Temple. The footpath was worn into the hillside, white rocks jutting out on either side. At times she jumped from one rock to another.

"Oh . . . !" she balanced herself. "I am not as agile as I was before . . . ." The thought of her pregnancy warmed Mary. Within her body was a human being, placed there by God. She now bounced across the rocks just a little heavier than a few months ago.

"Maybe it is best if I stay with Elizabeth for a while," she had told her mother, concerned about what the people in her community would say. It would not be long before everyone would see the telltale signs. First she would gain a little weight, but she could disguise that by arranging her clothes. Eventually, however, her pregnancy would show and there would be no hiding the life growing inside her.

Mary asked directions to the home of her cousin Elizabeth. Zechariah, her husband, was a priest who had just retired from active service in Jerusalem. Someone pointed out the white stone dwelling at the end of the road. There were several houses attached to each other in terraces, stretching up the hill. Pointing to the last house in the row, the stranger said, "Zechariah and Elizabeth live there."

Mary approached the dwelling and stood for a moment in front of the open oak door. The angel Gabriel had directed her here, but she felt strange walking in on relatives unannounced. The angel had said Elizabeth was pregnant, though she was too old for children. Thus far the angel's words had proven true.

Mary breathed a silent prayer. *God help me to know what to say.* She was fearful. *Please help me . . . .*

Mary walked into the room without knocking. An elderly woman sat in the kitchen, looking out the back door.

Elizabeth looked old and tired. Far beyond the normal age of having a child, she sat most of the time. Friends wanted her to stay in bed, but Elizabeth wouldn't surrender to the bed. Though her pregnancy was wearisome—and the dark lines of her face showed it—a quiet smile showed her contentment.

"Hello . . . I am Mary of Nazareth."

"Oh . . . oh . . . oh . . . !" Elizabeth cried out in pain, reaching for her midsection. Then, with a smile of relief she announced, "My baby just leaped in my womb!" She smiled at Mary. "My baby jumped like never before."

Then all at once Elizabeth grew warm and flushed, as though a desert wind from the south had blown through her very soul. And she knew.

Elizabeth exclaimed loudly to her uninvited guest, "Blessed are you among women, and blessed is the fruit of your womb!"

At the sound of Mary's voice, the baby in Elizabeth's ancient womb had leaped for joy, as if to announce the presence of God. Somehow, she knew, her unborn baby had recognized the presence of the unborn Messiah. "Why has the mother of our Lord come to see me?" she asked.

Sunlight streamed in through the cracks in the window and door, bathing the women in light, though it was dark in the room. Elizabeth asked why she had come, but Mary couldn't give an earthly answer. Mary hadn't known what to do, so she came to see Elizabeth. And here she had seen the truth of all that the angel had told her. Mary lifted her voice and praised God:

"My soul magnifies the Lord,
    And my spirit has rejoiced in God my Savior.
For he has regarded the lowly state of his maidservant.
    From this day forward, all generations will call me blessed.
For he who is mighty has done great things for me,
    And holy is his name."

Elizabeth and Mary talked until late in the evening. From the innocence of marriage begun, to the knowing wisdom of love completed, Elizabeth instructed Mary in the depths of perfect love. Zechariah was not at home to interrupt them, so the ladies talked from one dwindled candle to another. The wisdom of elderly Elizabeth was poured into a young, eager receptacle. All that Elizabeth had learned about living with a man of God was absorbed by young Mary.

"What about Joseph?" Elizabeth was skeptical. "What does Joseph think?"

Mary admitted that Joseph had at first sought to divorce her, to break their betrothal, for he was a righteous man. She had been crestfallen, but before Joseph could gather the necessary witnesses, an angel of the Lord appeared to Joseph in a dream. He confirmed everything Gabriel had said to her, that her child had been conceived by the Holy Spirit. The angel had then instructed Joseph to take Mary as his wife and to call the baby Jesus.

"What did the angel tell *you* to name the baby?"

"Jesus," Mary formed the name on her lips softly. "Jesus, the same name the angel said to Joseph."

"Jesus is a lovely name." The wrinkled smile on Elizabeth's face closed her eyes in joy. "Our Messiah will be named Jesus, for he will save us from our sins."

And Mary remained with her about three months, and returned to her house.

LUKE   1:56

chapter four

HIS NAME IS JOHN

LUKE   1:57-80

Zechariah sat with friends on the smooth bench in front of his white stone dwelling. He could hear the moans of Elizabeth coming from inside the house. He had never heard his wife cry as much as she had in the past few hours. She was a gentle woman who never complained, never raised her voice like so many of the wives in town. When some wives yelled, their voices could be heard two houses away through open windows. But Elizabeth had a quiet demeanor.

Today, however, was different. Everyone in the yard could hear her cries. *Lord, make this delivery easy for Elizabeth,* was all old Zechariah could think of to pray. Then Zechariah heard the unmistakable wail of new life.

"Wa-a-ah . . . Wa-a-ah . . . Wa-a-ah!"

Zechariah smiled. The neighbors also heard the cry and came running.

"The baby is born!" A teenage boy cupped his hands to yell down the street for everyone in the village to hear. Families left their evening meals, drawn to Zechariah's home by curiosity. *Is it a boy or a girl? Is it healthy? How's the mother?*

"It's a boy!" the midwife announced as she emerged from the house, wiping her hands on the apron around her pudgy waist. "He's a healthy boy."

A cheer went up from the crowd gathering in Zechariah's yard. One man reached out to shake the new father's hand, another slapped him on the back. Zechariah was not just a new father like some of the young men in town. Zechariah was older than most *grandfathers*. This baby's birth was a special event in Abia. It was a special baby and would have a special job. All the men in town were Levites, the family of priests that revered God. The men in Abia believed in God, and they wanted to believe God could do anything. But none had seen God do something *this* unusual. No one wanted to call it a coincidence—but no one wanted to call it a miracle.

"Zechariah, who is older than our fathers," someone declared amid the congratulations, "has himself become a father in his old age."

Laughter rippled through the crowd. Two or three women ducked into the house; they had to see the baby even before he was cleaned up.

"No men may come in yet," the midwife announced.

Shortly, a sister of Elizabeth emerged from the house with a baby neatly wrapped in swaths of cloths.

"Wa-a-ah . . . Wa-a-ah . . . Wa-a-ah!" the bawling baby commanded everyone's attention. His aunt couldn't shut him up. His puffy red cheeks were engulfed by his wide mouth.

"Wa-a-ah . . . Wa-a-ah . . . Wa-a-ah!"

Eight days later, the traditional ceremony to circumcise the baby boy was held.

"Call the baby Zechariah," an uncle announced when the deed was done and the village had gathered once more to celebrate. It was the custom to name the firstborn son after his father.

"Yes! Zechariah," the relatives agreed. "Call the baby Zechariah after his father."

"Yes!" the crowd joined in support for the name.

Zechariah jumped to his feet and waved his arms vigorously in protest. He violently shook his head. Zechariah tried to speak. "Ugh . . . ugh . . . ugh . . . ."

The people were embarrassed for the ancient priest. Zechariah had been faithful to God, yet now in this joyful moment he couldn't speak. Zechariah made a motion with his hand like he was writing. He was motioning for a writing slate. Zechariah couldn't talk but he could still write.

"What are you going to name your son?" someone asked.

Zechariah reached for the slate and chalk. The boisterous crowd grew silent. They pressed around Zechariah, wanting to see what he was writing. With his shaking hand, Zechariah wrote in large bold letters so no one could mistake what he was writing:

HIS NAME IS JOHN.

The angel Gabriel had told him in the Temple to name the child John. At the moment Zechariah finished writing, he felt something strange in his throat. He rubbed his neck with both hands, then tried to say something. He looked at the words he had just written and read aloud. The entire village then heard the man speak who had been mute.

Zechariah said, "His name is John."

Everyone who heard this wondered about it, asking,
"What then is this child going to be?" For the Lord's hand was with him.
And the child grew and became strong in spirit.

LUKE 1:66,80, NIV

chapter five

WHERE ELSE SHOULD A KING BE BORN?

LUKE 2:1-7

"I could have made the trip without the donkey." The petite but very pregnant girl shut her eyes to the constant pain. "We can't afford this animal."

"The price is not important," replied her young husband, carefully picking a smooth path through the rocks. They had taken a shortcut from Jerusalem to Bethlehem and were now following a shepherd's path to find a place to sleep before nightfall.

"Look," she pointed, "we can see Bethlehem on the next hill."

The young couple both had family roots in Bethlehem, but neither had ever lived there. Bethlehem was the home of their parents, and the Roman authorities had commanded everyone to return to his hometown to register for a census.

"We have to make this trip for taxes," the young husband had explained as they were preparing for the journey. "It's another way for Rome to get rich."

"Why now?" his wife had moaned. The weather was too blustery for travel. The first winds of winter had surrounded the Holy Land with vicious intent, like predators surrounding a cornered prey.

"Why now?" she repeated as they neared their destination.

"Because . . . ." The young husband couldn't think of an answer so he repeated, "Because." The raw wind flapped his tunic about his chilled legs.

"Oh!" she clutched her midsection. "It's a labor pain."

"Hold on, Mary," he counseled. "That's just the first sharp pain. Count the time between the pains as they come."

Joseph was frantic as he banged at the heavy wooden door. The sun had dropped behind the horizon hours ago. Mary pulled her cloak tighter against the biting wind. Her labor pains were closer together with every inn that turned them away. Bethlehem was swamped with pilgrims who had returned home for Rome's census.

A shaft of light and heat seeped from inside. The harried proprietor refused to open the door more than a crack. "No room in this inn!" came the gruff voice from behind the door. Just enough light escaped to entice Joseph and Mary. They heard the laughter of people around the supper table. They felt the warmth they needed.

"I've been to every inn in town. We've got to have a place!" Joseph's youthful beard was blown by the evening breeze. "She's having labor pains . . . a baby's coming!"

Quickly the innkeeper stepped out, closing the door behind him. Wiping his hands on the greasy apron, he walked over to Mary sitting on the donkey. Providentially, a pain hit and Mary moaned.

The innkeeper's eyes flinched. He recognized legitimate pain. His wife had a multitude of children. "There," he pointed to the stable. "You'll be out of the evening chill; you'll find plenty of straw. You can deliver your baby in there."

Mary looked at the ramshackle stable leaning against a giant rock wall. A warm, orange glow inside the stable emanated from a crude lantern hanging from a rafter. The light swayed gently in the breeze; obviously the stable wasn't windproof.

"There's a cave in the rock where you'll be out of the breeze." Away from the overcrowded hostelry, the crusty demeanor of the innkeeper was slowly giving way to his natural warmth and hospitality.

"Thank you," was all Joseph could say as he led the donkey towards the light.

"This your first one, Missy?" the innkeeper tried to be comforting. "Don't worry, my wife has given birth everywhere, even in an open field!"

He grinned and returned to his customers.

The women in Nazareth had told Joseph how to deliver a baby. He knew courage comes from a cause bigger than any danger, and he was not afraid of the task ahead of him. Although Joseph had never been a "midwife," he knew that if there was a job to do, he could do it. Joseph had the confidence to try his hand at anything.

He found some fresh hay for Mary to lie on, then he found some swaths of clean, white cloth on a shelf. A carpenter by trade, his hands were as skillful as any midwife in Nazareth. He prepared everything, just as he was told, then he sat beside Mary to wait. Knowing this baby was from God, Joseph had to ask himself the question, *What kind of birth will this be?*

Two hours later, it happened—just as the angel said it would. A healthy baby boy was born. Joseph didn't have to swat him. The baby waved his outstretched arms, sucked air into his lungs and cried as all newborns cry. The baby's red face let out a bawl.

"Don't cry, Jesus," Mary reached for her son. "There," she said as she kissed away the tears. Baby Jesus nestled into her loving arms.

"Jesus . . . do you like your name?" the new mother asked.

Joseph heard her call the child Jesus and smiled in support. Gabriel had said, "You shall call his name Jesus, for he shall save his people from their sins."

The baby slept in Mary's arms. She tenderly stroked his brow and kissed his forehead. All the fears she harbored in the past nine months were now gone. She forgot about the rumors in Nazareth, now that the gossip was almost a hundred miles away. The frigid night was peaceful since the wind had died down. Her baby was worth it all. At peace with the world, Mary fell asleep.

She gave birth to her firstborn, a son. She wrapped him in cloths and placed him in a manger, because there was no room for them in the inn.

LUKE 2:7, NIV

chapter six

THE SHEPHERDS AND THE LAMB OF GOD

LUKE 2:8-20

His was a hard face. His grizzled beard had been hacked off with a dull knife by hands that didn't care to have a handsome face. "The breeze has died down," the shepherd whispered to his younger companion, keeping his voice down so as not to frighten the sheep.

"No storms tonight . . . not a cloud on the horizon." The young shepherd glanced from the eastern sky to the west with distrusting eyes. The moon looked like a bowl of milk, full and clear, but the young man was unmoved. He thirsted for something more.

The snapping fire burned low, the red coals still warming their bare feet. The shepherds had taken shelter from the wind among low, flat limestone rocks, where they built a fire down in a small pit concealed from the breeze. Under the larger rocks the dirt had washed away, leaving shallow caves that afforded the shepherds some protection from the elements. Several shepherds in the largest cave were already wrapped in their tunics—sleeping—waiting for their watch.

"Nothing happens this early in the evening," the younger shepherd moaned, complaining again about his assignment to the early watch. His body was cold, his mind was cold, his world was cold. Everything warm in life had been snatched from him.

"When nothing happens," the older shepherd said impatiently, "maybe then we'll have peace." He had lost his faith in God. The only thing he believed in was the tyranny of Rome. He believed in the Roman sword because its sharp edge was his teacher. He believed in punishment, sweat and the scourge, because he had experienced them. But he hated what he believed. He hated Roman taxes and Roman laws. He was filled with revulsion at the sight of every Roman soldier.

"When the Deliverer, the Son of David, comes, we'll have peace," said the younger man. Despite his circumstances, the flame of faith still flickered within him.

"Ha!" snorted the older shepherd. Then, derisively, "Yes, when the *Deliverer* comes, I can go home . . . rather than hide up here in the hills." He paused, scratched his ugly beard and thought of a crime he committed when he was but a young man. Hardened by years of running from the Roman authorities, he had finally taken work as a shepherd to hide in obscurity from the soldiers. *If—when the Messiah comes*, he thought, almost wanting to believe, *I'll go home.*

The younger shepherd was lost in his own thoughts. He still believed in God. He had prayed for God to send the Messiah, but for a different reason from that of his companion. He had sinned deeply against his family, against his village, against God.

"When the Savior comes," the young man broke the silence, "He will purify my memory."

"What is *that* supposed to mean?" the older voice barked, suddenly regretting the whole subject had come up.

"I've done something," the young man confessed. "I try to forget, but I can't."

The young shepherd told his story, some of which his older companion knew, but much of it was unfamiliar and took him by surprise. The younger man had tried many things to eradicate his past, but the memory of his deeds relentlessly pursued him, like a hungry wolf stalking a lost sheep. The young man had worked as a soldier, a camel driver and shepherd. He had even associated with a band of thieves for a while, but everywhere his sin dogged him.

A warm wind flushed the shepherds' faces, whipping their tunics in the breeze. The older shepherd, who had found himself caught up unexpectedly in his young friend's tale, now found himself puzzled by the sudden, unseasonable heat. He glanced at the undisturbed youth, who was still talking.

Then the night exploded in LIGHT!

Light from the heavens obliterated the darkness, blinding the two shepherds keeping watch over the flocks. With their hearts in their throats and their eyes stinging as if ablaze, the shepherds covered their heads with their tunics and hid their faces from the brilliance around them.

The dazzling light pierced the closed eyelids of the sleeping shepherds. Even those in the deeper caves couldn't escape its radiance. It was as though a blanket of stars had dropped out of heaven and ignited the rocky outcropping. Fear choked the shepherd band like an executioner's hands. Their mute tongues . . . their paralyzed hands . . . their minds immobilized with fear.

"Do not be afraid," came a voice from the other side of the light.

"Wh-wh-what is it?" the young shepherd finally managed to ask.

"The voice is from heaven. Only heaven can be this bright," the older shepherd managed to say, surprised at his own words.

"What does God want with us?" his young friend asked.

"I don't know."

As their eyes began to adjust, the younger shepherd shouted, "I see people in the sky!"

The older man squinted toward the heavens. The glorious light appeared to be emanating from a breach in the night sky. And flooding through the opening in the sky were indeed people—angels. Thousands upon thousands of angels. And they were singing.

"Look . . . look . . . !"

The shepherds forced their eyes to look. For most of them it was painful—like looking directly into the sun.

"There's so many I can't count them!" the youth cried. "There's hundreds . . . thousands . . . millions."

"Do not be afraid," the voice behind the light repeated. "I have come to bring you good tidings of great joy to all men." The shepherds exchanged glances.

"Your Savior was born tonight in Bethlehem. He is Christ the Lord," the angel proclaimed. "You will find a baby wrapped in cloths, sleeping in a manger in a stable behind an inn."

The younger shepherd glanced again at the old shepherd when he heard the word "Savior." The older shepherd was thinking, *Can a child so poor that he sleeps in a feed trough deliver us from Rome? Is this child capable of driving the centurions from our shores?*

Then a magnificent sound flooded the night—the loudest thing they had ever heard, yet a harmonious sound that flooded out the noise of past failures. They tasted music that had never been enjoyed by humans—music far superior to the Levitical singer in the Temple, and a thousand times more beautiful.

The great company of the heavenly host praised God, singing:

"Glory to God in the highest,
And on earth peace, goodwill toward men!"

The shepherds were transported beyond their appointed place in time and space into the presence of God. They knew they were hearing the very music that God in heaven enjoyed.

Then just as suddenly as the angels came, they were gone. Almost immediately the nippy winter night closed on the shepherds, like the chilly darkness that floods an area when a warm fire is extinguished. The older shepherd tugged at his tunic to block the chill.

"Let's go!" The younger shepherd leaped to his feet, waving his arms for everyone to get up. *"Let's go now!"*

"Where?" one of the shepherds asked, unsure whether he might still be asleep and dreaming, albeit more spectacularly than usual.

"Bethlehem!" the young man shouted and laughed. "Didn't you hear? The Savior is in the stable at an inn in Bethlehem."

The shepherds began to stir, but slowly. They had seen the light and heard the angel. They were in shock . . . their senses singed . . . they didn't know how to react.

The shepherd in charge was now fully awake. He thought about what he had heard and about all they had experienced. He had been sleeping when the light first fell upon them. When awakened, he had known instinctively this was not sunrise. He had somehow known the light was heaven coming down to earth. He now spoke up. "If he is a Savior," the head shepherd instructed the group, "we must bring the Savior an offering."

The head shepherd understood that sinners were to bring a gift to God when seeking salvation. He had sold many lambs to worshipers, and he had come to recognize a look in the eyes of those who truly wanted salvation. He saw this look now in the eyes of the young shepherd and the men around him. If the Savior were indeed in a stable inn at Bethlehem, he knew what gift they must bring.

"We must bring the Savior a gift," he told the others. "A lamb." ·

"Why a lamb?" someone asked.

"Because the Jews have always brought a lamb. We have always brought a lamb as a gift to God our Savior."

"Mine," the young shepherd volunteered as he walked over to the flock. Searching through the flock he found his prize lamb—a perfect lamb. "My lamb for the baby Savior."

Mary and the baby were asleep. Joseph dozed on the straw beside them. The journey had been long, the search for lodgings emotionally exhausting. But Joseph's mind was still more active than his body was tired. He bolted upright, fully awake, when he heard the noises coming from outside the stable.

Creeping to the stable door he tried to be silent, but the door resisted. The donkey stirred, waking Mary, but the baby Jesus went on sleeping.

"Who is there?" Joseph spoke into the dark courtyard. In the darkness he saw a dozen faces; not the faces of thieves coming to steal from him, but expectant faces.

"We are shepherds," the humble voice of the lead shepherd replied. "Was there a baby born here tonight?"

"Yes."

"We must see him. We have been told the child is from God." The other shepherds nodded their agreement. They all heard the angels and saw the light.

The shepherds had brought a lamp, and they now set the wick of the lantern to give more light. The light was held high, and Joseph saw the yard was filled with shepherds. He opened the obstinate stable door wider.

"Mary," he whispered, so he wouldn't awaken the baby. "Some shepherds want to see Jesus."

Mary stepped to the door, the light revealing the soft features of her face to Joseph. *She is more lovely than ever before,* he thought. His own mother had taught him that a woman's satisfaction makes her more beautiful than she is, and giving birth is among the greatest accomplishments in life. But to Mary, he knew, this birth meant much more. She had obeyed God, and her son would be called the Son of the Highest. Mary was at peace with her dreams.

At Joseph's behest, the shepherds crowded through the stable door, their faces alive with anticipation. But when the light shone upon the baby, the shepherds quickly dropped to their knees with their faces to the ground. They prostrated themselves on the hay in silent adoration.

Several minutes passed as the shepherds worshiped, motionless on the ground. Mary and Joseph were transfixed by the sight. Then one of the shepherds lifted his head and repeated the song of the angels:

"Glory to God in the highest,
And on earth peace, goodwill toward men!"

As one by one the shepherds looked up at the baby, Mary saw their eyes—crying eyes framed by scruffy beards. Their faces, blackened by the soot of campfires layered upon the dust of the open fields, were now streaked with tears. Mary thought, *These are adoring eyes.*

"I don't understand . . ." Joseph broke the silence.

The lead shepherd told them how they had been keeping watch over their flocks by night, how a host of angels had appeared to them in the fields. He told how the shepherds had looked into the light of heaven itself and heard the singing of angels.

The older shepherd stepped forward to gaze at the little one in the manger. "The angel called him our Savior," he said, his cold heart warming to the child. He found he no longer doubted God or his promise of salvation. He adored the baby, and Mary saw belief in his eyes.

The young shepherd whose secret sin had brought him to this place arose, the small, spotless lamb in his arms. He approached the feed trough where Jesus lay sleeping. Placing the lamb in the straw, he said simply, "For you."

"This lamb is in my place."

The shepherds returned, glorifying and praising God for all
the things that they had heard and seen.

LUKE 2:20

chapter seven

AN UNUSUAL DEDICATION FOR AN UNUSUAL BABY

LUKE 2:21-35

The young couple walked slowly through the Golden Gate into the Temple. The frayed edges of the young mother's well-worn shawl obscured an inviting smile reflecting an inner peace. Her young baby, wrapped in swaths of cloth, slept quietly in her arms.

"I hope we won't have to wait too long," said the young father, Joseph, craning to see whether there was a long line in the place where as many as eight hundred babies were dedicated each day, and where new mothers offered sacrifices for their own purification.

Joseph led his wife Mary through the crowded entrance toward the women's court. Several priests leaving the Temple pushed past, oblivious to the presence of the young couple and their infant. Joseph thought them callous but said nothing. Mary lovingly patted the child and he remained asleep.

The winter sky was cloudless for a change. Low clouds commonly brought rainy, dreary winter days to Jerusalem, and Joseph's faded tunic and

Mary's thin shawl offered little protection against the damp cold. But today the sun kindly warmed their backs.

Joseph walked a few feet in front of Mary, searching intently the stalls where businessmen were selling birds and animals to sacrifice in the Temple. Joseph couldn't afford a large bull or even a small lamb, but according to the Law they could offer a turtledove or two young pigeons. Joseph spotted some crude handmade cages holding wild turtledoves and pigeons—one poor man recognizing the endeavors of another to make money.

Joseph went to bargain for a turtledove while Mary waited in the shade, shielding the face of her infant from the sun. She was grateful for Jesus' mild temperament, for he seldom cried, even when surrounded by a sea of unfamiliar faces amid the noise and bustle of Jerusalem.

Joseph returned with a fragile cage of wooden sticks, held together by tender vines. Mary heard the bird cooing and smiled.

Forty days earlier Mary had given birth to Jesus in a stable in Bethlehem. While Mary believed every birth of every baby was a mystery, she had never before heard of a birth announced by angels and attended by shepherds. Now she and Joseph had come to Jerusalem in accordance with Levitical law. On this day, Mary would offer animal sacrifices in the Temple for the ceremonial cleansing. The law considered her unclean because of the blood associated with the birth of a baby.

"Will they accept us?" Mary nervously asked her husband.

"Why not?" The young father was bewildered that his wife would ask such a thing. "We are good Jews. We pay our tithes. We bring a sacrifice."

"Yes . . ." hesitated Mary, "but they may have heard the rumors from Nazareth. They may count back nine months and know the time is wrong, that we were not yet married."

"We've done nothing wrong!" Joseph protested his obedience to God. "We've done everything right—just as the Lord commanded us." With that, Joseph lifted his head and walked boldly ahead. He would not let anyone question his wife or disturb his child. They were doing what God expected of them.

"STOP!"

Mary and Joseph heard someone yelling as they were about to enter the gate to the women's court. "Stop! I must see that child!" came a strong but aged voice behind them. The courtyard was bubbling with loud conversation, laughter and the braying of animals. Few paid attention to the cries of an old man.

Turning, Mary and Joseph saw an elderly man with outstretched arms beckoning to them. *"Please . . . I must see the child."* Joseph thought perhaps he was a Temple official, but he was not dressed in the white robes of a priest. His robe was gray from repeated washings, and shabby from repeated wear. The old man held out friendly arms to them.

His warm smile disarmed Joseph and Mary. The wrinkles on his face and tousled gray hair brought to mind a kindly grandfather. They smiled back. Joseph and Mary traded uncertain glances and walked tentatively over to where the old man stood. As they approached, he announced to anyone who would listen, "I have been waiting to see this child for years!"

Mary and Joseph looked at each other, but said nothing. They had come to expect the unexpected when it came to their child.

"I have come to the Temple to see this child," the elderly man, Simeon, explained to the young couple. "This morning the Spirit told me to come to the Temple—today. Many years ago, God spoke to me with a promise that I would not taste death until my eyes had beheld the Messiah."

"Today," he whispered, "my vigil is over!"

This was the tomorrow that Simeon had long awaited, the fulfillment of his life and destiny. Many times this righteous man had come to the Temple in faith, waiting for the Messiah who would save Israel. Through thousands of unfulfilled yesterdays, Simeon had remained faithful, believing the promise of God.

"Let me have the child." Simeon reached out with both arms. Mary looked at Joseph. He nodded, and she handed the child to Simeon, with just a little concern that the aged man might drop Jesus.

"It is all right," Simeon said to the young mother.

Taking Jesus in his ancient hands, he lifted him toward God, just as a priest would dedicate a baby to God . . . just as fathers dedicated their children . . . just as grandfathers dedicated their grandchildren. Ancient Simeon lifted the baby Jesus high above the crowd to God.

Joseph recognized the act; he had seen his father and uncles do the same. This Simeon was doing what a priest would do. Perhaps the Lord in

heaven knew there were no Temple priests worthy to dedicate Jesus, so the
Lord searched among the godly men of Israel to find a worthy one. *The Lord,*
he thought, *has chosen Simeon.*

Jesus was lifted above the throng of passing people. He was dedicated
where Simeon knew he would one day minister—among the multitudes,
crowds of people pressing in, looking for answers . . . looking for salvation.
Not in the quiet sanctuary of the Temple, for the Temple would not be his
place of ministry. As life went on around them, no one stopped to observe
an old man holding a baby to the sky. It was a common rite in Israel, as
ancient as love. Hundreds of babies would be dedicated that day in the inner
court, so no one gave Simeon a second thought. People brushed by on both
sides going about their business.

Simeon held the baby up to God, saying, "Sovereign Lord, as you have
promised, you now dismiss your servant in peace. For my eyes have seen
your salvation, which you have prepared in the sight of all people, a light for
revelation to the Gentiles and for glory to your people Israel."

The elderly man blessed the parents of the child, then spoke directly to
Mary. "This child has come to cause the fall of many people—and the rising
again of many more." Simeon's raspy voice was bold for his age. "This child
is a sign to all, but many will reject him because he will reveal their thoughts."

Then, in an oddly comforting manner, he said to Mary, "The sword
shall pierce your soul because of this child."

Mary marveled at this strange pronouncement of blessing, taking only
fleeting notice of Simeon's prophecy of personal tragedy.

Old Simeon then folded baby Jesus into his arms and bowed his head in
silent prayer amid the hubbub of the Temple. The baby did not whimper,
even as tears trickled from Simeon's closed eyes, then disappeared into the
heavy lines of his face. The old man finished his prayer then looked deeply
into the eyes of the baby. Simeon smiled, and his joy brought more tears.

"Just a moment." He clung to the baby as though Jesus were a newfound
treasure. Mary knew this look of adoration; she had seen it in the eyes of the
shepherds.

Simeon then handed the child back to his father. Baby Jesus had been
still throughout the ceremony, but now, perhaps sensing the dedication was
over, Jesus began stretching. Joseph gathered the baby in his arms, pulling

the swaths of cloth around his kicking legs.

"Now your servant can depart in peace," Simeon said. The old prophet had finished the task for which he was born, and now he was ready to leave. Without saying good-bye, Simeon turned away and sighed, "My eyes have seen our salvation."

Joseph and Mary had done everything required by the Law of the Lord.
LUKE 2:39, NIV

chapter eight

IN SEARCH OF THE KING
MATTHEW 2:1-12

"This house is wonderful," Mary chirped as she tidied the table.

The finely crafted furniture reflected a certain pride of ownership. Joseph had helped furnish several homes for the residents of Nazareth, but he had done some of his best work here in Bethlehem for his wife and son.

"This house will do for a while," he said, not looking up from his work.

Mary and Joseph had chosen not to return to their hometown of Nazareth, because the ugly rumors there made them uncomfortable. The people of Nazareth had refused to believe the talk of angelic visitations or miraculous conceptions in their midst. "The day of miracle births has passed," the people said.

So Joseph and Mary remained in Bethlehem, the birthplace of their son. "We'll be close to the Temple for the baby," Joseph had reasoned. "If Jesus is to be the leader of our nation, he should live near the City of God."

"But what will we do in Bethlehem?" Mary the dreamer had learned something of the practical necessities of life under the tutelage of her cousin Elizabeth.

"I will find work in a carpenter shop," Joseph insisted. "Bethlehem will be our new home."

Mary had to admit she loved their small but cozy first home, though it was simply one large room, with one front door and a smaller back entrance. Because the "house room" was attached on both sides to other houses, there were no side windows. On this day, Mary had opened both doors to allow the cool morning air to ventilate the house as she cleaned up after their morning meal. Joseph sat on a stool in the corner, hand carving intricate designs on a table leg for one of his more discriminating customers.

"Look at the camels!!" a small boy yelled outside their door.

The streets of Bethlehem were only just awakening, but some untold excitement had roused the neighbors from their homes. Melki, the unofficial town crier, ran from door to door yelling, "Come see the caravan!"

Mary gathered Jesus in her arms, and she and Joseph stepped into the street, blinking against the hazy morning sunlight as they looked toward the east end of Bethlehem. There a large crowd of villagers gathered about a string of camels. Caravans stopped in Bethlehem all the time, but this was no ordinary caravan. Camels with two humps like these were seldom seen in Judea.

The lead camel driver was talking to Melki, the young man with the loud voice. The local youth lifted his arm and pointed a finger toward Joseph. Above the crowd of villagers, several strangely colored turbans whirled around. Now all eyes were staring at Joseph down the narrow street lined with small houses. Everyone stared at Joseph and Mary—and the baby.

A man in a rich, gold turban whispered hurriedly to a servant in a bright pink tunic, and they both turned their necks to see Joseph. The gold turban motioned and the servant ran towards Joseph.

Not knowing if there might be danger, Joseph spoke quietly to Mary. "Go in the house," he said. She gathered young Jesus to her breast and obeyed, closing the heavy front door between them.

The servant bowed to Joseph in greeting. "They tell us you are the father of a young child."

Joseph nodded.

"We are searching for the one born king of the Jews."

At the phrase "king of the Jews," Joseph started. The angel Gabriel had told Mary that Jesus would indeed sit on the throne of David, but they hadn't dared breathe a word to anyone that Jesus would be a king. *How do they know?* Joseph thought before answering. *What do they know?*

Sensing Joseph's apprehension, the servant again bowed deeply. His milky brown skin was smooth, the cotton of his tunic beautifully woven, not like the coarse cloth found around Bethlehem. Joseph recognized the curled toes on the man's sandals as a Persian fashion.

"May we visit the young king this evening?" the servant asked. "We have gifts for the king."

Joseph again nodded. He was almost too shocked to speak, and besides he didn't know what to say.

"After the evening meal," the servant suggested. "We shall visit the child king after the evening meal."

Joseph retreated inside the house to tell Mary that the caravan had come all the way from Persia to visit their toddler who was the king of the Jews.

That evening, Mary nervously checked everything. She had spent the day fervently preparing to receive guests, sweeping, dusting and cleaning the white stone house as though the visitors were coming to inspect the facilities.

Young Jesus sat under the meal table playing quietly with a small toy carved by his father. As the twilight faded and the evening grew dark, the toddler grew tired and he tugged at his mother's robe. Mary supposed the house was as clean as it was going to get. She lit all the candles they had in the house and finally sat down for the first time that evening. Jesus crawled up into his mother's lap and dozed off in her arms.

"THEY'RE COMING!" Joseph heard Melki yelling from down the street. Moments later there came a rapping at the door. Opening the door to their visitors, Joseph was greeted by the sight of a massive camel outside the house. The driver beat a stick on the camel's knee, and it knelt. The rider looked straight ahead, his finely woven tapestry robe unfurling to the ground as he dismounted.

At the door, the servant who had spoken with Joseph earlier in the day bowed. "Why did they ride?" Joseph asked. "It's a short distance from your camp."

"Royalty does not walk in dirty streets," the servant said without superiority or condemnation, as though he held no personal conviction one way or another as to the cleanliness of Bethlehem pathways. He unrolled a red runner to stretch from the camel to the door of the house. Another servant scurried through the door past Joseph with a small chair. He found an appropriate place for his master to sit, returned to the door and nodded.

With the tapestry robe held in one hand, the camel rider stepped onto the rug. His exotic features were fixed without expression, revealing nothing of his intentions. He walked halfway to the house, then turning, he snapped his fingers. Two servants lifted a heavy chest and followed him into the small house. Once his master was seated, the servant at the door nodded and a second camel was led to the door of the little house. A gaggle of neighbors stood off to the side gawking at the proceedings.

The second and third camels dislodged their distinguished riders in equally elegant fashion. Nothing was said or done officially until all three dignitaries were seated in front of Mary and the child.

The room was tightly packed with nobility and servants. Joseph stood behind his wife. Jesus slept, unimpressed with the finery of the visiting dignitaries.

"We have come to worship the king of the Jews," the first and eldest of the noblemen spoke in flawless Greek with just a hint of an accent. He leaned forward to gaze upon the young child. Mary brushed back the simple cotton swath that hid Jesus' face. The other two noblemen strained forward to see him.

Jesus let out a yawn, and they smiled when they saw it.

"Why do you call our son 'king of the Jews'?" Joseph demanded with all the humility he could muster. His concern had not faded since the arrival of the foreigners in town that morning.

"We study the stars," the first nobleman explained. "The stars tell us God has sent a Savior." He said they were called *magi*, or wise men, because their lives were dedicated to studying the scrolls of the ancients.

"How did you know where to find us?" Joseph asked.

The elder wise man did not answer immediately. He looked from one colleague to the other, as though asking permission to share a secret.

They nodded.

"We studied copies of your scrolls . . . called the holy books of the Jews, the Word of God," the wise man began. "After reading your Scriptures, we believe the God of gods is *Elohim*, the Creator."

The magi waited. Joseph stood motionless, uncertain how to respond. He had always believed that Elohim was the only God and that he was the Creator of all things. But these men lived in a land of many gods . . . and many different explanations for the origin of the universe.

"Your Scriptures promise a Deliverer, saying he will come from among the Jews," the voice spoke again carefully.

"We believe this to be true," another of the magi spoke up.

"Your Scriptures also tell us the Deliverer will be born as a child."

The turbans of the other wise men nodded agreement.

"Your Scriptures tell of a star that will be a sign of his birth, so we began searching the sky for his star."

The third visitor, who had been silent, now spoke, his voice quavering with excitement. "For years we have studied the stars, looking for your Messiah."

"About a year ago," the elder continued, "a star that had not been in our sky just . . . appeared."

"*His* star," the third wise man insisted.

Mary shifted Jesus from one arm to the other. He slept through the conversation, blissfully unaware they were talking about him. The wise man politely waited for Mary to get comfortable, then continued.

They had prepared gifts for the journey. It was their custom to honor a child born to be king, and the new star told them this was no ordinary king. "His star began moving; we followed," the wise man's eyes flashed. "The star moved through the sky—unlike other stars. We obeyed its direction."

The star led them westward for several months, then settled over Judea. "When we arrived in Jerusalem, we went immediately to see the one called Herod the Great to inquire of this child." Joseph listened carefully as the wise men told of their audience with King Herod. They described Herod as a fat, arrogant, greedy man with food stains on his velvet clothes.

"I AM THE ONLY KING OF THE JEWS!" Herod had blustered at the magi and demanded they tell him where the boy king could be found.

"We do not know," was their response. "We followed only the star."

Herod consulted with his religious advisors, asking where the Scriptures said this Deliverer would be born. To a man they answered, "Bethlehem, the City of David."

"Go then," Herod had told the wise men. "Go follow your star. Find him and bring me the location . . . I will come to worship the child with you."

Joseph's brow furrowed. Herod was widely known to be ruthlessly cruel. He had executed his own wife and then his two children. Joseph knew this king was a killer. An unsettling fear lodged in the back of the mind of the young father.

The wise old leader silently acknowledged Joseph's apprehension and clapped his hands for his valet. A small cedar chest with cast-iron fittings was placed on the floor before Mary and the sleeping child. Bending, the old man slowly opened the chest. All present saw the light from the candle flames flicker off the pristine gold coins. Then, bending even farther, the old man bowed his face to the ground and spread his hands in praise.

"Bless the Lord, O my soul," the wise man prayed in the Hebrew tongue. "Bless the Lord with all that is within me . . . Bless his holy name."

Another of the magi then brought an expensive flask filled with myrrh, a rare, aromatic sap, and offered it to the child. He then also worshiped him.

The third dignitary set a cask of frankincense before Mary. He opened the top and released the elegant fragrance into the room for all to smell. Mary had never experienced a scent so heavenly in her life, even in her trips to Jerusalem.

"This fragrance is for a king," the third wise man explained, then bowed in solemn worship.

After a time, the three magi arose from the floor of the humble dwelling. The oldest glanced to his traveling companions for approval, then he asked, "May we get a closer look . . . ?" His words were unsure; he did not want to impose on the parents. "We've come so far . . . . We want to learn his features. One look and we will never forget."

Mary again unfolded the cloth from the child's face, then smiled warmly at their guests. Then Mary saw it. The wise men had the same eyes as Simeon and the shepherds. Their adoring eyes were like deep pools of still water, as if this child had unlocked the mysteries of the ages to them.

And having been warned in a dream not to go back to Herod,
[the wise men] returned to their country by another route.

MATTHEW 2:12, NIV

chapter nine

ESCAPE TO EGYPT

MATTHEW 2:13-18

Mary and Jesus slept peacefully. The little town of Bethlehem dozed beneath a silent blanket of stars. A dog barked in the distance, then let out a lonesome whimper. Joseph was awake, but it was not the dog that had roused him, nor was it his concern for the safety of the expensive gifts the unusual visitors had brought to Jesus. A fearful shadow stood in the back of his mind. Something was terribly wrong. Joseph had been startled out of his sleep, frightened by a dream.

He was working in the shop. Working on a table. A skilled carpenter, Joseph was growing frustrated with his seeming inability to balance the table's three legs, so he set it aside and instead put the finishing touches on a cradle he had fashioned for the royal family. He stood back to admire his handiwork and realized he had mistakenly made not a cradle, but a feed trough! Terror gripped his heart as a long shadow fell across the trough from the direction of the doorway. Had the king come for his cradle?

He turned to greet his highness, but it was not the king who had entered the shop. There stood a beautiful, but familiar figure who towered above everything in the room. Joseph was certain he had seen this man before.

"Get up, Joseph," the visitor warned. "Danger lies on the other side of dawn." Joseph knew this voice, but from where?

"An enemy is coming to kill the child."

Then Joseph knew. This was the messenger from God who had foretold the birth of Jesus. Joseph stood stunned, almost afraid to move. He didn't know what to do. He stared at the angel wide-eyed.

"Hurry," the angel warned. "There is no time. Death comes after sunup."

Herod! Joseph knew immediately the angel spoke of King Herod. He thought, That heartless killer is coming for my child.

"Go to Egypt. Take the child and his mother and stay in Egypt until I tell you," the angel said: Joseph bowed his head and nodded his willingness to obey.

"Leave now," was the angel's final warning.

There was a faint light in the eastern sky when Joseph led Mary out to the donkey. He helped her up then brought her the bundled child. He threw two sacks filled with gold, frankincense and myrrh over the animal, then tied them securely.

"We'll have money to live in Egypt," he said, patting the treasure sacks. He knew their contents, but hoped everyone else would think the sacks were filled with utensils for cooking.

The animal's hoofs clicked on the stones as they left their home. When the donkey halted to feel his way in the dark shadows, Joseph urgently pulled on the reins. "Hurry," he pleaded. By the time they made their way out of Bethlehem, the light in the east had grown bold enough to reveal the dark trees and stone walls that lined the road, though sunrise was still at least an hour away.

A few miles out of Bethlehem the donkey refused to go any farther, jerking his head angrily against Joseph's direction. The donkey pulled Joseph toward a little stream at the side of the road.

"What's wrong?" Mary was concerned.

"He smells the creek water," Joseph explained, "We left so quickly. I didn't give him water."

Mary decided it was a good time to feed Jesus and found a secluded spot out of the breeze among some rocks. Joseph led the animal into the stream to drink.

Moments later, he heard shouts coming from the direction of Jerusalem. Then Joseph heard the unmistakable tramp of Roman soldiers. These soldiers were not aimlessly strolling toward Bethlehem. Joseph heard the clamor of full-battle march.

He pulled the animal down the creek into some bushes and prayed the donkey would not let out a bray in protest.

"I hear them," Mary whispered to Joseph.

"Stay hidden in the rocks," Joseph instructed his wife.

The troops were led by a centurion dressed in battle gear, proudly astride a prancing white steed. Spotting the stream, he stopped to give his horse a drink, signaling the troops to continue their sonorous march. The horse waded into the shallow water near the rocks where mother and child were hidden. The centurion leaned back in his saddle and patted the rump of his horse.

Mary silently prayed, *Lord, don't let Jesus cry*. The toddler closed his eyes and slept.

The horse turned around in the stream, looking for firm footing amid the slippery rocks. In the darkness before the dawn, the Roman officer couldn't see into the bushes where Joseph hid with the donkey, but Joseph could see the centurion clearly enough. Joseph saw angry eyes staring back at him. He wanted to run, but held his ground. Escape was impossible, for the horse would certainly outrun him. And even though the distraction might enable Mary and Jesus to get away undetected, the angel had instructed Joseph to take his wife and child to Egypt, so he was determined to remain hidden.

The donkey swished its tail, and Joseph prayed, *Please don't let the donkey give me away*. The donkey stood silently.

Suddenly, the centurion jerked at his reins and the white horse ascended the bank from the stream and took up its trot beside the procession of soldiers. One hundred soldiers marched steel-eyed. They looked neither to their right or left. With hands on their swords and death on their minds, they marched on toward Bethlehem.

Quickly Joseph and Mary were back on the road. Now Joseph picked up his pace, heading for Egypt. By mid-morning, they had traveled far enough from Bethlehem that their fears slowly subsided. The sun washed away the dread of the night. The more babies and small children they saw along the way, the safer they felt.

Three nights later they were halfway to Egypt. Everything in sight was different from their hometown of Nazareth. Back in Galilee, the homes were built out of white fieldstone; as they drew nearer to Egypt, the houses were made of clay, their dirty walls caked with mud. Uncomfortable with the local accommodations and thinking it would be best to keep his family from the prying eyes of the opportunistic local authorities, Joseph stopped for the night at an oasis. The young family rested among strangers under the tall royal palms. They were almost ready to go to sleep when a gruff voice was heard approaching from the other side of the oasis.

The burly new arrival dropped his pack. Sticking his aching feet, sandals and all, into the cool water, he complained of walking all day to anyone who would listen. A few mumbled in agreement, but neither Joseph nor Mary said a word.

"I never want to see another Jew!" the boisterous voice carried over the water to Mary and Joseph. "Those crazy Jews kill each other." This remark was met with silence, though a few nods were exchanged.

"Yesterday," he bellowed, "King Herod killed all the baby boys in Bethlehem!" The traveler went on to describe in graphic detail how the Roman soldiers had stacked the bodies of the babies near the well in Bethlehem. The word on the streets of Jerusalem was that Herod had ordered the death of all male children two years old and younger because of a rumor that a rival to his throne had been born in Bethlehem.

"Herod, a Jew himself, sent a hundred soldiers to slaughter all the babies and any parents who got in their way. Terrible!" The agitated traveler swore again at the Jews. "I never want to go back there."

Mary looked at Joseph through the evening shadows; he returned a knowing glance. She silently wondered, *Why was our Jesus saved . . . and all those little boys slaughtered?*

She looked at Jesus sleeping in her arms and whispered to him, "Remember always, God loves you and will protect you."

> *Then was fulfilled what was spoken*
> *by Jeremiah the prophet, saying:*
> *"A voice was heard in Ramah,*
> *Lamentation, weeping, and great mourning,*
> *Rachel weeping for her children,*
> *Refusing to be comforted,*
> *Because they are no more."*
>
> MATTHEW 2:17,18

chapter ten

GOING HOME TO NAZARETH

MATTHEW 2:19-23

Mary and Joseph had settled in a small Egyptian town. Because everyone there wanted to live near the river Nile, houses were built on top of each other. Mary and Joseph lived in a small house built on the roof of a larger house, their front porch surrounded by a tall wall so Mary wouldn't have to worry about young Jesus falling off the roof. Joseph worked in a carpenter shop, making exotic furniture for his Egyptian customers. Because of their unique Judean designs, many people ordered chairs made by Joseph.

As Jesus was learning to speak, Mary taught him the great psalms of Scripture. She would constantly say, "Repeat after me, 'The Lord is my shepherd....'"

Little Jesus would repeat, "The Lord is my shepherd...."

"I shall not want...."

Jesus repeated the words of his forefather, King David. Mary said to her young son, "You must know everything that your forefather David knew. You must be able to say everything that David said."

At soon as he could talk, Mary began teaching Jesus the Hebrew alphabet. He sat in his father's chair as Mary prepared the meals. "Say aleph...."

"Aleph," Jesus would repeat the first letter perfectly.

"Say beth...."

"Beth," Jesus repeated the second letter.

"Gimel...."

"Gimel," Jesus repeated.

"Now say aleph ... beth ... gimel...."

Everything that Jesus needed to know, Mary taught him. He had a knack for memorization and learned quickly as he grew. Despite his supernatural birth, Jesus appeared in all respects to be a normal, healthy child.

The breeze fresh off the Nile made the Egyptian nights comfortable, even after the hottest of days. Living on the second floor put Mary and Joseph above the squalor of the small city, where the evening breeze habitually swept away all the smells of the town.

One night a sudden gust of wind blew through the room and Joseph awoke in the darkness. A rooster had crowed, rousting him from a sound sleep, but clearly dawn was not near. Then the rooster crowed again. Joseph tossed in his bed, but sleep eluded him. As he always did on sleepless nights, he prayed, *Lord, what are you trying to say to me? Let me understand your voice.*

Joseph listened, but nothing came to him and he soon drifted off.

He was back in his shop in Bethlehem. Working on the table . . . again. Two years, and he had been unable to balance the three legs. Joseph was widely known as a master craftsman. People came from far and near to drink from the trough he had built, but he was simply unable to make this table stand properly. Joseph stood in the center of the shop, perplexed as the table wobbled before him. Then his young son entered the shop. Little Jesus walked over to the table and, taking a saw in his small hand, shortened the errant leg. Then he stepped away from the table and looked up at his father for approval.

Joseph nudged the table, but it no longer wobbled. Upon closer inspection, he found the legs to be precisely the same length. He turned to Jesus. "How did you do this, my son?"

Jesus smiled again and said, "I must be about my father's business." He then looked past Joseph toward the door, and Joseph turned to follow his son's gaze. There, towering above the doorway once again, was the messenger of God. Joseph found he had been expecting the angel's return.

The visitor spoke. "Take Jesus and his mother and return to the land of Israel. Herod who has wanted to kill the child . . . is dead."

Then the angel smiled and said, "Go to your home . . . ."

During the next few days, Joseph wrapped up his business and finished the chairs at the shop. He wanted to keep his commitment to his customers. Mary cleaned the house immaculately, remembering the joy she had known there teaching little Jesus.

Joseph purchased a donkey for the long trip home. On the appointed day, he helped Mary onto the animal, jerked on the reins and they left Egypt, never to return.

Three days later they stopped at the same oasis where they had spent the night on their flight from Bethlehem. Joseph sought out the same tree, settling in the same place. As the sun went down, Joseph and Mary remembered together the stranger who had come into the oasis late at night with news of the slaughter back home. They rejoiced that even now God was taking care of them and guiding them.

"In a few days we will be back in Bethlehem," Joseph reassured Mary. She thought of their little house sandwiched in a row of houses where the magi had visited. She wondered if the little house was vacant and whether they might live there again.

A traveler came into the oasis late that evening, speaking the Hebrew tongue. Mary and Joseph had not heard others speaking Hebrew in a long time. *The language of God*, Joseph thought. Quickly they made acquaintance with the stranger, hungry for news about Bethlehem and Jerusalem. They inquired as to happenings in the Holy City.

"Archelaus is reigning in the place of his father Herod," the traveler told Joseph. This news disturbed Joseph. *Will Herod's son have the same hatred as his father?* Joseph tried to put the thought of danger out of his mind, but it kept coming back. *Will the son of Herod try to kill Jesus?*

That night Joseph lay on his pallet in the tent, trying to sleep. As on other nights when he couldn't sleep, Joseph asked God, *What are you trying to tell me?* He soon slipped into a deep sleep and dreamed.

The angel once again visited his shop. "Won't you sit down?" Joseph offered his guest a chair. "My son helped me to build this table."

"Do not go to Jerusalem," the angel said to Joseph. "There is danger waiting there for Jesus."

"What about Bethlehem?" Joseph asked. "Will my son be safe there?"

"There is danger in Bethlehem also. You must not go there."

"But shouldn't the Messiah be near the Temple? To be near God?"

"Return to Galilee," the angel said.

Joseph thought about Galilee. They had fled because of the rumors. He was afraid they would criticize Mary. Then Joseph realized all that faced them in Nazareth was embarrassment. In Jerusalem, his son faced death. So Joseph decided to return to Galilee. "It will be as you say," he said to the messenger of the Lord.

Then the angel said, "Go, live in the city called Nazareth."

"I will return to Nazareth."

And with the confidence of his destination and home in mind, Joseph turned over and slept soundly until the dawn.

"Almost home!" Joseph told his little son who was seeing Galilee for the first time. Joseph pointed up to the rocky top of Mount Carmel, which jutted out into the Mediterranean Sea. Then, after crossing the plain of Armageddon, they began climbing up the foothills, higher and higher, until they came to a bowl-shaped valley encircled by hills. Nazareth was built on the western slope of the bowl.

"When you get older," Joseph said, pointing out over the valley of Armageddon, "you can walk up here to study the famous battles in Jewish history." It had been two weeks since his dreams and their departure from Egypt, and Joseph was finally beginning to breathe easier as they spotted familiar landmarks from his boyhood.

They arrived on the outskirts of the village of Nazareth about dusk. Mary noted that the women were still gathering at the well, as was their custom. They came to draw water for the evening meal, but it was also a custom that young girls offered water to weary strangers and caravans.

"Some water for you?" A young teenage girl brought a jar to Mary for refreshment.

At first, people didn't recognize the young child or his mother as Joseph helped them dismount from the donkey. The shy, yet fearless face of this beautiful young woman was older and more mature than when she had left Nazareth just a few years earlier. But soon they were surrounded by eager relatives and friends welcoming them home. No one mentioned the rumors, the innuendoes. No one mentioned that the child had been conceived before marriage. Everyone seemed happy just to have them back home.

Several families invited Joseph and Mary to stay with them awhile, as their old home had fallen into disrepair. Joseph's parents had passed away and the house was deserted. It would take Joseph days, maybe weeks, to make the house habitable once again.

The morning after they arrived, news of Mary and Joseph's return quickly spread. In those first few days, the lamps burned longer than usual at night as Mary and Joseph greeted neighbors who came to call and shared with them their strange and thrilling experiences in Bethlehem and Egypt. Of course, not everything that had happened could be told because the people wouldn't understand the supernatural events; nor would they believe.

After the first excitement of their return home had died away, Mary and Joseph settled into their repaired house and took up the regular duties of everyday living. One idyllic Nazareth morning, Mary sat near the door of their home dressed in a dark robe with a spotless white scarf on her head and shoulders. Across her lap was an unfinished tunic which she had been sewing for Jesus. She looked out the door at her young son playing in the yard, but she was not thinking about this day. Mary had kept all those things about his birth in her heart . . . and she pondered them carefully.

And [Joseph] came and dwelt in a city called Nazareth, that it might be fulfilled which was spoken by the prophets, "He shall be called a Nazarene."
MATTHEW 2:23

chapter eleven

GROWING UP
LUKE 2:40

Mary and Joseph had lived in Nazareth for three years, residing on the outskirts of the city in the home that Joseph had once helped build and later restored after the death of his parents. Upon his return to the city, he had claimed his family inheritance on the edge of a vineyard—enough property for a house, with a small garden and a lot for a few small animals.

Near the back of the house, Joseph had built a carpenter shop and once again set about the business of making chairs and other items of household furniture. As young families needed homes, Joseph also built houses. Using the gray brick he found among the white limestone in the nearby hills, Joseph became a popular contractor in the city of Nazareth.

Now the family was expanding: Mary was pregnant with their third child. Joseph remembered the house on the second floor in Egypt and built an outside stairway that led to new main living quarters above the workshop. There they enjoyed the fresh breezes off the Galilean hills and slept above the commerce of the streets.

Life in Nazareth went on pretty much as it did in other villages, as it had for many years. Caravans came from far-off places, passing through Nazareth, many times stopping for water. Once in a while travelers on foot, donkey or camel would spend the night in one of the guest rooms in Nazareth. Peddlers, storytellers, even teachers with their small groups of followers—nearly all were willing to talk with anyone interested about what was happening in other parts of the world. The Nazarenes enjoyed standing around listening as visitors regaled them with stories, legends and news from faraway lands. Whenever possible, Jesus was in the crowd, ever learning.

Sometimes a traveler would have a broken wheel or saddle to be mended and would find his way to Joseph's shop. There the little boy Jesus watched his father make the necessary repairs, and now and then with a tool in his hand, Jesus helped his father.

On this day, the boy Jesus, dressed in a white tunic with a sash tied tightly around his waist, stood next to his father's knee. One hand clutched a nail, the other held a hammer. Joseph affectionately watched his son learning how to drive nails into the soft mountain pine. Even though Joseph enjoyed his work, he paused whenever possible to help his son learn the carpenter's trade. When the work was finished and the day was done, Joseph would sit down and try to answer as best he could the strange and discerning questions of which his young son seemed to have so many.

There was pride in Joseph's face as he paused at the workbench. He looked at Jesus, who even at this early age showed promise of becoming one of the best carpenters in all Galilee. Unlike the other village boys, who found their greatest happiness in running, playing or just being with other boys, Jesus spent long hours with his mother and father, learning whatever they could teach him. Of course, Jesus also enjoyed playing with the other boys, learning life skills which boys seem to learn only from one another.

Mary called her son into the house. "Jesus, it is time to learn how to write." Mary handed him a stylus. "Hold this pen between your fingers like this."

Mary put her tender hands over the small, ready hand of her son. Jesus drew large pictures in sand spread out over the kitchen table. As his fingers became more agile, the pictures became smaller, but the coarseness of the sand didn't permit minute work.

Eventually Mary taught her son to write on papyrus. Dipping the stylus in a bottle of charcoal—soot and olive oil—Jesus began making letters on paper.

"Write an aleph like this." Mary took the pen and wrote an aleph on the paper. Jesus copied the aleph on his sheet of paper.

Within a year, Jesus was copying his favorite psalms. "Jesus, if you're going to be a king," Mary would say to him, "then you must learn to do the things a king will do." Mary explained that the Law required the king to copy the Scriptures for his personal possession. She quoted the words of Moses:

> "It shall be, when the king sits on the throne of his kingdom, that he shall write for himself a copy of this law in a book. And it shall be with him, and he shall read it all the days of his life, that he may learn to fear the Lord his God and be careful to observe all the words of this law."

"Jesus," Mary instructed her son, "you must write a complete copy of the Scriptures, just like a king." She explained that a thought doesn't belong to a person until he can write it down in his own words. "Then the thoughts of Scripture will belong to you."

"That's a big job for a little boy," Jesus thought aloud.

"No task is too big for you," Mary told her son. "To be a great king, you must do great things." So each day Jesus copied a different psalm, then he memorized the psalm, repeating it flawlessly to his mother.

"We must finish up our work and clean the shop," Joseph said to Jesus late one Friday afternoon about a year later. The sun would soon set behind the hills and the Sabbath day would begin. Every devout Jewish home observed the Sabbath, and on Fridays everyone busied themselves with last-minute tasks in preparation for the Lord's day.

"Remember the Sabbath day, to keep it holy," Mary would remind her children.

She had already prepared the meal for the following day, so a fire wouldn't burn nor any food be prepared on Saturday. The Sabbath was strictly observed and held in reverence in their home. While Joseph and Mary would have made every day a holy day, the Sabbath was a special day— a day they gave to the Lord.

> *Though He was a Son; yet He learned obedience.*
>
> HEBREWS 5:8

HIS TWELFTH YEAR

LUKE 2:41-44

"Look, Mary!" Joseph called to his wife ahead of him and pointed toward the shining city on the mountain rising before them under the noontime sun. "I always get a thrill when I first see the Eternal City set high on Mount Zion."

Mary and Joseph had left home three days earlier from Nazareth with a caravan of family and close friends. The annual pilgrimage to Jerusalem for the Feast of the Passover was a festive occasion, a family experience. Each evening, they enjoyed sitting around the fire, eating and sharing stories, talking with other pilgrims on their way to Jerusalem, the children playing at the edge of the campfire light with other children. By day they walked mostly in silence—the women and children at the front of the procession—sharing smiles and knowing nods with those closest to them.

Joseph and Mary were taking their twelve-year-old son, Jesus, for his first visit to the Temple. As a "son of the Law," Jesus was now of an age to observe the requirements of Jewish law, and the Law required that Jewish men attend the feasts of Passover, Pentecost and Tabernacles in Jerusalem. Jewish customs and their timing were very precise. The child had been weaned at approximately age three, when he began wearing daily a fringed coat. Mary had taught her son the Scriptures, line upon line, precept upon precept. A conscientious Jewish boy would have memorized the entire book of Leviticus by age twelve. Jesus could recite the entirety of the Law from memory.

"Jesus!" Mary called to the pack of boys climbing rocks and exploring the terrain along the side of the road, well ahead of the main group. "Don't get lost . . . ." She let her words trail off. She fussed over her children like all mothers. But Mary was pleased that whatever the circumstances of his birth, whatever his destiny, Jesus enjoyed a wonderfully natural childhood.

Her boy's skin was tanned olive, like the other children walking with him. Jesus' hair was windblown and had caught some straw blown from a field. He wore the usual boy's white tunic, bleached by many washings and always clean with the smell of lye. Mary would have it no other way; she had lived twelve years on the rim of excellence. Raising Jesus was easy work, and she was doing what she wanted to do. It was living above one's expectations. Jesus had never given her a moment of worry, and yet . . . .

"Jesus!" Mary again called ahead to her son, "Stay close."

Jesus scooted up the path ahead of his parents toward Jerusalem. He seemed to know where he was going as though pulled to the city's presence. His tough bare feet were hardened to the hot rocks and sharp cinders, and dust flew from the weeds as he ran across a field. The sparkle from the sun radiated from his smile. He skipped a rock across a still pool of water. He drank in the world about him with a vigorous thirst. Jesus was all boy.

"He will be a carpenter," Joseph boasted to Mary as they came near to Jerusalem. According to tradition, when a son turned twelve years of age, the father announced his son's trade at his *bar mitzvah*. Immediately upon returning home, Jesus would begin learning that trade. It was a father's privilege and responsibility to choose a trade for his son.

"Jesus, the oldest of our children, will be a carpenter like me." Joseph glanced from one son to the other: James . . . Joseph . . . Simon . . . Judah. They would all have trades, but Jesus would be taught carpentry. He would be like his father.

"Come, children," Joseph announced, "let us sing the psalm of ascent." They had been taught that when entering the Eternal City of Jerusalem they must sing the psalms that God had given pilgrims to sing.

"This is the day the Lord has made," the young family chanted together. "We will rejoice and be glad in it." Spring had come in starts and spurts. Some days were cloudy, wet and cold, but this warm April morning was perfect for traveling. The high cumulus clouds stretched from horizon to horizon. The eastern breeze off the mountains refreshed them after the heat of their steep walk up Mount Zion. Temperatures would climb into the nineties after noon.

The family was celebrating the Feast of Passover: seven days of worship and feasting. Besides sacrificing the Paschal lamb, Passover was a family reunion. Each night Joseph would eat with different family members— sometimes with his family, other evenings with Mary's family. Friday evening was the Passover meal. As they walked, Joseph looked over at Jesus playing with the boys and thought of the last words of the Passover meal, *Until Elijah comes . . . .*

Joseph knew from Scripture that the prophet Elijah would one day return to announce the coming of Messiah to the nation of Israel. Joseph had many dreams for his son, but he recalled the unusual events at Jesus' birth and wondered, *Is my son Messiah? If so, where is Elijah? Why has he not spoken?*

Early the next morning, Jesus gently shook his father who was still asleep. "The sky is growing bright," the eager twelve year old said to his father. "Soon the sun will be up. May I walk down to the Temple and be the first to enter for worship?"

Joseph turned over in his bed, rubbed his hands through Jesus' hair and reminded him that already a priest was standing at the highest pinnacle in the Temple, watching for the first rays of the sun. As soon as he saw the sun, the priest would signal the trumpeter who would lift a silver trumpet and sound an announcement throughout the Temple area. Then the great gates of the Temple would be opened for anyone to enter. "You can't go in until the gate is opened," Joseph explained. "Let us wait here for the trumpet call."

Young Jesus did not seem to be discouraged. Joseph told him they would be among the first at the Temple, where they would see the white-robed priests going about their duties. Soon there would be the chanting of the psalms and singing by the Levites. "We want to worship when all is ready," Joseph told his son. "We will all go together and worship the Lord."

So while the dawn strengthened the day and the dark shadows disappeared, Jesus sat in the doorway and watched the brow of the hill that surrounded Jerusalem, waiting for the sun. The household slowly stirred and preparations for the day began. Then, they heard the trumpets. The sky was full of a clear radiance, a soft breeze stirring the trees and vines that hung over the walls. The first low call of birds was heard throughout the city.

Hastening through the crowded corridors of the city, the family entered the Temple by way of the Gate Beautiful. The clamor of the streets died away and the sweet peace of the psalms rippled through the Temple courtyard. Jesus had never before heard the music of harps and cymbals. Looking up from the Gate Beautiful into the Temple was like looking into heaven, and the boy stood to gaze about the whole Temple. Before him lay fifteen golden steps upon which the singers stood. Farther up were more golden steps leading to the Holy Place. Already the smoke of burnt offerings ascended into the blue sky, while priests repeated the sacred prayers for worshipers who brought their lambs to sacrifice. Some people were kneeling with their faces toward the altar; others had their heads bowed in prayer; still others stood with hands outstretched to heaven.

Suddenly Jesus dropped to his knees beside Joseph. This was where he longed to be, in the house of his heavenly Father, the place where his forefathers had come to worship. He was only a little country boy visiting the Temple for the first time. He had never seen a sacrifice, though he had read of it in the Law and heard it taught in the synagogue. This experience had been a long time coming, and Jesus wanted to drink deeply from it.

The priest before him began repeating the *Shema*, the creed that all Israel learned by heart. Jesus had learned it from his mother. Without coaxing, his childlike voice blended with the deep resonant sounds of mature priests as they repeated, "Hear, O Israel: The Lord our God is one Lord! You shall love the Lord your God with all your heart, with all your soul and with all your strength." Even though the priest was ministering to another family, Jesus entered wholeheartedly into what he heard, for it was the prayer of his heart.

As they walked past another family, Jesus stopped as he saw the priest lift his hand and give the benediction to the family:

"The Lord bless you and keep you;
The Lord make his face to shine upon you,
And be gracious to you;
The Lord lift up his countenance upon you,
And give you peace."

After Joseph and Mary brought their sacrifice and prayed to the Lord, the service was ended. More worshipers entered as Joseph and Mary left the Temple, the boy Jesus in hand. But Jesus thought to himself as he walked down the golden stairs toward the Golden Gate, *I will return again, again and again.*

It is written, "Zeal for Your house will consume Me."

JOHN   2:17,   NIV

chapter thirteen

TEACHING SCHOLARS BEFORE HIS TIME

LUKE   2:45-52

The family had left Jerusalem at noon for the return home to Nazareth. Walking half a day, they reached El Birech, an oasis about eight miles north of Jerusalem. The first day after Passover was anticlimactic; the festivities were over and a long walk home awaited them. Today's trek had been most difficult because of the winding path up and down, over one hill after another. Difficult, because they had been away from home for more than a week. Difficult, because the April sun was especially torrid this day.

"We'll set up camp over there," Joseph pointed to a grassy place between a small wild olive tree and a large rock. He nodded to his son James, a few years younger than Jesus. "Find your brother Jesus and gather some sticks for a fire so we can cook supper."

Mary began unpacking utensils from the bags. Joseph unrolled the greasy meat cloth, pulling out some dried goat's meat to be broiled over the open flame. The younger children played nearby.

"I can't find Jesus," James said when he returned.

Mary's heart jumped. Because the women and men walked separately in the caravan, each parent had thought that Jesus was with the other. "Run up ahead and check the campsites," Joseph immediately commanded his son James. "Ask in every campsite if they have seen Jesus today." Then he added, "All day . . . ask if they've seen him at all."

Mary and Joseph traded worried glances. "Don't worry," the concerned father said to his wife. "I'll search the road. He probably wandered off with friends and hasn't caught up to us yet."

Joseph left the oasis and began retracing their route from Jerusalem, asking anyone he met along the way about Jesus. Mary busied herself cooking the meat for the evening meal. James returned and reported that no one had seen Jesus all day.

Evening was darkening, the sun as red as the coals in the fire when Joseph walked into camp, his shoulders slumped, dejection showing. He had not found his son.

Mary fearfully dropped her eyes. She felt a stab in her heart, remembering the prophecy of Simeon: *A sword shall pierce your soul.*

"Pack up everything," Joseph barked to the younger children. "Jesus must still be in Jerusalem." Mary immediately began stuffing utensils in a bag. She prodded the children into action.

"We leave right away for Jerusalem," Joseph said. Within minutes, the family was on the road back to the Eternal City.

The following day, Joseph and Mary went from one home to another searching for Jesus. Mary had aunts and cousins in the city, but Jesus was not in any of their houses, nor had they seen him. Joseph too had relatives in the city, but they had not seen Jesus either.

By the next day, the parents were frantic. The city was still teeming with tens of thousands of pilgrims. Normally Jerusalem boasted a population of thirty thousand, but during Passover week more than two hundred thousand Jews crowded the city along with the peddlers, thieves and assorted predators who thrive wherever people congregate in mass quantities. Rooms were not available. Vendors inflated their prices for food and supplies. Conditions were insufferable. Joseph and Mary knew that Jesus could take care of himself in Nazareth, but this was the city. Nevertheless, deep down they knew the Lord's own hand was upon Jesus; God would protect and provide for their boy. But they still had to find him.

"What other relatives do we have?" Joseph searched his memory for where Jesus might be.

"Could he have left Jerusalem to visit some other relative?" asked Mary. "Would he have gone home with them and not told us?"

They were at their wits' end, until Joseph remembered the strange look on his son's face when they worshiped at the Temple. "Let's look in the Temple," Joseph said. Mary was willing to look anyplace. Together they hurried to the Temple. The closer they got, the faster they ran. They entered the Temple out of breath, but Joseph managed to ask the first priest he saw, "Have you seen a young boy here? Beautiful olive skin? A child's white tunic, well-washed but worn?"

"All the children here look like that," the kindly priest laughed at the thought of hundreds of boys who fit that description. Then the priest suggested, "There is a child sitting with the teachers of the Law; he's causing quite a commotion . . . ."

Joseph and Mary didn't wait for him to elaborate. Dashing into a court-yard, they saw a tightly grouped crowd of people. From what they could see, all the people on the outside were standing on their toes, trying to look over the people in front of them. Someone was the center of attraction.

Jesus so loves to learn, Mary thought. *Perhaps he found a fascinating teacher and became so enthralled while listening that he forgot what day we were supposed to go home.*

Joseph pushed his way through the crowd. He was a determined father and he had worried long enough. There at the center of the crowd was Jesus, standing in the midst of several bearded teachers and scholars. Mary herself pressed through the crowd to look over Joseph's shoulder. She had distinctly heard her son's voice.

"Let me put this question to you . . . ," Jesus directed his question to the scholars. They were all sitting, while Jesus was standing. They were sitting at the feet of Jesus! The boy was asking; the old men were thinking.

This cannot be! Joseph thought. Everybody knew that young boys sat at the feet of scholars. Here, the roles were reversed. *Always the student sits at the feet of the master. My boy is teaching these learned men.*

From back in the crowd, Mary could not contain herself any longer. With a voice of concern mixed with relief, she called out, "Son!"

Jesus stopped in the middle of a question, and turned to look at Mary, for he recognized his mother's voice.

"Son," Mary said, the crowd parting to let her through. "Why have you worried us?"

The crowd was silent. No one dared speak. They had heard the questions of children before. A true teacher wants to help a child learn, so they allowed him to ask his questions. The questions of children were often meaningless, but this boy was clearly different. His questions were deep, challenging even the wisest of the men assembled there. The scholars were pushed to the limits of their knowledge. Jesus asked questions they couldn't answer. Since the greatness of a mind is measured by the depth of its questions, the teachers recognized they were standing in the presence of a brilliant young man.

"We have searched all of Jerusalem for you . . . ," Mary said.

Twelve-year-old Jesus sensed deep anguish in his mother's voice. Hers were feelings of anxiety, of relief. They were feelings of panic, feelings of love. "Why didn't you look first in my Father's house?" Jesus asked, genuinely puzzled. "Didn't you know that I would be about my Father's business?"

And the child grew, and waxed strong in spirit, filled with wisdom:
and the grace of God was upon Him.
LUKE 2:40, KJV

chapter fourteen

LEAVING THE CARPENTER SHOP

LUKE 2:52

Jesus carefully sawed the board, then nailed it into the empty space on the chest he was making for a family in the nearby town of Nain. His strong hands had been forged by years of work in the carpenter shop. His unerring eye had helped him to become an excellent cabinetmaker . . . some said the best in all Galilee. *Perfect!* he thought, but his thoughts were interrupted by a scream from the street in front of the carpentry shop.

"HELP!"

Jesus rushed from the shop amid cries of panic from the neighbors. The commotion centered on a large, disabled oxcart slouching in the road with a broken wheel. Produce lay scattered on the ground. A crying boy lay pinned beneath the axle of the cart. The weight of the wagon didn't rest on the boy, but he was decidedly trapped.

"My boy!" a terrified mother shrieked over the cries in the street.

Two older men grabbed the wagon, straining with all their might, but they were unable to lift the tremendous burden off the lad.

"MOVE!" Jesus commanded his elders to step aside. "I can lift it." Putting his shoulder under the wagon, he began to strain at the load. "Get the baskets off this cart," Jesus yelled, and the bystanders quickly unloaded the remaining produce. Jesus' back muscles rippled under his workman's tunic as the wagon slowly lifted. The older men quickly pulled the boy to safety and into the arms of his weeping mother.

Jesus wiped the dust from his clothes as he stood up from underneath the wagon. "Jesus," the mother sobbed, "you saved my son."

A smiling Jesus tousled the boy's hair. He had done what anyone with his strength would have done. His physical strength came from working with wood and from digging limestone from a small rock quarry for the foundations of homes that he and his brothers had built for new residents.

A few years earlier his father, Joseph, had died, leaving the carpenter's shop to Mary and the family. As the oldest son, Jesus stepped into Joseph's shoes. After a time of grief—for Jesus loved Joseph—he supervised the family business, guiding his half-brothers James, Joseph, Simon and Judah in their daily tasks. The business prospered under Jesus' leadership.

Every Sabbath, Jesus was to be found in his favorite seat in the synagogue. He had never missed a service due to illness. His habits were an example to careless worshipers in Nazareth. He was always on time, though he never seemed to hurry. When he was chosen to read from the Law, his diction was clear, his pronunciation flawless. Old Solomon, who often rudely spoke out to correct the reading of others, never corrected Jesus. Once when Solomon stumbled over a word—whether he couldn't read or couldn't remember because of advancing age was unclear—he turned to Jesus for the correct reading.

"Jesus ought to be a rabbi," the women of Nazareth often said to the elders, who themselves had observed Jesus' mastery of the Scriptures. Many believed he should go and study in Jerusalem under Gamaliel, the celebrated scholar of the Law.

"Too bad Joseph died," old Solomon had been known to say. "Jesus could have been a great doctor of the Law. But the family business . . . ." He would let the words trail off wistfully. Then, stroking his silver-gray beard, Solomon would add, "Jesus will be an excellent elder one day. He's so strong, he'll outlive us all."

Because he was not married, Jesus sat toward the back of the synagogue. The honored seats were reserved for married men. Nor did he have a permanent seat because he was not yet thirty years old, but that would change in just a few weeks.

As a young businessman in a boisterous community, Jesus mixed well with all kinds of people, and he was liked and admired by all. His hair was long, soft and hung to his shoulders. His face was kind; he had his mother's dark, smiling eyes. There was something in his countenance that made people smile when he greeted them.

Jesus listened to the troubles of his customers and sympathized with neighbors when they lost a loved one. He heard the people complain of corrupt priests and politicians. He agonized when he heard of Roman soldiers needlessly beating people as they collected taxes. Jesus listened to travelers from all over the Roman Empire tell of their unending servitude to demanding kings. But Jesus knew a kingdom was coming—not a kingdom born of military power and conquest, but of love, peace and honesty.

He would begin soon. The day was coming when he would lay aside his carpenter's tools and minister to people with hurts like those he witnessed every day. He would not always be a carpenter.

Jesus saw men addicted to alcohol slowly destroying their families; he would offer freedom. Jesus knew of a hermit in town bound by a demon; he would cast it out. He watched as men and women broke their marriage vows; he would teach them faithfulness and offer them forgiveness. In the Temple, disillusioned Jews sought God amid the vendors and venality of the priests. Soon Jesus would announce, "I am the way, the truth and the life."

One day, word came to the village of Nazareth that a prophet of God was preaching repentance and baptizing people in the Jordan River. The men of Nazareth didn't know what to make of the rumors. God had been silent for four centuries, yet multitudes were flocking to hear John the Baptist preach because his sermons were said to be filled with power. It was said he was announcing that their Deliverer was coming at last. Hundreds were being baptized to get ready for the Messiah.

Late one evening, Jesus approached his mother as she sat at the family dining table. Mary's hands were always busy; she was sewing up a tear in a tunic.

"Mother," he said respectfully, "I will soon be thirty years old." He reminded her that a young Levite was consecrated into the office of priesthood at thirty and that young men became fully recognized as adults at that age. It was winter and the month of his birth. "I must be about my Father's business."

Mary remembered the first time she heard Jesus say those words in the Temple—and the waves of panic and relief that had swept over her in that place. Now those same feelings came rushing back. Mary understood that

Jesus was a gift from God. She had often pondered his miraculous conception and birth, never forgetting these things. She had treasured every day, every moment with him. She knew she could not hold on to her son forever, nor did she have any right to expect him to remain home. This day of separation was long coming, and she was ready to accept it, if only as a show of faith and her love for God.

"James can take over the carpenter shop," Jesus told her. "The other boys will work for James." Jesus had everything prepared in the shop for the others to carry on the business. James would take over tomorrow.

Jesus did not plan to tell the elders at the synagogue of his mission. He did not want their blessing, nor their authority. If they offered to recognize Jesus—their hometown product—he would have to turn them down. Jesus had been sent by his heavenly Father and had the authority of God on his life. The men from the synagogue in Nazareth would hear about his sermons and his works soon enough. He knew they would understand, for they had always expected him to be a teacher—but he also knew they would likely reject his claim of heavenly origin from God.

Mary and Jesus talked into the night. They revisited wonderful memories of God's providence for them. Mary was understandably proud of her son.

"I'll pack a lunch," Mary said, reluctant to forego her motherly role in his life. "I'll make sure your extra tunic is ready."

"No," Jesus said. He explained to her that he would trust his heavenly Father to provide for all his needs. He reminded her, "The Lord is my Shepherd, I shall not want for anything."

The candle was almost extinguished when they finished talking. "I will leave before sunrise," he said, rising.

And so Jesus left the carpenter shop that had been his home and business for many years. He trusted God, however, and didn't worry about the future. Yet a dark shadow which he did not yet fully understand lingered in the back of his mind. It was the shape of a cross that cast an ominous shadow over the joyful anticipation of his new ministry.

And Jesus increased in wisdom and stature, and in favor with God and men.

LUKE 2:52

chapter fifteen

A VOICE IN THE WILDERNESS

MATTHEW 3:1-17

Jesus walked through the bushes toward the Jordan River near Bethabara, a small village south of the Sea of Galilee. The foliage here was thicker than any he had seen in the hills surrounding Nazareth. As he slowly navigated the overgrown, little-used path, vines clutched at his legs, branches swatted at his face. The sound of water dancing and tripping over rocks told him the river was close. The sound of birds in the wetlands was different from the sound of birds that frequented the hilltops. A dead branch splintered under his foot; an unseen serpent slithered out of his way.

Then he heard a voice, barely audible. He couldn't make out what was said, but someone was shouting in the distance. As he reached the crest of the riverbank, the words became more discernible. He paused, listening to the now recognizable voice. As Jesus stepped out of the underbrush, the piercing bass voice of John the Baptist rang out, "REPENT!" The preacher paused for emphasis. "Prepare the way of the Lord. Make straight his path."

Jesus smiled when he saw John the Baptist. Wild and uncivilized in his appearance, John wore a tunic made of coarse camel's hair gathered at the waist by a wide leather belt. He stood in the water up to his ankles as he spoke, his long, unkempt hair blowing in the afternoon breeze. Around him on the bank were large rocks . . . people were sitting on the rocks. Up and down the river, hundreds of people were gathered, listening intently to John the Baptist. Jesus quickly surveyed the crowd, noting that all kinds of people had come to hear John—slaves, Roman soldiers, businessmen, mothers with their children sitting in friendly clusters. There were no roads nearby, so they had not just happened upon this unusual forum. All of them had been drawn to this spot. They had come just to hear the Baptist preach.

Then Jesus noticed a cluster of men who were not enjoying the sermon. These were religious leaders, scribes and Pharisees frowning at the orator and his fiery words. Huddled together, they whispered in angry tones. Finally, one of the religious leaders interrupted the sermon, yelling out without any attempt to disguise his hostility, "Who are you?"

These who called themselves keepers of the Law looked awkward on a riverbank in their tapestry robes. Standing in the hot afternoon sun, sweat trickled into the immaculate beards half hiding the scowls on their stern faces. The Pharisees practiced an elaborate and ritualistic obedience to the Law of Moses. They hoped that by doing so they would hasten the coming of the Messiah, who they believed would rid the country of the Roman overlords and usher in a time of peace and prosperity for the nation of Israel. But Jesus knew that in their hearts they denied everything proclaimed by John the Baptist.

Another of the hostile scribes repeated the question: "Who are you?"

"I am the voice of one crying in the wilderness," John answered.

"Are you the Deliverer?" another demanded to know if he was the Messiah. "No!"

"Are you Elijah? Are you one of the prophets?" another called to John.

"I am here to prepare the way for Messiah." John had lived in the wilderness, apart from the villages and their inhabitants for many years until called by God to this ministry. He subsisted on a diet of locusts and honey and had very little use for the trimmings and trappings of the social elite and the religious establishment. He would answer their questions, however, knowing they would not understand . . . or believe.

"We have been sent to find out who you are," an older priest spoke with a strong but condemning voice. "Tell us so we can answer those in Jerusalem who sent us."

"I am but a man sent from God. I am sent as a witness to the Light. The Messiah alone shall bring light to every man born into this world."

The religious leaders put their heads together, dissecting his answer. They clearly disapproved of John the Baptist. One man pointed an accusing finger at John while arguing vehemently. Finally, the men agreed on their next question.

"Then why are you baptizing?"

They didn't care that John preached, and certainly they didn't care that the multitudes heard him. But John was usurping their authority. He baptized people for the cleansing of their sins rather than sending them to the Temple to offer sacrifices. Only Gentiles who wished to become Jews were required by the Law to undergo the ritual cleansing by water. By baptizing Jews, John made no distinction between the Gentiles and God's chosen people.

But John knew their hearts and said, "You say to yourselves, 'We have Abraham as our father.' I tell you that God can raise up children of Abraham out of these stones."

One of the scribes spoke up angrily, saying, "Are we also to be baptized?"

"You brood of vipers!" John shouted, now incensed. "Who warned you to flee from the coming wrath? The axe is already at the root of the trees, and every tree that does not produce good fruit will be cut down and thrown into the fire."

"What should we do then?" someone in the crowd called out.

John turned and answered, "Bear fruit worthy of repentance. The man with two tunics should share with him who has none, and the one who has food should do the same."

A tax collector, hated in the Jewish community as a thief and a traitor, asked, "What must I do to be saved?"

"Don't collect any more than you are required to," came the answer.

A Roman soldier sitting with a few comrades stood up. "And what should we do?"

John replied, "Don't extort money and don't accuse the people falsely. Be content with your pay."

The people murmured among themselves, again wondering if John might be the Christ, their Deliverer. John answered them, saying, "I baptize you with water. But One more powerful than I will come, whose sandals I am not fit to carry. Even now he is alive and among us. He will baptize you with the Holy Spirit and with fire."

John the Baptist then glared once more at the religious leaders and said, "His winnowing fork is in his hand. He will clear his threshing floor and gather the wheat into his barn, but he will burn up the worthless chaff with unquenchable fire!"

Agitated and scandalized, the scribes and Pharisees refused to hear any more of this slander. Shaking their heads violently, the religious leaders scooped up fistfuls of sand and threw it into the air, cursing John. Then, stalking down the path, they departed from the river.

John had quickly become known throughout Judea as the Baptist, for he called upon the people to repent of their sins and be immersed in water to symbolize the cleansing of their sins in the sight of God.

His father had been a priest who ministered in the Temple. Because his father was a Levitical priest, John, too, could have ministered in the Temple in Jerusalem. He could have been clothed in rich, colorful robes or in the spotless white robes of a priest offering sacrifice for the sins of the people. But John had chosen to wear animal skins and to live in the wilderness. His long, flowing hair had not been cut since birth. John was a Nazirite, a man who had made a vow of holiness before God. John the Baptist had separated himself to his calling. His platform for ministry was the rocks of the Jordan, not the Temple.

The following day, John again preached to the hundreds assembled at the river his message of repentance and baptism. When he gave his invitation to the people to be baptized, a lone figure stepped away from the crowd. Jesus stepped from rock to rock, onto a sandy beach, then into the river. The river was clear; since there had been no floods, the water was not muddy. On this overcast day, the Jordan River was as clear as drinking water.

Jesus was unremarkable in appearance, his features plain and in most respects quite ordinary. He walked with strength and purpose though without tension, his movements deliberate but graceful. The carpenter's lean but muscular frame and sun-drenched skin showed him to be a laborer, a man who had known hard work; yet his carriage and demeanor spoke of a gentle man of quiet strength.

When John saw Jesus coming to him, the Baptist stopped in mid-sentence. His heart leaped, for John knew this was the event for which he had been born; this was his life's purpose. With the confidence of heaven and assurance in his heart, John pointed to Jesus, then lifted his deep voice for all to hear.

"Behold, the Lamb of God who takes away the sin of the world!"

After a moment of stunned silence on the banks of the Jordan, a murmur started low but grew steadily into a general commotion as the people talked among themselves. "Does John know this man?" "Who is he?" "What does the Baptist mean, 'Lamb of God'?" "Surely John doesn't believe this man is the Messiah, the Anointed One he's waiting for. We don't need a lamb; we need a lion to drive the Roman soldiers from our land!"

Undaunted, Jesus splashed through the shallow water to the place where John was standing. There was no need to introduce himself—John knew him. He recognized Jesus as the promised Messiah. He didn't understand all that he knew—and didn't dare voice his doubts—but John knew that this man was indeed the Anointed One of God.

Jesus fixed his eyes on John, and the Baptist returned his gaze. Neither spoke. Each man looked into the other's soul. A hush fell over the crowd, as if sensing the moment. Finally, Jesus broke the silence. "I am ready to be baptized," he said, smiling. His eyes revealed a heart that was light and free of worry.

"You are the One sent by God," John said. "I need to be baptized by *you*. Why do you come to me? I'm not worthy to tie the cords of your sandals."

"It is time," Jesus answered plainly.

John the Baptist hesitated a moment.

"Allow this," Jesus said, "because it is the right and proper thing to fulfill all that God requires." Jesus did not amplify his answer. Baptism was a matter of obedience to God, plain and simple.

John knew that Jesus was about thirty years of age, and the thought occurred to him that a Jewish priest was dedicated into office at the age of thirty, the age of maturity. From the time of Moses, priests had been washed from head to foot when initiated into office. Jesus had not come to repent; he was here to begin his ministry.

So, John the Baptist placed his hands on the chest and back of Jesus and dipped him into the cool waters of the Jordan River. When he raised him from the river, Jesus was smiling broadly. The crowd on the riverbank did not understand what they had just seen. There had been no confession of sin, nor had John called on this man to repent.

Jesus stood praying there in the shallow waters when there came a sound like thunder from above. Then John saw him. Silently . . . harmlessly . . .

just as a dove lightly rests on the branch of a tree, the Holy Spirit descended from heaven and rested gently on Jesus standing in the water next to him.

Then came a voice from heaven. The sound of the voice echoed off the rocks and through the trees. Everyone heard it, though many were unsure of what they heard. Some thought they heard a thunderclap; they looked around for the dark clouds of an approaching storm, but there was no storm. Others distinctly heard a voice, but didn't understand the words, their doubts muddling the evidence of their senses.

Those who truly believed, whose hearts swelled at this remarkable visitation, heard clearly the voice of the living God. His words had been spoken before in many languages to obedient sons around the world. This time, God spoke the words of a father: "You are my beloved Son, in whom I am well pleased."

And John bore witness, saying, "I saw the Spirit descending from heaven like a dove, and He remained upon Him . . . I have seen and testified that this is the Son of God."
JOHN 1:32,34

chapter sixteen

"COME AND SEE"
JOHN 1:35-42

The young fishermen had grown up together in the squalor of Bethsaida—not even a town, just a few shabby fishing huts at the headwaters of the Sea of Galilee. Andrew and John trusted each other, as men in their profession are wont to do, and as followers of John the Baptist they had often talked late into the night about the promised Messiah. "Get ready for his coming," the Baptist preached, so both young men expected momentary victory over Rome.

Yesterday, Andrew and John had witnessed the baptism of a man named Jesus, whom John the Baptist declared to be the "Lamb of God." Both friends had heard the voice of God thunder from heaven, declaring, "This is my beloved Son, in whom I am well pleased."

Andrew was a well-mannered, black-haired young man in his early twenties. His black eyes—round and bigger than on most men—could see things others didn't see. Andrew looked past the skin of men into their souls. Nonetheless, Andrew loved people and when his friends needed help, Andrew was always there. Hence, he had many friends. On this day, Andrew was busy explaining baptism to people waiting in line for a satisfactory vantage point at the water's edge. John was talking to a delegation of soldiers at the edge of the throng.

John's thin frame resembled a tall, solitary stalk of wheat, and next to the professional soldiers in their breastplates and helmets, his gauntness was almost comical. But he was not weak. The 17-year-old apprentice fisherman could hoist a catch of fish twice his weight on his own . . . and he was known to erupt on occasion with a violent temper. Young John was polite to all until offended or wronged; then he would snap and bellow at anyone within hearing.

The cold bitter wind whipped down the Jordan Valley, but the people were sheltered among the trees at the riverside. John the Baptist was again preaching to the multitudes: "Repent!" He continued to call on the people to make straight the way of the Lord—to mend their ways and prepare their hearts for the coming King.

When they saw Jesus walking among the crowds, Andrew and John followed him, at first from a distance. After a few moments, Jesus stopped and confronted the two young men. "What do you seek?" Jesus asked, almost as if the question were a command.

Andrew spoke up. "Rabbi . . . ," he spoke the title "rabbi" with deep reverence, surprising John with his use of the honorific word for "teacher." Andrew and John had long reserved this title for Rabbi Zebulun, their own beloved teacher. They had planned never to call any other man by that name. But then, something told Andrew that Jesus was no mere man. He knew Jesus could teach them much.

"Rabbi, where are you living?"

"Come and see." Jesus knew the real purpose they had come to talk with him, and he was prepared to deal with their searching faith. He said, "We'll eat together."

The vermilion sun kissed the peaks of the Judean mountain range. Soon it would be winter dark—that pitch-black night immediately after sunset and before the rising moon brought some warmth to the winter sky. Jesus, Andrew and John settled around a simple meal of roasted lamb and bread. The young men barely ate; their mouths were filled with questions.

"If you are the Messiah," Andrew asked, "why did you not preach to the multitudes today?" Andrew believed the Jews would eagerly acknowledge their Deliverer and follow him. So why didn't Jesus reveal himself to the multitudes? John pointed out that more than a thousand men had been present that day at the river; they could have formed the nucleus of a formidable army.

"My kingdom will not come by war," Jesus explained to the young ears. "I must rule the hearts of people. I must rule in their lives before I can reign over their villages or cities."

The young men listened intently.

"I must rule within before I rule without."

"But the Messiah will rule the world with an iron fist," John blurted out, revealing not only his mistaken assumptions but also his hotheaded approach to life. "If you are Messiah, you must sit on David's throne."

"First I must sit on the throne of the heart." Jesus reminded them that their Father in heaven had no interest in mere outward displays of worship. Love that is forced is not love at all, he said, reminding them of the first and greatest commandment: "You must love the Lord your God with all your heart."

"When will Messiah's kingdom come?" Andrew asked.

"With time. But seek first the rule of the kingdom of God in your heart. When you let God reign in your heart, these other things will be given to you."

Jesus taught them what the Messiah would do, tracing God's plan for the redemption of mankind as revealed in the Holy Scriptures. Beginning with the Torah—the first five books of Scripture—through the books of the prophets, Jesus showed them what God had said about his Anointed One.

The conversation lasted late into the night. The young men shared the questions of their hearts, but the difficult questions did not go just one way. Jesus had piercing questions for these young men.

"What does God want you to do with your life?"

Neither man was sure how to answer.

"When will you begin searching for God's will?"

"Now," they promised.

"Come, follow me." Jesus said they must learn of him. "Then you will go tell others about the kingdom."

The next morning the young men were gone. They did not tell Jesus where they were going, they just left. Jesus knew they had not rejected what he taught them; these were true seekers whose hearts were open to the things of God. Jesus knew where they had gone. The message of love must be shared with those whom they loved. Thus, the kingdom would go forward one person at a time.

Later, as Jesus was returning on the road to Galilee, Andrew came walking swiftly from the other direction. Someone was with him. When they got within shouting distance, Andrew waved, then yelled, "This is my brother." His big black eyes crinkled with excitement. "I told my brother you are the Messiah."

A tall man with a broad, muscular chest, Simon was ten years older than Andrew and looked nothing like his brother. Whereas Andrew's hair and beard were black as burnt wood, Simon's hair and beard glowed a flaming red.

"Are you the Christ?" Simon yelled as they approached. Before he was introduced to Jesus, Simon asked his burning question using the Greek form of *Messiah*. Simon was a blunt man, his head as hard as his life as a fisherman on the Sea of Galilee.

Jesus laughed at the boldness of the man, then looked into his eyes as if examining his soul. "You are Simon, son of Jonah," Jesus said to him, "but from now on you shall be called Peter." Jesus smiled. "You will be like a rock." The name Peter was translated "a stone."

"Peter, you are a blunt speaker," Jesus noted. "You say what's on your mind, whether people like it or not. I will need you to help build my kingdom." Jesus knew that hard times awaited those who followed him. When the Father needed a tough, hard man, he would send Peter to do the job.

Turning to Andrew, Jesus said, "I will need your sensitivity and insight in the kingdom. You are careful of people's feelings."

Reluctantly, Simon Peter walked with his brother and listened to Andrew's new rabbi. Soon they met young John and his brother James hurrying up the road to greet Jesus. Simon was interested in hearing what James would have to say about all this. Whereas John was young and often impolitic—he had followed the raving Baptist into the wilderness—James was highly reliable and unquestionably trustworthy.

James was as stocky as John was thin. Brawny and tall, James didn't say much, though like his brother he had a fiery temperament. He worked the nets in his father's boats along with the servants, usually outworking them.

"I don't like to speak," James said to Jesus, "but if you are who they say, I'll do anything you ask."

[Andrew] first found his own brother Simon, and said to him,
"We have found the Messiah" (which is translated, the Christ).

JOHN 1:41

chapter seventeen

CAN ANYTHING GOOD COME OUT OF NAZARETH?

JOHN 1:43-53

The following day, Jesus and his four new friends walked north into Galilee. By mid-afternoon they arrived at Tiberias, the fortified Roman city on the southern shore of the Sea of Galilee. Jesus was leading the way. The two close friends, Andrew and John, walked together while Peter talked with James, who just listened.

Tiberias was famous for its warm mineral springs. Herod Antipas, the reigning tetrarch of Galilee, had recently moved the capital there from Sepphoris. The city's forbidding black lava walls were as hostile as the Romans' dark prisons. When the city walls of Tiberias were in sight, young John felt a pang of revulsion. There was no way around the city he hated. Its protective walls stretched from the mountains out into the sea. They would have to walk through Tiberias.

John dropped back to walk between Peter and James. They were big men and his small frame was nearly hidden between them. John had had a number of run-ins with Roman troops and he wanted nothing to do with the three soldiers now standing guard at the gate, casually observing the travelers entering the city.

Jesus paid no attention to the soldiers. As he and his friends entered the city, a Roman guard called out, "Hey!" The soldier directed his question at Jesus: "Where are you going?" Rumors of a Deliverer among the Jews had reached the ears of Herod, and his centurions were ordered to suppress any attempts by the Jews, however futile, to form an underground rebel army. Therefore, they were always suspicious when Hebrew men traveled in a group.

Jesus turned and smiled at the soldiers. "I am going to Cana where my cousin is to be married," he answered. "These men are my disciples . . . I am a teacher."

"JOHN!" a voice rang out from inside the gate.

Young John, already nervous in the presence of the guards, nearly bolted when he heard his name shouted. Yet there was something familiar about the voice and the way his name was called.

"PHILIP!" John immediately forgot about the soldiers and instinctively stepped through the gate to greet his childhood friend from Bethsaida.

Philip was short and skinny and, to the soldier's trained eye, was an unlikely recruit for a military uprising. The Roman guard waved Jesus and his friends through the gate and went back to his post.

The young men embraced. "Where have you been?" Philip interrogated John in the way old friends have of asking for news. John explained that he had been with John the Baptist at the Jordan River until he met Jesus. Then John turned quiet and serious. "Remember Rabbi Zebulun . . . our teacher who expected the Messiah to come at any moment?"

Philip indeed had fond memories of Rabbi Zebulun, who ended each class by saying, "Maybe the Messiah will come today."

John said, "The Messiah is here!"

"Here?"

"Yes."

John told him of how Jesus had taught them from the Scriptures, showing them the kingdom of God and revealing himself to be the one they had been waiting and searching for.

"Do you believe in him?" Philip asked.

"Yes."

Jesus stepped over to where the two friends were talking, and Philip looked knowingly at Jesus. Some men need all their questions answered before they will take action, but Philip was a simple, straightforward man. He believed what his friend John said about Jesus. He trusted what he saw.

Jesus said only, "Come. Follow me."

Philip left Tiberias to follow Jesus. Five friends who had grown up in Bethsaida were now reunited by a deep-seated yearning planted by their forefathers and cultivated by their former teacher. Each had a dream of independence for Israel, yet each had doubts about his own personal relationship with the man they believed to be the Messiah.

As they neared Cana, Philip left the group to walk ahead into town. Philip sought his friend Nathanael, who lived just outside Cana on a small farm. They were unlikely friends—Philip from poor parents who lived in an obscure fishing village; Nathanael, who was also called Bartholemew or "son of Ptolemy," had royal blood flowing in his veins. A descendant of Ptolemy, who had ruled Egypt after the death of Alexander the Great, Nathanael lived in oversized surroundings and carried himself like royalty. His parents and brothers, who harbored the hope of the Ptolemaic line one day being restored to the throne of Egypt, lived in a world of unrealized dreams, making them cynical. But Nathanael was different. His hope lay in the coming of a far greater kingdom.

Philip found his friend behind the large, white flat-roofed house on the hill. Nathanael was there reading a scroll from the Scriptures under a fig tree, as servants tended cattle and planted the fields in the distance. The fig tree was his favorite place to pray and meditate. Philip saw that he had been reading the words of the prophet Isaiah, who had written much about the coming Messiah.

"We have found the Messiah," Philip said, "the one Moses predicted would come . . . the one Isaiah and the prophets described." Philip sat with his friend to tell him the Messiah was not a warrior like the Son of David they expected. Philip shared what his new master, Jesus, was teaching concerning the kingdom of heaven.

Nathanael liked the idea that this Messiah was different. Other messiahs—patently false messiahs—rallied the people with promises of political power, the slaughter of their enemies and the plunder of the gold of the Roman Empire.

"Who is this Messiah?" Nathanael asked.

"He is called Jesus of Nazareth, the son of Joseph."

A scowl darkened Nathanael's face. "Nazareth! Can anything good come out of there?" He had nothing against Nazareth per se, but the sleepy village was politically and culturally insignificant—most definitely not a birthplace of kings. Besides, as a careful student of the Scriptures, he expected the Messiah to come out of Bethlehem, the City of David.

"Come and see for yourself," Philip answered. "Listen to Jesus, then make up your mind."

The two left Nathanael's house and walked to where Jesus and his tentative band of followers were staying in Cana. It had been raining and the road was muddy, making it difficult to walk with any haste. A Roman officer galloped by, the horse's hooves splashing mud on Nathanael's woven tapestry cloak. The dirtied garment spoiled his enthusiasm for meeting Jesus. Nathanael understood the necessity of proper apparel when royalty met royalty.

Jesus met Philip and his friend in the street. When he saw Nathanael, Jesus announced, "Behold, an Israelite in whom there is no deceit! Nathanael, you are a sincere seeker. . . ."

"How do you know me?" Nathanael asked. "You haven't talked to me, nor have we met." Nathanael believed himself to be a sincere person, a fair person; he always listened first before making up his mind. But that was the proper way of royalty, which was the way Nathanael looked at life.

"I saw you under the fig tree where Philip found you praying," Jesus explained. "I have seen your heart and know you seek first the kingdom of God."

Nathanael looked to Philip. No one else had been there . . . but Jesus knew. *Only God knows all things,* Nathanael thought. *I am indeed standing in the presence of one who is close to God.* With his head bowed in reverence, he said, "Rabbi, you are the Son of God! You are the King of Israel."

Jesus lifted Nathanael's head and looked into his eyes. "You believe, just because I saw you under the fig tree? Follow me, and you'll see far greater things."

"I am ready to follow you," said Nathanael. Though heir to an earthly throne, Nathanael would submit to the reign of another king—a king who would rule his heart.

> *And He said to him, "Most assuredly, I say to you,*
> *hereafter you shall see heaven open, and the angels of God ascending*
> *and descending upon the Son of Man."*
>
> JOHN 1:51

chapter eighteen

A WEDDING FEAST

JOHN 2:1-11

"JESUS!"

The young Galilean men gathered around Jesus turned to see a middle-aged woman waving to them from the backyard. She was placing a ceramic mixing bowl on the food preparation table.

"Jesus," she warmly repeated the name of her oldest son. Then, holding out her arms to embrace him, she walked across the yard. Jesus and his mother lovingly embraced, then she stood back to look at him.

"It's good to see you, Mother," Jesus said.

"Thank you for coming to your cousin's wedding feast," Mary answered. "I am supervising the food."

Jesus recognized her blue robe as the one she wore to special occasions. Even though age had faded some of its luster, the robe looked elegant on Mary, not because of its quality or price, but because of Mary's mature beauty.

They were interrupted by a demanding voice from the direction of the house. "Mary, the wine is already running low!" Levi, the master of ceremonies at the feast, was an elderly man, short and extraordinarily thin, so much so that Mary was hard-pressed to see him in the doorway. His voice was quiet, but insistent, so as not to alert the guests to their predicament.

"Jesus!" Levi raised his voice when he recognized his nephew. Jesus introduced his disciples—Peter, Andrew, John, James, Philip and Nathanael—to his uncle, who in turn responded, "You must all come in to the marriage feast." Levi's role as master of the feast was to make everyone comfortable . . . and happy. "Come and eat with us."

After meeting the guests and the families of the wedded couple, the young men took their places at the foot of the table. Almost immediately, everyone returned to his or her conversation.

"Bring them a plate of food," Mary instructed the servants to look after Jesus and his friends. Quickly, warm bread appeared before them, and a large bowl of lamb stew.

"M-m-mmm," James sniffed the lamb stew. He was a hard worker and a hearty eater.

The loaf of bread was handed to Jesus. He broke off a morsel, dipped it into the lamb stew and ate. He passed the loaf to John, who followed his example.

When the main portion of the meal was finished, children were excused to play. Children were not interested in politics and family gossip. At the head of the table, Levi was telling stories. Though ancient of body, Levi possessed a keen mind and recalled heartwarming and embarrassing details of the childhood of nearly everyone at the table. There was much laughter and more than a few red faces.

While Levi was speaking, Mary came behind Jesus, bent over and whispered into his ear, "There's no more wine outside." She pointed to the pitcher on the table. "The pitchers are almost empty."

Jesus didn't answer.

"What am I to do?" Mary asked her son.

"Why do you come to me? You are responsible for the food at this wedding," Jesus said to her.

"But I am not the one who will bear the shame," Mary thought aloud. "Levi and this poor young couple will suffer the humiliation of failing to provide for their guests. This should be the happiest day of their lives." Mary was uncertain why she had told her son that the wine was gone; but in her heart, she knew Jesus could do something to help them.

Jesus knew the thoughts of her heart. "My hour is not yet come," he answered her.

James and John looked at one another, unable to comprehend just what Mary was asking him to do—or the enormity of her request.

From the time of his extraordinary birth until now, Jesus had done nothing to indicate that he possessed supernatural abilities, but Mary knew they were there nonetheless. She didn't know when he would use his power or how. She wasn't entirely sure what to expect when he did.

Mary turned to the servants standing by the wall. "Whatever he says for you to do," she gave them an order, "do it!"

Jesus left the festivities and walked outside to the back of the house. The servants wondered what Jesus was looking for back there. They simply followed, watching him.

Against a corner of the house were six water pots, each of a different size and color. Some were large, holding more than twenty-five gallons of water; others were smaller. These were rain pots used to catch rainwater off the roof. Since people walked on the roof of the house, any rainwater collected in the pots was dirty. According to Hebrew law, it was required that the dirty water stand for a prescribed number of days until all impurities had settled to the bottom of the pot. Then the water could be used for washing, cooking and on some occasions, even drinking.

Jesus looked into the pots as if inspecting their contents. Then he turned to the servants and said, "Fill each one up to the very top with water." Jesus held his finger to the lip of the pots. "Be sure they are filled to the brim."

Looking at Jesus, the servants just nodded.

Then Jesus said, "Take the water pots to Levi, the master of the feast." One servant jerked his head to look at a fellow servant. There was anxiety in his eyes. If they brought water when old Levi wanted wine . . . . It was not beyond old Levi to beat them with his walking stick.

"There is no wine," Jesus told the servants. "Fill these pots with water and take it for them to drink."

The persuasive power of Jesus was greater than the servants' fears. They quickly took small vessels and filled the larger water pots . . . to the brim. Then, picking up the pots, they started toward the door. Mary opened the door for the servants.

"Attention, everyone!" Levi commanded. He managed to conceal his relief at the arrival of additional jars of wine. "Let's have a toast to the bride and groom."

The table grew silent. Panic flashed in the servants' faces. They had hoped to set the water pots down and quickly leave the before their master realized what they had done. Servants placed a large pot on the floor on either side of Levi. The small pots were brought in and placed on the table. Levi took his cup and dipped into the water pot. A little spilled over the spout and down the edge of the pot. Since it was customary for the master of the feast to drink first, he put the cup to his lips. His hand shook slightly from advanced age, and a few drops of red liquid spilled onto his beard.

"Ah-h-h," he sighed, and the guests entered into Levi's happiness, laughing and raising their glasses in salute to the newlyweds.

Then Levi's crinkled eyes and deep smile suddenly vanished. He stared unbelievingly into his cup. The servants on the edge of the crowd nervously backed away from the table. The bride and groom looked at one another, wondering what was wrong with the wine. It was the groom's job to provide wine. *Was the wine not acceptable?* Old Levi furrowed his brow, then looking at the groom, he asked, "Why have you hidden the best wine until now?"

The groom said nothing, not knowing how to answer.

"This wine is the very best we've had all day!" old Levi exclaimed.

A smile spread across the face of the groom. He reveled in the compliment from old Levi. "Every man sets out the good wine first. And when the guests are full, *then* the host sets out the inferior vintage. But *you* have saved the best for last!"

Levi laughed. The groom laughed. The guests all laughed. The servants standing on the edge of the crowd did not laugh. They knew they had carried in pots full of rainwater, yet everyone was rejoicing over the quality of the wine in the very same pots. The servants began jabbering among themselves, each confirming what the others had experienced. As the servants babbled excitedly, John overheard them. He listened carefully as one servant after another told the same story. Then John turned to his brother James and whispered, "The servants claim Jesus turned water into wine."

"What?!"

"They say this wine we're drinking was water."

The disciples talked excitedly between themselves. Was this possible? Was Jesus responsible for this miracle? Was their Messiah more than they imagined him to be?

"Tell us what you are saying!" the voice of Levi called to James and John over the general din. He pointed to them and beckoned them to stand and address the guests, his demeanor plainly chiding them for their ill manners.

"Please, tell us what you are saying." Attention was suddenly focused on the two young men, their faces red with embarrassment and more than a little fear.

John spoke carefully. "The vintage you are drinking came from the pots that catch rain. An hour ago, it was not wine at all, but water."

Levi commanded that the servants be brought to him. "Where did you get this wine?" he demanded.

The head servant spoke with his eyes downcast. "Your nephew, the son of Mary, commanded us to fill the pots to the brim with water and to serve the guests from the same pots. We do not know how he did it, but the water became wine!"

The room fell supernaturally silent. The guests looked into their cups, then they looked around at one another. All eyes then turned to Jesus and his disciples, but Jesus was not there. He had departed before the miraculous wine had been served.

This beginning of signs Jesus did in Cana of Galilee, and manifested His glory; and His disciples believed in Him.

JOHN 2:11

chapter nineteen

TEMPTATION

MATTHEW 4:1-11

Dark clouds scurried across the winter sky above the mountains. The raw winter wind whipping down off the Sea of Galilee chilled his flesh. Jesus was tiring. He had traversed one hill after another toward this, his destination in the Judean mountains: an uninhabited peak barren of plant and animal life save for a few resourceful predators and the scavengers waiting for them to die of starvation.

The Spirit of God had led Jesus to this desolate place, but he was not alone; an evil presence shadowed the man from Nazareth.

Jesus crossed the Wadi Qelt and began to climb the rocks, then stumbled into a remote mountain pass flanked on either side by formidable cliffs. Because of its rugged ascent, climbing through rocks and narrow ravines, a casual observer would likely dismiss this path as a dead end. However, the Spirit kept leading Jesus upward until he reached a narrow ledge overlooking a deep canyon.

Nearby, a spring of water trickled through the rocks and Jesus drank from it. Although he was fasting, Jesus allowed himself life-sustaining water while abstaining from solid food. He followed the spring to a cave that would protect him from the elements.

A red serpent hissed and slithered out from under a rock and slid a short distance down the path. The serpent coiled in a murky, wet crevice and watched Jesus. Across the ravine, two ravenous wolves stood in a darkened cave, also watching the human who had invaded their canyon. Jesus ignored them. Soon, he knew, a far more dangerous predator would stalk him to this place.

Jesus lay exhausted on the cave floor, but could not sleep. He had committed himself not to eat of any food for forty days, but there was an emptiness deep inside that bread and wine could not fill. He longed for the presence of the One without whom he was incomplete. Jesus was hungry for God. "Father!" he cried out, "I will seek your face. I will do your good and perfect will . . . ."

The days passed, the weather turned mean. A storm rumbled through the valley, the dark underbellies of the clouds unleashing their frigid contents upon the mountain with stinging fury for several days. Jesus shivered in the cave, out of the wind and rain. His bones creaked, his muscles ached. He pulled his cloak tightly about him.

As Jesus approached the end of his fast, he found that he was lonely. He had not heard the friendly sound of another human voice for forty days. *Life is good,* Jesus reminded himself, *and made to be shared.* Jesus smiled as he remembered his family . . . meals . . . sitting with friends drinking in the beauty of the Galilean hills.

A snowflake softly lit on the back of his folded hands. Then another. And another. Lifting them to his eye, Jesus tried to see their unique patterns, but the overcast sky and the darkened cave kept them hidden in darkness. Though rare, snow did fall sometimes high in the Judean mountains. Jesus prayed again before dozing peacefully with the white flecks drifting gently in the ravine.

The next morning Jesus awakened to a sound—a sound out of place—like the squeak of a chariot wheel. Then he recognized the chirping of a bird. A bird was singing. Morning washed away the night, and Jesus saw shadows across the ravine. The sun peered through the canyon walls down into the ravine, like sunshine through a crack in a closed door. "The sun," Jesus said aloud, smiling as a golden sliver warmed his tired body. "God is good." He thanked the Father for the dawning of a new day. He was ready to do battle.

His adversary, Satan, had been waiting and watching, having followed Jesus to this desolate location. And now that Jesus was in a physically weakened condition, the devil would call upon every device, every wile, every work of evil to bring down the Son of God. Satan knew something of the power that lay within Jesus' grasp, and he wanted that power. He wanted Jesus to dangle helplessly like a puppet at the end of his string.

The devil came to Jesus in the small clearing. "If you are the Son of God," he challenged Jesus, "command these stones to become loaves of bread. You must be hungry. You have the power to change the stones into bread."

Memory can be a terrible master, for it reminds us of better days and tempts us to return to a past that is prohibited to us, and Jesus now remembered the bread his mother used to bake in the community oven in Nazareth. The stones he saw now were brown like small, round loaves of bread. The aroma of fresh bread drifted through Jesus' memory. He could do it. He could turn the stones to bread . . . bread just like his mother baked . . . with butter, if he desired. But the Father had sent him to serve mankind, not himself.

"No," Jesus said. "For it is written, 'Man shall not live by bread alone, but by every word that proceeds from the mouth of God.'" Jesus knew the strength of resolution—and its nourishment to the soul—that comes from the words of God.

Satan, still confident of victory, changed tactics. The two enemies were then transported to the pinnacle of the Temple in Jerusalem, where they could look down on Jerusalem—and Jerusalem could see them. There they stood atop the religious world. Satan challenged Jesus: "Since you are the Son of God, throw yourself down!"

Satan paused for dramatic effect. "Surely you are not afraid. Is it not also written, 'God will command his angels to protect you, and they will lift you up in their hands, so that you will not so much as strike your foot against a stone'?" The devil, too, could quote Scripture, though twisted for his own purposes.

Jesus neither moved nor responded.

"The people want miracles," the devil urged. "Throw yourself off the pinnacle. The angels will save you . . . people will believe in you."

Jesus would indeed do miracles, but he would not do one for Satan. He would do only the will of his Father, and this was not his will. Jesus answered the devil, saying, "It is also written: 'Do not tempt the Lord your God.'"

Then they were whisked to the peak of a great mountain. From there, they looked out on the beauty, the majesty, the glory of all the kingdoms of the world. "Look at the people," the devil said to Jesus.

In one transcending moment, Jesus saw the nations of the earth. People who were made in the image of God, people that God loved. *They are the reason why I have come*, he thought.

"I am the god of this world," Satan boasted, "and these are my people." Jesus did not deny this; he was familiar with the devil's claim. Satan reigned on earth, and he enslaved its people. Jesus' heart ached for the millions held captive by sin.

"If you bow down to me . . . ," the devil sounded so convincing. "If you bow down to me," he propositioned, "I will give all these people to you."

No mortal man will ever know how deeply Jesus was tempted to strike this bargain with the devil, because mortal men cannot fathom the depths of God's love. They will never love the people of the world as Jesus loved them at that moment.

"The world will be yours! Only kneel down . . . ," the devil coerced. "Worship me. NOW!"

"Away with you, Satan!" Jesus answered. "For it is written, 'You shall worship the Lord your God, and you shall serve him only.'"

Then the devil left Him, and behold, angels came and ministered to Him.

MATTHEW 4:11

chapter twenty

FISHERS OF MEN

MARK 1:16-20

A severe spring storm had rumbled across the Sea of Galilee the previous evening. Waves had pounded the shore, angrier than usual, and the fishermen who braved the storm were unable to catch anything during the night. But morning broke over the sea with an unusual calm. The silent early morning mist evaporated in the first rays of the sun. The sea was eerily mirror-like in its sudden stillness. Simon, whom Jesus called Peter, looked in the water and saw a perfect reflection of his red beard and red eyes. He needed sleep.

"We'll have to work all morning." Peter let out a laugh as he began pulling on the rain-soaked nets. "We have to make up for lost time."

Andrew didn't answer but jumped up to help him. The brothers usually caught their fish at night, slept in the early morning, then went out fishing again in the late afternoon. But today, there would be no morning sleep.

"Let's cast near the shore," the still boisterous Peter said to his brother. "The fish may be hiding among the shoals." Andrew piloted the boat toward shore, near the place where their friends James and John sat on the beach with their father Zebedee, mending their nets which had been damaged in the storm.

Peter clambered out of the boat and waded knee-deep into the lake, the hair on his legs turning auburn in the water. Andrew began tossing the wet nets from the boat, hoping that fishing around the shallow shores might indeed be profitable this morning.

"Any more news of Jesus?" Peter asked his brother between tosses of the net. They hadn't seen Jesus for weeks; not since the wedding . . . and the wine. "He was a good teacher . . . ."

The brothers discussed their doubts. Jesus was not at all what they expected of a Messiah. They had been looking for a strong, charismatic warrior who would lead Israel into battle. Peter had envisioned a Messiah who, like Samson, would tower over his enemies. Andrew thought that perhaps Messiah would be nimble and cunning like David, the boy hero who grew into a mighty king.

The brothers and their friends had followed Jesus for almost a week, asking questions and listening to his answers before returning to their fishing boats. They had all seen the miracle of the wine.

"Was it really a miracle?" John was asking his brother James on the beach, where they were carefully sewing up the holes in their nets for afternoon fishing.

"You drank it," James answered. "What did it taste like to you?"

Young John asked, "James, do you believe Jesus is the Messiah?"

James didn't answer immediately. He weighed his answer carefully. Finally, he nodded his head, answering simply, "Yes."

He waited a little longer then added, "But Jesus is not the kind of Messiah we expected."

Two months had passed since John and Andrew had witnessed the baptism of Jesus at the Jordan. Now the first signs of an early spring had come to Galilee. Unseasonably warm winds and rain had transformed the dull brown fields around Capernaum into sprightly green meadows. Fruit trees along the lake budded white, their blossoms a promise of new life.

While the fishermen worked and discussed the Messiah, they didn't see Jesus coming toward them, walking along the beach. A large crowd was following in his wake. It was the crowd the fishermen saw first, and John recognized Philip and Nathanael among them. Then the fisherman saw Jesus and they stopped what they were doing, his presence commanding their attention.

Jesus stepped out onto a few large rocks in the water near where Peter and Andrew had been fishing. Then he called to them, "Come!" He beckoned to the brothers. "Follow me, and I will make you fishers of men."

Peter knew in his gut and in his heart that Jesus was much more than a teacher. He realized all at once that he believed Jesus to be the Messiah who would usher in God's kingdom, and that it would be a different kind of kingdom. Peter was ready to learn about that kingdom. He made the decision to forsake all to follow Jesus.

Simon Peter immediately dropped his nets and sloshed through the shallow water toward Jesus. Andrew folded his nets over the side of the boat, then followed Peter to Jesus.

Then Jesus walked to where James and John had overturned their boat and were laying out their nets on the hull to dry in the morning sun. The young men eagerly looked up at Jesus, as if waiting for an invitation like the one he had just extended to their friends. They didn't want to be left out.

Jesus smiled at them. "Come and learn from me," he motioned to the sons of Zebedee. "From now on you will catch men."

James and John immediately dropped their nets and followed Jesus.

As young John put aside the nets, he knew he would not return to fishing. When he followed John the Baptist, he was running away—running from Rome and its taxes, running from the legalistic traditions of money-driven priests, running from a meager hand-to-mouth existence on the Sea of Galilee. His choice to follow Jesus was different.

John would help establish God's kingdom on earth. Jesus was the Messiah and the people must be told. And he was certain Jesus held the answers to his many questions.

They immediately left their nets and followed Him.

MATTHEW 4:20

chapter twenty-one

A DEVIL IN GOD'S HOUSE

MARK 1:21-31

The white marble synagogue in Capernaum lay nestled among tall sycamore trees. It was a quiet Sabbath day much like any other, but the calm soon gave way to a festive excitement that swept a small horde of villagers toward the synagogue. Jesus and his disciples walked at the front of the crowd, laughing and talking excitedly. After the services, Jesus, John and James would spend the Sabbath with Peter and Andrew at the house they had inherited from family in Capernaum.

As the people entered the building, each man reverently draped a prayer shawl over his head. Although excitement lingered because of the presence of Jesus, everyone joined in singing psalms in strictest solemnity.

Five elders stood to read from the Law. When the Law had been read, an elder then nodded his head to Jesus to read from the *Haphtarah*. Jesus approached the scribe who handed him the scroll. Unrolling the scroll with reverence, he knew the words as though he were the author. He read declaratively from the text.

Jesus spoke deeply from his heart, and the people listened with hearts eager and hungry for the things of God. They were astonished by his teaching. Jesus taught with the authority of God, not the empty, legalistic threats of the scribes. Truly, an otherworldly anointing rested on Jesus the teacher as he followed the Jewish custom of *charaz*, teaching the people verse to verse, passage to passage, like pearls on a necklace.

As Jesus approached the end of his lesson, he called for commitment and obedience to the heavenly Father. Suddenly a demonic voice shrieked from the rear of the synagogue: "Eeeeeeeeeekkkk!"

Some people jumped, others cried out. The women in the balcony lurched back from the guardrail. The elders craned their heads in disbelief to see who dared to irreverently disturb the sacred service.

"Eeeeeeeeeekkkk!" came the shriek again.

"Quiet." The calm but penetrating voice of Jesus hushed the crowd as he stepped down from the lectern to confront the disruptive force. The authority in his voice demanded attention. When he said, "Quiet," everyone became silent.

Jesus walked to where a man stood shaking. From deep within the man came a guttural sound like a voice echoing in a dark cave. The man who had cried out began shaking violently. Yellow saliva dripped from the corner of his mouth, and his eyes rolled back into his head. "Leave us alone, Jesus of Nazareth," the voice pleaded, using the man's lips. "What do you want with us? Have you come to destroy us?"

The crowd watched in horror. They recognized the strange man; he was thought to be a harmless recluse, a simpleton who lived in a small shack at the edge of town. He begged coins and food in the street and would go house to house offering to work odd jobs for a meal. Yet every Sabbath day he showed up in the synagogue, clean and prepared for worship.

Demon possession was not new to the worshipers. Some had heard about evil spirits in their travels, while others had seen actual manifestations. The rabbinical teachings described people who were demonized, particularly noting the paralyzing effects on the nervous system of the possessed individual. Somewhere between the spirit and mind, somewhere between the conscious and unconscious, a vulgar personality had invaded this man and taken possession of his personality.

Snorting and shaking violently, the man vomited, then yelled out, "You have no control over me, Jesus of Nazareth!"

Jesus was not intimated. He stood calmly, giving no indication that he would communicate further with the demon, nor did he attempt to restrain the man. One purpose of Jesus' mission, he knew, was to destroy the works of the devil, but he had not come to destroy this man or to harm him.

Again, the deep resonate voice of the demon challenged Jesus: "I know who you are." Everyone in the room waited for Jesus to do something. "I know you are the Holy One of God."

The demon spoke in Hebrew, calling Jesus by the name Satan coveted, the title used to describe God. The demon had called him *El Elyon*, "Possessor of Heaven and Earth."

Jesus, however, wanted no recognition or worship from the pit of hell. He would not allow a demon to proclaim him as Messiah. Such testimony was entirely unfitting and unacceptable in the house of the Lord or anywhere else.

"Be quiet!" Jesus commanded the demon, and the voice was gagged. The man retreated in fear, as the evil spirit within him cowered in fear of Jesus. The possessed man tried to protest but could say nothing. Jesus commanded the demon to relinquish the man's body: "Come out of him!"

The man slumped in his seat, falling against the rear wall. The crowd saw nothing leave the body, and yet everyone knew that the evil spirit within the victim had been unable to resist the authority of Jesus. No one doubted that the voice they had heard was gone . . . forever. The people were astonished.

Jesus returned to the lectern and rolled the scroll he had read from back into place. He gave the scroll to the scribe to be replaced in its container. Then he motioned to his disciples, walked to the door and left the synagogue. But the people were reluctant to follow. They sat in stunned silence for a few minutes, then gradually began to talk among themselves. Amazed at his teaching, amazed at his power, they said to one another, "Even the evil spirits obey him."

Jesus walked with his disciples away from the synagogue toward the lake. Shaded with sycamore trees and cooled by a constant breeze off the Sea of Galilee, Capernaum was comfortable year-round.

The home of Simon Peter and Andrew was located on the main thoroughfare that stretched from the front steps of the synagogue to the public dock on the lake. Jesus indicated to the disciples that they would stop there.

Their family was not the richest in town, but the house was large and had a prestigious location at the center of town because it had been in the family for years. Due to the gentle climate, Capernaum was the town of choice among Galileans. Wealthy families continued building new homes there and had made offers to the family, but Peter had thus far refused to sell.

As Jesus and the disciples approached the house, Peter's wife met them in the street and took her husband aside.

"Don't bring Jesus home," she told Peter. "My mother is sick . . . ." She looked at Jesus. "Very sick."

Peter stepped out of earshot of the others to whisper sternly into his wife's ear. It was obvious to all that Peter was scolding his wife. It was imperative for Galilean men to offer hospitality to one's friends.

"Where is she?" Jesus interrupted the husband-wife discussion.

Peter's wife led him to an inner bedroom where her sick mother lay. The older woman was asleep, a folded wet cloth draped over her forehead. A bowl of water to keep the cloth damp was next to the bed. Jesus tenderly bent over and took the woman by the hand.

"Fever . . . ," Jesus' voice was soft but commanding, "leave her."

She immediately awakened, and Jesus helped her sit up. He had not touched her forehead; he merely spoke to the fever and it left.

"My fever's gone," Peter's mother-in-law said, getting to her feet. "My headache is gone."

She looked to Peter. "This is Jesus," he said to her. "He has made you well. He is my teacher . . . he is the Messiah."

What a meal to end the Sabbath! The food had been prepared the day before—lots of it, for Peter loved good food. His wife always prepared the best for him and any guests he brought home, and this meal would be a banquet. Her mother now helped her to serve the feast.

The guest of honor was Jesus, and those who had witnessed the events of the day gathered around him in celebration, giving thanks to God.

Peter clanked his spoon on a clay cup to get attention, then announced to all, "If Jesus had not healed my wife's mother, this evening meal would not have been possible."

Everyone cheered in approval.

And immediately His fame spread throughout all the region around Galilee.
MARK 1:28

chapter twenty-two

JESUS HEALS THE SICK AT EVENING

MARK 1:32-39

As those inside the home of Simon Peter and Andrew enjoyed the Sabbath meal, a crowd was slowly gathering in the street out front. The lame, the injured, the sick and the demon-possessed of Capernaum lay on pallets in the street, while the whole of the city gathered around them and waited. Politely they waited, for until now they had had no hope. But now there was a man in town who could help them.

After the Sabbath service, word had spread throughout the community that Jesus of Nazareth had cast an evil spirit out of a man in the synagogue. Many had heard the demon cry out in the presence of Jesus before fleeing at his word. They had seen the transformation in the once-possessed man and they were astonished. After the services, they had run to their friends and neighbors to tell what they saw.

"Come with us," they encouraged all who were sick. "Come with us, and we will take you to Jesus."

Now they waited quietly, even those who wanted to cry out in pain. Fathers, widows, wives, children, grandparents. People who hurt, those who were depressed, those who had no hope, those who were facing death. All waited for Jesus to appear. It was a solemn crowd—hushed, awed, waiting at the front door for the happiness inside to subside, so they could find some peace.

The last vestiges of sunset faded. Two stars could be seen high above the sycamore trees. A cool breeze off the lake brought with it the scent of coming rain. The door finally opened, and all eyes were on Jesus as he stepped into the street, followed by John and James.

No one called out, and Jesus said nothing, but began going from pallet to pallet touching the sick and healing them. His voice was quiet and compassionate, and no one dared speak louder than Jesus. He cast out several demons, but would not allow any of them to speak, because they knew him. One by one the people thanked him, and he moved on.

"He'll be here in a little while," a mother whispered to her blind son. "Be quiet and still."

John observed the scene but remained emotionally detached. Jesus continued to confound his expectations. Rather than recruiting soldiers from among the Jews, the Messiah attracted an army of the sick and the helpless—people who couldn't take up arms against the Romans. These were people fighting to stay alive. And yet Jesus inspired fierce devotion. Perhaps, if the people were organized properly . . .

The next morning, before there was any movement in the house, Jesus arose and quietly left the home of Peter and Andrew. The roosters of Capernaum had not yet announced the new day, nor had the fishermen returned to the dock with their nocturnal catch. The people of Capernaum slept; those who had been healed rested peacefully for perhaps the first time in years.

Shortly after sunrise, John and James arrived at Peter's house looking for Jesus. A sparkling sun had broken across the Sea of Galilee, the white mist on the lake melting under the insistence of the sun. The blue sky didn't have a hint of a cloud.

Banging on Peter's door, John called, "Wake up, Peter!"

The youthful voice awakened everyone in the house except Peter. A sound sleeper, Peter could sleep through barking dogs, crying babies and howling winds. Andrew rousted Peter then answered the door.

"Where's Jesus?" John asked as he entered. "We're ready to get started."

But Andrew knew Peter would insist on being fed. "First, let's eat," he said to his friends and invited them in.

"Jesus is not here," Peter thundered as he stormed into the room. "I went to call him for breakfast and he wasn't in his room. I've looked everywhere in the house, and he's not here."

The four disciples spread out to search Capernaum for their master. One went to the synagogue, another searched for him on the beach. Peter inquired about him in the marketplace, where merchants were setting out their wares for the inevitable day-after-Sabbath crowd.

Then, looking out across the fields outside town, James caught sight of a trail left in the morning dew, where someone had clearly walked within the last few hours. James found John and Peter, and together they followed the trail through the wet grass.

A mist still lingered in the low ravines and hung heavy over a pond where cattle drank. There near the pond, they found Jesus praying among the rocks. He was kneeling with his hands spread toward heaven.

"Jesus!" Peter called out. "We have looked everywhere for you." John looked at Peter askance, concerned that Jesus would be angry with them for disrupting this rare moment of solitude.

The disciples ran to his side, and Jesus got up from his knees. Peter blurted out, "We've been looking for you. Why are you out here . . . alone?"

Jesus embraced his friends, clearly glad to see them. He reveled in their company. As they walked back to town, Jesus taught them the importance of prayer for renewing spiritual strength after an exhaustive day of ministry.

But John was not listening to Jesus, for his mind was elsewhere. "The people of Capernaum are ready to follow you," he announced. "Now is the time to rally the people."

Peter nodded with enthusiasm. The crowds were truly enamored with Jesus: Perhaps the time was right for him to proclaim himself king. Peter wasn't quite certain *what* to do, but Peter wanted to do it *now* and he wanted to do it *big*.

"No," Jesus said, dashing cold water on their enthusiasm, though his own did not wane. "We will first go to the other villages of Galilee," he said, grinning at their youthful exuberance. "They also must hear of the kingdom of God."

Jesus crested a hill, then turned to point to a village sitting high on a far mountain. Peter knew the village well; there were three valleys between them and this particular village. From their vantage point, Peter could see several villages in the area. Jesus was asking a hard thing.

Jesus looked at Peter and said, "It is for this purpose I have come."

So he traveled throughout Galilee, preaching in their synagogues
and driving out demons.
MARK 1:39, *NIV*

chapter twenty-three

A LEPER IS HEALED

MARK 1:40-45

Jesus and his disciples left the home of Peter and Andrew shortly after breakfast, and by noon they were winding their way up the mountain to a village that could be seen from Capernaum. John walked apart from the others, following at a distance and deep in thought, still trying to reconcile his expectations of the Messiah with the events of the previous day. Jesus healed and delivered those who came to him, not as a show of power, but simply because he loved them. He saw their pain and reached out to them with relief and restoration.

The main group followed the path that ran along the wall of the small city, then, abruptly turning left through a gate, they went out of John's view. Before John could catch up, he heard noises coming from the other side of the wall—shouting and the clunking of stones falling to the ground. At first he feared for Jesus' safety. Then he heard the distinct shout: "Keep away! Unclean!"

Young John rushed to where Jesus and the other disciples had stopped just inside the village gate. He knew the cry, "Unclean." It was a warning that a leper was near. While there were many physicians and even false messiahs who claimed to have the power of healing, no one claimed to heal a leper. Leprosy was the father of defilements, the epitome of uncleanness. Priests and scribes confessed themselves powerless to deal with leprosy. Leprosy was creeping death. Slowly, a leper's skin rotted, scales of dead skin dropping to the ground.

From the village came limping a man, a leper, pursued by a small group of men and women hollering and throwing stones at him. The leper's clothes were filthy, his hair disheveled. The lower part of his face was eaten away by scabs, and his upper lip was covered with sores. When the leper saw Jesus, he cried with a loud voice what he was required by law to announce when approaching anyone: "Unclean . . . Unclean . . . ."

John looked at Jesus. As a young boy, John had been taught that leprosy was a disease inflicted on an individual as a result of serious sin. He had heard the rabbi say many times, "Leprosy does not kill; sin kills." He remembered listening to a sermon that identified eleven sins that caused leprosy. John had been terrified by the sermon and vowed never to commit any of the eleven sins.

This leper, wrapped in the mourner's garb of funeral clothes, retreated against the city wall to let Jesus and the disciples pass. When the leper stopped at the wall, the villagers halted their pursuit and backed off a few steps. Jews were not to come within six feet of a leper. If walking downwind of the afflicted, a hundred feet was scarcely sufficient for a healthy Jew to remain pure.

After what he had witnessed the day before, John fully expected that Jesus would do something to help this man, too. *But if this disease is the result of sin*, he thought, *would Jesus be willing to heal this man?* But then a deeper question came: *Does Jesus have the power to heal a leper?*

As he cowered against the wall, the leper's eyes darted from his pursuers to Jesus and his followers. No one moved. Jesus stood silently and looked at the man. Much to the surprise of the disciples and the villagers, the leper tentatively began approaching Jesus, his eyes haunted with recognition. Then he suddenly fell with his face to the ground and cried out, "If you are willing, you can make me clean."

John wondered, *How does a leper know of Jesus? And does he know what he's asking? No one has been cleansed of leprosy in hundreds of years!* Only Moses' sister Miriam and Naaman the Syrian were known to have been healed of leprosy, and then only by the intervention of God.

The eyes of the disciples fixed on Jesus, for this was not just another miracle; this was leprosy, for which there was no cure. Those who fell into this pit were never retrieved.

Jesus looked down at the man with deep compassion and tenderness in his eyes, and young John knew Jesus would heal him. Then to his horror, Jesus knelt and reached his hand toward the leper. *No!* A scream tore through John's soul. All those who touched a leper were considered unclean, just as the leper was unclean. Leprosy was highly contagious. *If Jesus were contaminated*, John thought, *would he be able to heal himself?*

"I am willing," Jesus said, placing his hand firmly on the head of the leper. "Be clean!"

Jesus removed his hand, and after a moment the man stirred. He slowly looked up at Jesus, and John caught sight of the man's face. *His face is whole!* John was shocked. The man had been immediately and completely healed. The sores, the scabs, the rotted flesh—all were gone. His face was instead wet; he was crying. He grinned through the tears, appearing refreshed like someone who had just stepped out of a bath.

Jesus commanded the man to stand up, then he said to him, "Now you must go."

"But . . . ," the man began.

Jesus cut him off with a strong warning. "See that you tell no one about this. But go, see the priest. Offer the sacrifices that Moses commanded for your cleansing, as a testimony. Let the priest tell the people that you are healed."

The disciples knew the words of Moses well. When a person had a rash that appeared to be the first stages of leprosy, that individual would be quarantined by the priest for seven days. If the rash disappeared, the priest announced that he or she had been cleansed. If the rash intensified, the person was designated a leper, then quarantined. This man's only way back into public acceptance was through the public pronouncement of the priest.

"Now go and do as I tell you," Jesus said to him.

John wondered if the wiser course would be to have the leper stay with them, for he bore a tremendous witness to the power of Jesus. And yet, he knew that Jesus tended to shrink from public recognition. Jesus had made it clear to them that he did not want crowds following him out of curiosity, nor did he want sightseers who came for temporal benefits. He had come to teach and preach the kingdom of heaven: already, on several occasions, Jesus had pointed his disciples away from the miracles to his greater mission.

Unfortunately, the man did not remain silent. He ran into the town shouting that Jesus had cleansed him. John could hear him running through the streets, calling, "Clean! I am clean!"

Instead he went out and began to talk freely, spreading the news.
As a result, Jesus could no longer enter a town openly but stayed outside in
lonely places. Yet the people still came to him from everywhere.
MARK 1:45, NIV

chapter twenty-four

JESUS CLEANSES
THE TEMPLE

JOHN 2:12-25

When it was nearly time for the Jewish Passover, Jesus and his disciples made the four-day journey to Jerusalem. As when he was a child, Jesus was immediately drawn to the Temple upon entering the Eternal City. But something was different now. A poor, unfortunate few were always there outside the Temple begging for alms in silent desperation; now as Jesus and his disciples approached the Golden Gate, a throng of able-bodied beggars blocked their way, shouting and pleading with outstretched hands for a couple of mites. But it wasn't the sight of beggars that took away from the magnificence of God's house.

Trash was everywhere. The steps had not been swept. Large gouges in the masonry and tarnish on the Golden Gate reflected a lack of care and upkeep. The distinct odor of livestock and cattle made the Temple smell like a stable.

As Jesus and his disciples entered the gate, a ram bolted out of the Temple, followed by a young teenage boy. The protestations of the ram, punctuated by the yells of its pursuer, caught everyone's attention. The crowd surrounding the gate laughed at the boy's fruitless attempts to capture his elusive quarry.

Peter saw it first. A scowl had come over the face of Jesus. His usually calm demeanor had dissolved into visible irritation. *What had upset him so?* Peter wondered. *Is it the ram? The beggars? The disorder outside the Temple?*

Inside the Temple, loud voices filled the courtyard. The Galileans had expected to hear the voices of Levites singing the psalms of Israel. They had expected to see priests and worshipers talking and praying together. But instead of quiet reverence, they saw a tumultuous crowd laughing, jostling, haggling. People were buying and selling in the outer courtyard, the Court of the Gentiles. This had all the earmarks of a bazaar, not a Temple.

Tables and booths filled the courtyard. Moneychangers were negotiating with worshipers to change their foreign coins into acceptable Hebrew currency. Each year at the time of the Passover, every adult Jewish male made an offering of half a shekel to the Temple treasury. But because the Law prohibited carved images or likenesses, the Jews could not give an offering using foreign coins bearing the image of Caesar or any other figure. Naturally, the moneychangers charged a "small" premium for their services.

Then there was the selling of livestock and birds for the required sacrifices. Row upon row of cages holding pigeons and turtledoves were sold to the poor. One farmer held several oxen by a harness. Another had a small pen for lambs. Still another had a gigantic bull he was trying to sell to people who looked like they had committed the most heinous of sins. "If you have a big sin, I have a big bull," he hollered.

"Ten shekels is nothing . . . ," a sleek businessman yelled at two dark-skinned worshipers, who were apparently not from the Holy Land.

"Cheap!" another hawkster called to passersby. "I'll change your money cheap!"

"No one will sell you a lamb for less than I!" shouted a farm boy clad in the skins of the mountains.

Jesus and his followers stood and surveyed the unruly mob before them. Nearby, a stack of coins tumbled to the floor, creating a frenzied scramble for loose change. Worshipers were assaulted from all sides by the clamor of business and the cries of animals, especially from those being dragged off to the brazen altar to be sacrificed. Worse than the odors of animal refuse, the stench of greed covered the Temple courts.

Jesus shook his head. He looked about for a priest, for they were responsible for reverence in the house of God. Jesus was looking for priests who would be praying for the people, who would be teaching the people, who would be ministering to the people. But the priests were nowhere to be seen.

His nostrils flaring, his jaw clenched, Jesus picked up three leather cords laying near him on the ground. These tethers had been used to harness an animal, but he began to deliberately weave the cords together, leaving the three ends flayed. The disciples had never seen such a look of righteous indignation in his eyes.

Jesus walked up the stairs and out onto a small wall where he could be seen by all. Then lifting his voice, he cried out, "How dare you turn my Father's house into a market! This is not a house of merchandise!"

Laughter erupted from the businessmen near him. Others dismissed his protests as just another voice among the general din.

"Stop!" Jesus yelled out over the crowd. Now a few more people stopped their haggling. They turned to see a daunting figure, standing on a wall commanding the attention of everyone. Silence began to ripple out to the edges of the courtyard like ripples on a pond dousing everyone within hearing distance of Jesus.

"This is a house of prayer," Jesus' voice echoed in the courtyard. "Take your business outside the Temple. Now!"

No one moved.

There was absolute silence.

The owner of the bull, who was almost as large as his animal and accustomed to bending others to his will through sheer intimidation, took a menacing step toward Jesus. He pointed at Jesus and shouted, "Why don't you take *your* business outside."

He laughed at Jesus. Others laughed with him. The crowd that had been given over to unrestrained haggling now united in angry scorn.

Leaping down from the wall and stepping over to a table, Jesus kicked it over with a thunderous crash. The sound of coins splashing across the marble floor sobered the worshipers.

The merchants grew silent.

Jesus now unleashed his wrath on the moneychangers' tables, overturning each of them in succession. No one challenged him. Coins flew every which way, but no one moved to retrieve them. Cages crashed to the ground as Jesus stormed through the courtyard, turtledoves and pigeons fluttering free into the open skies. Jesus pulled down a rickety pen holding several rams.

With his makeshift whip in hand and his face flushed with anger, Jesus stepped toward the man with the big bull. The man stumbled backwards and the bull bolted toward the exit, its hooves trying desperately to gain a foothold on the marble floor. The bull's owner scurried after it in mortal fear.

Merchants and customers alike scattered like leaves before the fury of

Jesus. Moneychangers left their coins lying on the stones, their fear of the man with the whip greater than their greed.

His disciples recoiled in shock. They had never seen this side of Jesus. The Jesus they knew was a marvelous companion. People walked for miles just to be near him. He was kind, compassionate, forgiving. A patient teacher with a wonderful sense of humor. Always willing to make time for little children, he delighted in their simple faith. The Jesus they knew inspired devotion in his followers. But this Jesus . . . this Jesus was terrifying.

Suddenly the crowd was gone. The animals were gone. The courtyard was as reverent as intended by God, although overturned tables littered the area. Cages were smashed, the pens holding the animals were broken. Yet even their destruction seemed to glorify God. The businessmen had escaped, but many honest worshipers were still there. They were stunned yet scared, not knowing what Jesus would do to them for participating in the commerce that defiled the Temple of God.

"My Father's house is to be a house of prayer," Jesus announced to them, breathing heavily. "For people of all nations . . . this is a house of prayer."

Peter turning to the disciples, whispered, "What drove him to do this? Businessmen have always been here selling their cattle. And worshipers have always been here buying. The priests have allowed this for as long as I can remember."

John said somberly, quoting from a psalm, "Zeal for God's house has consumed him."

Slowly, priests began appearing in the courtyard as though from nowhere. One by one they appeared through small doors and from behind columns. They congregated and whispered among themselves. They surveyed the coins on the floor, the broken pens and the overturned tables.

"They should have cleaned up the Temple," James said to the disciples standing nearby.

One of the priests walked over to Jesus. Jesus saw him coming but paid him no attention. When the priest drew near, he said, "By what authority do you clear the Temple?"

Jesus didn't answer.

"The priests are the keepers of the Temple," the Levitical spokesman said. At this point the other priests nodded their heads, grunting their approval.

"What right do you have to do this?" the interrogator asked.

Jesus ignored him.

"Are you not Jesus of Nazareth?" he asked. Word had already reached Jerusalem of a Galilean by this name reportedly doing miracles with wine. So the priest goaded him, saying, "Show us a sign then," as he looked to the other priests for their approval. They chuckled and nodded their agreement. The priest turned back to Jesus and asked once more, "What miraculous sign can you show us to prove your authority to do this?"

"If you destroy this Temple," Jesus now acknowledged the priest's presence and said in answer to his request, "I will raise it again in three days."

"It has taken forty-six years to build this Temple," the priest mockingly answered Jesus, "and you think you can rebuild it in three days?"

No one fully understood what Jesus meant, nor did he attempt to interpret what he said. The priests were looking for the source of Jesus' authority. But Jesus spoke of his own death and resurrection which he knew was coming.

Jesus remained in Jerusalem for the seven-day feast of unleavened bread and Passover. He continued teaching, performing miracles, healing the sick and the lame and explaining the way of salvation to all who would listen. The Temple merchants stayed out of his way and for the rest of the week they kept their merchandise out of the Temple. The priests continued to discuss Jesus among themselves. They knew that it was their duty to keep the Temple clean, and in their hearts they knew what Jesus did was right. But he had embarrassed them and challenged their authority. They would have to take action.

Now while he was in Jerusalem at the Passover Feast, many people saw the miraculous signs he was doing and believed in his name.

JOHN 2:23, NIV

chapter twenty-five

A NIGHT INTERVIEW
WITH A LEADER

JOHN 3:1-36

A cool breeze rustled the palm branches at the edge of the flat-roofed house. April was hot in the daytime but chilly at night. The Passover moon was so bright the Torah could be read by its light. With no clouds in the sky, the stars created a perfect canopy for an evening discussion.

Jesus sat with John, James and Peter on the rooftop, waiting for Nicodemus. A Jewish leader among the most influential in Jerusalem, Nicodemus would be severely censured by the Sanhedrin if they knew of this meeting. The other sixty-nine members of the council did not consider Jesus to be a legitimate teacher. And, after Jesus had expelled the merchants from the Temple, he was considered a menace.

But the taciturn shadows would hide all, the outside stairway allowing Nicodemus to slip upstairs unnoticed for his meeting with Jesus.

Passover was a week for celebration. Many banquets were held during Passover. People got together to discuss current events, family matters or just to renew old friendships. New friendships were also begun in this festive atmosphere. What began as a formal discussion would often end up in intimate conversation. This discussion between Jesus and Nicodemus was such an appointment, but Nicodemus wasn't ready to let his peers know about it, and Jesus understood this. Power . . . position . . . prestige . . . . Nicodemus was a man with much to lose.

Young John had not said anything all evening. He was suspicious of priests, scribes, anyone who represented the religious establishment. Nicodemus was a Pharisee and a respected member of the Sanhedrin, the ruling council that exercised authority in all Jewish religious matters. The Roman governor was the final authority in Judean civil matters, but as part of the occupational agreement, the Romans allowed the Jews to take charge over their own religious affairs—as long as they didn't interfere with the Roman government.

James gave voice to his brother's concerns. "Nicodemus is the most influential teacher in Jerusalem," he said. "He may have been sent here to spy on us."

But Jesus said nothing, and they waited.

When Nicodemus arrived with his academic attachés, he found two prominent chairs set on the roof, the first an ornate oak chair, padded with blue leather. This was the taller chair. Nicodemus would sit in the exalted chair, surrounded by his lieutenants. Across from him, a stool, lower in height, had been placed for Jesus. Behind Jesus was a bench set against the wall. On the bench sat John, the impulsive youth. Next to him was Peter, the stubborn, outspoken fisherman. Beside Peter sat James, the quiet but fiery one.

According to custom, it was the privilege of the elder Nicodemus to choose the topic of the evening. By all standards, it would have been inappropriate for Jesus to set the agenda for discussion. Nicodemus had a reputation for arguing the significance of historical events and the Talmud, those areas in which he excelled. Sometimes the discussions were nothing more than monologues, with Nicodemus discoursing all evening on a particularly fascinating topic. He was a brilliant scholar, and people invited him to their evening feasts just to glean something of his magnificent wisdom and understanding.

As they took their seats under the stars, Nicodemus and his three fellow scholars presented a formidable challenge for anyone wishing to engage in a religious debate. They held within their grasp a world of knowledge and learning that was feared by most illiterate people. Before them was Jesus, an itinerant teacher with no formal education, and three unlearned fishermen.

The disciples fully expected that the Pharisee would try to intimidate Jesus. But the shadows hid the face of Nicodemus, and his intentions were unclear. When at last he spoke, he did not attack Jesus, nor did he challenge him with a question. Nicodemus leaned forward into the light, lowering his own head in clear deference to Jesus.

"We know about the miracles you have been doing in Jerusalem. We know about the miracle of turning water into wine . . . ." Nicodemus' eyes were soft and pleading. They did not flash hot, nor were they ready for academic battle. "Rabbi, we know that you have come from God," he said, "because no one could perform these signs if God were not with him."

To the disciples' surprise, Nicodemus had spoken to Jesus as an equal.

Nicodemus, as the first to speak, had complimented Jesus. It was customary among such men that the compliment be returned.

Nicodemus waited for Jesus' reply. All eyes on the rooftop turned to Jesus who was sitting in the full moonlight. There were no shadows to hide Jesus' reaction. Jesus waited for a few seconds to make sure it was his turn to speak. But rather than return the compliment, Jesus bypassed the niceties of rhetoric and went straight to the heart of the issue—the reason Nicodemus had come. Jesus told him, "Unless a man is born again, he cannot see the kingdom of heaven."

The body language of three scholars-in-tow stiffened; they didn't like what they heard. They expected Jesus to compliment Nicodemus on his wisdom or his influence with the Sanhedrin. But Jesus was blunt.

Nicodemus did not take offense at the slight. It was as if Jesus had known what the Pharisee had come seeking and answered his unspoken question. But Nicodemus was puzzled by the logical impossibility. "How can a man be born when he is old?" he asked. "Surely he cannot enter a second time into his mother's womb to be born!"

"I tell you the truth, unless a person is born of water and of the Spirit, that person cannot enter the kingdom of God."

The three lieutenants to Nicodemus were disarmed by the intimacy of the discussion. Though offended when Jesus didn't compliment their leader, the warm, inquisitive response of Nicodemus told them the discussion was going well.

"Flesh gives birth to flesh, but the Spirit gives birth to spirit." Jesus explained, "When a man is born into this world that man is flesh, like the parents who gave him birth. But when a man is born of the Spirit, his life will be rooted in the spiritual."

Nicodemus understood the simplicity of Jesus' logic; there was a profundity in its simplicity. *But what does it mean to be "born again"?* he wondered silently.

Jesus looked deep into the eyes of Nicodemus. "You shouldn't be surprised when I tell you, 'You must be born again.'"

A swift evening breeze swept up the street and over the house. "Being born again is like the blowing of the wind," Jesus said to help Nicodemus. "You hear the sound of the wind, but you cannot tell where it comes from or where it is going. So it is with everyone born of the Spirit."

Nicodemus' eyes were still searching. Jesus continued. "Sometimes the wind stops blowing. Other times it blows briskly. No one can tell the wind where to blow, or when to blow. The wind blows wherever it pleases. So the world cannot fathom a man born of the Spirit."

"How can this be?" Nicodemus asked.

"You are Israel's teacher," Jesus said to Nicodemus. "You claim to know about God, and yet you have difficulty understanding the simplest teachings of the kingdom."

Jesus arose from his stool and walked to the wall. Nicodemus followed him, listening as they walked. The others remained seated. Jesus looked out on the people in the street below. People were still walking, returning home from work or an evening meal. From the house next door there came the sound of congenial laughter. Everywhere Jesus looked, there were people who needed to hear about the kingdom of God.

Jesus turned to Nicodemus and said, "I have spoken to you of earthly things and you do not believe. Then how will you believe if I speak to you of heavenly things?"

Jesus folded his robe over his arm and returned to his stool. Beckoning to Nicodemus, he motioned for him to sit with the others. This was no longer a discussion between two great scholars, but a lesson from a master teacher.

"As Moses lifted up the serpent in the wilderness, so must the Son of Man be lifted up. Whoever looked at the snake on the pole, did not die of poison, and whoever believes in the Son of Man will live forever.

"For God so loved the world, that he sent his only Son, that whoever believes in him will not perish, but have everlasting life.

"For God did not send his Son into the world to condemn the world, but to save the world through him. But whoever does not believe stands condemned already because he has not believed in the name of God's one and only Son."

Nicodemus did not know what to say to this.

"God has sent his Son as a light into the world . . . ," Jesus explained. Just then a cloud covered the moon. The rooftop went black, as though a cosmic hand had extinguished its light. Almost immediately with the blackness, they heard a wicked laugh from the shadows in the street below . . . a chilling laughter.

The scholars and the disciples traded glances. Jesus, sensing the moment, said, "Men love darkness rather than light because their deeds are evil and the darkness hides what they are doing. But he who lives according to the truth will come into the light, that his deeds may be clearly seen, that they have been done in the name of God."

Nicodemus nodded. A spark had been touched in his own soul, and he determined to do whatever he could within the Sanhedrin to allow Jesus to teach openly. And Nicodemus himself would watch . . . and listen.

He who believes in the Son has everlasting life; and he who does not believe the Son shall not see life, but the wrath of God abides on him.

JOHN 3:36

chapter twenty-six

TELLING A WOMAN ALL ABOUT HER PAST

JOHN 4:1-43

As the scorching April sun neared its zenith, the disciples trudged up yet another charred Samaritan hill. Jesus had been led by the Holy Spirit to make the difficult trek through Samaria on their return home from Jerusalem, where they had celebrated the Feast of Firstfruits. At this feast a few of the early heads of blossomed wheat were brought to the Temple by the Jews as a promise to God that they would bring a tithe from the full harvest come autumn. Fields of new wheat stretched before the disciples as they crested the hill.

"If we had gone by way of the Jordan Valley," young John complained, "we could have avoided these hills and saved ourselves a few blisters."

"Ha!" Peter laughed. With his lighter complexion, his red eyebrows were beginning to blend into a sunburned face. "I don't mind how we get there, as long as we're heading home," he said, keeping in mind that his master had chosen this route. "Let's not complain . . . ."

John pointed to the sun directly overhead. "It's nearly noon. We need to stop and let Jesus rest."

"The village of Sychar is up ahead."

"Jacob's Well is closer," John reminded him. "Let's stop there."

Jesus looked to John as though he could go no farther. Several days of intense ministry to the people in Jerusalem had seemed to drain him. Peter gave Jesus a needed shoulder to lean on. The small olive trees surrounding the well would be in sight just a few paces up the road.

Jacob's Well was located in the middle of the broad, flat valley with wheat growing in the fields on either side of the road. The fields were flanked by two mountains rising several hundred feet from the desert floor, forming a beautiful backdrop. To the disciples' left was Mount Ebal, the Mount of Blessings, where Joshua had once sacrificed to the Lord for the great victory over the northern kingdom. To their right was Mount Gerizim, the Mount of Cursing. The mountains stood like sentinels guarding the deep well that had been dug by Jacob, the father of the twelve tribes of Israel.

Now the area was populated with Samaritans, and most Jews had very little to do with the Samaritans because of their apostate faith. Still, the Jews revered the well of their forefather and would make the pilgrimage to this place just to drink from the well and pray to the God of Jacob. Some Jews were even superstitious, believing that a drink from Jacob's Well would ward off disease and misfortune.

Jesus nearly collapsed onto the stone wall next to the well, under the shade of a small olive tree, where he promptly fell asleep.

"Let's go into town and get something to eat," Andrew said to John. "No one will bother Jesus. It's too hot to come for water at this hour of the day." So the disciples left their master sleeping by the well, and they made their way to Sychar.

Jesus was dozing in the shade and didn't hear the bare feet coming down the powdery road toward the well. He sat up when he heard the squeak of a leather bucket being lowered into the well. A Samaritan woman was there. She wore dark clothes—a black robe similar to that of a widow or an unmarried woman. A dark blue shawl protected her from the sun.

"Oh . . . ," she said, startled by the presence of a stranger at the well. She let go of the rope and her bucket fell with a distant splash a moment later. "I didn't see you resting in the shade."

Jesus greeted her kindly, then seeing her jar asked, "Could you give me something to drink? I am very thirsty."

"But you are a Jew and I am a Samaritan woman," the woman said, her curiosity winning out over fear and hatred. Looking past their cultural differences, she knew it was highly unusual for a Jewish man to talk alone with a woman. And yet there was something different about this man . . . .

"How can you ask me for a drink?" she demanded.

Jesus did not immediately answer.

"Jews have no dealings with the Samaritans," she reminded him.

Jesus was not interested in such distinctions. He was, however, interested in the life of this woman. He knew she was why the Holy Spirit had led him and his disciples into the hills of Samaria.

"If only you knew the gift of God," he said, smiling at her reluctance. "If you knew who it was that asked you for a drink, you would ask for water from me. Anyone who drinks from my living water will never thirst again."

"Where would you get this 'living water'? Sir, you have no bucket. You have no rope, and the well is deep."

Jesus continued to smile at her.

"Who are you?" the woman asked. "Are you greater than our father Jacob who gave us this well and drank from it, as did his sons, his flock and his herds?"

"Everyone who drinks this water will be thirsty again," Jesus answered, "but whoever drinks the water I offer will never thirst. Indeed, the water I give you will become in you a spring of water filling your heart and over-flowing into eternal life."

"I want this water," the woman said, "so that I don't have to come to this well to draw water again. I want eternal water."

"Go call your husband," Jesus said to the woman. "Tell your husband about the water of eternal life, then bring your husband here to see me."

"I don't have a husband."

"I know you are telling me the truth," Jesus said to her, "for you have had five husbands in your lifetime, and the man you are now living with is not your husband."

Stunned, she said nothing for a moment. She had never met this man. How could he know all about her life? Her closest friends in Sychar did not know of her five marriages. She blurted out, "Sir, you must be a prophet of God. You know the secret things about me."

So she tested him to learn whether he was indeed a prophet. "The Samaritans worship on Mount Gerizim where Joshua worshiped," she said, "but the Jews say we should worship in Jerusalem . . . ."

Jesus had not come to argue religion with the Samaritan woman, so he didn't answer her.

"Where should we worship?" she asked.

"Woman, the hour is coming when you will not worship on a mountain or in Jerusalem. A time is coming when true worshipers will worship the Father in Spirit and in truth . . . . These are the kind of people the Father seeks to worship him."

She did not have an answer for this, but said to Jesus, "I know the Messiah is coming. When he comes, he will explain everything to us."

"I who speak to you am he."

When the disciples returned with food and found Jesus talking with the Samaritan woman, they were taken aback but said nothing out of respect for their teacher. Nevertheless, the woman turned and ran swiftly away, leaving behind her water jar, rope and bucket.

"Wait . . . !" Peter yelled after her, but she continued running.

The disciples drew water for Jesus and gave him a drink from Jacob's Well. Unfolding their food cloth, they began distributing bread and dried lamb for lunch. Embarrassed by finding Jesus alone with a woman, the disciples maintained an awkward silence.

Finally, Peter spoke. "Take some bread, Rabbi."

But Jesus shook his head and said, "I have food that you know nothing about."

The disciples looked at one another, wondering who could have brought Jesus food while they were gone.

When he saw his disciples wondering at his words Jesus said to them, "My food is to do the will of my Father who sent me and to finish his work." Jesus drew his strength from feeding others, as he had done for the Samaritan woman.

"Don't say there are yet four months until harvest," he said to them, pointing. "Lift up your eyes and look on the fields now." But Jesus wasn't pointing toward the wheat fields.

The disciples looked toward the village. Coming down the road from Sychar were dozens of men—all in white turbans—walking fast toward the well, looking like a field of whitened wheat waving in the wind.

Jesus said, "The field is white for harvest."

The woman had gone back to the city, babbling to everyone she knew, "Come see a man who told me everything I ever did." She ran from one group of men to another. To each group she said the same thing: "This man is from God."

Upon hearing about the man who knew the secrets of the heart, many Samaritans quickly ran out of Sychar toward Jacob's Well. They listened to Jesus and urged him to stay with them. So Jesus and his disciples departed the well and went into Sychar.

That evening in the town piazza, Jesus taught the crowd from the Scriptures concerning himself. Many believed that he was the Christ. As he finished speaking, an elderly man stood, his stringy beard bouncing from his chin as he talked, "Now we believe you are the Messiah. We have heard for ourselves, and we believe you are the Savior of the world."

Now after the two days He departed from there and went to Galilee.
So when He came to Galilee, the Galileans received Him, having seen
all the things He did in Jerusalem at the feast.

JOHN 4:43,45

chapter twenty-seven

HEALING THE ROYAL OFFICIAL'S SON

J O H N   4 : 4 6 - 5 4

From Samaria, Jesus and his disciples journeyed to Galilee and arrived in the town of Cana, the village where he had changed water into wine. Jesus sat and talked with his disciples in the sweltering city market, the cool evening breezes still hours away. Business at the booths and stalls in the market was already dwindling as the shoppers hurried home to escape the afternoon heat and prepare their suppers. Children were playing their games here and there, hiding behind the tables to the amusement of the merchants, whose dispositions were buoyed by a morning of brisk business.

The children darted out of the way as a dignified man came hurrying up the street, his manner of dress indicating he was a man of some importance. An officer of Herod's royal court, he had come to the marketplace searching for Jesus. Word had reached him in Capernaum that Jesus of Nazareth had returned to Galilee; the official had been anxiously awaiting his return since he heard of the healings Jesus had done in Jerusalem. His own son was extremely ill and on the verge of death, despite the attention of the best physicians available. In an act of desperation, the concerned father had set out at first light for the hill country of Cana to find this miracle worker. He covered the distance quickly, driven by his conviction: *If Jesus will only touch him, my son will be made well.*

The courtier understood power; he knew that men of wealth and stature traveled great distances to make their requests of Herod in person— if they hoped to have their desires granted. He was willing to beg an audience with Jesus for the life of his son.

When he arrived in Cana, it didn't take long to find the man he sought surrounded by his disciples. Jesus was well known in Cana; they still talked of the excellent vintage he had provided them at the wedding feast. The royal official dashed into the marketplace and knelt at Jesus' feet.

"Rabbi," he said, "my son is at death's door. Please . . . you must come to Capernaum and heal him."

Jesus looked into the courtier's heart and sighed, because this man did not believe he was the Messiah; all he wanted was a miracle. "Unless you people see miraculous signs and wonders," Jesus told him, "you will never believe."

The royal official accepted the rebuke but would not be deterred. He wasn't sure who Jesus really was, but he knew the rabbi held his son's life in his hands. "Please . . . ," he begged, "please come before my child dies."

Jesus was moved with compassion for the distraught father. He knew that the man's belief in miracles was a first step to real faith. "Go back home," Jesus told the court officer. "Your son will live."

The officer got up off the ground and bowed his head. He understood what a royal edict meant. When Herod gave an order, it was carried out. The courtier believed Jesus had authority, just as he believed Herod had authority. He said to Jesus, "Thank you," and he backed off a few steps as a subject would back away from a king. He said again, "Thank you for healing my son."

The encounter had taken only a few minutes. The court officer turned and walked swiftly down the street, heading out of the village of Cana. He would not reach Capernaum that night, but would have to find lodging along the way.

The following day, as he wound his way down the hills toward Capernaum, he saw a familiar figure down the road. One of his servants was running to meet him.

"Your son is well!" the servant called out from a distance. When he reached his master, the servant said breathlessly, "Yesterday the fever broke. He sat up and asked for water . . . immediately he got up . . . he is healed!"

The court officer was stunned by the news, but he gave praise to God, then asked, "What time yesterday was my son healed?"

"The fever left him at the seventh hour," he was told, which was about one o'clock in the afternoon—the very hour he had spoken with Jesus of Nazareth.

The court officer needed no further proof. Jesus was no charlatan, nor was he merely a worker of miracles. The royal official believed that Jesus was truly the Messiah of Israel, and when he returned home, his whole house believed with him.

This was the second miraculous sign that Jesus performed,
having come from Judea to Galilee.

JOHN 4:54, NIV

chapter twenty-eight

CONFRONTATION IN NAZARETH

LUKE 4:16-30

The crowd was much larger than usual for Sabbath services at the synagogue. Word had spread quickly through the small village. The son of Mary and Joseph had returned to his hometown of Nazareth and had been asked to speak at the synagogue, though his mother and brothers had since moved to Capernaum. Jesus was remembered in the village as a favored son, but since his departure, rumors had reached Nazareth of the carpenter-turned-rabbi who spoke with power and great wisdom and performed miracles.

Jesus entered the synagogue and took a seat reserved for visiting speakers. It was the custom for five different elders of the community to stand and read from the Law; that is, the five books of Moses, the portions of Scripture most revered by the Jews. First a priest, then a Levite, and then the other elders. Then a distinguished visitor would read a passage from the Prophets—the *Haphtarah*—to conclude the services.

When the time came for Jesus to speak, the leader of the synagogue arose, went to the box containing the scrolls and selected the writings of Isaiah and handed the scroll to Jesus. The scrolls on which the prophets were written were different from the five books of the Law. They were accepted as Scripture, but were not considered to have the same authority as the Torah. Usually the concluding speaker would read no fewer than twenty-one verses from the Haphtarah, unless he were going to preach a sermon after the Scripture, then he usually read two or three verses before the sermon.

Jesus carefully unrolled the scroll to where Isaiah prophesied concerning the Messiah, then he read aloud:

"The Spirit of the Lord is upon Me, because He has anointed Me to preach the gospel to the poor; He has sent Me to heal the broken-hearted, to proclaim liberty to the captives and recovery of sight to the blind, to set at liberty those who are oppressed; to proclaim the acceptable year of the Lord."

When Jesus read this, he stopped, rolled the scroll back into place and returned it to the leader of the synagogue. Then Jesus sat down. Every eye in the room looked at him. They had heard of his miracles. It was said that the blind saw, the lame walked and lepers had been healed. The room was breathless in anticipation. They were waiting for the sermon, the *pethichah*.

But all Jesus said was, "Today this Scripture is fulfilled in your hearing."

First the minister of the synagogue shook his head in disagreement. At his cue, the other elders began shaking their heads in disapproval. To them, the words of Jesus were peculiar, foolhardy, even vulgar. The passage he had read referred to the coming Messiah. The word that jumped to their minds was "blasphemy," but no one wanted to say that word. This was Joseph's son who grew up in their midst. They loved him and knew him to be a good man. But what Jesus had said was out of character. They had expected a sermon. Instead, Jesus had publicly claimed to be the Messiah.

"No!" one of the elders dared to say out loud. "You may be a worker of miracles, but you cannot call yourself Messiah!"

Jesus knew their hearts; he knew they came to see miracles but did not believe in him. He said, "Many of you want me to do miracles here in Nazareth, my home, as I have done at Capernaum and at Jerusalem."

The elders nodded slightly. They did want to see miracles.

"But I say to you, no prophet is accepted in his hometown."

The people were perplexed. They had come looking for a miracle, but Jesus was refusing to do one. The minister of the synagogue, who was accustomed to dialoguing with the sermon, asked, "Why will you not show us what you can do? If you are the Messiah, give us a sign."

Jesus didn't answer him directly, but spoke to the congregation. "There were many widows in Israel in the days of Elijah the prophet, when God stilled the rain for three years and six months, and there was a great famine throughout all the land. But when Elijah was given a miracle to feed a widow, he fed a foreign Gentile in the land of Lebanon. He was not sent to the widows of Israel because of their unbelief."

But the people still did not comprehend, so Jesus added, "In the time of Elisha, there were many lepers in Israel, but none of them were cleansed except Naaman, a Syrian. I cannot do miracles in my hometown of Nazareth because of your unbelief. You will not believe that I am who I say I am."

The elders and congregation had heard enough. The synagogue erupted in holy indignation at this brash sermon. As much as the elders loved the son of Joseph, they loved the Law more, and the Law provided for instant death without formal trial in the case of open blasphemy or profanation. Jesus had claimed to be their Messiah, yet he told them they were not fit for miracles.

Voices began to swell like thunder rolling across a rain-stricken sky, and the Nazarenes drove Jesus out of their synagogue. Jesus did not resist, but departed the building with the enraged crowd pressing in about him. They cursed him and forced him down the road to the outskirts of town.

Just outside the village of Nazareth, the road to Capernaum passed dangerously close to a forty-foot cliff, and the danger of the cliff pulled the crowd toward it like the scent of blood calling to a predator. They pushed Jesus up the hill toward the cliff, determined to throw him off. Jesus allowed himself to be pressed forward by the menacing crowd until they reached the brow of the hill.

Then he turned and looked upon his pursuers, and the angry mob was immediately silenced. They held their collective breath, waiting for Jesus to speak.

Jesus said nothing. He simply walked down the hill, passing through the midst of the villagers, and went his way.

And he was amazed at their lack of faith.

MARK 6:6, *NIV*

chapter twenty-nine

GETTING A FRIEND TO JESUS

MARK 2:1-12

Autumn had come to Galilee. There were a few early snowfalls in the mountains that year, coaxing Jesus and his friends to leave the open-air gatherings and relative anonymity of the hill country and retreat to Capernaum.

Unbeknownst to the disciples of Jesus, more than just large crowds awaited them in the city. Religious authorities in Jerusalem had sent representatives to observe Jesus of Nazareth and report on his activities and teachings to the Sanhedrin. If possible, they were to entrap Jesus, to find something they could use to discredit him as a teacher or even have him arrested by the civil magistrates. So Pharisees and scribes of the Law had come to Capernaum from the neighboring towns of Galilee and from Jerusalem to scrutinize the so-called Messiah.

Early one morning, Jesus knocked at Peter's door, even though his friends knew that Simon Peter was a sound sleeper and a late riser. But this morning, Peter was up, sitting at the breakfast table with Andrew.

"Come in," Peter motioned to Jesus. "Sit down and eat with us."

In short order, the room was filled with disciples. James and John had come from their father's home, telling people along the way that Jesus would be teaching this day. One by one, neighbors came to Peter's door asking, "May we come in? We want to hear what the rabbi says . . . ."

The priest from the synagogue came to the house, and with him came visiting rabbis from Jerusalem and doctors of the Law from local villages. Because rabbis always occupied the places of honor, they sat near to Jesus, while everyone else was left to the other places in the room.

Sitting at the breakfast table, Jesus explained to his listeners that the kingdom of God is like a city built on a hill. "It cannot be hidden. Everyone can see it. Likewise, you are to be lights to the world." Jesus saw a lot of heads nodding in the back of the room. He challenged them, "Let your light shine so men might see. Do not light your candle and put it under a basket. Put your candle up high so you can share the light with all men who will come to you."

As usual, the majority of the listeners were responsive to Jesus' teaching. Some were just curious; others were hungry to know God. But positioned between the crowd and Jesus were the Pharisees and scribes. The religious leaders were not warm and responsive; doubt hung on their faces for all to see.

Peter's home was located on the main street. Although surrounded by wealthier homes made of ornamental stone, granite or marble, his was a simple house made of fieldstone—well built, quite comfortable and larger than average. It was a flat-roofed house as were all the structures in Capernaum. On the roof was an *aliya*, the "prophet's chamber," an upper room for studying and praying.

Outside the back door was a covered gallery that stretched around two sides of the home. There was a courtyard in the back and various small guest chambers that opened onto the courtyard. It was here that Jesus resided while in Capernaum. Stone stairs led to the roof, where Jesus and the disciples had spent many enjoyable evenings talking, singing and laughing.

Jesus was teaching in the large family room, which was crowded to overflowing. Outside the room and outside the house, others who wanted to hear Jesus were pressing to get inside the doors.

About the third hour of the day, down the main street of Capernaum came four men carrying a small bed between them. On the bed was a friend, a paralytic man. They had started out before dawn from a town seven miles away, bringing their crippled friend to see Jesus. They arrived in town about mid-morning and asked in the marketplace where they could find Jesus. They were told he was teaching in Simon Peter's house. But when they reached the home of Peter and Andrew, they were unable to get to the front door.

They said to the people blocking the doorway, "We have a sick man who needs to see Jesus." But the crowd didn't move nor did they respond. They were absorbed in the words of Jesus.

"Please," the friends pleaded. "Let us through to see Jesus."

"Sh-h-h!" someone hushed them.

Picking up the bed with their friend, they went around to the back door, but again a crowd of people blocked the way into the building. Again one of the men politely asked, "May we bring our friend to see Jesus?"

No one even turned around to respond. With the courtyard crowded and people at every window, access to Jesus was simply impossible.

"Shall we wait until everyone leaves?" the spokesman asked his friends. "Or come back at a more convenient time?"

But they had come so far, and their friend had been sick for so long. And they knew that if they could get to Jesus, he would heal their friend. There was a sense of urgency among these men—they had to do something and they had to do it quickly.

"Then if we cannot get in to see him through the usual means," one of them said, "we will have to make a way."

The four men lifted their paralytic friend and carried him up the stone stairs that led to the roof. No one took notice of them as they mounted the stairs; all attention was focused on what was going on inside the house. On the roof they found hard-packed dirt covering the flat stone tiles underneath. The large stones had been laid one next to the other, paving the roof of the house like some cities paved their main streets. A low wall was built about the perimeter of the roof, so that no one could fall from the roof to the ground.

The four men set the bed down gently and began digging at the dirt with their hands. Then, finding flat smooth stones, they used them as shovels to clear away the dirt and reveal the large flat stones. They had caught a glimpse of Jesus through a window and knew approximately where he sat teaching. With a stick, they pried up a covering tile above the family room, and sunlight poured into the home of Peter and Andrew.

"What are you doing?!" Peter hollered, while his visitors shouted in protest against the loose dirt and pebbles raining down on them. Jesus raised a hand to hush the crowd. Then looking at Simon Peter, he put his finger to his mouth, gesturing Peter to be quiet. Jesus had been sitting at the table talking for more than an hour, and every eye had been on him. But now no one could resist looking up at the widening hole as the four men continued removing tiles.

Then the men backed away from the opening they had created. Moments later the crowd was stunned to see the form of a man in a large blanket being lowered through the hole in the ceiling. Several men seated nearby stood to grab the pallet and assisted in lowering it slowly to the floor. The feverish face and glistening eyes of the paralyzed man turned up to Jesus. The room was silent, more still than if the room were empty.

Peter forgot about the damage to his roof for the moment, touched by the intense devotion of four friends who had worked feverishly to get their friend to Jesus. And though he marveled at their love, Peter understood such devotion, for he himself was a man of great passion. He was similarly devoted to the very person whom these men had gone to such great lengths to see.

Thus far, the suffering paralytic had not opened his blanched lips to speak to Jesus. He did not ask for healing. The broken ceiling and the sun streaming in through the hole in the ceiling were, if nothing else, a bold testament of the faith of his four friends.

"Be of good cheer," Jesus said, looking into the man's heart.

Some of the religious officials in the room believed that suffering could cleanse a sick person from sin. They argued that the loss of an eye or a tooth liberated a person from the bondage of sin, and so much so that the suffering of the whole body would free the soul from its guilt. Jesus knew better.

He said to the man, "Son, your sins are forgiven."

The scribes and Pharisees in the room dared say nothing, surrounded as they were by Jesus' friends and supporters. But they exchanged contemptuous looks, asking the same questions in their hearts and minds: *Why does this man speak blasphemy? Who can forgive sins but God?*

Simon Peter saw that the religious authorities clearly rejected the words of his master. He, too, had been taken aback for a moment. No one in the room doubted that God alone can forgive sins. And if Jesus were merely a man, albeit an honored teacher and a healer, then the keepers of the Law had every right to their criticism. But if Peter's growing suspicions were correct, if Jesus were—incredibly—who Peter believed him to be, then Jesus stood there to condemn their worst imaginings.

Then Jesus turned to the scribes and Pharisees and said to them, "Why are you thinking these things? Which is easier: To say to the paralytic, 'Your sins are forgiven,' or to say, 'Get up, take your bed and walk'?"

Peter suppressed a laugh. Jesus smiled and said, "But that you may know that the Son of Man has authority on earth to forgive sins . . . ." Jesus then turned to the paralyzed man and said to him, "I tell you, get up, take your bed and go home."

Immediately, the man stood up, gathered up his pallet and walked through the crowd and out the front door to the accompaniment of unabashed cheers and praises to God.

And the chagrined religious leaders covered their heads with their robes as they were showered with dirt and pebbles shaken loose under the feet of four dancing friends.

He got up, took his mat and walked out in full view of them all. This amazed everyone and they praised God, saying, "We have never seen anything like this!"

MARK 2:12, NIV

chapter thirty

EATING AND DRINKING WITH SINNERS

MARK 2:13-22

The road from Damascus to Egypt ran alongside the outer wall of Capernaum; the calls of camel drivers to their animals drifted over the protective wall to the consternation of those who lived on the edge of town. Jesus and his disciples exited Capernaum through the city gate, turned left on the Roman road and began walking south in the direction of Judea.

Almost immediately, they encountered the customs booth where taxes were collected. Philip, a keen observer of details, quickly counted the number of camels in front of him, then remarked to his friend Nathanael, "It will take us a long while to get through the tax line today."

Philip was annoyed, but it couldn't be helped. Capernaum was the convergence of most traveled roads in Galilee, so that's where most of the taxes were collected. Just south of Capernaum, the road from Damascus forked. One highway ran south along the Jordan River toward Egypt; the other route turned west, trailing over the mountains through Nazareth on its way to the Mediterranean Sea. There the highway turned south again and continued along the shore toward Alexandria. The civilization of the known world passed Capernaum when traveling between Syria and Egypt.

Everything that went through customs was taxed—grain, wine, cloth, produce of all kinds. In addition, a toll tax was collected, a levy for each person twelve years old and older. To add to the burden, Levi, the son of Alphaeus and chief tax collector for Herod in Capernaum, collected *ad valorem* on just about everything that passed his table: axles, wheels, pack animals and anything else he could think of to tax. Like most tax collectors of his day, Levi collected not only for Herod and the Romans, but he also took an additional portion for his own coffers; thus he had become extremely wealthy.

Under Levi, a number of publicans ran about doing actual inspection, bartering and bickering with the travelers. If there was too much bickering, Levi got involved, and beyond him there was no appeal, defense or escape. Roman soldiers enforced the tax collector's edicts. Because they ruled supremely over everything that passed through their particular domains, all tax collectors were thought to be *mokhes*, or oppressors. The Jews viewed them as criminals and considered them inferior to animals. Rabbis expelled at once any Jew who accepted a job collecting taxes for the Romans. Excommunication from the synagogue for such a traitor included his whole family. Rabbis said, "When one becomes a mokhes, the whole family becomes a mokhes. When they die, they are carried unmourned to the grave."

Levi was philosophical about his ejection from the synagogue in Capernaum, because rejection came with the territory for a tax collector. But deep down he knew he was a sinful man in need of salvation more than most. Levi had seen the crowds listening intently to this new teacher, Jesus of Nazareth, at the seashore and in town. The locals constantly talked about Jesus with travelers waiting in the tax line. Levi recognized hope in the faces of those who followed him. *Is there hope in Jesus?* he wondered. He was personally acquainted with the fishermen, Andrew and Simon Peter. The man he knew as Simon was one whose loyalties were not easily gained, but once obtained his devotion was fierce. Nevertheless, Levi had no reason to believe that, as a tax collector, he would find acceptance with the rabbi Jesus who, after all, didn't even have a synagogue.

Yet when he looked up to see Jesus in the tax line, Levi wanted to say something to him, but he didn't want to ask personal questions in front of a crowd. He didn't even know how to greet him.

As Jesus stepped to Levi's table, he paused, not to pay taxes, but to offer the tax collector the salvation that had eluded him. With a burning deep in his eyes, Jesus said to him simply, "Follow me."

With this simple invitation of Jesus, Levi saw his entire past swallowed up before him. His sins . . . his greed . . . his oppression . . . his alienation from the commonwealth of Israel. And an overwhelming sense of relief washed over him.

Jesus dropped a coin on the table and walked past the tax booth. Philip and the disciples followed Jesus past the booth; they did not look back expecting to be hailed by the collector for unpaid taxes. To a man, the disciples expected Levi to do as Jesus had commanded.

Levi left the booth to follow Jesus.

"Where are you going?!" one of the Publicans shouted after Levi, but the tax collector did not look back. He decided to follow Jesus, no turning back.

"Come back!"

Levi had been surprised by the unexpected display of love he felt from Jesus. Because he was a mokhes, he had seen only hatred from those he legally robbed. He ran to catch up with the teacher.

Jesus looked at him and smiled. He said, "You will be called Matthew, for you are a gift of God."

That evening, after teaching by the sea, Jesus and the disciples joined Matthew at his house for the evening meal. A number of publicans who worked under the tax collector were also invited. Some came hoping that associating with Jesus would give them a new standing in the Jewish community. Some came out of respect for Levi; others because the meal was free.

After the meal was over, Jesus began teaching those assembled about the kingdom of God. As was the custom in Capernaum, visitors from town squeezed into the large dining room after the evening meal to share in the talk around the table. This was how news was spread, and Jesus shared good news, offering illumination and insight to those who drew near to him. But just as a light in the darkness draws bugs, so the light of Jesus attracted the religious pests from the synagogues—those who hated Jesus.

A Pharisee slipped behind Philip, knowing that Philip observed the details of the Law, and whispered into his ear, "How can your master eat and drink with tax collectors and sinners?"

But Jesus overheard this and answered aloud, "Those who are well have no need of a physician—only those who are sick. I did not come to save the righteous; I came to call sinners to repentance."

That evening, when Jesus and the disciples departed the home of Matthew, followers of John the Baptist confronted them outside. They had heard that Jesus was feasting at the house of a tax collector and they were disturbed. Moreover, they knew that Jesus and his followers did not fast. John the Baptist was a Nazirite, a man of the vow; he had separated himself to God by his diet, and so had his disciples. They expected Jesus to follow the Baptist's example, so they said to him, "Why do the disciples of John and of the Pharisees fast, but your disciples do not fast?"

Jesus said to them, "When people go to a wedding, they do not fast. They eat and enjoy themselves. As long as the bridegroom is with them, they will eat at the feast. But when the bridegroom is taken from them, then they will fast until his return."

Jesus could see the lack of understanding in their faces. Even his own followers had questioned the wisdom of attending dinner at Matthew's house, knowing how it would look to the Jews and the religious authorities. But they also understood that Matthew and the publicans needed God, while the Pharisees wanted only to enforce rules. The disciples of John the Baptist were clinging to the old ways of outward conformity, so Jesus sat down to teach them.

"No one sews a piece of new cloth on an old garment to repair a tear, because the new cloth will shrink and pull away from the old garment, making the tear worse than it was before it was repaired.

"Likewise, no man puts new wine into old wineskins. If he does, the new wine will ferment and burst the old wineskins and everything will be lost. You must put new wine in new wineskins. My message is a new message. The old will pass away, but I bring new wine that must be put in new containers."

"And no one, having drunk old wine, immediately desires new; for he says, 'The old is better.'"

LUKE 5:39

chapter thirty-one

THE POOL OF BETHESDA

JOHN 5:1-13

When Jesus returned to Jerusalem to observe the Feast of Passover, he had gained popularity with the people. His reputation with the religious authorities had only worsened, however, since he had cleansed the Temple one year earlier. Nevertheless, he would make no concessions by avoiding the Eternal City and those who would silence his ministry.

As Jesus and his disciples walked to the Temple to worship on the Sabbath day, Andrew drew their attention down the street to where a throng had gathered at the pool of Bethesda, blocking their way to the Temple. During the week of Passover, this street was all but impassable. Any other time of the year, there were no more than twenty or thirty people to be found waiting at the pool for the stirring of the water. It was said that an angel stirred up the pool from time to time, and the first person to enter the pool after the water erupted would be healed.

"There must be more than two thousand people at the pool today," Andrew cautioned Jesus. "They will all want you to heal them." He pointed to a small street off to the left and suggested, "If we go that way, we can bypass the crowd and go directly to the Temple."

Jesus shook his head and continued walking the direct route to the Temple, which would lead through the mob of people at the pool of Bethesda.

As they approached the pool, they heard moaning and groans of anguish, punctuated by the sounds of an argument. Jesus walked into the midst of the crowd, but no one took notice of him. At the edge of the pool, people were elbowing for position near the waters.

"I was here first," a voice rang out.

"But that's my place!"

"I was here yesterday," another protested.

"This has always been my spot."

The disciples were amazed. Whereas back in Galilee everyone wanted to touch Jesus or to be touched by him, Jesus was completely ignored here in Jerusalem. In Galilee, the sick were respectful . . . quiet . . . almost praying for healing. Here at the pool of Bethesda, the boisterous crowd was loud . . . mean-spirited . . . selfish.

Slowly Jesus eased through the crowd, looking from one ashen face to the next forlorn set of eyes. He seemed to be looking for someone, a special someone. Then seeing a man against a wall, Jesus immediately began walking toward him, as though the sick man were a long-lost friend.

Jesus was jostled by two men leading a blind man to the pool. But Jesus continued walking toward the man he had spied sitting against a wall. The poor man's worn pallet showed the wear and tear of being rolled and unrolled every day for thirty-eight years. Each day during that time, the lame man had waited in vain for the moving of the waters, knowing full well that when the waters were stirred he could not be the first in.

The pool of Bethesda was surrounded by beautiful marble columns that reached into the sky. When crowds did not overrun the area, it was an oasis in the middle of the city. What was designed as a resting spot in the middle of Jerusalem had come to be occupied by the sick and oppressed.

The lame man had waited day after day, each time disappointed when the waters bubbled up. The man slumped against the wall, his hope long since depleted. The chin of his balding head rested on his chest, his flesh sagging like his spirit. The empty stare in his eyes looked down at his mangled legs. Those who saw his eyes knew that he was not looking at the legs he saw. His eyes were remembering a time when he could walk. In an act of rebellion against God nearly four decades earlier, something happened to cripple him, leaving him with nothing but guilt and self-doubt. Because of one act of rebellion, he had never walked again.

The shadow of Jesus fell across the man, but still he did not look up. None of the two thousand people crying for help recognized Jesus, nor did he look to them. Jesus had chosen this helpless man, perhaps because he was the most helpless of all those at Bethesda.

"Do you want to be healed?" Jesus asked.

The man slowly lifted his head toward Jesus, his eyes blinking in the midday sun. He shielded his eyes from the glare. It was a strange question, and he didn't know how to answer. He was obviously there to be healed; why would anyone ask him if he wanted to be healed? He had seen his hopes dashed many times. Many times the water had rippled, but he couldn't make it into the pool. Now all hope was gone.

He answered, "Sir, I don't have anyone to help me into the pool when the water is stirred. When I try to get in, someone else goes down ahead of me."

Jesus had seen this same desperation in the faces of the other sick. He saw their eyes. Their eyes gazed at the pool; they were not looking to God. They waited in anticipation of the slightest ripple, so that they might reach the water first. Their faith was in the water. Their faith was in a quick response. Their faith was in an unseen angel. The kingdom of God was standing in their midst, and they didn't know it.

Jesus commanded the lame man, "Rise. Get up! Pick up your mat and walk."

Instantly, the man felt energy enter his legs. He felt sensations he hadn't felt for thirty-eight years. His silently commanded his toes to move. They wiggled. He told his left foot to move. It responded as he pulled the foot toward his body. He pulled himself up, and found himself rising as anyone with normal legs would. He stood! No one around him noticed, and he did not yell, scream or dance. He had been told to take up his mat and walk, so he obeyed. He bent over and began rolling his pallet, closing the door on his life as a cripple. He then threw the pallet on his shoulders and walked away from the pool.

Jesus, having finished his task, continued walking through the crowd, making his way toward the Temple. Because all eyes were fixed on the water, none had seen the miracle transpire near them. Less than a block away, the Temple was filled with priests, self-seeking men who trifled with their religious acts, ignoring the multitude of people suffering nearby.

A pair of Jewish leaders walking to the Temple almost immediately spotted the healed man carrying his pallet. "THIS IS THE SABBATH DAY!" they shouted at him. "PUT THAT MAT DOWN IMMEDIATELY!"

The Sabbath day had been instituted as a sign of God's covenant with his people. Just as God rested from his work on the seventh day to reflect on his creation, so the Jews were to work six days and rest on the seventh. Moses' instruction not to do any work on the Sabbath day seemed simple enough. This was supposed to be a day set aside for worship, prayer and rest, but through the years Jewish leaders had developed so many regulations concerning what was work and what was not, the original meaning of the Sabbath had become hopelessly obscured.

Under the rabbinical interpretations of the Law, carrying a pallet was considered "work" and was therefore illegal on the Sabbath. The two Pharisees accosted the once-lame man, grabbing him by the sleeve of his tunic. Within minutes of his miraculous healing, the man's joy was stolen from him and replaced by fear.

"It is not lawful for you to carry your bed on the Sabbath day. Why do you do this?"

"The one who healed me . . . ," he tried to explain. "The man who made me well said to me, 'Pick up your mat and walk.'"

"Who is this person who told you to pick it up and walk on the Sabbath?" they demanded.

"B-but this is a wonderful thing . . . ," the man sputtered in defense of his healer. "I have not been able to walk for nearly forty years."

"What was the man's name?" the Jewish leaders insisted.

"I don't know. I didn't ask his name."

The healed man looked around the crowd but didn't see Jesus. The Pharisees also looked to the same direction, searching for the man who had broken their Sabbath law. By now, a few others had recognized that the lame man was standing on his own legs, without help. They gathered in a tight knot around the confrontation between the healed man and the two Jewish leaders. Their voices were getting louder as the crowd got bigger.

One of the Pharisees again demanded, "WHO HEALED YOU?!"

"You're standing!" an old friend of the man exclaimed. "Did the waters stir? Did you make it into the pool? How were you healed?" His loud voice brought others to the scene of the confrontation.

When he was lame, the healed man had been ignored as he sat alone at the edge of the crowd. No one was concerned about him; no one helped him into the pool. Now he was the center of attention.

"Who healed you?"

"Where is the healer?"

"PUT YOUR PALLET DOWN!!!" the repetitious Pharisee could only bark one command.

No one seemed to be happy that the man was healed. Many were curious about his healing, however, and the crowd began looking for the healer that had been in their midst.

"Heal me! Heal me!"

But the one who was healed did not know who it was, for Jesus had withdrawn, a multitude being in that place.

JOHN 5:13

chapter thirty-two

JESUS CLAIMS EQUALITY WITH THE FATHER

JOHN 5:14-17

The commotion at the pool of Bethesda had gone on for longer than the once-lame man cared. To get away from the Pharisees, he was forced to throw his pallet to the ground. Even though Jesus had told him to take up his pallet and walk, he threw the crumpled pallet into a doorway. The healed man no longer wanted a souvenir of his lameness, but it was his only possession. He left his pallet in a doorway, and just as quickly, a thief came along and took it.

The healed man walked strongly from the pool of Bethesda to the gate of the Temple. He knew well the commandment in Scripture, that those with physical ailments could not enter into the House of God. For thirty-eight years as a lame man, he had not been inside the Temple. On many days he had begged near the Gate Beautiful, outside the presence of God. But now with strong legs, he walked up the granite steps past the Golden Gate into God's house.

A haunting memory of past voices still scared him. He remembered a priest turning away the physically impaired who tried to sneak into the presence of God, screaming, "Get out of the Temple! God commands you to stay out . . . ."

Now his two good legs carried him through the gate; no one would turn him away.

Many people were standing about in the courtyard of the Temple, waiting for the afternoon call to prayer. The healed man waited among them, looking up to the pinnacle. There stood a Levite in a spotless white tunic, a silver trumpet held in readiness. It was a lifetime ago that he had last seen the trumpeter place the musical instrument to his lips to call God's people to worship.

Now inside the Temple, the once-lame man was no longer the center of attention. He was left to his thoughts, and he looked forward to the time of prayer. He wanted to sing with the psalmist:

Bless the Lord, O my soul,
And all that is within me,
Bless his holy name . . .
Who forgives all your iniquities,
Who heals all your diseases.

He wanted to say to God, "Thank you for healing me."

Suddenly, Jesus was there. The man had not seen Jesus approaching through the crowd, nor did anyone else seem to recognize Jesus. Jesus had walked unobserved through the crowd and now stood next to him.

"God has heard your prayers," Jesus said to the man.

"You . . . !" the healed man said to Jesus. "You are the one who told me to take up my mat and walk." His eyes welled up with tears of gratitude; there were so many things he wanted to say. But Jesus did not seek the man's gratitude, he sought the man's heart.

Jesus cut him off sharply, saying, "See, you have been made well." Jesus searched the man's eyes. "Do not go back to the sin that crippled you."

The once-lame man looked into his own sinful heart, nodding his head; he knew why he had been stricken lame. There had been days when the man had forgotten what he had done, like clouds blocking his memory of the sun. But then there were other days when he remembered vividly his sin against God. These were days when the sun shone brightest into the darkest corners of his heart. The man looked down to see healthy legs; but he remembered crippled feet. Jesus had pricked his conscience.

Jesus said to him, "Do not sin again, or something worse may happen to you." Then Jesus turned and melted into the crowd.

Unknown to the man, the Pharisees had been watching him. The healed man had broken their Sabbath rules by carrying his pallet. They had followed him to see if he would break another law, but they stumbled onto a bonanza. They had recognized Jesus, and they immediately approached the man.

"Was that the man who healed you?" they demanded.

The healed man nodded yes.

"Did he tell you to pick up your bed and walk?"

"Yes."

Immediately the priests stormed through the crowds after Jesus, pushing worshipers out of the way. To them it was imperative that they catch Jesus and confront him. Jesus had knowingly broken their law. Not only had he healed the lame man—surely this must be defined as "work"—but he had incited the man to break the Sabbath himself! Like hungry dogs running through the streets of the city, their howling soon attracted other priests who joined in their pursuit of Jesus. They finally caught up to him near the Gate Beautiful, where he stood talking with a handful of his disciples. The priests assaulted him with questions all at once.

"Did you heal a lame man at the pool?"

"Did you command that man to carry his pallet?"

"Who gave you this authority?"

"Why do you violate the Sabbath?"

Jesus smiled a knowing smile and nodded his head. This told them what they wanted to know. But Jesus was ready to give them much more than they had bargained for.

He said to them, "My Father is always ready to work on the Sabbath day, and so the Son must work while he is on the earth."

"Blasphemy!" a priest shouted. The priests' countenances screwed into violent hostility. Jesus had boldly proclaimed himself to be the very Son of

God. He had called God his Father, thus declaring himself equal with God. They knew Jesus understood fully what he was saying. This was blasphemy, and the punishment for blasphemy was death.

By now a large crowd was gathering about them, drawn by the shouting of the priests. If they had been outside the Temple where rocks were at the ready, the crowd would have stoned him. Their hatred choked them, like a thirsty man gulping too much water chokes for air. Jesus saw the rage in their hearts, but he continued speaking.

"I tell you the truth, the Son can do nothing by himself. He can do only what he sees his Father doing, because whatever the Father does the Son will also do. For the Father loves the Son and shows him all things."

Many who heard these words walked away from Jesus, refusing to listen further to what they considered to be a blasphemous diatribe. Others surrounded Jesus, wanting to question him, but they dared not interrupt. This man spoke with an authority not of this world.

"The very work that the Father has given me to finish, and which you have seen me doing, testifies that my Father has sent me. You have never heard his voice nor seen his form, nor does his word dwell in you, for you do not believe the one he sent."

The priests retired to themselves to determine what they would do about Jesus of Nazareth.

One enraged priest said aloud, "May God send Jesus to damnation for what he has said." His anger was so deep that he didn't recognize that he himself had broken the fourth commandment by taking God's name in vain.

The Jewish authorities put their heads together to discuss what they had just heard, and they plotted how they could put Jesus to death.

Therefore the Jews sought all the more to kill Him, because He not only broke the Sabbath, but also said that God was His Father, making Himself equal with God.

JOHN 5:18

chapter thirty-three

A SABBATH CONTROVERSY

MARK 2:23-28

The disciples walked with Jesus as they returned to Galilee from the Feast of Passover in Jerusalem, a handful of Pharisees trailing in their wake. The Pharisees had been sent to spy on Jesus, in hopes of catching him in further blasphemies or other sin or inconsistencies.

Jesus turned on an overgrown path leading over the hills, a path most travelers didn't follow. The path stretched along a rocky wall that separated the land of two grain farmers. The disciples followed and the Pharisees traveled behind, in tow and not out of sight. It was early afternoon and the disciples had not eaten since breakfast. Peter was the first to spot the patch of ripened wheat lining the path.

"Look!" he said. "This field is already ripe. Let's roll grain . . . ." As boys, they had all learned to strip kernels of wheat off a stalk, rub them briskly in their hand, then blow away the chaff. Then, rubbing even more briskly the grain became powdery . . . flour. Then they added water making a paste that could be eaten.

"Pick only in the corners," Philip said to his fellow disciples in observance of good manners. God's law allowed the poor to pull the heads off standing grain to eat the raw kernels. But when the Pharisees saw them picking grain, they immediately broke into a trot.

"This is the Sabbath day!" they yelled at the disciples. "You've broken the Sabbath."

"We've not broken the Sabbath law," Philip protested. "The rabbis taught us we can take three heads of grain for food. We're not stealing."

"But you were picking the grain. You were reaping, and that is work," argued the Pharisees. "It is *not* lawful to work on the Sabbath day."

Jesus was not intimidated by their charges, but accepted this as an opportunity to teach his followers the true meaning of the Sabbath. He waited for the Pharisees to catch their breath then said to them, "Haven't you ever read what David did when he was in need and hungry, how he went into the house of God when Abiathar was high priest, and David ate the showbread, which is not lawful to eat except for the priests?"

The Pharisees did not answer him. So Jesus asked another question. "What about the priests who fulfill their duties in the Temple on the Sabbath day? Aren't they breaking the Sabbath when they work?"

Again, the Pharisees did not answer Jesus. So Jesus said to them, reminding them of God's words to the prophet Hosea, "If you knew what this means, 'I desire mercy and not sacrifice,' you would not condemn those who are not guilty."

Jesus tried to teach them that grace and mercy were more important than legalistic adherence to the stringent rabbinical interpretations of the Law. Still the Pharisees would not listen.

"God did not make the Sabbath day to be another rule to be followed," Jesus said, "but rather God gave the Sabbath day so that man might rest and regain his strength." Up until now Jesus had argued doctrine and the finer points of the Law. But what he said next infuriated the Pharisees, stopping any further discussion.

"The Sabbath was made for man, not man for the Sabbath. Therefore the Son of Man is also Lord of the Sabbath."

The spies continued following Jesus, snooping around Capernaum and listening to Jesus' sermons, looking for any accusations they could bring against him. The next Sabbath day, according to his custom, Jesus went to the synagogue. As the Pharisees prepared to follow Jesus into the house of worship, they caught sight of a middle-aged man approaching the building, his shriveled hand dangling useless at his side. The keepers of the Law followed the man into the synagogue, knowing that if Jesus were to heal the man on the Sabbath, they could accuse him before the Sanhedrin.

They watched the man sit down, hiding his lame hand under his robe, not seeking to draw attention to himself or the withered hand.

The worship proceeded normally, though the Pharisees were preoccupied with observing the healer from Nazareth. Tiring of their machinations in the house of God, Jesus was determined to bring the situation to a head. He stood and spoke boldly to the man with the withered hand: "Step forward."

The worshipers gathered there looked about to see who it was that Jesus addressed. The man in question panicked; he had tried to be as inconspicuous as possible. But he could not ignore the call of Jesus. Slowly he stood and stepped to the center of the meeting house, his withered hand dangling for all to see. The people anxiously anticipated a miracle in their presence.

Jesus turned to the visiting Pharisees who had hounded him for several weeks. Under different circumstances, the Pharisees would have relished a debate of theological issues, but Jesus had a sympathetic audience and a perfect platform to prove a point. Jesus asked them, "Is it lawful on the Sabbath to do good or to do evil?"

His question was greeted with silence from the Pharisees. Their eyes dropped into their laps; any answer they gave would play into Jesus' hands. If they were to say a good act is lawful, Jesus would then heal the man's hand as a good work. Of course, they couldn't say it was unlawful to do good, so they said nothing.

So Jesus asked a second question. "Is it lawful on the Sabbath to save a life or to kill?"

Again, they refused to answer the question. They had already made up their minds that Jesus was a blasphemer. They were only looking for proof and did not wish to discuss any alternatives.

Jesus was angered by their hardness of heart. He knew they were not concerned about the Law as a matter of obedience to God. He grieved that the appointed leaders of God's people should completely reject him, just as they had rejected John the Baptist.

Then he said to them, "Who among you with just one sheep, if it fell into a pit on the Sabbath, would not lift it out? Of how much more value then is a man than a sheep? Therefore, it is lawful to do good works on the Sabbath."

Jesus turned his attention to the unfortunate man and said to him, "Stretch forth your hand."

At first the man didn't move; the muscles in his hand had not flexed in years. The fingers had not twitched, neither had the nerves from his brain made their connection with his fingertips. The man slowly looked up, his eyes catching the steady gaze of Jesus. Rather than looking away, he received assurance from compassionate eyes. He nodded his head, knowing he would be able to comply. Then he looked at his hand and saw the rigid fingers slowly clench into a fist. He released the fist to flex the fingers, holding out the hand for all to see. He pointed with a finger . . . he clapped . . . he flexed the fingers again.

"It's whole! My hand is restored as whole as the other!"

The entire congregation gasped, even though the healing was not unexpected. Many had heard about Jesus' healing in Capernaum. Now that they had seen it for themselves, they joined together in praise of God.

Then the Pharisees went out and plotted against Him,
how they might destroy Him.
MATTHEW 12:14

chapter thirty-four

CHOOSING TWELVE DISCIPLES

MARK 3:13-19
LUKE 6:12-19

Knowing the religious authorities plotted against his life, Jesus withdrew with his disciples to the Sea of Galilee, for there was still much to do and his time to die had not yet come. A great multitude from Capernaum and the surrounding villages of Galilee followed him to the sea, and many more came from Syria and Phoenicia to the north and from Judea and the lands beyond the Jordan River to the south, where news of his miraculous works had reached.

The crowds pressed in on Jesus so much, he was unable to talk privately with his disciples. Nor could he preach or even eat a meal. Turning to those closest to him, he asked that a small boat be kept ready to take him across the sea should the crowd grow unruly. The sheer numbers of people were making it difficult for him to help anyone.

"I want to touch him," one man cried, elbowing his way through the horde, almost causing a scuffle.

"I was here first," another yelled.

When Jesus tried to walk, people grabbed at his tunic because they wanted some power or blessing or healing from him. Those with unclean spirits fell down before him and cried out, "You are the Son of God!"

He needed help to minister to the multitudes. Jesus had many followers and many wanted to be his disciples, but they were not particularly well organized. There were more than seventy who pledged loyalty to him, but Jesus needed a smaller number of men, close associates whom he could personally direct and guide. This smaller circle of men would learn from his example, then they would teach others and help him to minister to the people. Just as there were twelve tribes of Israel, so he would choose twelve men to be his closest companions.

Jesus climbed into the boat and sailed away, leaving the crowd on the shore. Arriving near Magdala, Jesus left the small craft on the beach and climbed a steep hill, looking for a secluded place where he could be alone this night. When he reached the brow of the hill, Jesus turned to see Tiberias on his right and Capernaum on his left. The blue waters of the Sea of Galilee stretched out before him. A gentle breeze blew across the lake surface, as the sun slowly set behind him. Tonight, on this spot, Jesus would come to the most important decision in his ministry,

All those who faithfully followed him were known as his "disciples," a title that meant follower or learner. Jesus would call his chosen twelve by a different title; he would call them "apostles," a Greek word that meant sent ones. The twelve apostles would be the ones he would send to carry the gospel, or good news, to the entire earth.

Falling to his knees, Jesus began praying and continued into the night. "Lord . . . help me look into the heart of these men. Help me choose those that can be trusted with your words." Even as he prayed, Jesus yielded the decision to his Father, saying, "Your will be done . . . ."

Jesus prayed all night. When the sun peeked over the eastern mountains beyond the Sea of Galilee, Jesus came down from the hill to where the disciples were waiting for him. Still there were more than seventy, each one waiting to serve him.

"A disciple is a follower," Jesus said to them. "All of you will continue to follow me. You will all be called my disciples.

"Only twelve will be chosen as apostles," Jesus explained. "An apostle is one that I will send in my name. These will be your leaders in ministry. First they will be with me . . . learn from me . . . pray with me . . . help me in ministry. They will preach and be given power to heal sickness and cast out demons."

Jesus looked from face to face, searching for confirmation of his choices. "Simon will be first," Jesus nodded to the strapping fisherman. "Simon will be called Peter, for he will be strong . . . firm . . . a hardened leader. He will fearlessly preach the gospel."

His next choice was James, the son of Zebedee. Everyone was surprised by this choice, because James was so quiet yet quick to anger. James was always the first to pull a net, first to the oars, first to pick up any burden. James was not afraid of work, but the disciples were hard-pressed to imagine him as a preacher. The third choice was his brother John, the youngest of all the disciples and the one with the most volatile personality.

Jesus said, "James and John are as thunder; they will quickly roar like the thunderstorm at sin or iniquity. The Sons of Thunder will be prophets who preach against unrighteousness."

Jesus selected Andrew as his fourth apostle. Once a follower of John the Baptist, Andrew was the brother of the bombastic Peter, but Andrew had people skills to relate to others. He was sensitive to the needs of people and would bring many to salvation.

"Philip, you too will be an apostle." Surprised at being chosen, Philip stepped forward, ready to do anything for Jesus. Philip was a doer; his hands were always busy keeping things in order. Philip thought little of himself, but compensated for his perceived shortcomings with hard work and attention to details.

"Philip will be in charge of the next three apostles and will supervise the crowds and will arrange for accommodations and other details in our travels." Jesus appointed three other apostles to serve with Philip: his friend Nathanael, who was also called Bartholomew; Matthew, the former tax collector and oldest of the disciples; and Thomas, who was known for his pragmatism.

"The ninth apostle will be James, son of Alphaeus," Jesus nodded to the shortest of his disciples. There were several followers named James, and to keep them straight, everyone called the smallest of them James the Less. Jesus instructed James, "Your group will be in charge of our money."

To work with James the Less in this last group of apostles, Jesus also called Thaddeus and Simon the Zealot, who had once been a guerrilla fighter.

The first eleven men that Jesus chose were from Galilee. They spoke with a Galilean accent, and they understood the area from which Jesus came.

Then Jesus announced, "The twelfth apostle will be from Judea. Judas Iscariot will be my twelfth apostle. He is the one especially chosen by my Father to be one of our disciples." And he assigned Judas to carry the money bag.

And when He had called His twelve disciples to Him, He gave them power over unclean spirits, to cast them out, and to heal all kinds of sickness and all kinds of disease.

MATTHEW 10:1

chapter thirty-five

THE SERMON ON THE MOUNT

MATTHEW 5 – 7

The morning broke soft over the hills around Tiberias. Jesus left the highway and began to climb up into the hills. He pointed to the top of a small hill.

"Up there," he said.

Arriving at the top, they had a vantage point overlooking Galilee from which they could see several miles in every direction. At the pinnacle of the hill, the mount flattened out and Jesus sat on a large, white limestone rock with his disciples clustered about him. Jesus had promised he would tell the disciples about the kingdom of heaven. Here they would learn about the kingdom he was going to establish on earth—with their help. More than a sermon, this was their training class.

However, they would not be alone. The multitudes had followed Jesus from the road into the hills. Every day, more and more people were coming from every region of Palestine to be near him. They came to hear him teach, of course, but there was something more. People genuinely liked being with Jesus. Where he went, there also was joy.

Jesus had chosen this hill precisely because it would comfortably accommodate a few thousand listeners. When he sat, the people scurried for position as near to him as possible, where they could see and hear him clearly. The breeze bent the grass lightly, the clear air of this bright summer day refreshing the crowd as he taught them.

"Blessed are you who depend only on the Father, for yours is the kingdom," Jesus said to the people.

"Blessed are you who mourn, for you shall be comforted.

"Blessed are you who are humble, for you shall inherit the earth.

"Blessed are you who hunger and thirst after righteousness, for you shall be filled.

"Blessed are you who show mercy to others, for you shall obtain mercy.

"Blessed are you who have a pure heart, for you shall see God.

"Blessed are you who make peace between warring factions, for you shall be called the children of God.

"Blessed are you who are persecuted for doing what is right, for yours is the kingdom of heaven.

"Blessed are you when men hate you, persecute you and lie about you because of me. Remember, they also lied about the prophets. Rejoice and be glad, because great is your reward in heaven.

"I did not come to do away with the Law and the prophets, as some have said; I have come to fulfill the Scriptures. Everything written will happen as God said. Until heaven and earth pass away, not the smallest letter, not the least stroke of a pen will disappear from Scripture. God will fulfill all his promises."

Jesus taught them that the kingdom of God was not a place that could be seen or visited, but that the kingdom lived within those who believed. And contrary to what they had been taught by the keepers of the Law, this was not a kingdom founded on rules. Outward conformity to a set of rules meant nothing if one's heart was not right, Jesus said. Obedience was a matter of the heart.

He explained, "The Law says, 'Do not murder.' But I tell you do not get angry with your brother or even think about killing. The Law says, 'Do not commit adultery.' But I say to you do not even think lustful thoughts in your heart."

Simon, the one called the Zealot, wasn't sure he liked Jesus' sermon. Simon had been a freedom fighter, a member of the Zealots, a fanatical band of patriots committed to overthrowing Herod's corrupt rule and driving the Romans into the sea. Simon had left his comrades to follow Jesus because he believed this miracle worker could rally an army to destroy Rome.

But Jesus was saying, "Love your enemies. Bless those who curse you, do good to those who hate you and pray for those who spitefully use you."

Simon the Zealot was perplexed by this sermon of Jesus. *What about the glory of the kingdom?* he wondered. Jesus instead described a kingdom based on trusting in God.

"Do not worry about your life, what you are going to eat, what you are going to drink. Do not worry about your body or what you will wear. Life is more than food, and your body is more than clothes. Seek first the kingdom of God, and all these things will be given to you.

"Look at the birds in the sky. They do not sow, nor do they reap like farmers or store their food in barns, and yet they have all the food they need. Your heavenly Father feeds the birds of the sky, and he will take care of you.

"None of you can add one inch to your stature by worrying about such things. Look at the lilies of the field and see how they grow. They do not labor, neither do they spin. Yet I tell you that not even Solomon in all his splendor was dressed like one of these flowers. If that is how God clothes the grass of the field, how much more is he able to take care of you?

"Have faith in your heavenly Father. He knows that you need food, drink and clothing. Therefore, do not worry about tomorrow, for tomorrow will take care of itself."

Still Simon struggled. The Zealot was a man of action. He had been trained to capture a kingdom by force, but Jesus said the kingdom of God comes from within.

"Do not give your money to God by sounding a trumpet so that your good works are seen and praised by men. This is what hypocrites do. I tell you they have received their reward. But give your money secretly so that your left hand doesn't know what your right hand is doing. Then your Father who sees what is done in secret will reward you openly.

"Do not pray on the street corner with loud prayers and vain repetition. Hypocrites do this to be seen by men, and so they have their reward. But when you pray, go into your room, close the door and pray to your Father in secret. Then your Father, who sees your heart, will reward you openly."

Then Jesus taught the people to pray:
"Our Father in heaven, holy be your name.
Your kingdom come.
Your will be done on earth as it is in heaven.
Give us each day our daily bread.
And forgive us our sins as we forgive those who sin against us.
And do not lead us into temptation that will destroy us,
But deliver us from the evil one.
For yours is the kingdom and the power and the glory forever.
Amen."

Jesus said, "Ask and it will be given to you. Seek and you will find. Knock and the door will be opened to you."

Simon the Zealot marveled at this teaching. Jesus was simply throwing open the gates to his kingdom, and anyone who would come to Jesus and follow him could enter.

"So in all things," Jesus said, "do to others what you would have them do to you, for this is the law of the prophets."

And the people were astonished, because this is not what they had been taught in the synagogues. Yet Jesus taught with authority far greater than that of the keepers of the Law. So the people listened to Jesus and believed his words because he loved them.

For the law was given through Moses,
but grace and truth came through Jesus Christ.
JOHN 1:17

chapter thirty-six

THE CENTURION'S SERVANT

LUKE 7:1-10

When Jesus returned to Capernaum, a delegation of elders was waiting for Jesus and his disciples inside the city gate. When Jesus entered, he was walking in the midst of a large crowd. The elders brushed past the common people thronging about Jesus, making their way to the center of the procession. One of the synagogue leaders said to Jesus, "Master, we have a desperate problem that perhaps you can help us solve."

The elders quietly hated Jesus; but they tolerated him in public, even using the honorific title "Master," so as not to raise the ire of the public with whom he was so popular. Now they needed his help, so they approached the teacher with false humility.

The elder's voice trembled with urgency. "The centurion who commands the Roman forces in Capernaum has a servant who is tormented with palsy and is near death."

The crowd grew silent at the mention of the hated Romans.

The Jewish elders explained to Jesus that this Roman centurion had heard how he had healed the sick and the lame, even a leper. He had also heard that Jesus dined with tax collectors and had helped an officer of Herod's court. The centurion believed that Jesus could heal his Gentile servant.

The elders usually hated Roman soldiers, but they were politicians who buttered both sides of their bread. If they could be kind to this Roman soldier, he would be kind to them. The elders told Jesus, "The centurion is a worthy man. Will you heal his servant?"

The elders stood anxiously awaiting a decision from Jesus. They looked carefully into his eyes searching for any sign of willingness to heal the servant. The elders could see they had not convinced Jesus of their mission, so they added, "The centurion is an unusual Gentile who loves the Jews. He paid for building the synagogue for us." They pointed down the street to the white limestone synagogue in Capernaum, where Jesus had worshiped many times.

Jesus knew what he was going to do; he had been waiting to force the elders to admit their motives. They were clearly seeking to help the centurion for political reasons. Jesus said, "I will heal the servant."

The crowd began running ahead of Jesus toward the home of the centurion. Jesus slowly followed with the elders in tow. A servant ran ahead of the crowd to tell the centurion, "Jesus is coming."

The centurion knew Jesus could heal his servant. The only question in his mind had been whether he would. Unlike the elders who doubted the source of Jesus' miraculous power, the centurion believed that Jesus was a true healer. His question was one of crossing ethnic barriers. His home was unclean according to Jewish law, so if Jesus were to enter his home, he would defile himself, becoming unfit or unworthy. The centurion did not want to cause problems for Jesus, so he planned to meet Jesus in the street.

Seeing Jesus in the crowd only a half a block away, he uncharacteristically ran through his courtyard, out the gate and cautiously approached Jesus. He stopped Jesus, saying to him, "Lord, I beg you come no further. I am not worthy that you should come under the roof of my house."

The centurion turned to point out his Gentile home. Then turning back to Jesus, he said, "You come in great authority. I also am a man under authority, with soldiers serving under me. I tell this soldier, 'Go,' and he goes. To that one, I say, 'Come,' and he comes."

To prove his point, the centurion turned to one of his soldiers, who immediately snapped to attention. It was evident to every Jew in the crowd that the Roman soldier would do exactly whatever the centurion commanded, even to the point of falling on his sword. The rigid, statuesque Roman soldier was mute testimony of the centurion's great authority.

The centurion said to Jesus, "Just say the word . . . ." The centurion didn't want more. "Say the word and my servant will be healed."

When Jesus heard this, he was truly astonished. He turned and spoke to those following him, saying, "I tell you the truth, I have not found anyone in Israel with such great faith."

The elders drew back in horror, teeth gnashed and fists clenched. They wanted to lash out at the Nazarene, because he had said that a Gentile had greater faith than they. So they tried to reason with Jesus. "But Master, the centurion is not circumcised. He does not know the Law."

Jesus answered them, "I say to you that many Gentiles will come from the east and the west, and will take their places at the feast with Abraham, Isaac and Jacob in the kingdom of heaven." It was a common belief among the Jews that in the day of the Messiah, the redeemed nation of Israel would be gathered to a great feast together with the patriarchs and heroes of the Jewish faith. According to tradition, Gentiles could have no part of that feast.

But Jesus said, "Not every son and daughter of Abraham will be seated at the banquet. Those who do not have faith will be thrown outside, cast into the darkness—*Gehinnom*—where there will be weeping and gnashing of the teeth."

The crowd sobered, not believing what Jesus had just said, not even believing that they heard Gentiles would be welcome at the banquet of the Messiah. To make matters worse, Jesus had announced this in front of the centurion; if they reacted violently, they would be punished.

The Jewish leaders were furious. The chief elder, who had led the delegation to make the request of Jesus, muttered his hatred for the carpenter under his breath. For this heresy, he despised Jesus.

Before the crowd could react to his startling declaration, Jesus turned to the centurion in kindness and said, "Go to your house. Because you have believed, it is done."

The centurion did not reach out to clasp Jesus' hands, as he would an equal. Instead, he knelt before him in deep gratitude, as a centurion would kneel before Caesar, acknowledging the divinity to which he laid claim.

And his servant was healed that same hour.

MATTHEW 8:13

chapter thirty-seven

THE WOMAN WHO WAS FORGIVEN MUCH

LUKE 7:36-50

Jesus sat on a stone bench in the marketplace of Tiberias, teaching the multitudes the Word of God. People gathered tightly about him, many sitting on the ground at his feet, leaning in as if pulled by the magnetic power of his words. It was the custom of the day to maintain a respectful distance from rabbis and revered "holy men." But Jesus encouraged people to draw near to him. At the end of his message on this day he issued an invitation. "All who labor with sin and are heavy laden with guilt, come to me and I will give you rest from your heavy burden.

"For when you follow me, you will no longer follow sin, but you will have new life. Take my yoke upon you and learn from me, for I am gentle and lowly in heart, and you will find rest for your souls.

"For my yoke is easy and my burden is light."

Crouching in the doorway nearby, a woman full of sin pulled her dark robe tightly to her neck. No one in the crowd saw her, as she was around the corner, out of sight. But as the wind drives rain around the corner of a wall, so the Spirit of God can drive his Word around the barriers of sin. On this day, the words of Jesus sought out this woman to quench the thirst of her sickened soul.

The woman heard . . . grasped . . . believed . . . and she felt cleansed. For the first time in her life, she felt truly forgiven. She had not received forgiveness from the priest, nor could she find forgiveness at the Temple. She had believed Jesus, and she knew God had forgiven her, simply because she had believed.

When Jesus finished, a prominent Pharisee named Simon walked across the clearing in front of everyone to invite Jesus to his house for the evening meal. Jesus accepted the invitation. And as Simon retreated, the Pharisee smiled at the apostle Matthew, knowing that the one-time tax collector had also put on an elegant meal for Jesus. But Simon the Pharisee planned a better meal. He had better cooks, finer eating utensils, and his banquet would be superior.

Then Simon turned and announced to the crowd, "Jesus is coming to my house to eat tonight." The Pharisee smiled at his conquest. "Come . . . you are invited to hear Jesus teach at the end of the meal." It was the custom that after a large banquet, neighbors were permitted in the banquet room, where they would be entertained by music or challenged by the speaker of the evening. A murmur went through the crowd; everyone seemed to be saying, "I will be there."

No one saw the woman in the doorway smile. The Jews excluded her from society because her sins were grievous. But this was not a Jewish feast; this was a banquet for Jesus. *Jesus has forgiven me*, she reasoned in her heart, *so I will be there—first. They can't keep me out.*

After the meal was over, after the sun was set and night had spilled into the room, no one saw the woman making her way into Simon's house.

Wearing a black dress, her face covered, she stepped into an open door, up the veranda steps and into an antechamber, then into the large, festive banquet hall. Without asking anyone, without being greeted, she found herself standing behind Jesus.

Right there in front of her were the feet of Jesus. According to custom, the men were resting on pillows, their feet turned away from the table toward the wall, their left elbows resting on pillows.

The words of the afternoon sermon—"Come to me and I will give you rest"—still shined in her heart, and now she looked with love upon that one who had forgiven her. She felt free of her heavy burden of sin. She dropped to her knees and wept in gratitude.

Absorbed by her shame, she had been unable to live a normal life. Now the fountains of the woman's heart broke open and before she knew it, tears had dripped from her cheeks onto the feet of her Messiah.

He was the only one in the room that mattered to her, and now her tears were dampening his feet. She had not come to do this; her tears surprised her. She quickly stooped and wiped the teardrops from his feet with a long lock of hair that fell from her shoulder.

Reaching into her tunic, she removed an alabaster flask—like those that women carried on a chain around their necks, that hung close to the heart. The small bottle contained *palyeton*, a fragrance favored by the women of Palestine to sweeten the breath and perfume the body, as baths were not always available. Opening her flask, the woman anointed the feet of Jesus, just as a servant anoints with oil the feet of an honored guest.

Then she began to kiss his feet . . . again and again . . . out of deep gratitude for the forgiveness of her sins.

Jesus stopped talking to look at the woman. When he became silent, the whole room looked to see what was happening. Jesus was no longer the focus of attention. Everyone stared at the woman as she quietly wept over his feet, then quickly wiped away the tears. Only Jesus smiled, saying nothing but accepting her worship.

When Simon the Pharisee saw this, he said to himself in disbelief, *If this man were a prophet, he would know who is touching him and what kind of woman she is; he wouldn't allow her to touch him, for she is a sinner with a terrible reputation.*

Breaking the silence of the room, Jesus turned to Simon saying, "Simon, I have something to tell you."

"Tell me, Teacher," Simon said genially, careful not to betray his thoughts.

"A certain man had loaned money to two persons," Jesus said. "One man owed him five hundred denarii; the other man owed him fifty denarii. Neither man was able to pay him back, so the lender freely forgave both of them the debt they owed. Now, which man was more grateful to the money lender?"

Simon had listened carefully to the parable and replied, "The one who was forgiven more, he was the more grateful."

"You are right," Jesus pointed out. Then turning to the woman behind him, Jesus said to Simon, "Do you see this woman? You did not give me water to wash my feet when I came unto your house, but this woman has washed my feet with her tears and wiped them with her hair.

"You did not greet me with a kiss. But this woman has not stopped kissing my feet.

"You did not anoint my head with oil as you would an honored guest, but she has poured her precious perfume on my feet."

Simon should have been embarrassed for being a poor host, embarrassed that Jesus recognized his thoughts. But the Pharisee hardened his heart.

Jesus said to him, "This woman's sins, which are many, have been forgiven. Hence she has shown me great love."

The room was uncomfortably silent. Jesus had done the unthinkable: He had accused Simon of being an ingracious host. But Jesus was not chiding him for neglecting a few acts of hospitality.

He looked directly into Simon's eyes and said, "But he who has been forgiven little loves little."

Jesus turned away from Simon and gazed lovingly at the woman, who was not embarrassed, for she was comfortable in his presence. He said to her, "Your sins are forgiven."

The room erupted in whispered protests, the guests saying to one another, "Who does he think he is? Does he think he can forgive sins?"

Then Jesus released the woman with a final benediction, "Your faith has saved you. Go in peace."

Now it came to pass, afterward, that He went through every city and village,
preaching and bringing the glad tidings of the kingdom of God.

LUKE 8:1

chapter thirty-eight

PLUNDERING THE HOUSE OF SATAN

MATTHEW 12:22-45

The city of Magdala was a short journey from Tiberias. Celebrated for its dyeworks, the city's main commerce was the manufacture and sale of fine woolen textiles. Magdala was famous for its springs and small creeks where shellfish were caught and dye from them was boiled to various colors.

The last time Jesus had journeyed through Magdala, a woman in black had come running down the road, hissing and spitting at him. Grotesque in her appearance as a result of a number of physical infirmities, Jesus was moved with compassion for her. He cast out seven evil spirits from within her and healed her infirmities. In gratitude, this woman, Mary, had gone from home to home in Magdala telling everyone about Jesus.

Now when Jesus returned to the city, Mary the Magdalene again met him in the road. Peter stepped between them to protect his master, but Jesus put a reassuring hand on his shoulder. This was an entirely different woman, clothed in white, healthy, respectful. She smiled shyly as she pleaded with him.

"We must follow you," she said, pointing to a group of women nearby which included her friends, Susanna and Joanna, the wife of Chuza who served as Herod's steward.

"We want to help in any way possible," Susanna spoke up.

Mary Magdalene asked, "May we follow you at a distance?"

Jesus laughed joyfully at the woman's remarkable transformation and gave his permission gladly.

As Jesus traveled from one village to another, the twelve apostles stayed close by him, while the other disciples followed from a short distance. Mary Magdalene and the other women fell in behind them, and trailing them were the inevitable crowds. But among the multitudes was a group of Pharisees, Sadducees, scribes and other critics of Jesus, drawn anew by reports that he had raised a young man from the dead in the village of Nain. Suspicions had risen among the religious authorities that Jesus was working miracles in the power of Satan. Therefore, they were watching and waiting for occasions to make formal accusations against him.

As Jesus traveled through Magdala, some people brought to him a young man who was blind and mute, being possessed by a demon. The boy with arms outstretched seemed to be reaching in every direction for Jesus, babbling and grunting. Jesus cast the demon out of the young man, just as he had done on other occasions, and the boy was healed.

He began speaking clearly . . . plainly . . . continually. "I'm healed! I'm healed!" The boy went running through the crowd telling everyone, "I can see!" He ran up to an old man. "I can see your bald head . . . ."

The crowds witnessing this miracle were amazed and began to ask among themselves, "Could this be the Messiah, the Son of David?"

The Pharisees, infuriated at the response of the crowd, put their heads together to try to determine how to stop the madness. Finally, a Pharisee confronted Jesus, saying loudly, "You are not the Son of David, because you do not perform miracles by the power of God."

The Pharisee could not deny that the people had seen a miracle. The people believed in Jesus, but the Pharisee would have to change their minds. He turned to the people and proclaimed, "It is only by Beelzebub, the prince of demons, that Jesus of Nazareth drives out evil spirits!"

Peter, enraged at this slander, took a menacing step toward the Pharisee, but Jesus put a hand out to stop him. He would answer these outrageous charges, not because he himself was under attack, but because they had demeaned the power of the Holy Spirit.

Jesus announced to the Pharisees, "A kingdom divided against itself will be ruined, and every city or household divided against itself cannot stand. If Satan drives out Satan, he is divided against himself. How then can his kingdom stand?

"And if I drive out demons by the power of Beelzebub, by whom do your own priests drive them out? But if I drive out demons by the Spirit of God, then the kingdom of God has come upon you, and you must believe in me."

Then to the crowd Jesus said, "How can anyone enter the house of a strong man to carry off his possessions unless he first ties up the strong man? Then he can rob his house. So I have come to take what belongs to Satan.

"He who is not with me is against me, and he who does not gather souls with me is scattering them."

Jesus' voice was rising with his anger. He turned to the Pharisees and thundered, "And so I tell you, every sin and blasphemy you do against me will be forgiven you, but the blasphemy against the Spirit who casts out these demons will not be forgiven! Anyone who speaks a word against the Son of Man will be forgiven, but he who speaks against the Holy Spirit will not be forgiven, either in this world or in the world to come."

The Pharisees decided it was time to change the subject. Another of them approached Jesus with a mocking request. "Master," he said using false reverence, "perhaps we have misjudged you. Please, give us a miraculous sign."

Peter again wanted to answer the Pharisees with something more than words, to point to the young man in the crowd that Jesus had just healed. He could see, he could talk, and the demon was gone. Wasn't that miracle enough?

But it was not Peter's place to answer the Pharisees. Rather, Jesus said to them, "A wicked and adulterous generation asks for a miraculous sign! But none will be given to you except the sign of the prophet Jonah. For as Jonah was three days and three nights in the belly of a huge fish, so the Son of Man will spend three days and three nights in the heart of the earth.

"And the men of Nineveh will stand up at the judgment and condemn this generation, for Nineveh repented at the preaching of Jonah, and now one greater than Jonah is here calling *you* to repentance. But you will not repent."

The Pharisees, stunned by the rebuke of Jesus, turned on their heels to stalk off through the crowd.

Then Jesus explained to the people, "It is not enough to cast the unclean spirit out of a man. The demon will travel through arid places seeking rest, and if it does not find a new home, it says, 'I will return to the house I left.' When it arrives, it finds the house unoccupied. So it brings with it seven other demons more wicked than itself, and they go in and live there.

"When you cast a demon out of a man, you must fill him with the Spirit of God and the Word of God. If you don't, that man will be much worse off than before."

"But I tell you that men will have to give account on the day of judgment for every careless word they have spoken. For by your words you will be acquitted, and by your words you will be condemned."

MATTHEW 12:36,37, *NIV*

chapter thirty-nine

THE SERMON BY THE SEA

MATTHEW 13:1-58

Golden rays from the rising sun found the Sea of Galilee and twinkled with pleasure at the new day. As fresh breezes rippled across the placid water, the fragrance of springtime invited early risers into the fields. Butter-yellow tulips and narcissus, white and scrubbed clean by the Creator, were sprinkled over the green fields surrounding Capernaum.

Jesus left Peter's house and walked with his disciples toward the seaside, but before they could reach the water's edge, an eager crowd surrounded them. They begged Jesus to teach them, so he waded into the water, climbed into a fishing boat, then nodded and smiled at the surprised crew. Without question, they pushed off a little distance from the shore, then dropped the anchor. Quickly the crowd jostled for position on the shore, hoping to gain the best spots to listen to Jesus without getting wet.

Jesus began his sermon with one word: "Look!" He pointed off across the small inlet to a farmer sowing wheat in his field. When Jesus pointed, every neck strained to see what he saw. Quiet covered the crowd.

"Behold," Jesus said, "a farmer sowed wheat in his field. As he scattered the seed, some fell on the path that ran around the field, and the birds came and ate it up. Some seed fell among rocks where there was not much soil. The wheat sprang up quickly, because the soil was shallow. But when the sun came up, it scorched the wheat, and the wheat withered because it had no roots. Some seed fell into thorns, which grew up and choked the plants. Still other seed fell on good soil and brought forth a crop that was thirty, sixty, even a hundred times more than had been planted.

"He who has ears, let him hear what I am saying then apply it to his life."

Jesus stopped preaching for a few minutes, allowing the people to think about the story he had just told. James and John sat with Peter nearby in their own fishing boat. Since the recent passing of their father Zebedee, the boat was kept ready at the shore to serve their master. John asked Jesus, "Why do you speak to the people in parables?"

The story was clear enough, but his disciples did not understand its meaning. Until now Jesus' teachings had been plain and straightforward. He had performed miracles, and he had preached that the kingdom of God was coming. He had revealed much to the multitudes, but this sermon was different. Because the Pharisees were busy sowing seeds of doubt regarding Jesus, from now on his sermons would be filled with parables to further separate the two factions—believers and nonbelievers—among his listeners. His parables would lead the true believers to a clearer understanding of the mysteries of the kingdom of God. On the other hand, those who refused to believe would come to regard these mysteries as wholly unintelligible and reject him outright.

Jesus said to his disciples, "I am teaching in parables to explain why some people reject the Son of Man while others follow him." Jesus nodded his head toward a contingent of Pharisees who had occupied a prominent rock ledge on the shore. "They do not have spiritual discernment to understand what I am saying. You know the secrets of the kingdom of heaven, but they do not. Whoever has this knowledge will be given more, and he will have an abundance. Whoever does not have it, even what he has will be taken from him.

"This is why I speak to them in parables. In them is fulfilled the prophecy of Isaiah: They will hear but not understand. They will see but not perceive. For the hearts of this people have grown dull."

Then Jesus continued his sermon to the people. "Blessed are your eyes for they see, and your ears for they hear. Many prophets have desired to hear the things you hear and see the things that you see. Therefore hear the parable of the sower:

"When anyone hears the word of the kingdom, and does not understand it, then the wicked one will come to snatch away what was sown in his heart. This is the seed sown along the path.

"But the one who received the seed that fell on rocky places is the man who hears the word and immediately receives it with joy. But since he has no root, he lasts only a short time. When trouble or persecution comes because of the word, he stumbles.

"Now the one who received the seed among the thorns is the man who hears the word, but the worries of this life and the deceitfulness of wealth choke the word, and he becomes unfruitful.

"But the one who received the seed that fell on good soil is the man who hears the word and believes it. He produces a crop, yielding thirty, sixty, even a hundred times what was sown."

Then Jesus gave a second parable.

"The kingdom of heaven is like a man who planted good wheat in his field, but as he slept, his enemy came and sowed weeds among the wheat. When the wheat sprouted, the weeds also appeared. The owner's servants came to him and said, 'Sir, didn't you sow good seed in your field? Where then did the weeds come from?'

"'An enemy did this,' he replied. The servants asked him, 'Do you want us to pull the weeds?'

"'No,' he answered, 'because while you are pulling the weeds, you may root up the wheat with them. Let both grow together until the harvest. Then the reapers will sort out the weeds to burn them, but the good wheat will be stored in the barn.'"

When Jesus finished the second parable, many began whispering among themselves as to its meaning. A voice rang out over the water. "Don't give us stories . . . ." The voice was not angry, but inquisitive. The man asked, "Preach to us in plain language." But Jesus did not always answer in kind. Instead, he spoke another parable.

"The kingdom of heaven is like a mustard seed, which a man took and planted in his field. Though it is the smallest of all your seeds, it grows into the largest of garden plants and becomes a tree, so that the birds of the air may come and perch in its branches."

Later, Jesus explained the parables to his disciples. "The harvest is the end of the age, and the harvesters are angels. As the weeds are pulled up and burned in the fire, so it will be at the end of the age. The Son of Man will send out his angels, and they will weed out of his kingdom everything that causes sin and all who do evil. They will throw them into the fiery furnace, where there will be weeping and gnashing of teeth.

"Then the good wheat will shine like the sun in the kingdom of their Father."

Then Jesus explained for them the parable of the mustard seed that grew into a tree so large that the birds of the world found shelter in it. "This is the power of the gospel, that when it is planted in the world the kingdom of God will grow to give shelter to all who seek its shelter."

Jesus then gave his disciples another series of parables.

"The kingdom of heaven is like a treasure hidden in a field. When a man found it, he hid it again, and then in his joy went and sold everything he owned to get enough money to purchase the field, and to possess the treasure.

"Again, the kingdom of heaven is like a merchant looking for fine pearls. When he discovered an exquisite pearl of great value, he went away and sold everything he had to buy the pearl.

"Have you understood all these things?" Jesus asked.

"Yes," the disciples said, recognizing the kind of commitment he was asking from his followers. But Jesus was also assuring them that the ultimate reward of eternal life was well worth the sacrifice they would make.

"Once again, the kingdom of heaven is like a net that was let down into the lake and caught all kinds of fish," Jesus told them. "The fisherman gathered good and worthless fish. When he got to the beach, he sorted the fish, throwing away the useless ones but keeping those that can be eaten. This is how it will be at the end of the world. The angels will come and separate those who have chosen the world from those who have chosen to follow me."

Jesus spoke all these things to the crowd in parables;
he did not say anything to them without using a parable. So was fulfilled
what was spoken through the prophet: "I will open my mouth in parables,
I will utter things hidden since the creation of the world."

MATTHEW 13:34,35, *NIV*

chapter forty

JESUS STILLS THE STORM

MARK 4:35-41

Jesus was fatigued. Teaching under the early morning sun had drained him. The crowds did not leave but still pressed in on him at the shore, preventing him from eating the food brought to him by his disciples. So Jesus beckoned to James.

"Let's cross over to the other side," Jesus said, pointing to a village some five miles across the lake. James hoisted the sail and soon a strong wind lurched the boat forward, and they headed into deep water. An exhausted Jesus lay his head against the leather-covered seat, the gently rocking boat and the cool wind quickly lulling him to sleep. James pointed the boat toward the village of Gadera and all seemed well.

The Sea of Galilee is set in the bottom of a large geologic bowl. Surrounded on four sides by high mountains, the Sea of Galilee is nearly seven hundred feet below sea level. As the hot winds rush off the surrounding plateaus, they tend to mix with cool air over the water, creating sudden, violent thunderstorms.

When Jesus and his apostles left to cross the lake, the sky was a deep blue, not a threatening cloud in sight. But as Jesus slept, out of the western desert came streaks of dark gray clouds, followed by a wild wind that rushed down the western mountain gorge toward the little Sea of Galilee. Within minutes the waves began raising the boat, tossing it lightly then slapping it down into deepening troughs between rising waves. It wasn't long before large, white, foamy waves were breaking over the sides of the boat, covering the apostles' feet with water. They dropped sail and began bailing.

Several of the apostles, who knew the lake well, were not sure they would make it to Gadera alive. But Jesus did not stir; he was undisturbed by the howling wind or the flurry of activity around him.

James leaned all his weight into the helm, trying to keep the boat steady into the wind. John joined Peter in bailing seawater out of the bottom of the boat, but they were unable to keep pace with the rising water being deposited there by the wind and the waves.

WHOOSH! A large wave broke over the boat, flooding in with more water than they had bailed since the storm began. The apostles urged Peter to awaken Jesus.

John threw his bucket aside, shouting to be heard above the storm. "Give it up, Peter! There's nothing more we can do!"

Peter stopped bailing, fear choking off all hope. He shook Jesus and cried out, "Don't you care that we are about to die?!"

"Lord, save us!" John cried out to him. "We're going to drown!" His was not a vague, undefined belief in Jesus; he was simply a scared fisherman yelling for help when there was no other hope at hand.

Jesus stepped to the middle of the boat, holding on to the mast. He lifted his hands to rebuke the wind, saying, "Quiet! Be still!"

The voice of Jesus could barely be heard above the roaring of the storm, but when he rebuked the wind, he was heard. Suddenly the wind died down, and the sea was calm. The flapping ropes fell limp on the mast; wet clothes clung to the disciples. There was silence.

Jesus looked at Peter and said to the twelve incredulously, "Why are you so afraid? You have so little faith?"

There was no response.

As Jesus returned to his resting place, Peter and John bailed out the boat and James readied the sail to get under way. The three of them said nothing, ashamed that at the first sign of trouble, they had not believed that Jesus would save them.

And they were afraid, and marveled, saying to one another, "Who can this be? For He commands even the winds and water, and they obey Him!"

LUKE 8:25

chapter forty-one

THE DEMONIZED IN GADERA

MARK 5:1-20

The boat had been blown off course, and now James was faced with a choice. Should he land at Khersa, a small village two miles to the north, or should he head for Gadera, their original destination and the largest village in the area three miles to the south? The problem was there was no wind; the sails drooped listlessly from the mast. After Jesus had calmed the storm, there was not so much as a gentle breeze, as though the wind dared not blow.

Tired and famished, the apostles would have to take up oars and row in either direction. The coast in front of them was a cliff with no beach on which to land. Then they spotted small cove with only a narrow sliver of beach. There they would rest and assess the damage sustained to the boat.

They passed beneath the steep limestone cliff and rowed the boat into a small inlet that was hidden from much of the lake. Once inside the tiny harbor, the apostles were heartened at the sight of a steep but navigable slope leading upwards from the minuscule beach to a grassy plateau, where they saw a herd of pigs grazing.

A shadow fell over the face of James as he pointed off to their right. Burrowed into the side of the cliff to their right were dozens of caves and chambers. Markings on the walls told them the caverns were tombs; this was a burial place for the dead. Small, dark-green bushes growing out of the caverns did little to dispel the foreboding appearance of the place. The boat ground into the sandy beach.

The men clambered out of the boat and secured it to shore. As Jesus stepped off the boat, a long, chilling scream emerged from the caverns, as if to announce his arrival. The apostles were frozen in their tracks, staring nervously up into the caverns, not knowing from which cave the menacing voice had come.

Within moments, two men emerged from separate caves. One appeared docile. Clothed in rags, he was stooped and drooled heavily, seemingly uncertain of where he was or what was happening around him. The other man stood upright, completely naked, waving his fists in defiance. He repeated his maniacal, blood-curdling scream.

"EEEEEEEEEEEEAAAAAARRRRGGGGGHHHHH!"

The residents of the area, who believed that evil spirits dwelt in lonely, desolate places such as this, relegated their lunatics and the demon-possessed to the tombs. The larger of the two men had often been bound with shackles and chains to prevent him from injuring himself and others. But with superhuman strength, he had torn the chains and broken the shackles to prowl where he chose. Day and night, the demonized man roamed the area, crying out and cutting himself with sharp stones.

Now an irresistible compulsion drew him into the presence of Jesus; something about Jesus compelled demons to confess themselves in his presence. The large man rushed down from the cliff, jumping from ledge to ledge, swinging from tree roots and limbs. Peter and James stepped in front of Jesus to protect him, convinced the lunatic would physically assault their master. He continued yelling as he hurtled himself headlong across the beach. As he approached Jesus, the man fell on his face, his hands outstretched toward the master, sobbing and pleading.

"What have I to do with you, Jesus, Son of the Most High God—possessor of heaven and earth?"

The disciples listened carefully. They saw the man move his lips, but his mouth did not match the words. What they heard was an echoing voice, almost as if dozens of people were speaking simultaneously from within a dark well. This was the voice of evil.

"I implore you by God, do not torment me," came the voice again.

"What is your name?" Jesus asked the man.

"My name is Legion," the voice answered, "for we are many."

"Come out of this man, unclean spirit," Jesus commanded. "Leave this man and release him."

"Please!" the demon pleaded with Jesus. "We have no place to go. We will be confined to the abyss."

The man looked about wildly. "There!" The man pointed to the herd of pigs feeding on the mountain. "Send us into the swine . . . . We must possess something . . . ."

Jesus gave his permission and commanded the demons to come out of the man. Up on the plateau above the cliff, two thousand pigs calmly grazed, oblivious to the unfolding events. As the demons left the man, they entered into the swine, and the swine reacted violently. Screaming in frenzy, they began rushing toward the sea. Many dashed madly down the slope and into the water, while others tumbled helplessly down the cliff, bouncing from rocks to ledges through the bushes onto the narrow beach and out into the sea. In a bizarre scene of unsurpassed terror and vivid destruction, two thousand squealing pigs stampeded over one another to a watery grave. Then silence.

Within minutes the keepers of the pigs came running to see what had happened. They looked down the slope to see the once-demonized man that had terrorized them—he was standing calmly next to Jesus. Philip, always the tidy one, ran to place a cloth around the loins of the naked victim. The swineherds also saw the last of their helpless animals drowning in the Sea of Galilee.

The owners of the swine showed up with other men of Khersa, drawn by the commotion. The swineherd pointed down to Jesus and his disciples in the small inlet. "Those men were here. They saw everything!"

The owners and keepers of the pigs made their way down the slope to demand, "What did you do to our herds?"

"We didn't kill your pigs." Peter stepped forward, then pointed to the man calmly sitting next to Jesus. "When Jesus cast demons out of this man, they entered into your pigs. The pigs went mad, then ran over the cliff and killed themselves."

The pigs' owners stepped back when they recognized the man sitting at the feet of Jesus. The madman was clothed and seemingly in his right mind. How was this possible? Awed and greatly terrified by a power mightier than that which had possessed the demonized man, the men of Khersa begged Jesus, "Leave us. Depart from our shores."

Their fears fueled by superstition—and anger over the lost herds—the people were unwilling to find out what Jesus could do for them.

"Go now," they cried.

Jesus nodded to his disciples to prepare the boats for departure. As Jesus began walking to the boats, the former lunatic grabbed Jesus by the feet, pleading, "Let me go with you. Allow me to serve you."

But Jesus denied his request. "Go to your home," he said. "Go to your friends and tell them what great things the Lord has done for you."

The man released Jesus' feet and rose to look deeply into his eyes.

Jesus turned to step into the boat. As James and Peter shoved off, Jesus called to the man, "Tell how God had mercy on you and forgave you of your sins."

> *So the man went away and began to tell in the Decapolis how much Jesus had done for him. And all the people were amazed.*
>
> MARK 5:20, NIV

chapter forty-two

THE DAUGHTER OF JAIRUS

MARK 5:21-42

Jesus and his disciples sailed away from Gadera with the evening breeze at their backs and and the afternoon sun in their faces. The sails billowed, pushing them westward back across the Sea of Galilee to Capernaum. It had been a long day since the sermon of parables by the sea.

As the boat arrived back at Capernaum, there was an anxious crowd waiting at the beach in hopes that Jesus had survived the storm. Jesus was welcomed, surrounded and soon thronged by the people. Some were concerned about the storm; others were there to be healed. Still others were just curious, for the curious gathered wherever Jesus went.

As Jesus left the shore, Philip and his helpers formed a wedge through the crowd, so that Jesus could return to Peter's home to rest. As they entered the streets of Capernaum, a leader of the synagogue came running toward them, his dark-green tunic unfastened and flying behind him as he ran. His *sudar*, the garment tied around his head, tilted crazily. Those who knew Jairus were certain something was dreadfully wrong.

The crowd parted before Jairus as he reached Jesus. Doing something a man of his status rarely did, he prostrated himself on the ground before Jesus, begging.

"My little girl is at the point of death . . . ." His red eyes and trembling lips demonstrated his sincerity. "She's my only child . . . she can't breathe . . . when I left the house, she was gasping like it was her last breath."

Being one of the chief elders in the synagogue, Jairus had met Jesus on several occasions, and he knew how Jesus had healed the centurion's servant.

Jairus pleaded, "Come and lay your hands on her. Heal her, so she can live."

"I will heal her," Jesus replied, then began walking with Jairus toward the area of Capernaum where the wealthy resided.

As they walked, a woman in the crowd was following Jesus, her body covered with sores. Blood had been oozing from them for twelve years. She had given up all hope of being healed, but upon hearing the reports of the miraculous power of Jesus of Nazareth, she had come to see him. She knew that if he could help her he must be the promised Messiah.

Twelve years earlier, when the sores had first appeared, the physician had told her to wash daily and use every ointment and astringent available, but nothing worked. Another physician told her to roll in the ashes of various burnt woods. Another packed her in clay then baked her in the sun. She fell into poverty, having spent everything she had on worthless prescriptions and superstitious cures. Still the blood flowed, her sores spread and the pain intensified.

The loss of blood over the years had taken its toll, leaving her pale and weak. A pitiful wretch, she could no longer bear to bathe or put water on her skin. Any clothes brushing against her skin sent waves of agony through her body when she moved. She walked with her eyes cast downward in shame; she was unclean according to Levitical Law, and so was anyone who touched her. But in spite of this, she pushed through the crowd toward the one man who could help her.

As Jesus walked with Jairus through the marketplace toward the elder's home, they slowed their pace because of the sudden surge of people. This was the woman's opportunity. She squeezed through several of Jesus' followers to get behind their master. His long, white tunic was in front of her. But even now she hesitated to touch it. Not wanting to defile him, she reached out to touch just the very edge, the hem of his garment. *If I only touch his cloak, I will be healed.*

Within her imperfect knowledge, there was a seed of faith that was beginning to grow. Hers was a superstitious faith. She had thought a touch would make her whole. Yet there was strength in her weakness. She believed in Jesus, so much that she felt all she had to do was touch him.

Suddenly, Jesus stopped and looked about. His searching eyes captivated the crowd. Everyone halted. The longing eyes of Jesus were seeking someone. Then he asked, "Who touched me?"

"Everyone is crowding around you," John blurted out. "And there are so many people, how can you ask 'Who touched me?'"

Jesus ignored the question. He continued looking from face to face. Jesus was not simply looking for the person who touched him; he was looking for the person with faith.

"Someone touched me. I felt power go out of me," he said to those around him. A miracle had happened that was unwilled on his part. The power that resided in him had been called out of him by faith. He continued to look from one set of anxious eyes to another until his knowing eyes found the one who had touched him.

The woman knew Jesus was looking for her, because she knew what had happened. The moment she touched Jesus, she had felt something in her body. Just as a person touching the flame of a candle experiences heat, when she touched the hem of his garment she experienced healing.

Jesus would not let her superstitions go unchallenged. She had to know that it was not the touch of his garment that had healed her. Jesus explained to her simply, "Daughter, your faith has made you whole."

He smiled and said to her, "Go in peace and be freed from your suffering."

Jairus waited anxiously, standing at the edge of the crowd. He wanted to beg Jesus to leave the miserable woman and go immediately to his house; his daughter was at the point of death. Then a servant came up to whisper in his ear, "Your daughter has died. Do not trouble the teacher further. All is lost."

This news was too much. First, the slow-moving crowd, then the unplanned delay with the woman, and now his daughter lay dead. Jairus could maintain his composure no longer.

The anguished cry of Jairus filled the marketplace.

But Jesus went to him and said, "Do not be afraid. Just believe."

Jairus had run through the streets of Capernaum because he believed that Jesus could heal his little girl just as he had healed others. Where there is life there is hope, but now the little girl lay dead. He could only look blankly at Jesus with uncertain faith.

The crowd that had followed Jesus from the shore had been swept happily along, fully expecting Jesus to heal the little girl. When they heard the girl was dead, their bouyant mood was deflated. After all, what could Jesus do now?

When they reached the gate of Jairus' home, Jesus dismissed the remainder of the crowd, instructing all but three of his apostles to keep the people in the street. Taking Peter, James and John, he entered the courtyard to the sound of mourners—real and hired—and flutes playing for the departed.

Because Jairus was rich, the paid mourners had stayed near, ready to rush into the house the moment the little girl died, like vultures swooping down on the carcass of an animal in the field. Since the amount of their fee was measured by the loudness of their weeping, their sobs were great. Their mournful discords flooded over the walls out into the streets, overwhelming the disciples and the few onlookers who were still there.

"Why all this commotion and wailing?" Jesus asked as he entered the house. He pointed the professional mourners to the door. "You may leave now. You are no longer needed here. The little girl is not dead," Jesus smiled. "She is only sleeping."

The mourners gasped, stunned at this pronouncement. Then they burst into laughter, mocking him.

When Jesus did not reply, the mourners saw his strength and began leaving one after another. There would be no pay this day.

Jesus, motioning to the father and mother, said to his three companions, "Come with me." He led them toward the inner chamber where the body of the child lay.

The flame of Jairus' faith was burning low but had not gone out. Jesus tenderly approached the bed where the corpse lay. The Levites—had any been present—would have told Jesus not to touch the body, because he would have become unclean. But taking the hand of the corpse, he said, "Get up, little girl!"

At first her eyes fluttered, then blinked; she rubbed them with both hands, as though rubbing sleep from her eyes. Her parents watched in amazement the transformation from death to life, but they were too stunned to respond.

Then as a child waking up in the morning, the girl sat up and threw her legs over the edge of the bed. She raised both arms to stretch as if to welcome a new day. Then she looked at her guests to say, smiling, "I'm hungry."

Because the parents hadn't sufficient time to grieve, now they were unsure how to rejoice. They didn't know whether to laugh . . . cry . . . or smother their daughter with hugs and kisses. So they looked to Jesus for their cue.

Jesus said matter-of-factly, "Give her something to eat."

And her parents were astonished, but He charged them
to tell no one what had happened.

LUKE 8:56

chapter forty–three

SENDING THE TWELVE

MATTHEW 9:27–10:42

Jesus of Nazareth healed many people, and though a healing may not be noteworthy to the casual observer, it meant everything to the man or woman whose life was changed.

One day as Jesus was walking among the people, two blind men followed him from a distance crying out, "Son of David, have mercy on us!"

When Jesus arrived at the home of Peter where he was staying, the two men came to him to make their request in person. Jesus asked them, "Do you believe I can make you well?"

"Yes, Lord."

Jesus touched their eyes, saying, "According to your faith, it will be done to you."

Instantly their sight was restored, but Jesus sternly warned them, "See that no one knows about this."

But the blind men in their jubilation went throughout the region telling others what Jesus had done for them.

As Jesus traveled from town to town, he preached the gospel of the kingdom. He healed people of every kind of disease and illness. Jesus had compassion on the crowds because they were overwhelmed by the circumstances of life. Confused, hurting and helpless, they were like sheep without a shepherd.

Jesus said to his disciples, "When you see a great potential harvest and few workers, pray to the Lord of the harvest to send workers out into the field to bring in the harvest."

He then called the twelve apostles to him and commissioned them to go out among the people in his name to preach the good news of the kingdom. He gave them authority to drive out demons and to heal every disease and sickness they might encounter.

Jesus would not go with them, but sent them out two by two with the following instructions: "Do not preach the gospel to the Gentiles, nor should you go to any Samaritan town. Go only to the lost sheep of Israel.

"Every place you go, preach this message: 'The kingdom of heaven is near.' You will heal the sick, raise the dead to life, cleanse those who have leprosy and cast out demons. You have received this power from me freely. Now freely use this power for the glory of God.

"Do not take with you any gold or silver or money. You will take no bag, no bread and no extra clothing. The Lord will provide for your needs.

"When you go to preach in a town, those who are worthy of the kingdom will have you as their guests. Stay with them until the time has come to leave that city. Your presence in their homes will bless them.

"And whoever will not receive you nor hear your words, when you depart from that house or city, shake off the dust from your feet as a testimony against them. Assuredly, I say to you, it will be more tolerable for Sodom and Gomorrah in the day of judgment than for that city!

"I am sending you out like lambs into a pack of wolves. So be wise as serpents and harmless as doves. All men will hate you because of me. When people mistreat you in one town, go preach in the next town."

The apostles listened carefully to what Jesus said. They were willing to follow the example of Jesus, but the part about rejection and persecution raised concerns.

"Do not be afraid of men," Jesus continued. "They may kill you, but they cannot harm your soul. Rather, fear God who can destroy both your body and soul in hell.

"Your Father in heaven knows your needs and will take care of you. Two sparrows are sold for but a penny, yet your Father knows when any one of them falls to the ground. He even knows the number of hairs on your head, so do not be afraid. You are worth more than many sparrows.

"When you tell others that you belong to me, I will tell my Father in heaven that you are my followers. But if you deny me before men, I will disown you before my Father in heaven.

"Do not think that I came to bring peace on earth. I did not come to bring peace but a sword. When anyone believes in me, there will be members of their family that turn against them—sons against fathers, daughters against mothers—their worst enemies will come from their own families.

"If you love your father or mother more than me, you are not fit to be my apostle. If you love your son or daughter more than me, you are not worthy of me. You must take up your cross . . . daily . . . and follow after me. If you try to save your life, you will lose it. But if you will give up your life to me, you will find it.

"When people receive you, they are receiving me and him who sent me. Those who welcome you also welcome me, and I will give them the same reward that I will give you."

Now it came to pass, when Jesus finished commanding His twelve disciples,
that He departed from there to teach and to preach in their cities.

MATTHEW 11:1

chapter forty-four

JOHN THE BAPTIST IN PRISON

LUKE 7:16-35
MATTHEW 14:1-12

From his prison cell high in the fortress of Machaerus, John the Baptist looked out to see the world of his past. In the west, across the Dead Sea, he saw Hebron and the hilltops of Jerusalem in the distance. To the north he saw the Jordan River, like a silver thread winding its way through the desolate Jordan valley past the jeweled city of Jericho. The Baptist could see these places clearly from his cell. The only question was, how long would he keep his head to be able to see?

John the Baptist had been imprisoned for publicly denouncing the relationship between Herod Antipas and his brother's wife, Herodias. Of course, this relationship was no secret. Everyone in Tiberias—and every other of the cities of Palestine—knew of Herodias' treachery. Herodias had been married to her older half-uncle Philip, the son of Herod the Great, whom she had married for wealth and power. Although Philip had indeed inherited an immense fortune, he had no political power. Instead he lived as a wealthy private citizen in Jerusalem, but his young wife wanted more. So Herodias seduced Philip's half-brother Herod Antipas, the tetrarch of Galilee. Antipas was just as treacherous and ruthless as Herodias; he had his own wife executed then took Herodias to be his wife, even while Philip still lived.

No one in the religious community dared to speak out against their adulterous union except John the Baptist, who called the marriage unlawful, denouncing Herodias as an immoral woman. Herod Antipas was inclined to overlook this outrage, because he liked the Baptist and had sought him out to interview him on many occasions, though he rejected John's staunch message of repentance. Certainly the tetrarch did not want to make a martyr out of the Baptist; he believed John was a righteous and holy man, and he also feared the anger of the people, who considered him a prophet. But his new wife, Herodias, was as vengeful as Jezebel and twice as mean. She vowed to rid herself of the hated preacher, and within a year she convinced Antipas to imprison him, though he refused to harm John.

The Baptist was arrested and imprisoned in Machaerus, a fortress high up in the barren, rocky mountains on the eastern shore of the Dead Sea. The fortress was surrounded by impregnable walls and flanked by towers, each one a hundred and forty feet tall. The fortress was flanked by a magnificent palace, with cisterns for water, storehouses and arsenals containing every weapon to defend itself against attack. Machaerus stood nearly four thousand feet above the salt water of the Dead Sea, a narrow road paved with stones winding four miles upward to the fortress. No army could break into Machaerus; no prisoner had ever broken out.

In this wretched prison, doubts plagued John the Baptist. Was the kingdom that he announced really at hand? He had sacrificed everything for the kingdom, denying himself food, home and marriage, to prepare Israel for the coming King. But was Jesus really the Messiah?

John's disciples had come to Machaerus to tell him of their own disappointment. If Jesus were the Anointed One of God, they asked, why was he eating with tax collectors and sinners? Why did Jesus not teach his followers to fast?

Lingering questions seeped into John's mind. Being alone in prison was different from being alone in the wilderness, where his feet could walk where his heart told him to go. Here, isolation was his affliction. He was unable to go and talk with Jesus himself, so John the Baptist sent his followers to Jesus with a message: "Are you the Coming One, or should we look for another?"

Like a serpent crawling out of the cracks in the wall to strike fear in the prisoner, doubts began to crawl into the heart of the Baptist suggesting that he had made a terrible mistake in identifying Jesus as the Messiah. *Did I lead the people into error?* All doubts are bitter, he knew, whether they come from the heart or the head.

Yet even the tiniest flame encourages the spirit in the darkest moments. *Do we wait for another Messiah?* John knew he was asking a question that could not be addressed to false messiahs. He had merely sought reassurance in his isolation and impending death. John the Baptist believed what the Spirit of God had told him, that Jesus was the Christ, the Coming One.

Jesus was preaching and healing the multitudes when the disciples of John caught up with him. They approached him and said, "John the Baptist sent us to ask, 'Are you the Coming One, or should we look for another?'"

At that moment a blind man was brought to Jesus. Jesus touched the man's eyes and immediately his sight was restored. Jesus turned and said to the messengers, "Go back and report to John what you have seen and heard: The blind receive sight, the lame walk, those who have leprosy are cured, the deaf hear, the dead are raised and the good news is preached to the poor."

Jesus understood why John had questions, so he reassured those who had heard the previous conversation. He did not want anyone to reject the Baptist because he had expressed doubts. Jesus said concerning John, "Did the people go out into the wilderness to see a reed blown by the wind? Did they go to see a man dressed in fine clothes? No, those who wear expensive clothes and indulge in luxury live in palaces. But what did they go out to see? A prophet? Yes, and more than a prophet. I tell you, among those born of women, there is no greater prophet than John. And yet the one who is least in the kingdom of God is greater than he!"

On an early, cool spring evening, one week before Passover, the palace at Machaerus was brilliantly lit up like a torch on the hill. The people in the town below could smell the tempting aromas and hear the drunken laughter from the festive banquet. The meal was extensive; one course of food followed another. Wine and alcohol were abundant. Finally, Herod Antipas called for his thoroughly drunken guests to be entertained. Clapping his hands, he commanded the dancers to commence.

To the surprise of everyone, Salome, the alluring young daughter of Herodias, danced into the light of the room. Salome danced magnificently, tempting and taunting the men with provocative movements and gestures. Herodias recognized the burgeoning charms of her young daughter—her husband was clearly attracted to the young girl—and had coaxed her into this wretched, fleshly amusement to achieve her own ends. When Salome reached the end of her spectacle, the entire audience erupted into applause. Antipas jumped to his feet, wildly cheering. Then, with his guests as witnesses, he made a drunken vow to Salome: "You shall have anything you want, even half of my kingdom."

Salome smiled, her mother's words leaping out of her mouth like the fangs of a cobra. "Give me the head of John the Baptist here on a silver platter."

Silence fell across the drunken assembly. The shock of her request sobered men who previously in the evening had willingly given their sense of morality over to the wine. Herod's countenance dropped. Anger gripped his heart, but having been put on the spot, he could not rescind his offer to Salome in front of his guests.

Antipas ordered his guards, "Go immediately and bring me the head of the Baptist."

The appointed executioner stepped out of the banquet hall into the cold spring night, walking up the steps from the palace to the prison. When he opened the rusty doors to enter with a torch, John the Baptist knew that his end was at hand. He knew he was to be sacrificed on the altar of Herod Antipas.

Within a few minutes, the guard was dashing down the stairs to the banquet hall, the silver platter in hand, the gory head of John the Baptist held high for all to see. The piercing eyes of the dead Baptist were open, accusing the man to whom the head was delivered. As the platter was offered up to Herod Antipas, John preached his final message: "REPENT."

Young Salome eagerly received the silver platter, then ran through the night to her mother Herodias, delivering to her the ghastly prize for which she had asked.

Then his disciples came and took away the body
and buried it, and went and told Jesus.
MATTHEW 14:12

chapter forty-five

FEEDING THE FIVE THOUSAND

JOHN 6:1-14

The twelve apostles returned shortly before Passover from preaching the gospel, elated with their successes and amazed at the power they wielded in their master's name. But their optimism quickly turned to fear when they heard that Herod Antipas had murdered John the Baptist. They found Jesus angered and heartbroken over the death of the prophet, so they encouraged him to speak out against this atrocity. The youngest apostle John agreed with Simon the Zealot that this might be the catalyst that would stir the Jews to war, to follow Jesus in seeking revenge. But Jesus did not want a confrontation with Herod Antipas, especially when his clashes with the bureaucrats in Jerusalem were growing more heated. This was not the battle he came to fight; his battle would take place on a later Passover.

The roads were filled with pilgrims on their way to Jerusalem for the Feast of Passover. Wanting to avoid the crowds and any speculation about what he would do—and needing some time to himself—Jesus got into a boat with his apostles and headed north, away from the multitudes, away from Herod Antipas. He and his apostles needed rest.

When men and women on the highway along the lake saw Jesus leave, many abandoned their pilgrimage and began following him along the shore as the boat headed north. Jesus' boat landed near a large expanse of grass about a mile wide before the plain arches up into the mountains. He went to the top of a small hill to pray in the spring afternoon sun, leaving his apostles at the foot of the hill. But soon the multitudes found them and gathered at the hill. When Jesus saw the people in need of hope, in need of healing, as always his heart was moved. He began teaching them; the question of rest was put behind him.

The crowd, predominately male, grew steadily throughout the day. Because only men were required to attend Passover, many of their wives and children had stayed home. Jesus looked out to see thousands of strong men. If ever a dictator wanted an army to recruit and train for his purposes, this was the occasion. If ever a dictator wanted a cause, the murder of John the Baptist would surely be the motivation. If ever a dictator wanted support, these sheep were looking for a shepherd. Jesus had only to proclaim himself their leader.

Jesus ministered all day, teaching the multitudes and healing those who were sick. The apostle Philip, who was responsible for crowd management, was the first to notice the shadows from nearby trees falling long over the crowd. The first evening had set in, when the sun is low in the sky and the whole earth quiets itself in anticipation of sunset. This was the time when men normally began to think of food, but the crowd did not seem hungry; they were being fed the bread of life.

But Philip, who looked after the needs of the crowds, did think about food, and he spoke to Jesus. "Lord, this is a deserted place, and the hour is already late. Send the multitudes away, so that they may go into the villages to buy food."

Since Philip was in charge of food and provisions, Jesus asked him, "Where can we buy bread so that these people may eat?" Jesus was testing Philip; he already knew what he would do. Jesus was looking into Philip's heart for faith, to see if Philip recognized that he was standing in the presence of the Living Bread from God.

Philip had already counted the crowd. He knew there were about five thousand men there, plus a few hundred women and children. Philip answered, "Why, eight months of wages wouldn't feed this many!"

Philip sent the apostles into the crowd to inventory what food was available. Only Andrew found food among the multitudes. Andrew said to Jesus, "There is a little boy here." He pointed to the young boy in front of the crowd. "This lad has five barley loaves and two small fish, but what are they among so many?"

Fresh grease stains on a white cloth the lad carried revealed a carefully prepared meal for a growing boy. The boy's mother had wrapped the five barley rolls and two fish in a clean cloth for the boy to eat on his way to Jerusalem.

Jesus said to Philip, "Make the people sit down on the grass, and bring the loaves and the fish to me."

Philip directed the men to sit in groups of fifty so they could organize the distribution of the food. The apostles weren't sure how they would be fed, but when Jesus gave them directions, they followed them explicitly.

By now, the dark shadows stretched across the crowd, the young spring grass turning dark green under their influence. The heat of the sun was gone, and a slight breeze floated off the Sea of Galilee. It was the end of a beautiful spring day.

Jesus took the loaves, held them to heaven and gave thanks to God, a prayer that all in the crowd could hear: "Blessed are you, Jehovah our God, who calls this bread to come forth from the earth."

He directed the twelve to gather some baskets. Baskets were plentiful among the pilgrims, who carried their belongings in either cloth sacks or wicker baskets.

Jesus began breaking the small loaves of bread, placing the morsels in a basket. He then picked up another piece of bread, breaking it and dropping it into the basket. He repeated the practice until the baskets were filled.

"Give this food to the people to eat," he said to Philip, who had watched the process. Then the apostles fanned out into the crowd, holding the baskets for each hungry person to take bread and fish. As food was taken from a basket, it was seemingly replenished. The baskets were never emptied, yet each person ate as much as he needed.

Jesus smiled at the contrast between two feasts. These men, in obedience to the command of God, were on their journey to Jerusalem to celebrate the elaborate Feast of Passover in the Temple, but here they were in the open fields enjoying a simple feast of bread and fish. For many Jews, the Passover feast instituted for them by God had become an empty ritual devoid of spiritual meaning. The priests who officiated at the Passover were the same men who would one day deliver Jesus to be crucified. The Passover feast in the Temple sanctuary could only satisfy the body; but in the sanctuary of God's creation, on the shore of the Sea of Galilee, a meal of bread and fish satisfied both body and soul.

As the sun set, Jesus said to his apostles, "Gather up the fragments that are left over."

When the apostles had gathered up the fragments, there were twelve baskets left, one for each apostle—enough food for three or four days.

So they all ate and were filled.

MARK 6:42

chapter forty-six

PETER WALKS ON WATER

MATTHEW 14:21-33

By the estimation of anyone in Palestine—Roman or Jew—five thousand well-fed men was a potential army. Certainly no rebel faction had ever been able to rally such forces against Rome.

Some of the apostles realized the potential set before them on the grass. Here were five thousand men who wouldn't be distracted by such trivial things as hunger—Jesus could feed them miraculously. If they were wounded in battle, Jesus could heal them. In the aftermath of the miracle with the fish and the loaves, the men were openly declaring Jesus to be the Son of David. They shouted, "Truly this is the Prophet who is to come into the world!" Surely these men could be motivated to follow the Messiah in a military campaign to liberate the Holy Land. Once the Roman interlopers were expelled, Jesus and his disciples would be free to preach the gospel of the kingdom to establish righteousness in the hearts of all its inhabitants.

But the same thoughts occurred to a number of the five thousand—that they formed a nucleus around which an army could be recruited, trained, deployed and inspired to attack Rome. The men quickly were carried way with the greatness of their potential and talked about making Jesus their king—by force if necessary. His army would not be defeated!

Quickly Jesus directed the apostles toward the boat, then pointing across the sea, Jesus instructed them, "Go to the other side. Go to Capernaum."

Jesus walked swiftly through the midst of several clusters of excited men, then he slipped between some high rocks into the hills. Before anyone realized it, Jesus was gone, and so were his apostles.

As the sun settled behind the western hills of Galilee, Jesus took advantage of the fading light to climb higher into the hills. He needed to be alone, to pray and commune with the Father. This was not the time for a military confrontation with Rome. That was not why he had come to earth.

Finding a secluded ravine, Jesus prayed, "Your kingdom come . . . your will be done . . . ."

A desert storm rolled into the Sea of Galilee, and the hot air from the eastern plains mixing with cool breezes off the cold water unleashed a brief torrential rain followed by a relentless, driving wind.

As Jesus was praying, he looked through the black storm to see the disciples caught in the grip of the storm. If they tried to make it to shore, the boat would be pounded to pieces on the rocks and they would be lost. If they stayed on the lake, the boat would surely capsize and they would all drown.

Immediately, Jesus left his place of prayer and went to them, walking out across the water.

The apostles meanwhile were fighting just to stay afloat. Most storms blew in and out of the basin within thirty minutes, but this storm had settled over the Sea of Galilee for the last two hours, and there was no letup in sight. The waves grew higher; even the apostles who were hardened fishermen were frightened. When the others sensed fear in the fishermen, their own fears intensified.

"Y-E-E-E-A-A-A-I-I-I!" one of the apostles screamed in terror. "It's a ghost!"

The scream startled the other apostles, who then caught sight of the apparition walking on the water toward them. They stopped pulling on the oars and stared, dumbstruck. Peter's strong back had been holding the rudder steady, but he let go and the boat lurched with the waves. Peter paid no attention to the howling wind but wiped the water from his eyes to get a better look.

One of the others yelled again, "It's a ghost!"

Peter didn't believe it. He recognized the figure, even as one senses the presence of another who is loved. Peter knew this was no spirit, but someone dear to him. He reached for a rope, steadying himself to stand and peer out through the sea spray. Then the stout, red-bearded fisherman yelled back to the men at the oars, "It's the Lord!"

Then Jesus called out to them, "It is I! Do not be afraid."

. Peter recognized the epic potential of this event. Ever impetuous, he moved to the edge of the boat to yell out over the water, "Lord . . . if it is you, tell me to come to you, and I will walk to you on the water."

This was the kind of faith Jesus had been waiting to see in his disciples. If they were to proclaim him as the Lord of nature, his followers would have to look to him in such times of crisis. Jesus said to Peter, "Come . . . ."

Instinctively, Peter leaped from the boat. He didn't expect to plunge into the water, nor did he expect to sink. Peter expected to walk on the water. Nevertheless, he was amazed to see that his feet barely got wet. He began walking toward his master, walking on the water.

At first, the eyes of Peter were riveted to Jesus. In faith, the big fisherman was doing something no other man had ever done before. But as Peter realized the impossibility of what he was doing, in a moment of speculation, he looked down to see what was holding him up. Then he saw the enormous waves swirling around him, he became afraid and slowly began to sink into the water. Again, Peter looked to Jesus with beseeching, faithless eyes. He cried out, "Lord, save me!"

Jesus stretched out a hand to him and caught him, then he gently lifted Peter up, asking, "O you of little faith, why did you doubt?"

When Jesus and Peter got into the boat, Jesus commanded the raging waves, "Peace . . . be still." And the wind ceased.

Then those who were in the boat came and worshiped Him,
saying, "Truly You are the Son of God."

MATTHEW 14:33

chapter forty-seven

"I WILL BUILD MY CHURCH ON THIS ROCK"

MATTHEW 16:13-28

Rising dramatically more than nine thousand feet from the Syrian desert, the snowcapped peak stood in stark contrast to the surrounding terrain. Mount Hermon marked the boundary of Palestine and dominated the northern landscape of Galilee. Here, near the village of Caesarea Philippi (Philip, the local tetrarch and son of Herod the Great, named the town Caesarea in honor of the emperor Augustus), Jesus found rest out of the reach of the massive crowds that followed him in and around Galilee.

Nestled amid three valleys on a terrace in the shadow of Mount Hermon, the village was almost shut off from view by cliffs and woods. The area had been beautified by Philip and boasted a medley of waterfalls, mulberry trees, fig trees and bubbling fountains, mingled with the music of birds and waters. Here Jesus was less well known—and safe from the watchful eyes of the religious authorities who sought to destroy him.

His ministry on earth was nearing its end. The attacks and accusations were growing more aggressive; soon the authorities would, in spite of his popularity, arrest him and charge him with imagined crimes against the people and against God. Jesus knew he had only a short time to live.

After a few days of rest, Jesus was ready to renew his challenge to the apostles, to redirect their thinking and prepare them for the coming time when he would no longer be with them.

"Who do people say that I am?" Jesus asked the twelve.

The apostles looked from one to another. Peter, usually the first to speak but still embarrassed at his recent failure to walk on the water, didn't answer. James the Less spoke up. "Some say you are John the Baptist." Indeed, this rumor had only gained popularity since the Baptist was beheaded.

Nathanael spoke. "Some say you are Elijah." The Jews had expected the return of Elijah the miracle worker before the great day of the Lord.

"Others say you are Jeremiah," said Simon the Zealot, "the prophet who will come to find the ark of the covenant and lead the people to defeat Rome."

Jesus had heard these speculations and knew the disciples were telling him the truth. Then he asked the twelve, "But what about you? Who do you say that I am?"

Simon Peter now stepped forward and answered in faith, "You are the Christ, the Son of the Living God."

Jesus didn't respond immediately, allowing the others to reach their own conclusions. The apostles looked at one another, and slowly they nodded their agreement. They had seen too much to believe otherwise. Jesus was the Messiah.

"Blessed are you, Simon Peter," Jesus said, "because my Father in heaven has revealed this insight to you. You did not receive this answer from men."

Then Jesus walked over to Peter, standing between him and the other apostles. "And I tell you that you are Peter," Jesus spoke slowly. "Peter, you are a rock; your words are solid like a rock."

After his two failures in the storms, Peter didn't feel much like a rock. He knew himself to be an impetuous, boastful man who often spoke without thinking. Like an empty barrel rolling down a hill, Peter made empty promises; he didn't always have the weight to back up his words.

But Jesus smiled, his confidence in Peter clear. He knew Peter could lead the disciples after he was gone. Jesus put a hand on Peter's shoulder and said, "On this rock I will build my church . . . ."

He used the word "church" in a way unfamiliar to the apostles. To them a church was an assembly—of politicians, soldiers or even ordinary people. But Jesus used the word in a new way. An unusual way. An important way. But the apostles did not understand.

Jesus said to Peter, "I will build my church upon this rock, and the gates of hell shall not be able to keep us out. I will give you the keys to the kingdom of heaven, and whatever you lock on earth will be locked in heaven; whatever you open on earth, will also be opened in heaven."

Then Jesus looked sternly at his apostles, catching the eye of every man. He warned them, "Do not tell anyone what I have just said to you. People do not understand what the Son of Man has come to do, and they do not believe he is the Christ."

The apostles nodded. They would not tell anyone.

"There is something else you need to know," Jesus said soberly to his apostles. "Soon we are going up to Jerusalem. There, I must suffer at the hands of the elders, chief priests and teachers of the law. They will kill me, but after three days, I will rise again from the dead."

Jesus explained carefully what was going to happen. He did not speak in parables, nor did he veil his speech. Yet his apostles did not understand, because they did not want to think about his death. Then Peter shocked all the apostles by blurting out what they were thinking. He leaped up in their midst and rebuked Jesus.

"Never, Lord!" Peter pounded a fist into his hand. "We will never let them kill you!"

Jesus wheeled about at Peter's arrogance to declare, "Get behind me, Satan! You are in my way, because you have not set your mind on the things of God, but on the things of men."

Peter was stunned. Only moments ago Jesus had called him a rock; now Jesus called him by the enemy's name. Peter dropped to the ground, pulling his tunic around him in shame.

"If any man will come after me," Jesus said to them all, "you must put aside any selfish ambition you have for your life. You must take up your cross and follow me. For what profit is it to a man if he gains the whole world, and loses his own soul?"

None of the apostles slept soundly that evening. They had come to the foot of this mountain for rest, but Jesus' message weighed heavily on their minds. Even though the days were still hot, the mountain breeze was crisp, and each man wrapped his tunic tightly about himself against the cool, evening air.

Then He commanded His disciples that they should
tell no one that He was Jesus the Christ.

MATTHEW 16:20

chapter forty-eight

THE MOUNT OF
TRANSFIGURATION

MATTHEW 17:1-13

Six days later Jesus spoke privately to the three men closest to him, his inner circle of apostles. "Peter, James and John," he said, "come with me." He pointed to the peak of Mount Hermon towering high above them.

They climbed all that day, higher and higher toward the snowcapped summit. The surrounding villagers often called this place "Old Man Mountain," because its top was crowned with white year-round. But quite often clouds hid the peak from view, and as Jesus and the inner three climbed, from time to time a cool, damp cloud enshrouded them.

What does Jesus want to tell us? John thought to himself—but dared not ask— whenever the going was difficult. *And why speak to us so high on this mountain?* Jesus climbed in solitude ahead of the others. He did not tell them where they were going or why.

Clouds had been intermittently covering the four men all afternoon. After the mountain breezes blew a cloud away, the blinding sun again warmed their damp skin.

How much farther? John complained to himself.

As John and his fellow apostles crested a plateau notched in the side of the mountain, the breeze picked up speed, blowing another cloud rapidly toward the plateau, where Jesus now stood about fifty paces away. John saw there was something unusual about this cloud. Rather than absorbing light, sunbeams danced off this cloud, causing it to sparkle differently than the other clouds they had seen. Every part of the cloud sparkled as though it contained a thousand candles.

The cloud settled over the plateau, covering them as a warm blanket; this was not a damp mist. Staying low to the ground, Peter, James and John looked for their master through the mist and then saw Jesus as they had never seen him.

"He's sparkling," John whispered.

"Shhhh," James silenced his younger brother.

Jesus stood transfigured before them. At first he appeared opalescent, as though reflecting the light from the cloud, but then John was certain the light came from Jesus himself. His face shone like the sun, and his clothes reflected gloriously white—brighter than lamb's wool washed with the strongest soap.

Then, through the mist, two men appeared at Jesus' side to talk with him, though the apostles couldn't hear what they were saying. Jesus conversed comfortably and amiably with the men as though they were long-lost friends.

"That's . . . that's Elijah," sputtered Peter.

"How do you know?" John asked, genuinely curious.

"Because he looks how I think Elijah would look," answered Peter. Then to reinforce his own opinion he said, "And the other one is Moses. I'm certain of it."

The three apostles watched silently, for what could they say? This was as awesome a sight as they had ever witnessed. Peter felt an urgent need to do something to celebrate this remarkable occasion. He jumped to his feet, calling out to Jesus, "Lord, it is good for us to be here! If you wish, let us make three tabernacles here. One for you, one for Moses and one for Elijah."

Suddenly, the shining cloud grew a hundred times brighter, the intensity of the light hurting the apostles' eyes. Peter crumpled to the ground beside his friends. Then a commanding voice spoke from the cloud all about them.

"This is my beloved Son, in whom I am well pleased. Listen to him!"

This was simply too much for the apostles. Terrified, they fell with their faces to the ground, pulling their tunics over their heads. For the next few moments nothing was said, nothing was felt, nothing happened.

Then Jesus knelt beside them. He touched them, saying, "Get up. Don't be afraid."

When at last they looked up, the apostles saw only Jesus. His clothes were no longer shining. Moses was gone, Elijah was gone, the cloud was gone. Peter slowly turned his head, searching the mountainside in every direction. Looking up, he could see the snow at the top of Mount Hermon, then turning he looked to the valley below.

*As they were coming down the mountain, Jesus instructed them, "Don't tell anyone
what you have seen, until the Son of Man has been raised from the dead."*

MATTHEW 17:9, *NIV*

chapter forty-nine

THE POWERLESS DISCIPLES

MATTHEW 17:9-23

Jesus descended from Mount Hermon with Peter, James and John. They
had gained a new knowledge of Jesus, having seen him transfigured in the
heavenly light.

The other apostles anxiously awaited Jesus' return to the small village at
the foot of Mount Hermon. While Peter, James and John beheld the glory of
the Lord on the mountain, hell had been loosed on the village below and the
remaining apostles were under siege.

Peter and James heard the terrible excitement as they approached the
village and broke into a run to come to the aid of their friends. People were
yelling, arguing and milling around as though they were spectators wagering
on a sporting event. The shouting crowd had surrounded the apostles.
Some were laughing at them, some watching, some shouting questions.
A few Sadducees had discovered their location here in the north of
Palestine, and now they were perched at the edge of the crowd, mocking the
apostles for their inability to cast a demon out of a boy.

As Jesus entered the village, a father was leading his lunatic son—the boy
the apostles were unable to free—out of town. The demon-possessed boy
was clearly unable to speak or hear. When the father saw Jesus, he left his
son and ran to him. Kneeling before Jesus, he said, "Lord, have mercy on my
son. He has a demon and suffers greatly. The spirit throws him into the
river; at other times into the fire. I brought the boy here for you to heal, but
I couldn't find you. So, I brought him to your disciples, but they could not
cure him."

Jesus surveyed the crowd that was now gathering around him. Jesus recognized the unbelief in the Sadducees and the growing frustration among his apostles. "Have you no faith? You cannot conceive of the kingdom of heaven even when it is shown to you. How long must I be with you before you will learn to trust me? Bring the boy to me."

The demon in the boy had been passively silent. But when the boy was brought into the presence of the Son of God, he fell on the ground, shaking violently and wallowing in the dirt. Yellow-green saliva foamed from his mouth.

"How long has the boy been doing this?" Jesus asked.

"Since he was a child. If you can do anything for us, have compassion . . . help us."

"If you can believe," Jesus said, looking into the eyes of the father, "all things are possible to him who believes in me."

The father knew he didn't have the faith that Jesus described, but without hesitation the father cried out, "Lord, I believe in you. Help my unbelief . . . ."

The grunts and yells coming from the boy grew louder, sensationalizing the moment. Tension and anticipation mounted, even among the Sadducees. Then Jesus spoke, rebuking the demon. "Deaf and dumb spirit! I command you, come out of this boy and do not enter him again!"

The demon shrieked, shaking the boy violently before leaving his body. The boy doubled over, then rolled onto the ground as though he were dead. Not a limb moved. There was no sign of his breathing. Someone yelled out, "He's dead!"

Jesus reached out, as if to take the boy by the hand. But the young lad opened his eyes and began to get up without help. He could hear what the people said, and he began speaking excitedly to his father. The father, joyfully reunited with his son, walked down the road out of town. Then the people of the village began leaving one by one.

As the crowd dispersed, Jesus and his apostles turned the opposite way, walking toward Galilee. Philip would not let the people follow him, nor were the Sadducees allowed to ask him any more questions.

Later that evening the apostles came to him perplexed by what had happened that day. Those who had tried unsuccessfully to heal the boy asked, "Why couldn't we cast out the demon?"

"Because of your unbelief," said Jesus. "Assuredly, I say to you, if you have the smallest measure of faith, even a faith as small as a mustard seed, you can say to this mountain, 'Move from here to there,' and *it will move.* Nothing will be impossible for you."

Jesus taught them that faith was the source of their power, and their lack of faith was responsible for their lack of power. Still, the apostles wondered why they did not have enough faith. They believed in Jesus; they knew he was Messiah. On other occasions they had cast out demons and healed the sick in his name, but this time they were not able to. Jesus answered, "This kind of spirit will not come out except by continued prayer and fasting."

Then they departed from there and passed through Galilee, and He did not want anyone to know it. For He taught His disciples and said to them, "The Son of Man is being betrayed into the hands of men, and they will kill Him. And after He is killed, He will rise the third day."
MARK 9:30,31

chapter fifty

EVEN HIS BROTHERS DID NOT BELIEVE IN HIM
JOHN 7:1-14

A chilling wind blew off the Galilean hills. Though the autumn sun was warm, the brisk breezes and frigid nights had turned the remaining leaves of the trees golden brown and orange. Already fallen leaves danced along the roads in crisp, colorful whirls.

As Jesus and the twelve entered Capernaum, they greeted a family departing for Jerusalem, where they would soon celebrate the Feast of Tabernacles and Yom Kippur, the Day of Atonement.

When they entered the village, Jesus parted from his disciples to visit his mother, Mary, and his half brothers. He hadn't seen them since summer and he looked forward to their company. With the crowds always pressing in, demanding his attention, times of quiet companionship with family were rare treasures. Mealtimes were usually spent listening to his disciples discuss the events of the day and, in turn, teaching them. A private meal with his family was always refreshing, and yet when he arrived at his brothers' home, a sense of discomfiture hung over the meal table.

"We are preparing to leave for the Feast," James his half brother said to Jesus during dinner. The Law required every Jewish male to go to Jerusalem for the Feast of Tabernacles. "We are glad you're here and able to travel with us."

Jesus said nothing. He had been unusually quiet all evening.

James looked around at his brothers, then returned his gaze to Jesus. "All good Jews will be in Jerusalem. There will be many who have not yet heard you speak."

Jesus ate in silence. James grew frustrated.

"Don't you want people to know who you are? To see what you do? No one does such works in secret; what good are signs and wonders in the small villages of Galilee? If you can really do the things they say you do, go to Jerusalem and show yourself to the world!"

James turned away, angry with himself for this outburst. He did not believe that his brother was Messiah. He believed Jesus was a wonderful teacher, and nothing more. But James hadn't intended to hurt Jesus by letting his unbelief show. He tried to make amends, adding kindly, "The people will see your miracles and believe in you."

Jesus smiled reassuringly, saying, "You go ahead to this Feast. I do not plan to go up to Jerusalem, for my time has not yet fully come."

His brothers were concerned for his safety, but they did not press him further. He was the eldest brother and they would abide by his wishes.

During the rest of the day the brothers of Jesus packed, while Mary busied herself in the kitchen preparing food for the journey. None of them said much to Jesus. They knew he was a conscientious Jew and would only miss the Feast for very good reason. The following day, the family left for Jerusalem.

The apostles and Jesus stayed in Capernaum for the next two days, while rain drizzled steadily from a dark, milky sky. Then Jesus announced to the twelve, "Get your things together. We are going to Jerusalem to celebrate the Day of Atonement and the Feast of Tabernacles. We will travel in secret by way of Samaria without attracting attention."

The path through Samaria was scenic but strenuous over rolling hills; they were usually climbing one hill or descending another. The rain had moved on, making way for a deep blue sky and an autumn day perfect for traveling. And yet as they drew nearer to Jerusalem, Jesus' mood was contemplative, for he knew a different kind of storm was on the horizon.

Traveling through the small, out-of-the-way villages of Samaria was not without difficulties. The Samaritans would have little to do with Jews. Most of them hated Jews, and their hatred was returned in kind. Often, innkeepers would refuse to rent them rooms or serve them meals.

Jesus stopped at a well outside a small Samaritan village, instructing James and John to go into the village to arrange lodgings for the night. While they were gone, Jesus rested against a tree. Sitting apart from his apostles, he did not take the opportunity to instruct them, nor did he fellowship with them. The apostles could see that Jesus wanted to be alone.

Within the hour, John came running down the footpath from the village with James a few steps behind. Jesus and the others could see their seething anger from a distance, but they were all accustomed to the volatile moods of James and John. Like thunder rolling across the Galilean hills before a rainstorm, the Sons of Thunder would often rumble into a rage at the first sign of trouble.

When they arrived at the well, John breathlessly bellowed, "They refuse to give us a place to sleep! They wouldn't rent us a room for *any* price!"

They had been turned away by Samaritans before, but John was tired from the arduous journey and still smarting from this rebuff. He turned to Jesus and in his youthful anger demanded, "Lord, do you want us to call fire down from heaven to destroy them?" John spat out the words.

Jesus would not let John influence him in anger. He looked away from the apostles toward the Samaritan town that just had refused service to them. "You don't know what you are asking for," Jesus told John. "The Son of Man has not come to destroy lives, but to save them."

Jesus and the apostles went on to the next village, where they found a place of lodging and food to eat.

Now at the Feast the Jews were watching for him
and asking, "Where is that man?"
J O H N   7 : 1 1 ,   N I V

chapter fifty-one

MARY AND MARTHA

LUKE   10:38-42

The Feast of Tabernacles, or the feast of booths, was the grandest and most festive of all Jewish celebrations. Booths—small dwellings covered by tree branches—were erected all over Jerusalem, in the streets and on rooftops. Many went outside the city to live in booths during this feast; they did this to remember how the children of Israel had lived in tents for forty years during their wilderness wanderings. Like no other Jewish feast, this weeklong celebration attracted strangers from such faraway lands as Arabia, Persia and India, their colorful costumes only adding to the gaiety of the proceedings.

It was early autumn and the days were growing shorter, but the great candelabras in the Court of the Women burned brightly, giving vitality to the Temple and the surrounding city. Several times each day the clear sound of the priests' silver trumpets called the entire city to worship. The Temple gates were open all night, the glare of torches on the city wall announcing these were exciting days.

The apostles were anxious to attend the Feast, so Jesus dismissed them to complete the journey to Jerusalem while he tarried in the nearby town of Bethany. A few months ago when Jesus had sent out the twelve, Andrew and John had ministered in Bethany, where they stayed in the home of Martha, her sister Mary and her brother Lazarus. The apostles found this to be a worthy home. The inhabitants had given a standing invitation for

Jesus to stay there. So Jesus now would spend the feast in this house.

Jesus sat under the leafy canopy in the rear of the home, enjoying the autumn afternoon. Martha, the older of the two sisters, was busily preparing for the evening meal, again and again passing Jesus as he sat teaching Mary about how to live in the kingdom of God. Mary sat at his feet in rapt attention.

Martha was determined to honor their guest with a clean home and a sumptuous meal. Meanwhile, Mary honored Jesus by listening carefully and learning from his words. She honored him, not by doing things for him, but by forsaking the cares of this world to give him her undivided attention.

Time after time, Martha passed the scene in the courtyard with mounting irritation at her sister's laziness. After a few hours, Martha could contain her frustration no longer. However, she did not address her sister, but spoke to Jesus.

"Lord, do you not care that my sister has left me to prepare the meal by myself? Tell her to help me."

Jesus said to her, "Martha, Martha, you're worried and troubled about many things." He did not tell her that looking after things was wrong, but he wanted Martha to put all things into perspective, to understand the eternal implications of her actions.

"One thing is needed," he said. "Mary has chosen to learn from me. These lessons will not be taken from her."

Jesus invited Martha to sit down with him. Then he smiled on her and said, "The basic necessities of life—eating, drinking, sleeping—are only temporary, for when you do them once, you must continually do them. Do not work for food that perishes, but for food that endures even to eternal life, which I will give you."

Martha said, "But Lord, how do I work for this food?"

Jesus said to her, "The work of God is this: to believe in the one he has sent."

Now about the middle of the feast Jesus went up into the temple and taught.

JOHN 7:14

chapter fifty-two

THE FEAST OF TABERNACLES

JOHN 7:37-53

During the Feast of Tabernacles in early autumn, the people of Israel camped outside their houses and in the streets, lodging in tents or booths to commemorate their forefathers' forty-year sojourn in the wilderness. On the last day of the weeklong festival, the Great Day of the Feast, immediately after sunrise the people left their booths to take part in the celebration at the Temple.

Every worshiper carried in his right hand the *lulabh*, a myrtle and willow branch tied together with a palm branch between them, waving it before the Lord. In his left hand was the *ethrog*, a native fruit symbolic of the fruit of righteousness to be waved before the Lord.

A third of the worshipers attended the preparation of the morning sacrifice. Another third erected a leafy canopy over the altar in the Temple. The remaining third of the worshipers left the Temple to follow a chosen priest carrying a golden pitcher on his shoulder through the streets of Jerusalem toward the pool of Siloam, located at the water gate on the south wall of the city. As they made their way to the pool, the multitudes waved their branches to the glory of God. Siloam was their destination because it was the only pool in Jerusalem fed with living water—a flowing spring. Six hundred years earlier, King Hezekiah decreed a canal be excavated through the solid rock under the city of David to divert the waters of the spring of Gihon. Thus the city would be supplied with water, even if under siege by an enemy.

When the Temple procession reached the pool of Siloam, the priest waited for the ceremonial blast from the trumpet, then filled the ceremonial pitcher from the pool. Then the procession marched triumphantly to the Temple, where a threefold blast from the silver trumpets greeted the arrival of the priest. As the priest and the worshipers wound their way up the terraces and through the gardens of the Tyropoeon Valley within the walls of the great city, the pilgrims chanted loudly the words of the prophet Isaiah:

"With joy shall we draw water out of the wells of salvation.

In that day we shall say praise the Lord, call upon his name, declare
his works among his people, exalt his name.

Sing unto the Lord for he has done excellent things that are known
in all the earth.

Cry aloud and shout you who live in Zion, for great is the Holy One
of Israel who lives in the midst of us!"

The priest with the pitcher of water arrived at the Temple to enter the
Court of the Priests. There he was joined by a second priest carrying sweet
wine as a drink offering to the Lord. The two priests walked up the twelve
steps to the great altar. One priest went to the east end of the altar and
poured wine into the appropriate funnel; the other priest poured water
from Siloam into a funnel on the west end.

To the accompaniment of flutes, the priests shouted, "Praise the Lord.
Praise, O servants of the Lord, praise the name of the Lord!"

The people responded by shaking their lulabh branches toward the
altar and shouting, "*Hallelu Yah*" which means "Praise the Lord!"

The priests shouted, "Oh, give thanks to the Lord, for he is good!"

The people responded, "For his mercy endures forever!"

The priests shouted, "Let Israel now say . . . ."

The people said, "His mercy endures forever!"

"Let the house of Aaron now say . . . ."

"His mercy endures forever!"

"Let those who fear the Lord now say . . . ."

"His mercy endures forever!"

The recitation of psalms ended when the priests shouted, "O Lord,
work now salvation! O Lord, send us prosperity!"

The people waited in awesome silence for God to hear their prayer. Only
the faint sound of pouring water was heard in the Temple.

It was in this momentous silence that Jesus of Nazareth stepped out of
the crowd, as if in answer to their prayer, and called with a voice that rang
throughout the entire Temple, "IF ANYONE IS THIRSTY, LET HIM COME
TO ME AND DRINK!"

No one responded, no one moved to silence him. The presence of Jesus demanded their attention.

"I am the water of life. Come drink of me and you shall live."

The voice was unmistakably that of Jesus. He had been teaching in the Temple for three days—to the consternation of the scribes and Pharisees. Even those who couldn't see him from where they stood recognized his voice.

"Whoever believes in me shall have rivers of living water flowing from within him," he said.

A murmur spread throughout the crowd. There was immediate division among the people. Some were frightened by the authority with which Jesus spoke; some were hostile toward him for the interruption of their solemn ceremony; others were thirsty for God and believed in his words.

The celebration degenerated into violent disagreement. Some who heard him said, "This man is the prophet that has come to announce the Messiah."

Others said of Jesus, "He *is* the Messiah."

"No," said others, "the Messiah cannot come out of Galilee. Doesn't the Scripture say the Messiah will come from the seed of David and be born in Bethlehem?"

There was great strife in the Temple that day because of Jesus. There were many differing opinions regarding his claims and his authority, but whatever was said about Jesus, none of it was lukewarm or neutral. Some hated him and wanted to kill him, but none dared to touch him.

The Temple guards were overwhelmed by the presence of Jesus. They stood amazed at his message, unsure whether to take action or not. The priests came running to the guards and demanded, "Why did you not arrest the troublemaker? Why did you not bring him to us?"

One of the guards answered their superiors, saying, "We have never heard any man speak like this . . . ."

"Has he deceived you, too?" One of the priests stepped forward yelling at the guards; the priest could not believe what he was hearing. Turning back to the other priests he said, "Is there one among us, priest or Pharisee, who believes in him?"

Nearby there stood a respected member of the ruling council, Nicodemus, who had come to Jesus by night. He stepped forward to defend Jesus. "Does our Law condemn a man before it hears what he has to say?"

The priests and Pharisees sneered at Nicodemus, asking, "Are you from Galilee, too?" They turned and stormed away, shouting, "Look at the Scriptures! No prophet has ever come out of Galilee!"

And everyone went to his own house.

JOHN 7:53

chapter fifty-three

A WOMAN CAUGHT IN ADULTERY

JOHN 8:2-11

On the Monday after the Feast of Tabernacles, the fields around Jerusalem were littered with dried-out branches and leaves from the discarded booths. Before the sun came up, Jesus was in the Temple to worship the Father, but even at daybreak the people were drawn to him. A few hundred gathered around him as he sat on a low wall in the Court of the Women to teach. The area was available to all. Some were sitting at his feet, while others stood to hear him clearly. The Pharisees and priests remained at a distance, but with a conspiratorial air about them.

Then a woman's cry was heard amid a rising commotion outside the gates of the Temple.

"No! No!" The protests and shouts grew louder until two Pharisees appeared in the Court of the Women, dragging a disheveled woman between them. A pack of scribes and Sadducees followed in their wake, barking, "Guilty! Guilty!" The woman's hair was in disarray, her eyes wide in panic. Her unkempt clothes seemed to indicate that she had been forcibly dragged from her bed. The woman was thrown onto the pavement in front of Jesus.

One of the Pharisees announced smugly to Jesus, "This woman was caught in adultery, in the very act of having sex with a man who was not her husband."

When the woman looked up at Jesus, she immediately pulled back, covering her head with her hands. She made no effort to deny the charges. Just as darkness flees from the presence of light, the woman was uncomfortably subdued by the presence of Jesus.

The Pharisee said to Jesus, "The Law of Moses commands that we stone her." He looked about him with a sneer, as if sizing up the crowd for potential executioners. Then he turned back to Jesus and demanded, "But what do you say?"

The authorities were well aware of this woman's affair and had been letting this particular stew of trouble simmer, waiting for just the right moment to serve it up to the healer from Nazareth. With a crowd of witnesses present, her sin would pose a prickly dilemma for the man who had become the bane of the religious establishment.

"Everyone knows the Law," an elder Pharisee had reasoned to the others a few days earlier. "If a man and woman lie together in adultery, they are to be stoned. If this Jesus is from God, he cannot deny God's Law."

"But Rome has taken away our authority to stone sinners," said another, "even if it is a religious matter. Only a Roman court can condemn a person to death."

"Precisely!" said another. "If Jesus says, 'Stone her,' he will be arrested for murder and inciting a riot. Then he will be Rome's problem, not ours."

"And if he says, 'Stone her,' where then is his gospel of forgiveness and mercy?"

"He cannot say 'I forgive her' without breaking the Law of Moses. And he cannot say 'Stone her' without breaking the law of the land!"

The Pharisees had no difficulty catching the woman in the act of adultery. For the past several days, the Jewish people had lived in booths and small tents pitched around the city of Jerusalem. It was a simple enough matter to spy on a woman with a questionable reputation and catch her in a compromising position. They had prudently and patiently waited three days for this opportune time. Now they had Jesus in a difficult position with no room to maneuver.

The woman sat up at the word "stone." She knew the Law and knew the prescribed punishment. But this was not a sentence that was usually carried out. Usually those who committed adultery were banished from religious

services, divorced and considered social outcasts. But few violators had been
stoned in recent years. Stoning was a terrible form of capital punishment. In
an organized stoning, the victim would be pinned to the ground with arms and
legs spread. If the executioners were merciful, they would crush the victim's
head with the first stone. If they wanted to prolong the suffering, they
would smash a massive stone into the rib cage of the accused, taking care
not to kill him with the first stone. Then the crowd would continue pelting
the body with smaller stones until every bone was broken.

The woman wondered, the Pharisees wondered, the people wondered:
What will Jesus say? If Jesus spoke the word, his listeners were ready to rise up
in moral outrage to stone this woman.

But Jesus said nothing.

He ignored the Pharisees; he had no obligation to answer them. Instead,
Jesus bent over to scribble in the dust with his finger, as though they had
never spoken.

The Pharisees began to grow uncomfortable. They had captured the
undivided attention of the crowd, but Jesus seemed completely oblivious to
their presence. So they persisted.

"Moses commanded that we stone a woman caught in adultery. What is
your verdict?"

Jesus looked up from where he was scribbling. Then he looked into the
faces of the Pharisees who had brought the woman before him. He stared
intently at the elder who had instigated this scenario to trap him. The older
man dropped his eyes.

Then Jesus' quiet pronouncement was heard by all: "Let he among you
who has never sinned throw the first stone."

The silent crowd refused to move. Then Jesus stooped down to continue
writing in the dust.

After a few moments of embarrassment, the oldest Pharisee, who was
the ringleader, folded his tunic around his waist, then turned to leave. Next,
two or three of the other leaders also left. One by one, the Pharisees slipped
away, trying to be inconspicuous lest their own sins should come under
intense scrutiny. Finally, only the woman remained, standing amid the
crowd before the teacher from Nazareth.

Jesus stood to look around. Seeing none of the religious leaders, he said to the woman, "Where are the people who accuse you? Has no one condemned you?"

"No one, sir," she said. "They've all gone."

"Then neither do I condemn you," Jesus said to the woman. "Go and sin no more."

The three large candelabras in the Temple were still lit, though their light was not needed. It was first morning—daylight before the sun comes over the horizon. As Jesus stood there, a solitary figure in the circle of listeners, the sun broke over the eastern mountains. A ray of sunshine penetrated between the buildings and sought out the spot where Jesus was teaching.

When Jesus spoke again to the people, he said, "I am the light of the world. Whoever follows me will never walk in darkness, but will have the light of life."

JOHN 8:12, *NIV*

chapter fifty-four

"BEFORE ABRAHAM WAS, I AM"

JOHN 8:31–9:7

"Who are you?" a voice called out to Jesus from the crowd gathered in the Temple for the Sabbath.

"I am just what I have been claiming all along," Jesus replied.

"Prove to us you are the Messiah!" another shouted.

"When you have lifted up the Son of Man," said Jesus, "then you will know that I am the one I claim to be."

As he continued speaking, many in the crowd put their faith in him. The twelve apostles sat near Jesus, waiting to minister to the people after he completed his teaching.

"If you are the Messiah, what must we do to follow you?" came another voice.

"If you obey my teaching, you are my disciples indeed," Jesus said. "Then you shall know the truth, and the truth shall set you free."

A broad, strapping man near the front stood and said, "But we have never been the slaves of anyone. How then can you say we will be set free?"

Jesus said to them, "I tell you the truth, everyone who sins is a slave to sin."

The Pharisees stood to the side listening intently . . . waiting. They felt this Messiah business had gone on long enough. Each of the Temple leaders hated Jesus and wanted him dead—an event they had been planning. They wanted him out of the way once and for all.

Jesus perceived their thoughts and answered them in front of the people, "You seek to kill me because my words have no place in your thinking."

The Pharisees yelled at Jesus, "We were not born in fornication as you were," referring to the rumors of Jesus' birth.

Jesus did not answer the accusation but told the Pharisees, "You belong to your father, the devil, and you want to carry out your father's desire. Satan was a murderer from the beginning, and there is no truth in him. He is a liar and the father of lies. Yet because I tell the truth, you do not believe me!"

"How dare you accuse us of consorting with the devil?!" a Pharisee snarled at Jesus and his outlandish claims. "You are the liar."

"Can any of you prove me guilty of sin?" Jesus now claimed to be sinless; the religious authorities knew what he meant.

The Pharisee shot back in angry hysteria, "You Samaritan dog! You must be demon possessed!" Even the other Pharisees were taken aback at this racial slur.

"I am not possessed by a demon," Jesus answered with a quiet voice, though his words were curt and direct. "But I tell you the truth, if anyone obeys my words, he will never see death."

"Ha!" the disdainful Pharisee jeered heartily. He threw both arms into the air, then turning his back to Jesus he answered, "Now we know you are demon possessed!"

The crowd of Pharisees laughed, while many of the onlookers withdrew in disbelief. This bitter confrontation was not what worshipers had come to the Temple to hear.

"Your father Abraham rejoiced to see my day," Jesus said. "He saw it and was glad."

The Pharisees laughed again. "This madman says he has seen Abraham!" said one.

Another said, "You're not even fifty years old, and yet you claim to have seen Abraham, who has been dead for more than two thousand years!"

Yet another stroked his beard in sarcasm. Ridiculing Jesus, he said, "You say that if anyone keeps your word, he will never taste death. Are you greater than Abraham? He died, and so did the prophets." Then lowering his voice, he spat out the unthinkable question: "Who do you think you are . . . God?"

"I tell you the truth," Jesus answered him directly, "before Abraham was born, I AM!"

A collective gasp went up from both Jesus' supporters and opposition. They all knew "I AM" was the title God used to identify himself to Moses. Jesus had just called himself "I AM." He had identified himself as God!

"Blasphemy!!!" someone shouted.

The Pharisees commanded the crowd, "Get stones! Stone this blasphemer!"

The apostles quickly moved to put themselves between Jesus and the angry mob. They heard the clink of stones as the people began gathering them into their arms.

Then someone shouted, "Where is he? Where did he go?"

The apostles turned to where Jesus had been standing, but he was no longer there. The crowd turned this way and that, milling about in confusion, while the apostles scanned the Temple court looking for some sign of their master. Then John spotted him walking unhurried and undisturbed through the center of the hostile crowd. As Jesus walked, the people parted in front of him as bread before a sharp knife, but no one took notice of him. Jesus looked neither to his left, nor to his right, and no one stopped him.

As Jesus left the Temple, John and the other apostles quickly ran to catch up with him. A shiver ran up John's back. He expected at any moment to feel a rock against his head or hear the feet of angry Pharisees chasing them. He was tempted to look back over his shoulder to see what the mob was doing, but he did not want to show his fear. With eyes ahead and wavering confidence, he marched forward.

When Jesus and the apostles reached the sunlit street, John's inclination was to put as much distance between him and the Temple as quickly as possible, even though it was unlawful to run on the Sabbath. Everything within him wanted to escape from that spot. He looked to the left, to the right, then back into the Temple to see if the Pharisees were following them. John could feel his heart quicken. In the Temple, he had reacted without thought or feeling during the tense minutes, as though his heart had stopped beating. Now he began trembling as he realized just how closely death had stalked him.

The apostles tried to hurry Jesus along, but the Messiah's attention was drawn to a blind man sitting outside the Temple begging for alms. His soiled tunic was stretched out in the street. Bugs and ants were eating the few remains of bread that had fallen into his lap. The blind man was propped against a stone wall, his vacant eyes wide open, staring into the space, seeing nothing. The sun shone directly in his eyes, but he knew it not.

Jesus knelt and said to the man, "Be of good cheer, my son. Salvation has come to you this day."

The man smiled and said, "I will gladly accept it. I have been blind since birth these forty years."

"Rabbi," Philip asked, "who sinned, this man or his parents, that he was born blind?"

John was irritated at Philip's inquisitiveness. This was no time to be asking theological questions; they had just escaped the valley of the shadow of death! Angry assassins were waiting just inside the Temple. John inwardly chided Philip for not appreciating the urgency of their situation.

The blind man couldn't see that he was the center of attention. The apostles gathered around Jesus to hear his answer.

"Neither this man nor his parents sinned," Jesus said, standing and turning to his apostles. "But there is a reason why he was born blind."

John stopped shaking to listen to Jesus. Jesus said, "This man was born blind that a miracle of God should be worked in his life."

John expected Jesus to touch the man's eyes to heal him, although on occasion Jesus had simply spoken and the blind saw. But Jesus did neither this time.

"I am the light of the world to the woman caught in adultery," Jesus explained to his apostles, "but I am also the light of the world to this man born in blindness."

The shadow of Jesus fell across the blind man's face, blocking out the glaring sun, but still the man did not blink. He couldn't discern the difference between light and darkness.

Jesus spat on the ground. Then he stooped to make mud with the saliva and clay from the ground. In the palm of his hands, he formed the clay into a thick paste. Then Jesus dipped the tip of his finger into the clay and rubbed the mixture into the man's eyes—not on his eyelids, but right into the eyes.

Jesus said to him, "Go wash in the pool of Siloam." John looked down the street, past the shops and tables, past the commotion of shoppers and businessmen in the bazaars in the direction of Siloam. He knew it was a long walk.

Then Jesus turned, saying to the apostles, "Let us go."

And they walked away in the other direction, knowing this task was done. Jesus had left the responsibility for the miracle with the one in need. It was now the blind man's responsibility to obey and be healed.

So he went and washed, and came back seeing.

JOHN 9:7

chapter fifty-five

"I WAS BLIND BUT NOW I SEE!"

JOHN 9:7-41

John was puzzled by the instructions of Jesus. The pool of Bethesda was only a half a block away. Why hadn't he sent the blind man to wash in Bethesda? Across the street, a donkey drank from a feed trough; it had water with which the blind man could wash the clay from his eyes. But the pool of Siloam was all the way down the Tyropoeon Valley on the other end of Jerusalem. It was a long, tedious walk through many narrow arches, across shopping bazaars and down terraced steps.

John was concerned for the ragged man, and yet the blind man seemed to know the way. He had not hesitated, but at Jesus' command had struggled to his feet, propping himself on a gnarled walking cane, and immediately set out for the pool as Jesus had instructed him. In fact, it was a trip the blind man had taken many times. *Tap . . . tap . . . tap . . .*, he instinctively began tapping his cane on the cobblestones, searching for a passage through the crowds. His steps were unsure on the uneven pavement, yet his feet had direction. He began walking toward Siloam. John turned and set off after the apostles, convinced that the old man knew where he was going.

The blind man picked his way through the crowds, passing tables and stacks of pottery. He was not distracted or detoured. Once the blind man walked into an unseen stack of grain sacks that had been unloaded from a camel by traders from the east. On another occasion, a small boy darted into him, knocking his cane to the ground. After retrieving the cane, the blind man tapped his way forward.

Near the pool of Siloam, the steps narrowed and descended steeply. The flow of water emerged from Hezekiah's Tunnel and, with a friendly gurgle, emptied into a larger pool. Palms and a large eucalyptus shaded the gardenlike setting tucked away under the shadow of the outer wall of Jerusalem. The freshwater usually attracted a large crowd, most of whom came to fill their water pots. But on the Sabbath, only a few moved about the pool enjoying a relatively cool autumn day. Slowly, step by step, the blind man descended. He instinctively reached out for a handhold that was not there.

Tap, tap, tap, the blind man stumbled toward the edge of the pool. *Tap . . . tap . . . SPLASH.* He found the water's edge. Dropping his walking stick to the ground, he bent over to lie flat on his belly at the pool's edge. Dipping his hands into the water, he splashed clear liquid into his muddied eyes. Then he splashed another handful of water into his face. Then he repeated the process again . . . and again.

Finally, he dried his eyes with the sleeve of his robe, then stopped suddenly, realizing he could see the fibers of his tunic. He jerked his head backward when he spotted his reflection in the water for the first time. He stared steadfastly at his face in the water, puzzled every time the waves of the pool distorted his vision. He lay on his stomach for a long time trying to match the image he saw in the pool with his previous self-perception.

Then rolling over onto his back, he gazed up into the blue skies. "Look!"

he said to no one in particular, pointing at the white clouds. Then he stared into the sun and for the first time in his life, he blinked, putting up his hands to shield his tender eyes from the sun's piercing rays.

The man stood. He had habitually used his cane to lift himself, but realizing the cane was no longer needed, threw it aside. He surveyed the pool of water, the trees and bushes, taking note of people going about their business, especially the women filling their pots of water. The once-blind man walked over to an older man sitting on the stairs.

"Shalom," he greeted.

The elderly man innocently returned his remark, not understanding the enormity of what had happened. The once-blind man recognized the voice and called the man by name. "You must be Caleb. I know you . . . I can see you . . . It's me . . . Nathan."

There was unbelief in the face of Caleb. He knew the blind man, but not personally. Caleb knew the man was blind, but not much more than that. So Caleb held up his hand asking, "How many fingers?"

"Five," said the now-seeing blind man delightedly.

"Aren't you the blind man that begs at the Temple gate?" old Caleb asked. He couldn't believe what he had just perceived, that a blind man was now seeing. "No," Caleb answered himself, "you look like the blind man, but you are not him."

But Nathan nodded vigorously. "I was blind, but now I see!"

Skeptically, Caleb asked, "How were your eyes opened?"

"A man called Jesus put clay on my eyes," Nathan said, "then he told me to wash in the pool of Siloam." He pointed to the waters of the pool. "When I washed, I could see!"

"Come," old Caleb pulled at Nathan's tunic. "You must show yourself to the priests. They must see this wonder . . . . You must offer a sacrifice of thanksgiving in the Temple."

Nathan protested, "I must see my parents! They will be glad for this miracle."

But the elderly Caleb prevailed and hurried him through the streets of Jerusalem back to the Temple. Nathan was certainly willing to make the required sacrifice of thanksgiving, but he protested the pace, wanting to stop along the way to gaze at the new world around him.

As they approached the Temple, a group of religious leaders were gathered at the gate in heated debate about the morning's events involving Jesus of Nazareth. Caleb led the once-blind man to the gate, waving his arms at the priests and Pharisees, shouting to get their attention. He told them of the miraculous healing while Nathan stood passively. The eyes of the priests widened at the mention of Jesus' name. One of the Pharisees went to Nathan and callously pulled his eyelids apart to inspect his eyes.

"Where do you live?" the Pharisee asked, and Nathan told him.

"Get this man's parents," a priest demanded, and a young Temple guard ran off on the errand.

The Pharisees asked Nathan directly how he had received his sight. He said to them, "Jesus put clay on my eyes, and I washed, and I see. It is a miracle from God!"

One of the Pharisees protested, "This man Jesus is not from God, because he does not keep the Sabbath."

But other of the religious authorities had their doubts. "How then can a man who is a sinner perform such signs?" asked one.

The Pharisees argued among themselves for several minutes, ignoring Nathan, just as they had ignored him for so many years when he sat begging at the same gate. Nathan tried to follow the discussion, but he was unable to fathom why his eyesight caused so much rancor, and he allowed curiosity to get the best of him. He peered into the Temple, his eyes drinking in the magnificent structure dedicated to the glory of God.

His reverie was shattered when finally one of the Pharisees confronted him, booming in rage, "I don't believe you were ever blind! You are a liar!"

"But . . . my parents will tell you I was born blind," the frustrated beggar pleaded, as a crowd began to gather around them, drawn by the dispute.

"You are one of the disciples of this rabble-rouser from Nazareth," the Pharisee accused him. "We will not allow anyone who follows Jesus to worship in the Temple."

Nathan gazed once more upon the splendor of this place dedicated to praising the Lord, looking upward to the dome on the engineering marvel that towered a hundred feet above him. If he told these men he believed in Jesus, these things would be taken away from him. *I see this exquisite Temple because of Jesus,* he thought. *How can I deny the one who gave me my sight?*

The tension was broken when the young Temple guard came rushing down the street, pushing two older people through the crowd. Terror clearly marked the faces of Nathan's parents. They had not been arrested, but the guard treated them as common thieves, refusing to tell them why they had been summoned by the authorities.

"Are you the parents of this man?" one of the Pharisees pointed to Nathan. "Is this your son?"

Both man and wife nodded, afraid to speak before the assembly of threatening faces.

"He claims to have been born blind," the Pharisee continued, "but clearly he is able to see. How is this possible?"

The mother's eyes were downcast in shame; she felt guilty for not running to embrace her son who had somehow been healed.

"We will deny you entrance to the Temple," the Pharisee threw down the challenge, "along with this man who claims to be healed by Jesus of Nazareth." He again indicated the once-blind man now staring intently at him. "If I do not get the truth, you will never return to this Temple to make sacrifice to God."

Then turning to the parents, he snapped, "Is this your son?"

"Yes," they whimpered.

"Was he born blind?"

"Yes," the mother nodded more vigorously than the father.

"How then does he now see?"

The parents knew they should be loudly praising God that their son could now see. Before he was born, they had had great hopes for their child, but from birth his eyes were dark and hollow. As the mother had held him in her arms, she knew her loving look was not returned. Their hopes for this baby were crushed by blindness, but now he could see. They should have thrown their arms into the air in thankfulness, but they cowered before a curious crowd and angry Pharisees, not wanting any part of this controversy.

"Speak up!" the Pharisee was shouting now. "How did he get his sight?"

"We know that this is our son," the father fumbled for the correct answer, a reply that would not incriminate them, "and that he was born blind. But how he now sees or who opened his eyes, we do not know." Then the father spoke clearly, disavowing his responsibility in the matter. "Ask him! He is of legal age. Let him speak for himself."

With that answer, Nathan's mother felt something die inside her, as if the opportunity to witness the goodness of God had just eluded her. God had somehow intervened in her life, answering forty years of prayers, but she kept silent instead of praising God.

But Nathan could contain himself no longer. He blurted out, "This is a miracle! Jesus is indeed a prophet."

"Jesus is a sinner," the Pharisee answered. "Give the glory to God."

"Whether Jesus is a sinner I do not know," Nathan answered, "but one thing I do know: I was blind, but now I see!"

"What did Jesus do? How did he open your eyes?" the Pharisee badgered him, as though cross-examining a hostile witness who grew bolder with each answer.

"I already told you, but you wouldn't listen," Nathan retorted in exasperation. "Why do you want to hear it again? Do you want to become his disciples, too?"

The crowd roared in laughter. This uneducated man was making fools of the religious scholars, his pragmatism confounding them.

"We are disciples of Moses!" the Pharisee proclaimed. He pulled his elegant robe around his bulging midsection, showing disdain for the simple man. "We know that God spoke to Moses, but as for this fellow Jesus, we don't even know where he comes from."

"Now that is remarkable!" Nathan laughed. "You don't know where he comes from, and yet he opened my eyes. We know that God does not hear the prayers of sinners; he listens to the godly one who does his will. If this man were not from God, he could not do miracles. He could do nothing."

The Pharisees were enraged. The healed man would not shut up. "You were corrupt in sin at birth. How dare you lecture us!" the leader yelled, pointing to the gate. "Get out! And do not return!"

The worshipers in the Temple did not keep this heated debate to themselves. Word spread quickly about the miracle of sight to the blind man, and how he had been expelled from the Temple. Jesus soon heard that the healed man had been barred from Temple worship. He found Nathan talking to a crowd of people; he was still telling the story of going to the pool of Siloam.

Jesus smiled inwardly at the man's faith. Then he interrupted him to ask, "Do you believe in the Son of God?"

"Who is he, sir?" Nathan asked. "Tell me so that I may believe in him."

"I am he." Jesus looked deep into the eyes he had healed. The eyes were no longer blinded, but were alive with love and faith.

"Lord, I believe," Nathan said. He knelt and worshiped Jesus.

> Jesus said, "For judgment I have come into this world,
> so that the blind will see and those who see will become blind."
>
> JOHN 9:39, NIV

chapter fifty-six

THE GOOD SAMARITAN

LUKE 10:25-37

Jesus and his apostles left Jerusalem and traveled across the Jordan River to Perea. News of his confrontation with the Jewish leaders in the Temple spread before him, and the crowds turned out in droves to hear Jesus speak. Standing on the edge of the crowd one day was a lawyer, a man studied in the intricacies of Jewish canon law. He wanted to test the rabbi from Nazareth, believing that if he could win a debate with Jesus, or at least trip him up with a difficult question, then his own reputation would grow throughout the region.

When Jesus came to a pause in his sermon, the lawyer interrupted with a question: "Teacher, what shall I do to inherit eternal life?"

Jesus perceived that the lawyer was not seeking salvation, but rather was only interested in debating him. Since Jesus was not interested in a rabbinic contest concerning a speculative problem, he threw the question back to him. "What is written in the Law?" Jesus asked. "How do you read the Scriptures?"

The clever lawyer was prepared with his response, answering, "You shall love the Lord your God with all your heart, with all your soul, with all your strength and with all your mind. And you shall love your neighbor as you love yourself."

The lawyer hoped to trip up Jesus with a question of fundamentals; he expected Jesus to say, "Repent" or "Follow me," but Jesus did not take the bait.

"You have answered correctly," Jesus told the lawyer. "Do this and you will live."

The lawyer, chagrined at Jesus' refusal to debate him, guessed that the teacher suspected his motivations. He knew in his heart he was incapable of fulfilling these commandments completely, and as a son of the Law, he believed there were many among his fellow man who did not keep the Law. So to justify himself, the lawyer asked, "And who is my neighbor?"

So Jesus told this parable: "A certain man was walking down the lonely road from Jerusalem to Jericho, when he was attacked by thieves. They stripped him of his clothes, beat him severely and left him for dead."

Most of those listening to Jesus knew the road of which he spoke—twenty-one lonely miles of road, mostly down a narrow path that hung precariously to the mountainside. Bands of thieves were not uncommon along this road, so wary travelers walked in caravans or large groups, because there was safety in numbers.

Jesus continued, "By chance, a priest was traveling down that same road, but when he saw the dying man on the road, he passed by on the other side. A Levite also came to that place and saw the beaten man. He, too, passed by on the other side.

"But a Samaritan traveling on the road saw the man and took pity on him. The Samaritan went to him and bandaged up his wounds, pouring oil and wine on them. Then he set the man on his own donkey, and brought him to an inn and took care of him.

"The next day when he left, he gave two silver coins to the innkeeper and said, 'Look after him, and when I return, I will reimburse you for any extra expense you may have.'"

Jesus asked the antagonistic lawyer, "Which of these three men was a neighbor to him who fell into the hands of robbers?"

The lawyer was on the spot. There was truth in the story. Clearly Jesus was trying to teach him that love was not a matter of theological discussion but of practical demonstration. Therefore, the lawyer could not choose either of the Jewish leaders, for they had neglected the beaten man. The lawyer—and everyone else who heard the parable—recognized the criticism of the legalists for their lack of love and concern for sinners, those they considered to live outside the Law.

But being a devout Jew, the lawyer could not even bring himself to say the word "Samaritan." So he answered, "The one who showed mercy on him."

Jesus said, "Go and do the same."

"On these two commandments hang all the Law and the Prophets."
MATTHEW 22:40

chapter fifty—seven

THERE WILL BE REJOICING IN HEAVEN

LUKE 15:1-32

Wherever he traveled in those days, tax collectors, sinners and outcasts flocked to Jesus of Nazareth. For the first time, they heard about God's unconditional love, and that God deeply cared about their lives and eternal destination. The rabbinical interpretations of the Law made it impossible to measure up to the demands of the letter of the Law. In contrast to the Pharisees, Jesus preached that their Father in heaven would gladly welcome them into his kingdom, if only they would repent and believe in his Son.

One day, the Pharisees were heard to mutter against him, "This man welcomes sinners and eats with those who rebel against God."

Jesus said to them and to all who were gathered about him, "Suppose one of you has a hundred sheep and loses one of them. Will you not leave the ninety-nine in the open country and go look for the lost sheep until you find it? And when you find it, you will joyfully put it on your shoulders and go home. Then you will call your friends and neighbors together and say,

'Rejoice with me, for I have found my lost sheep!'

"I tell you in the same way there will be rejoicing in heaven when one of these sinners repents. There is more joy in heaven over one of these who comes to the Father than over ninety-nine self-righteous persons who will not repent."

Jesus told yet another story to the multitudes to convey the universality of his message: He had come seeking those in need, offering help to those who could not help themselves.

"Suppose a woman has ten silver coins and loses one," he said. "Will she not light a lamp, sweep the house and search carefully until she finds it? And when she finds it, she calls her friends and neighbors together and says, 'Rejoice with me, for I have found my lost coin!'

"In the same way, I tell you, God rejoices in the presence of the angels over one sinner who repents."

Before the Pharisees could protest that God had no interest in sinful men, Jesus told them one last story to show the heart of his Father for lost sinners.

"There was man who had two sons. The younger of them went to his father and demanded of him, 'Father, give me my share of the estate.' So the father divided his property between his sons.

"Not long after that, the younger son got all his possessions together, set off for a distant country and there squandered his wealth on friends, women and wild living.

"After he had spent everything, there came a severe famine in that country, and he found himself in need of food. He went to his friends, but they would not take care of him. So he found a job feeding pigs in the field, and he was so hungry he ate of the food that he was feeding to the pigs.

"When he came to his senses, he said, 'How many of my father's hired servants have food to spare, and here I am starving to death! I will go back to my father and say to him, "Father, I have sinned against heaven and against you. I am no longer worthy to be called your son. May I become one of your hired servants?"'

"So he got up and went to his father's house. But while he was still a long way off, his father saw him and was filled with compassion for him. He ran to his son, threw his arms around him and kissed him.

"The son confessed, 'Father, I have sinned against heaven and against you. I am no longer worthy to be called your son.'

"But the father said to his servants, 'Quick! Bring the best robe and put it on him. Put a ring on his finger and sandals on his feet. Bring the fattened calf and kill it. Let's have a feast and celebrate! For this son of mine was dead and is alive again; he was lost, but now he is found.' So they began to celebrate.

"Meanwhile, the older son was in the field. When he came near the house, he heard music and dancing. So he called one of the servants and asked him what was going on. 'Your brother has come home,' the servant replied, 'and your father has killed the fattened calf for a feast because your brother is back safe and sound.'

"The older brother was furious and refused to go in. So his father went out and pleaded with him. But he answered his father, 'Look! All these years I've been slaving for you and have never disobeyed your orders. Yet you never gave me so much as a young goat so I could celebrate with my friends. But when this son of yours who has squandered your property with prostitutes comes home, you kill the fattened calf for him!'

"'My son,' the father said, 'you are always with me, and everything I have is yours. But now we must celebrate and be glad, because your brother was dead and is alive again; he was lost and is now found.'"

And [the Pharisees] could not answer Him regarding these things.

LUKE 14:6

chapter fifty-eight

AT THE FEAST OF THE DEDICATION OF THE TEMPLE

JOHN 10:22-39

Two months after the Feast of Tabernacles, Jesus left the hills of Moab to return to Jerusalem for the Feast of the Dedication of the Temple, also known as *Chanukkah*, or "the festival of lights." Jewish men were not required to attend this feast, so the disciples could not fathom why Jesus was going to Jerusalem, where recently the priests and Pharisees had tried to kill him. Concerned for his safety, Peter and John attempted to dissuade Jesus from attending the feast, but he would not be deterred.

Two hundred years earlier, after the Temple had been desecrated by Antiochus Epiphanes, the Jewish revolutionary Judas Maccabaeus had purified the Temple and restored its services. During the desecration, the Temple oil had been polluted by heathen hands. However, one flask of oil was discovered which was pure. The priests knew it was consecrated because it had been sealed with the signet of the High Priest, but the flask contained only one day's supply of oil to keep the sacred candlestick burning. By a miracle, however, the flask was continually replenished during eight days, until a fresh supply of oil could be obtained. To commemorate this miracle, the festival of lights was celebrated for eight days.

Winter had come to Jerusalem, and a cold, wet fog settled over the area. Jesus was bundled with an extra tunic when he walked onto the porches of the Temple, entering through the Gate Beautiful. Immediately, the people surged to him, barring his way.

A spokesman of the people asked, "How long will you keep us in suspense? Tell us plainly if you are the Messiah."

The Feast of the Dedication was for rejoicing and celebration. All fasting and mourning were prohibited, so it was a rather rambunctious crowd that gathered about Jesus on this day. With remarkable forbearance, Jesus said to them, "I told you I am the Messiah, but you do not believe. The miracles I do in my Father's name speak for me, but you do not believe because you are not my sheep."

"And why can we not understand your sayings?" the spokesman asked.

"You are not my sheep, therefore you do not understand my words. My sheep hear my voice, and they follow me. I give them eternal life, and they shall never perish. No one will snatch them out of my hand," Jesus replied. "My Father, who gave them to me, is greater than anyone, and no one can snatch my sheep out of my Father's hands . . . I and my Father are one."

"Blasphemy!" a priest yelled from the fringes of the crowd.

"Silence him! Don't let him speak blasphemy in the Temple!" another priest shouted from the other direction. The crowd began yelling and taking up stones with the intention of stoning him.

Lifting his hands, Jesus spoke quietly to the crowd. They quieted, still wanting to hear what he had to say. He asked them, "I have healed many and shown you many good works of my Father. For which of these miracles do you stone me?"

"We do not stone you for miracles," replied a young priest, "but for blasphemy! Because you are a mere man who claims to be God!"

"Do you accuse me of blasphemy just because I said, 'I am God's Son'? If I do not do the works of my Father, then don't believe me. But if I do miracles, even though you don't believe me, believe the miracles, so that you may know that the Father is in me, and I am in him."

"No!" The crowd erupted in a violent explosion of bitterness, and some men shouted, "Stone him! Stone the blasphemer!"

But Jesus turned his back to the crowd and walked toward the gate. No one hindered him or tried to restrain him. Jesus did not look back, nor was he afraid they would try to harm him, for he knew it was not yet his hour to die. He walked out the gate and into the streets, disappearing among the multitudes.

Therefore they sought again to seize Him, but He escaped out of their hand.
And He went away again beyond the Jordan to the place where John was
baptizing at first, and there He stayed.

JOHN 10:39, 40

chapter fifty-nine

RAISING LAZARUS

JOHN 11:1-14

Flames crackled from the small fire fueled by dead vines and pinecones. Jesus and the twelve huddled around the diminutive flame for warmth on this especially bitter January evening. They had tarried in the cold highlands of the Moab hills for what seemed to the apostles like all winter, though they had been there but a few weeks. There was snow on the peaks above them in the higher elevations of the mountains east of the Jordan.

"Someone is coming!" James the Less whispered urgently from his position on the perimeter of the camp. The apostles stood to meet the stranger, whose clothing identified him as a servant as he walked into the light thrown off by the small fire in defiance of the darkness.

The man was a messenger arriving from Bethany. Jesus immediately recognized him as the servant of Mary and Martha, his dear friends who lived in the small town less than two miles from Jerusalem. His memories of the warmth of their home and their gracious hospitality helped to fend off the frigid winds.

"Lazarus is sick." The servant anxiously spoke to Jesus in low tones. "Mary and Martha ask that you come immediately."

The twelve glanced nervously at one another, recognizing the implications of this message. Certainly Jesus would go to his friends in their time of need. The apostles also knew and loved Lazarus and his sisters, but a return to Judea at this time was ill advised. Twice the people of Jerusalem had tried to stone Jesus. If the Jewish leaders caught wind of the fact that he was within their borders, they would likely try to arrest him.

"This sickness will not end in death," Jesus told the servant. The twelve overhearing this were relieved. "No, Lazarus is sick for the glory of God," Jesus said.

"What shall I tell Mary and Martha?" the servant inquired.

"Tell them that God's Son will be glorified through this," Jesus answered.

During the next two days, Jesus did not mention Lazarus but explained to his apostles that soon it would be necessary for him to go to Jerusalem. There he would suffer at the hands of the authorities, be crucified and on the third day rise again. Even as he explained what would happen, the apostles did not understand, nor were their fears allayed.

After the two days had passed, Jesus awakened the twelve early in the morning. "Get up," he urged them. "We are going to Bethany. Now is the time."

There was frost on the leaves and the disciples could see their breath. Peter, usually the soundest sleeper of the bunch, was the last to the fire.

"Not now, Lord," the redheaded apostle protested. "This is the wrong time to go back to Judea."

"Rabbi," John pleaded, "a short while ago they tried to stone you. Why would you go back there?"

But Jesus quoted Solomon to them. "There is a time to be born, and a time to die," he said. "Look, there are twelve hours of daylight in which to walk. If we walk in the light, we will not stumble. But a man who walks by night will stumble, for he has no light."

Seeing their lack of understanding, Jesus smiled at his disciples and said to them, "Fear not, my friends, for there is still light to do our work. My time has not yet come."

The twelve pulled their tunics tightly around themselves to keep warm as they ate their breakfast. Jesus explained further the events that were about to unfold. "Our friend Lazarus has fallen asleep," he said. "But I am going to wake him up."

"Lord, if Lazarus is sleeping," Philip argued, "will sleep not restore him?"

Jesus said plainly, "Lazarus is dead."

The apostles were stunned. They had seen Jesus calm a storm, heal a leper and give sight to the blind. They all knew Jesus did not order his life according to death's timetable, nor to the schedule of any man. And they had seen Jesus heal the centurion's servant without going to him. Could Jesus not do something for his friend Lazarus at a distance?

"I am glad for your sakes I was not there to heal him," Jesus said. "But let us go to Bethany now."

As they cleaned up and prepared to travel once more, Thomas said to the other apostles, "If Lazarus is dead, let us go to Judea that we may die with him." Thomas could always be counted on to see the black side of a situation, but all the apostles were in a dark mood this day and no one bothered to contradict his doomsaying.

Jesus and the apostles crossed over the Jordan River and into the mountains of Judea heading in the direction of Jerusalem. Nearly every Jew experienced some level of holy excitement when approaching Jerusalem, but there was no excitement in the hearts of the twelve on this day. The cold, cloudy day further dampened their spirits.

As they drew near Bethany, one of the apostles instructed a young boy playing alongside the road to run ahead to the house of Mary and Martha to tell them Jesus was coming. Oblivious to the somber mood of these events, the young legs bounced up the path to the village.

Shortly, Martha came running down the path to meet Jesus, her mourning clothes flowing in the breeze. Her eyes were reddened and swollen from shedding many tears and as she approached Jesus, fresh tears fell down her face. Martha ran to Jesus and fell at his feet. Without greeting him, she blurted out, "Oh, Lord! If only you had been here . . . . If you had been here, my brother would not have died."

Lazarus had already been dead four days, during which Martha had said repeatedly to everyone within the sound of her voice that if only Jesus had been there, Lazarus would not have died. And yet, though Martha did not understand why her Lord had tarried, she still had faith.

She looked up from Jesus' feet to say to him, "Even though you were not here to heal him, I know that even now God will give you whatever you ask."

Jesus, smiling, said, "Your brother will rise again."

Martha stood, trying to muster her considerable emotional strength, and said to him, "I know he shall rise again in the resurrection at the last day."

But Jesus had more immediate plans. "I am the resurrection and the life," he said to her. "Those who believe in me will live, even though they die. And whoever lives and believes in me will never die."

He placed his hands on her shoulders, looked into Martha's eyes to ask, "Do you believe this?"

Martha didn't fully comprehend the question. But she knew what she knew, and she believed what she believed. She answered him, saying, "I believe that you are the Christ . . . the Son of God, who was to come into the world."

Jesus smiled and nodded, as Martha ran off to tell her sister that Jesus had arrived. But Jesus did not go to the house, knowing it would be surrounded by professional mourners. He had heard the wailing and commotion of those who were paid to mourn throughout his life, and Jesus did not want to hear their hypocritical grief for his friend. So he remained outside the village.

Soon Mary came hurrying down the path toward Jesus. The professional mourners followed her, doing what they were paid to do.

"Lord, if you had been here my brother would not have died," Mary repeated what Martha had said. She fell at his feet and began to weep bitterly.

Jesus, deeply moved by her grief, asked, "Where have you laid him?"

They walked into a narrow valley with limestone caves. Many of these caves had been fashioned into tombs. As Jesus approached the sealed tomb of Lazarus, a strange crowd convened around him—paid mourners wailing for the dear departed, two disillusioned sisters who had believed but now had doubts, twelve men devoted to Jesus who did not understand why he had risked his life to come here *after* his friend had died, elders from the local synagogue, plus neighbors and strangers drawn more by curiosity than grief.

As Jesus surveyed those gathered in this place, he realized that no one there truly believed. No one understood he held life in his hands. Not one of them would stand with him in the end. He had given up everything to come to his own, and his own had not received him. He grieved for the world.

Jesus wept.

Someone in the crowd saw the tears on his face and said, "See how Jesus loved Lazarus!"

Another said, "This man opened the eyes of the blind. Why didn't he stop Lazarus from dying?"

Their unbelief only brought more tears to Jesus' eyes. They did not understand who he was. They did not know what he could do. They were blind.

"Take away the stone," Jesus commanded, and four young men quickly put their shoulders to the stone, rolling it away from the opening to the tomb.

"But, Lord," Martha protested, "the odor! He's been in the grave four days." Rotted flesh was not how Martha wanted to remember her brother.

Jesus said, "Didn't I tell you that if you believed, you would see the glory of God?"

Four strong young shoulders had strained at the stone, releasing only a mild musty smell, nothing like the stench of rotting flesh they had all expected. Through the dark shadows where death held the body, the corpse could be seen wrapped in white soiled sheets that had been anointed with oil.

Then in front of all of the witnesses, Jesus lifted his face to heaven to pray, "Father, I thank you that you have heard my prayer. But I pray this for the benefit of the people standing here, that they may believe you sent me."

Then with a loud voice, Jesus shouted so all those gathered in that small valley could hear clearly.

"Lazarus . . . come forth!"

The body wrapped in linen sat up, silencing the crowd. The body that had been carried lovingly into the cave and carefully placed on a rocky ledge, now rose to leave the cave.

"Take the grave clothes off him and let him go," Jesus commanded. Quickly, several young men and apostles ran to Lazarus, unwrapping the cloths that had been wound about his body.

> *Therefore many of the Jews who had come to visit Mary,*
> *and had seen what Jesus did, put their faith in him.*
>
> JOHN 11:45, *NIV*

chapter sixty

TEN LEPERS ARE HEALED

LUKE 17:11-37

Many of those who had witnessed the raising of Lazarus from the dead now believed that Jesus was indeed the Messiah and became his disciples. Others knew that Jesus had raised this man from the dead by a miracle, but they did not believe in their hearts that he was Messiah. Still others refused to believe they had seen anything but a trick, a charade or a demonstration of satanic power. Nevertheless, the crowd dispersed to tell the story, each in his own way.

The elders who had officiated at the burial of Lazarus knew he had been dead. They hurried to nearby Jerusalem to alert the religious authorities of Jesus' presence. "Jesus is a threat," they declared. "Many among our people are ready to follow him."

So the chief priests and the Pharisees called a meeting of the Sanhedrin. After much deliberation among the council members, one stood and spoke to the others. "What are we accomplishing here? We must do something now," he said. "This man is performing miraculous signs across the countryside. If we let him go on like this, everyone will believe in him. And when the Romans hear of the people uniting behind this man, the soldiers will come and take away both our authority and our nation."

"If Jesus whips the crowd into a frenzy and they should attack the Roman soldiers . . . ," another cautioned.

"We will all perish in a fight with Rome!" another shouted, and everyone began talking at once.

But Caiaphas, being high priest that year, called them to order. He then reminded them all of a well-known proverb. "It is better that one man should die for the people, than the whole nation perish," he said.

Caiaphas suggested that they had waited long enough for the Nazarene to implicate himself in a crime against God or against the state. Far better that they execute a blameless man, he claimed, than to await the certain slaughter of multitudes of fanatical followers by the soldiers. A failed coup would bring severe Roman judgment upon them all. Therefore, he said, Jesus should be eliminated by their expeditious use of Roman justice.

"Jesus must die to save the people," Caiaphas declared. He could not know that he spoke a prophecy that day, or that by his judgment upon Jesus, he had spoken God's sentence upon himself. This would be the last prophecy he would ever utter.

While people in Jerusalem were buzzing over the resurrection in Bethany, Jesus and his disciples headed north through the hill country, staying awhile in Ephraim. The small city of Ephraim straddled the border of Samaria and Galilee, where it overlooked rolling green pastures and wheat fields partitioned by broken rock walls. From there, many went into Galilee to visit family and spread the news that Jesus was in Ephraim. A multitude of his followers gathered to him in this place, and Jesus remained there until he was ready to go to Passover. He then set his face like a flint toward Jerusalem, knowing this would be his final journey.

Leaving Ephraim, the entourage of disciples began a slow, circuitous journey to Jerusalem, first heading east and later south, always staying outside of Samaria and Judea. They eventually crossed over to the other side of the Jordan and into Perea. The residents of these parts did not think the large band of travelers particularly strange or unusual. Many such groups from all over the world passed through the region, making the pilgrimage to Jerusalem in the weeks leading up to the Feast of Passover. But this group was different. Whenever they entered a village, Jesus healed the sick and taught the people the word of God. Then hundreds from the village would follow him to the next village. From there, some would return to their homes, while others would continue on the journey with him.

One day, as they passed near a leper colony in a remote area, ten lepers met them along the road, having heard from family that Jesus was coming. A lookout had been set to keep watch for Jesus, and when they saw him coming, the ten lepers began calling to him from afar, "Jesus . . . Master . . . have mercy on us!"

The lepers came to the road, but would not enter the road in strictest compliance with Jewish law.

Jesus said to them, "Go show yourselves to the priests."

His disciples thought this an unusual command. He neither touched them nor commanded them to be healed. On at least one occasion Jesus had done the unthinkable and touched a leper to heal him. All they knew for certain was that the Law of Moses required a leper who was cleansed to be observed by a priest for ten days. Then the priest would pronounce to the village that the leper was in fact clean. Only then could he or she return to society and have normal contact with others. So Jesus sent these lepers to the priests.

The ten lepers did not question his command but obeyed Jesus, for they had nothing to lose. As they made their way to the nearest priest, a miracle happened—new life flooded through them. Leprous flakes of rotted skin began to disappear. Their act of faith and obedience released healing in their bodies, and before they reached the priests they were restored to full health.

Nine of the men continued into the village to show themselves to the priests and to celebrate their liberation from the curse of leprosy. The remaining man, a Samaritan, when he saw that he was healed was so over-joyed, he returned to the road where they had met Jesus, shouting all the way.

"GLORY TO GOD! GLORY TO GOD!"

Seeing Jesus and the multitudes from a distance, he began running. Falling at his deliverer's feet, he sobbed, "Thank you, Lord! Glory to God!"

Jesus looked down the road, but not seeing the others, asked, "Were not ten lepers cleansed?" Looking to the Samaritan, he asked, "Where are the other nine?"

Then turning to his disciples, he asked, "Were the others not willing to return and give praise to God except this foreigner?"

Nathanael the apostle said to Jesus, "The nine must be seeking the priest as you commanded. This man is a Samaritan and does not know the Law."

But Peter scoffed and said, "That's not the issue. This is nothing but stubbornness and ingratitude!"

Jesus shook his head. He would later teach them that the nine had been healed in body only, but this man had received healing in his heart and spirit. He turned, telling the Samaritan, "Rise and go your way. Your faith has made you well."

Andrew then asked, "Lord, will this man see the kingdom of God?"

Peter asked a question more to the point: "How will *we* know when the kingdom has come? You told the Pharisees the kingdom of God cannot be seen."

Jesus grew quiet, walking away from where the multitudes had gathered. The twelve followed him so they could talk in private. Jesus told them, "The time is coming when you will long to see the day of the Son of Man, but do not be deceived. Men will tell you, 'There he is!' or 'Here he is!' Do not go running off after them. There will be reports that I have returned, and people will go to different places searching for me. But when I return everyone will know it. As the lightning flashes out of the sky from one end of heaven to the other, so will be the coming of the Son.

"Just as it was in the days of Noah, when no one expected God to judge the earth, so it will be in that day. Everyone was eating and drinking and joining in marriage right up until the day when Noah entered the ark. Then the flood came and destroyed them all."

"But first He must suffer many things and be rejected by this generation."
LUKE 17:25

chapter sixty-one

THE RICH YOUNG RULER

LUKE 18:15-30

Spring swept into Palestine from the eastern mountains as Jesus and his followers crossed over the River Jordan into Perea. Up ahead was a little village off the beaten path, nestled among white rocks at the top of a hill. Jesus stopped to rest in the shade of a budding sycamore tree and sent a few of the apostles into town for food.

Shortly Jesus heard laughing and shouting coming from the direction of the village. "Jesus! Jesus!" children called as they came running down the mountain path followed by several mothers. Jesus had not intended to reveal himself in this region, but the children always seemed to know when he was near. Perhaps one of his apostles had seen a need and could not resist doing a kind deed in his name. Whatever the reason, Jesus didn't send the children away but stood to greet them.

"Blessed are you," Jesus said, smiling and placing his hands on the heads of the children. Then looking into heaven, he blessed them.

"Touch my child," a mother pleaded.

"Mine, too," said another.

The children pressed upon Jesus, pulling on his robe, grabbing him by the hand. The older children in the rear reached over the young to touch Jesus.

"Touch me!" a little one shouted.

"Touch me. Touch me first!"

"I'm next!"

Jesus laughed, amused by their youthful exuberance and simple faith. But Peter was irritated by the clamor and the demands being made on his master. He and Matthew began pulling the children away, grabbing them by the hand or a tunic. But as soon as they pulled a child away, he ran back into the melee, hoping to touch Jesus.

"Back up, children!" Peter sternly ordered them. "Get back!"

"Stop, Peter," Jesus said, still laughing. "Let the little children come to me." Jesus then said to his disciples, "Don't forbid children to come to me, for this is the way all people should come to me. The kingdom of God belongs to such as these."

Jesus then sat down, and the children became calm sitting at his feet. "Let children come to me openly . . . expectantly . . . happily," he explained to his followers. "They want me to bless them. I say to you, if a person does not receive the kingdom of God like a little child, he shall never enter God's presence."

Some of the men from the town had drifted out to see what was happening. They had watched Jesus and the children, and they heard what Jesus had said concerning the kingdom. One of the younger men—a wealthy leader—came forward and asked of Jesus, "Good teacher, what must I do to inherit eternal life?"

Jesus had heard this question many times, often as a prelude to an argument. But Jesus looked into the hidden compartments of the man's heart, seeing he truly believed himself to be good and desired the gift of eternal life. "Why do you call me 'good'?" Jesus asked the young man. "No one is good, except God alone."

The young man's smooth skin and high-pitched voice revealed he was young—younger than Jesus. Yet his wealth was evident from his regal tapestry robes and finely manicured beard. Even the way the young man held his head reflected good training.

"God wants us to obey his commandments," Jesus explained to the young gentleman. "You must not commit adultery . . . ."

"I have never done that."

"You must not kill . . . ."

"I would not harm anyone."

"You must not steal . . . ."

"I have never taken anything that doesn't belong to me."

"You must not lie . . . ."

"I endeavor to always tell the truth."

"You must honor your father and mother . . . ."

"All these things I have observed since I was a child," the rich young ruler said to Jesus.

Jesus silently stared at him. The apostles knew that look. Jesus loved the young man, but he was about to ask something difficult. Something hard to give.

"You still lack one thing. You must do one thing more," Jesus said, breaking the silence.

"Tell me," the young man pleaded. "Quickly, tell me what I must do."

"Go sell everything that you own." Jesus waited for a moment to let his pronouncement sink in. "Sell everything you have and give the proceeds to the poor, and you will have treasure in heaven."

Matthew watched the young man's face. Matthew had held a lucrative post as tax collector and had accumulated wealth in many forms; he had owned beautiful homes, elegant clothes, servants and riches hidden in many places. But Matthew left all to follow Jesus and had never regretted his decision.

"After you have given everything to the poor," Jesus said finally, "then come, follow me."

The young man was stunned. His countenance fell and he dropped his eyes to the ground in bitter disappointment. The young man had grown accustomed to a life of affluence, having accumulated much property and many servants. He had everything the world could offer, and he had believed his good works would earn him a place in God's kingdom. He hungered for God, for everlasting life, but this price was too high.

Jesus waited for an answer, but the ruler would not look up at him. Deeply grieved, the young man shook his head. He loved his life and the things of this world; he could not give up everything, not even for God. With a sudden move, the young man turned back toward the village and walked away.

As the young man walked away, Jesus said to those gathered around him, "How hard it is for the rich to enter the kingdom of God! Indeed, it is easier for a camel to squeeze through the eye of a needle than for a rich man to enter the kingdom of God."

Peter smiled inwardly; he knew of a place where people tried to squeeze a camel through the eye of a needle. It was the small gate in Jerusalem called the Needle's Eye. A camel could get on its knees to crawl through that gate, but it first had to get rid of all its baggage. Peter wondered to himself if money was the excess baggage keeping this man out of heaven.

"Who then can be saved?" Matthew interrupted his thoughts.

"Anyone can be saved," Jesus said. "Things that are impossible with men are possible with God."

Peter said, "Lord, we have left everything to follow you."

"You may be poor in this life," Jesus told Peter, "but those who have given up homes, parents, friends, family and even money for the kingdom of God shall receive greater things than money in this life, and in the age to come, they shall have eternal life."

They were on their way up to Jerusalem, with Jesus leading the way, and the disciples were astonished, while those who followed were afraid.

MARK 10:32, *NIV*

chapter sixty-two

ZACCHAEUS

LUKE 19:1-27

Jesus and his disciples crossed the shallow fords of the Jordan and were once again in Judea. Two hours later, they approached the outskirts of Jericho to drink from the ancient spring of Elisha. They rested in the shade of the Roman aqueducts that carried water from the springs to the surrounding fields. Jericho was a lush green island in an otherwise dry, sandy valley.

The Jewish people had occupied the city since the days of Joshua. After Pompeii nearly destroyed Jericho in his military campaign, Herod the Great first plundered, then partially rebuilt and later fortified and adorned the great city. A large wall now surrounded Jericho, with a fort located at each of its four corners to protect the city from conquest.

Herod had built a palace in this little paradise because, he claimed, he could be comfortable wearing nothing but linen there all during the winter months. A grand theater and large amphitheater were part of Herod's legacy to Jericho. His son Archelaus later constructed a new palace surrounded by splendid gardens of roses, sweet-scented balsam trees and extensive groves of palms of stately beauty. The narrow streets of Jericho were lined on each side with walls to protect the gardens, while sycamore trees graced the edge of the highway, reaching their covering branches over the streets to provide shade to its residents and many visitors.

However, the beauty of Jericho did not always extend to its people, a motley crowd drawn by the reputation of this jeweled oasis in the desert. Roman soldiers kept order, people seeking health cures came for the waters, courtiers came for the comfortable weather, and many merchants came seeking their fortune. A proportionate number of tax collectors were stationed in Jericho to gather Rome's share of the wealth, and all tax collectors on the road leading from Arabia to Damascus were under the command of Zacchaeus, the chief tax collector residing in Jericho.

During the past year, Zacchaeus had often wondered about his friend Levi, who now called himself Matthew. One of Zacchaeus' most efficient revenue agents, Matthew had resigned a couple of years earlier and given up his worldly possessions to follow Jesus of Nazareth, a man who had gained a reputation as a great teacher and worker of miracles. After a particularly difficult day, Zacchaeus would find himself thinking of Matthew and Jesus. *Has Matthew found happiness?* he wondered. *If he has, can I find the same?*

Jesus had only just entered Jericho when word reached Zacchaeus that the teacher was passing through the city. A massive crowd had gathered to see him. People were climbing the walls to catch a glimpse of Jesus, while most lined both sides of the street two and three deep. Mothers held their children high above the crowd to see him; some wanted Jesus to touch their children. Jesus walked calmly through their midst, followed by the twelve and, after them, a large company of men and women.

Zacchaeus left his tax office, determined to see Jesus. He was quite curious about the rabbi who had persuaded Matthew from collecting taxes. But when Zacchaeus ventured into the street, he found he was unable to get anywhere near the teacher because of the crowds. To make matters worse, Zacchaeus was very short. Had he thought of it earlier, as a tax collector in authority, he might have commandeered a soldier to clear his way. Zacchaeus ran along behind the crowd, looking for an opening in the throng. But as far as he ran, his view of Jesus was completely blocked.

If Zacchaeus had been driven solely by curiosity, he might have given up and returned to his tax office. But a flicker of faith burned deep inside him, shedding light on the emptiness of his unfulfilled and sinful life. Spying a sycamore tree just down the road, the diminutive tax collector quickly ran to the tree and shimmied up the trunk, just as he had done as a boy whenever great men and foreign dignitaries passed through the city. From his tenuous perch, Zacchaeus looked out over the crowd to see the approaching procession.

Jesus was walking slowly, almost strolling down the garden road. As he passed the people, the crowds, like an enormous river, swarmed in his wake, swallowing up his disciples. Jesus smiled, glancing to his left and to his right, nodding and acknowledging the people as he walked. Zacchaeus was surprised and delighted when Jesus stopped directly beneath him. As Jesus looked up, his searching eyes spotted Zacchaeus in the tree.

"Zacchaeus," Jesus called him by name, "come down from your tree."

The attention of the crowds shifted upward to Zacchaeus. The short man, who had always striven to have people look up to him, was suddenly self-conscious when his ambition was achieved.

"Come down quickly!" Jesus said, laughing. "I must stay at your house today."

Tremendous excitement filled the house of Zacchaeus when it was heard he was bringing Jesus of Nazareth home for the evening meal. In contrast, there was great displeasure among much of the crowd. "Jesus has gone to eat in the house of a notorious sinner," they said. "Zacchaeus is chief tax collector, the worst of backslidden Jews!"

But Zacchaeus, who had heard their protests and accusations, listened carefully to the message of Jesus and believed. His life was changed and his sins forgiven. That evening after dinner, Zacchaeus stood to announce to his guests, "From now on I will give half my money and possessions to the poor. And if I have cheated anyone out of anything, if I have overcharged anyone for their taxes, I will pay back four times the amount."

Jesus said to those assembled, "Today salvation has come to this house. This man is truly a son of Abraham. For the Son of Man has come to seek and save what was lost."

Now as they went out of Jericho, a great multitude followed Him.

MATTHEW 20:29

chapter sixty-three

MARY ANOINTS JESUS

JOHN 12:1-11

In the days leading to the Feast of Passover, the word on the streets was that the chief priest planned to arrest Jesus of Nazareth if he dared to show himself in Jerusalem. Because of this, many said, "Jesus will not come to Jerusalem. It is too dangerous for him here." Others argued that Jesus must come to Jerusalem to validate his claims; if he were truly the Messiah, he had nothing to fear.

The Pharisees and priests fully expected the Nazarene to come to Jerusalem, and they were indeed prepared to seize him before he could enter the Temple. They wanted no more of his teaching the multitudes or inflaming them with his "blasphemies." If he were to incite a riot, it would not go well with Rome—for him or for the priests. "If anyone knows where he is staying," the chief priests told their spies, "report it immediately so that we might arrest him."

Six days before the Passover, Jesus walked up the Geba Valley from Jericho, arriving that same day in Bethany at the home of Lazarus and his sisters, Mary and Martha. Jesus had sent word of his impending arrival two days before, and the people of Bethany had set about preparing a great banquet in his honor. This was, after all, the Passover season, a time of family and feasting. The banquet for Jesus and his apostles was to be the festive meal before the Sabbath.

The meal was held at a large horseshoe-shaped table, each person reclining on a pillow on his left elbow and eating with the right hand. Lazarus sat on Jesus' left in the place of honor. At the conclusion of the meal, people from the village and the surrounding areas—even Jerusalem—filled the banquet room and stood outside the windows to get a look at Jesus and the man he had raised from the dead. There were rumors that the chief priests were plotting to take the life of Lazarus, too, because on account of him, many Jews were proclaiming Jesus as Messiah and putting their faith in him.

During the meal, Martha served while Mary again sat at the feet of Jesus. She did not eat, but wanted only to be near him, to worship him. She listened when Jesus spoke, hanging onto every word as though it were a morsel of bread she needed to satisfy her emptiness. She wept when he again spoke of his death and resurrection, as he so often did in these days.

As the evening was drawing to a close, Mary arose suddenly and left the banquet hall. Soon she returned with a large alabaster jar she had kept in her room for many years. Inside the treasured container was a pint of the pure essence of *nard*, a perfume of India worth a year's wages in this quantity. Upon entering the room, Mary held the jar close to her heart, hoping no one would ask her what she had or what she was doing.

On many occasions at the banquets of the rich and powerful, the heads of kings and dignitaries were anointed with fragrant oils. Mary was determined to use the most precious of her possessions to anoint Jesus, the most precious person in her life, as her lord and king.

Breaking open the flask, Mary released the perfume. Before anyone could protest, she poured half the ointment over the head of Jesus, the opulent fragrance pouring into the banquet room like a desert rain running down a dry canyon. Then she knelt and poured the remaining perfume onto his feet, anointing them as well.

As only those who walk in sandals in hot climates know, it is not the mountain that brings the greatest displeasure in life, but the cinder pebble that gets lodged in the sandal. It was considered a great luxury to have one's feet anointed with oil.

"What a terrible waste of money," muttered Judas Iscariot, who carried the money bag for the apostles.

Then in a shocking display of humility in worship—no one expected it, nearly everyone was appalled—Mary began to dry the feet of Jesus with her hair, a Jewish woman's most prized feature. She could not look into his face as she wiped his feet, an expression of her deep love for the man who had taught her so much.

Though the people were transfixed by the sacrifice of Mary, Judas broke the spell by openly rebuking Mary. "Why wasn't this perfume sold and the money given to take care of the poor?" he asked. "We could have asked three hundred denarii for pure spikenard!"

The candles on the table threw their light onto the black beard and eyebrows of Judas, casting a dark, larger-than-life shadow on the wall behind him. He did not rebuke Mary because he cared about the poor, but because he was a thief. As keeper of the money bag, he had made a habit of helping himself to its contents.

The words of Judas hung suspended in the air. No one in the room applauded Mary or leaped to her defense. No one in the room challenged Judas' criticism.

But Jesus spoke up and said mildly, almost sadly, "Let her alone. It was intended that she should save the perfume for this day. She has anointed me for my burial."

The guests silently looked to one another to see if anyone understood his meaning.

"Mary has done a beautiful thing," Jesus said, "and she will always be remembered for this deed. I tell you the truth, wherever the gospel is preached throughout the world, what she has done will also be told."

Then he looked to his disciples and said, "You will always have the poor among you, but you will not always have me."

Then the chief priests, the scribes, and the elders of the people assembled at the palace of the high priest, who was called Caiaphas, and plotted to take Jesus by trickery and kill Him.

MATTHEW 26:3

chapter sixty-four

A ROYAL RECEPTION

MATTHEW 21:1-11
JOHN 12:12-19

Early Sunday morning, the day after the Sabbath, many of his followers went ahead of Jesus into the city of Jerusalem to spread news of the coming of the man they believed would be crowned king of the Jews.

Many inhabitants of Jerusalem had rejected his claims; they held little or no interest in his whereabouts. In contrast, excitement was spreading among the multitudes who had made the pilgrimage from throughout Judea and Galilee and all parts of the known world for the Passover celebration. These pilgrims intensified the festive atmosphere in the city. By midday, thousands had gathered at the city gate to see if the one they called Messiah, the Christ, would indeed come to the city. The chief priests and Pharisees also took a keen interest in the rumors that Jesus was coming. They immediately sent representatives to observe his arrival and arrest him, if possible.

Jesus and the twelve departed Bethany at mid-morning, again walking among the rocks and loose stones on the main caravan road leading from Jericho to Jerusalem. The mountainous path climbed Olivet, or the Mount of Olives, past the village of Bethphage.

As they came near to the village, Jesus instructed Peter and John, saying, "Go to the village ahead of you. Just as you enter the village, you will find a small donkey, a colt which no one has ever ridden, tied near the side of the road. Untie it and bring it here."

Peter and John looked at each other but did not question how Jesus planned to ride an unbroken animal.

Jesus said to them, "If anyone asks you, 'Why are you taking this animal?' tell him, 'The Lord has need of the donkey and will send it back here shortly.'"

As Peter and John entered the village, they spotted a young donkey tied next to its mother. Without hesitation, they untied the donkey and began to lead it away. The owner of the donkey was working nearby repairing a fence. He ran after them, shouting, "What are you doing? Where are you going with my colt?"

Peter turned and said to him, "The Lord has need of the donkey and will send it back here shortly."

During Passover week, Bethphage was filled with pilgrims unable to secure lodging in Jerusalem, and the rumors of the coming Messiah had already reached the ears of everyone in the village, including the colt's owner. "Jesus of Nazareth? Here?" he said excitedly. "If the Messiah needs my animal, please take it with my blessing!"

Leading the donkey to Jesus, Peter and John removed their tunics to drape them over the animal for Jesus to ride upon. Jesus sat upon the colt, which did not protest. Resuming their ascent of Olivet, the apostles broke into a psalm of praise. "Open to me the gates of righteousness. I will go through them, and I will praise the Lord," they sang. "This is the day the Lord has made. We will rejoice and be glad in it!"

Meanwhile, an enthusiastic crowd followed after Jesus. As they neared the summit of Olivet, the crowd joined with the apostles, singing, "Blessed is he who comes in the name of the Lord!"

The apostles marched victoriously, dazzled by the brilliance of the day and moved by the excitement of the crowd as they led the donkey bearing their Lord. When the procession swept over the ridge, the city of Jerusalem loomed before them. The magnificent gardens—terrace upon terrace—reached up the walls of the Eternal City, peacefully perched high on Mount Zion. Menacing towers protected the city walls, wherein lay the glorious Temple and the gleaming palaces of Herod, Caiaphas the high priest and Annas, his father-in-law.

The Roman road descended straight down Olivet across a rock bridge over the Wady Kidron. Then the road led up Mount Zion, through the Golden Gate and into the heart of the city. As the procession of Jesus and the multitude came into view, a massive cheer rose from the valley to greet them. Coming over Olivet, Jesus saw that thousands of people had lined both sides of the road leading into Jerusalem to greet him. Many had spread their cloaks on the road, while others cut palm branches from the trees to spread them on the road in honor of the Messiah.

The crowds ahead of him picked up the refrain of those that followed, shouting, "Hosanna!" meaning, Save now!

"Hosanna to the Son of David!" they cried. "Hosanna in the highest! Blessed is he who comes in the name of the Lord!"

The apostles were caught up in the excitement and did not notice that Jesus was untouched by their enthusiasm. A single tear fell down his face as he stared, not at the adoring crowds, but at the city of God—the city that had rejected him; the city that would finally crucify him. No one heard his lament as Jesus, in his moment of triumph, caught a glimpse of the city's terrible future. He saw before him a vision of destruction, an enemy camped around the city, tearing down its walls and destroying the Temple so that not one stone was left upon another. Jesus said quietly, "O Jerusalem, if you only knew . . . . This is a day of rejoicing, but the day will come when your enemies will trample down your walls, because you did not recognize the time of God's coming to you."

The Pharisees who had been sent out with the crowd from Jerusalem were caught up in the surge of the multitudes, struggling to remain with one another. There was no chance they could arrest Jesus when he was surrounded by so many supporters. "This is getting us nowhere!" one of them called out to the others.

Disgustedly recognizing the numerous nationalities of pilgrims among the crowd, another shouted, "Look at this! The whole world has gone after him!"

The Pharisees were shocked and appalled at the massive public reception for the Nazarene healer. They recognized that the Sanhedrin's worst nightmare was coming true before their eyes. Yet, though they knew the Scriptures by heart, they failed to recognize the fulfillment of Zechariah's prophecy of the coming Messiah: "Rejoice greatly, O daughter of Zion! Shout, O daughter of Jerusalem! Behold, your king is coming to you. He is just and having salvation, lowly and riding on a donkey."

"Peace in heaven and glory in the highest!" the people called out.

"Hosanna to the Son of David!"

The Pharisees continued to follow on the edge of the crowd, becoming more agitated as the crowd became more vociferous in their praise of Jesus. One of them forced his way into the road to confront Jesus on the donkey. With a measure of respect, but with agitation clearly in his voice, he said, "Teacher, rebuke your disciples! They are out of control!"

Jesus now broke from his silent reverie and smiled broadly, seeing the crowds cheering about him. He looked down on the Pharisee and said, laughing, "If they were to keep quiet, the stones would immediately begin to cry out in their place."

Jesus rode the donkey through the gate and into the narrow streets of the city all the way to the gate of the Temple. There he dismounted and looked about him at the crowds as the people cheered ever louder, and his mood darkened once more. Within a few days, these who worshiped him now at his triumphal entry would turn fickle and shout for his death. But today the tramp of their feet and the shouts of their voices would not be silenced.

As the hour was already late, He went out to Bethany with the twelve.

MARK 11:11

chapter sixty—five

NOTHING BUT LEAVES

MARK 11:12-25

A crisp, new spring day came to Judea, the air seemingly alive with the excitement of Passover week. Very early that Monday morning, Jesus and the twelve left Bethany, where they had spent the night, and walked up the Mount of Olives, heading for Jerusalem. As they passed Bethphage—the name of which means house of figs—Jesus departed the path and approached a solitary fig tree growing in a patch of rocky ground at the side of the road.

Of all the regions in Palestine, this was among the best for growing figs. Spring breezes blew up from the Geba Valley toward Jerusalem, warming Bethphage at the top of Olivet. As a result, fig trees in Bethphage blossomed earlier and, some claimed, bore sweeter fruit than any other trees in Judea. Back in Galilee, Jesus knew, the fig trees would not give their fruit for another two months. But high on the hills around Jerusalem, the figs of Bethphage were ready to be picked.

Jesus was hungry. Walking to the tree, he brushed back the leaves, looking for a ripened fig. But as he parted the branches, looking within, he found no fruit on the tree. "Nothing but leaves," he said.

Throughout the Scriptures, the nation of Israel was compared to a fig tree, a people among whom the fruit of righteousness was to be cultivated to the glory of God. Jesus, the promised Messiah, had come to the children of Israel to harvest their fruits, but instead he had found nothing but leaves.

Jesus backed away from the lowly tree and spoke to it, saying, "May no one ever eat fruit from you again, even until forever."

The apostles discussed among themselves the meaning of his curse on the fig tree as they continued on their way to Jerusalem. Upon entering the Temple, they were again confronted by the marketplace atmosphere they had encountered on their first visit in the company of Jesus three years earlier. Again, birds and livestock were being sold for sacrificing, and Roman coinage was being changed at exorbitant rates for *kosher* currency.

Jesus knew that the merchants who tied their money bags to their belts were not solely to blame. Caiaphas the high priest and Annas his father-in-law also profited from each transaction. The high priest gave the merchants permission to do business in the Temple and skimmed a percentage off all sales.

"Nothing but leaves," Jesus said quietly, and no one heard him.

As he had done before, Jesus stormed through the courtyard, upsetting the displays and overturning the tables of the moneychangers. "Out!" he yelled, pointing to the gate. "It is written, 'My house will be called a house of prayer,' but you are making it a den of thieves!"

The merchants began running for the exits, while the priests, who were charged with keeping the house of God clean and pure, disappeared behind columns and into little doors that shielded them from the public. Worshipers scurried in every direction. No one challenged Jesus or moved to stop him as he tore down the animal pens and released the birds from their cages. Within minutes, the porches were cleared of priests, merchants and animals, and in their place . . .

Silence.

After a few moments, worshipers began emerging from behind colonnades and pillars. First one, then another and then several. Then the blind, the lame and the sick were brought into the Temple, and they came to Jesus quietly . . . expectantly. He placed his hands upon them and healed each of them of their afflictions.

The apostles watched in amazement as the crowds parted to allow the sick to approach him. No one spoke but Jesus, who would say gently, "Be healed." In the sacred silence, there could be heard in the Temple the soft scrape of sandals shuffling across the paved floors and the rustle of clothes of those going to and from Jesus.

Then the silence was broken by the sounds of dozens of delighted children rushing into the Temple from the streets. They flocked about him, cheering and shouting, "Hosanna to the Son of David! Hosanna to the Son of David!"

Jesus laughed out loud and a spirit of celebration returned to the Temple.

Behind closed doors, Caiaphas gathered the priests together in urgent conference. Their hearts were not moved by the scene in the courtyard, but were indignant at the shouts of the children.

"This must stop!" one priest blustered.

"Everyone is being enchanted by this man's teachings," declared another.

"Why don't we just go out there and remove Jesus by force?"

"Arrest him!"

"Not now," Caiaphas spoke up. "All the people are following him, and they won't let us get near him. We must take him when he is alone."

Jesus joyfully continued to teach and minister to the people, undisturbed by the priests and scribes. When evening came, he and the twelve departed the Temple and returned to Bethany for the night.

Early Tuesday morning, as Jesus and the apostles walked back to Jerusalem, Peter was the first to see the solitary fig tree which Jesus had found to be barren of fruit the day before. "Rabbi, look!" Peter called out. "The fig tree you cursed has withered!"

Indeed, as they approached the fig tree, they saw that it had dried up from the roots. Thomas ran to the tree and took hold of a small branch, crumpling its dry leaves in his hands.

"Fig leaves don't dry this quickly," he said to the other apostles. Others examined the dead tree and found it dry right down to the roots.

"Have faith in God," Jesus said from behind them. "If you have faith in

God you can do anything. I tell you the truth, if anyone says to this mountain, 'Go, throw yourself into the sea,' and does not doubt in his heart but believes it will happen, it will be done for him.

"Therefore I tell you, whatever you ask from God in prayer, believe that you have received it, and it will be yours."

> *Every day he was teaching at the temple. But the chief priests, the teachers of the law and the leaders among the people were trying to kill him. Yet they could not find any way to do it, because all the people hung on his words.*
>
> LUKE 19:47,48, *NIV*

chapter sixty-six

THE CHIEF CORNERSTONE REJECTED

MATTHEW 21:22 – 22:22

Early Tuesday morning, as Jesus walked again toward Jerusalem, the people swarmed about him, wanting to be near him, hoping to touch him. Like a mighty river rushing into a narrow gorge, the crowd poured through the Golden Gate into the city. Jesus led the procession to the Temple and went immediately to Solomon's Porch, a place where scholars and teachers of the Law often debated the finer points of the Law and willingly instructed anyone who would hear them. Jesus sat to teach there, and the people rushed to claim seats where they could see and hear him.

The priests and scribes were livid at the overwhelming popularity of Jesus, as the people were gathering to him right under their noses in the Temple. They had sought to keep Jesus from teaching in their Temple and had thus far failed in their attempts to deny him entry, let alone arrest him. Now they reasoned that if they could publicly humiliate Jesus and discredit him in the eyes of the people, the crowds would leave him. The priests hoped the multitudes would turn their attention to the coming Passover festivities.

So, as he taught in the Temple, the priests standing at the edge of the crowd asked so that all could hear, "By what authority are you doing these things? Who gave you authority to teach here?"

The priests had often used this ploy to discredit any would-be rabbi they wanted to run out of the Temple, and it usually worked.

Jesus knew the priests were not prepared to recognize his authority, because they had repeatedly rejected him in the past. So he answered, "I will ask you one question. If you can answer me, I will tell you by what authority I teach."

Ah, a debate! The priests coveted any opportunity to display their knowledge in public and felt they could embarrass the teacher from Nazareth in such a forum. "Ask your question," a priest said, smiling like a shark about to feed.

"John's baptism—where did it come from? Was it from heaven, or from men?" Jesus asked pointedly. "By what authority did John the Baptist do this thing?"

The priests huddled together and discussed the question among themselves, frustrated that they had allowed themselves to be put in this awkward position.

"If we say, 'From heaven,' he will ask, 'Then why didn't you believe him?'" one said.

"But if we say, 'From men,'" another interjected, "the people may rise up against us, for they all believe that John was a prophet."

Finally, they turned to Jesus and announced, "We cannot tell."

"Neither will I tell you by what authority I do these things."

Turning his attention to the crowd, Jesus told a parable. "What do you think?" he said to them. "There was a man who had two sons. He went to the first and said, 'Son, go and work today in the vineyard.'

"'I will not,' the son answered, but later he changed his mind and went.

"Then the father went to the other son and commanded the same. This son answered, 'I will, sir,' but he did not go. Which of the two did what his father wanted?"

"The first," the crowd answered.

Looking to the priests, Jesus said, "I tell you the truth, tax collectors and prostitutes will enter the kingdom of God ahead of you. For John came to show you the way of righteousness and you did not believe him. But the tax collectors and the prostitutes believed and repented."

The priests were infuriated by the suggestion that the most vile sinners would make it into the kingdom of God before them.

Jesus, seeing their fury, said to them, "Listen to another parable: There was a landowner who planted a vineyard. Then he rented the vineyard to some farmers and went away on a journey. When the harvest time approached, he sent his servants to the tenants to collect the fruit due him. But the tenants seized his servants and stoned one and killed another.

"So he sent his son to them. 'They will respect my son,' he said. But when the tenants saw the son, they took him and threw him out of the vineyard and killed him. Therefore, when the owner of the vineyard comes, what will he do to those tenants?"

Someone in the crowd shouted indignantly, "He will bring those rebels to a wretched end! And he will rent the vineyard to other tenants, who will give him his share of the crop at harvest time."

The priests said nothing, for they recognized that he was speaking against them in the parable, because they rejected outright his claims to be the Son of God.

Jesus saw that they reasoned this way and said to them, "Have you never read in the Scriptures: 'The stone the builders rejected has become the chief cornerstone. The Lord has done this, and it is marvelous in our eyes'? Therefore I tell you that the kingdom of God will be taken away from you and given to a people who will produce its fruit."

Speaking of himself as the cornerstone, Jesus said to the people, "The one who falls on this stone will be broken to pieces then restored, but the one on whom this stone falls will be crushed beyond hope."

The priests would have arrested him then and there if they could have, but they feared the wrath of the multitudes who listened and believed in him. So they left him to his teaching and went away to plot against him.

Later, the priests sent the Pharisees and Herodians with a question they felt certain would entangle Jesus in his own words and perhaps even get him in trouble with the Roman civil authorities. Usually the Pharisees, Sadducees and Herodians opposed one another because each fought for control of the religious ruling council, the Sanhedrin. But today they were bound together in cobelligerent friendship because of their mutual hatred of Jesus of Nazareth.

"Teacher," they said respectfully, carefully baiting their trap, "we know you are a man of integrity and that you teach the way of God in accordance with the truth. You aren't swayed by men, because you pay no attention to who they are. Tell us then your opinion. Is it right to pay taxes to Caesar or not? Should we as Jews pay taxes, or shouldn't we?"

If they could get Jesus to advocate withholding the tax from the hated Romans, they could have him arrested by Roman soldiers for fomenting a rebellion. Or if he said they must pay the taxes, he would alienate his followers and they would desert him, leaving him vulnerable.

Jesus shook his head and said to them, "You hypocrites! Why are you trying to trap me? Bring me the coin used for paying the tax."

A Herodian instantly produced a Roman coin, holding it between his thumb and forefinger. Jesus didn't take the coin but asked, "Whose portrait is on this coin? And whose inscription?"

"Caesar's," the man answered. "Tiberius Caesar, son of Augustus."

Jesus smiled, then answered, "Give to Caesar the things that are Caesar's, and give to God the things that are God's."

And no one was able to answer Him a word, nor from that day on did anyone dare question Him anymore.

MATTHEW 22:46

chapter sixty—seven

JESUS TELLS OF THE LAST DAYS

MATTHEW 24:1 – 25:13

Toward the end of the same day, Jesus sat with Peter, James and John on the steps by the Temple treasury, looking out on the ebb and flow of worshipers, seemingly searching for someone in particular.

Alongside him were thirteen large, brass, trumpet-shaped containers into which offerings were received. The bell of each horn, where money was to be deposited, clanged loudly as coins were dropped into the chest. The greater amount of money that was contributed, the louder the sound and the greater the attention paid to the giver of the gift. A rich man came near and slowly, ostentatiously poured a bag of coins into one of the horns, announcing to everyone in the Temple with a tremendous *clatter, clang, zing, ping* and *bing* that he was making an immense offering.

Then Jesus saw the one for whom he waited. A widow clothed in black mourner's garb crept toward the offering box, ignored and unseen by most of the crowd. She held in her hands two *perutahs*—two minuscule coins—the smallest amount she could lawfully contribute.

All she had were two mites.

She crept inconspicuously toward the treasury, as though she were ashamed to mingle with the rich. The widow glanced about her and when she thought no one was looking, she humbly gave her two mites.

Jesus did not speak words of encouragement to the widow, for he could see she walked by faith. But he turned to his closest companions and said, "Truly, this poor widow has given more than all the rest, for in her poverty, she put in all that she had."

About this same time, as the sun dipped towards the horizon, several Greeks approached the apostle Philip in the Court of the Gentiles. "Sir, we wish to see Jesus," they said to him.

Philip assured them he would try to arrange the meeting and excused himself to speak with Andrew. Together, Andrew and Philip found Jesus and told him that a group of Gentiles were asking to see him.

"Even the Gentiles are drawn to you, Lord," said John, who was also there with James and Peter.

"The hour is come that the Son of Man should be glorified," Jesus responded.

John and Andrew looked at each other, hoping this statement referred to the establishment of his kingdom on earth. But somehow, they knew this was not what he meant.

Jesus knew his disciples were frightened when he talked about his death, so he said to them, "Unless a grain of wheat falls to the ground and dies, it remains only a single seed. But if it dies, it will produce much grain. When I am lifted up from the earth, I will draw people from all nations to me."

The day was coming to an end, as was his ministry. No one in the Temple that day knew they had seen the last public ministry of Jesus. He led his apostles out of Jerusalem, the Temple gate clanging shut behind them.

Jesus made his way through the Kidron Valley, climbing past the Garden of Gethsemane to the top of Olivet. The day had been unseasonably hot and the crowds demanding. Debating the religious leaders had taken its toll. Jesus was tired.

A flat, white limestone shelf jutted out from the grassy meadow, inviting Jesus and his apostles to rest. When they sat, Jesus looked back at Jerusalem, the City of God.

Peter pointed out the Temple proclaiming, "Magnificent! The Temple is exquisite, the most beautiful thing on earth."

But Jesus did not revel in the sight. He said to them, "Do you see those buildings? I say to you that soon not one stone shall be left upon another. Every stone will be thrown down, and Jerusalem will be destroyed."

This piqued the curiosity of the apostles. Peter asked, "Tell us, when will these things take place?"

John, the youngest of the apostles, had thought often about what Jesus had said about returning to judge the world, and he wondered if his return might be connected to the destruction of Jerusalem. "What will be the sign of your coming?" he asked.

James rarely said much, but he was concerned about all the prophecies in Scripture concerning the end of the world. He had no interest in seeing falling stars, earthquakes, the moon turning to blood . . . . In spite of his fears, or perhaps because of them, James asked, "What will be the sign of the end of the world?"

Jesus turned away from Jerusalem and spoke to them concerning the last days. "Take heed that no one deceives you. For many will come in my name, saying 'I am the Christ,' and will try to lead my people astray. You will hear of wars and rumors of wars, but these are only the beginning of the end.

"Nation will rise against nation, kingdom against kingdom. And there will be famines, epidemics and numerous earthquakes. All these are the beginning of the horrors. My followers will be tortured and killed, and they will be hated all over the world because they believe in me. Because sin will be rampant in the world, many will fall into sin and the love of many will grow cold. But those who endure to the end will be saved.

"The gospel of my kingdom will be preached in all the world and to all the nations, and then the end will come.

"Watch and be ready, for when you see all these things, you will know that the end is near, right at the door. Yet no one knows the day or hour of my coming, not even the angels in heaven, only the Father."

When Jesus had finished saying all these things,
he said to his disciples, "As you know, the Passover is two days away—
and the Son of Man will be handed over to be crucified."

MATTHEW 26:1,2

chapter sixty-eight

THE PRICE OF BETRAYAL

MATTHEW 26:14-16

Nervously, Judas Iscariot stood in the Temple at the place called the Court of Israel, where penitent Jews waited in line for a priest to offer sacrifice in atonement for their sins. A vain man, the apostle called Judas smoothed the wrinkles out of his tunic and ran his fingers through his hair and beard to comb them. All who saw him on this Wednesday afternoon could see he was agitated.

Judas shifted his weight from one foot to the other and back again. He wasn't thinking about sacrifices or atonement; he was uncomfortable in the presence of the enemies of his teacher.

Jesus was supposed to deliver us from the Romans, the confused and frightened apostle said to himself. *I followed him because he was supposed to be the Christ, the Messiah. Now he tells us he is going to die!* The enemies of Jesus were powerful men, and Judas did not want to find himself at their mercy. *If they are willing to destroy an innocent man for his teaching, what will they do to me for following him?*

Judas had heard the priests were looking for an opportunity to arrest Jesus. He had conceived of a plan to save his own skin by handing Jesus over to the Jewish leaders and in the process make some money on the transaction. He needed the money and it would not be the first time he had resorted to underhanded measures to obtain it.

Judas had been taking money all along from the money bag. He justified his actions as "pay" for the extra responsibility of overseeing the money, paying their taxes and dealing with merchants. Judas had been using the money he took from the bag to make payment on a small piece of land known as Potter's Field, where the claylike soil was unfit for growing anything except olive trees and grapevines. He had always dreamed of owning a little farm outside Jerusalem.

Probably no harm will come to Jesus, reasoned Judas. *He has escaped from angry mobs trying to stone him; he can escape from the Sanhedrin.*

His nervousness showed as Judas whispered to a Levite official, "I am one of the followers of Jesus." Judas looked about furtively to be sure no one overheard him. "I must talk to your superiors about the Nazarene."

The Levite whisked Judas through a door, down a hall and into the caucus room where Levites gathered before appearing in public. After greetings were exchanged and the Jewish leaders had confirmed his identity, Judas announced to them, "I can help you capture Jesus."

Smiles broke out all around, broadening the faces of the priests as they nodded to one another in gleeful anticipation. This was the opportunity they had been waiting for.

Judas explained his plan. "Jesus is popular and you cannot expect to take him when he is surrounded by thousands of followers. We are going to celebrate the Passover meal in Jerusalem tomorrow—just the twelve of us and the teacher. After the meal, Jesus will go to pray. I will lead you to him."

One of the priests asked, smiling, "What can we do to assist you in this?"

What Judas wanted was money to pay off the remainder of the land and live out his days in peace. But Judas knew he couldn't ask for a bribe; it was against the Law the priests had vowed to uphold. He had thought about the plan for several days—now was the time to see if it would work. "I carry the money bag for Jesus and his disciples. I am in charge of providing for the

poor and indigent," he lied. "What are you willing to give me for the poor if
I hand Jesus over to you?"

"Will thirty pieces of silver meet the needs of the poor?" the priest
asked, naming the legal price for a slave according to Hebrew law.

Judas nodded.

The priest motioned to an aide, who instantly left the room by another
small door. Shortly he returned, holding a leather sack with a small leather
thong tied tightly about the bag. The aide offered it to the priest, who shook
his head; he wouldn't touch it. The priest nodded for the bag to be placed
on the table in front of Judas.

Then the priest said, "The Sanhedrin counts it a privilege to contribute
to the poor." He smiled at the other leaders, who returned his grin. "Please
take the thirty pieces of silver as our gift to the poor. May your mission suc-
cessfully recapture the hope of Israel."

Judas left the room, holding tightly to the bag, tucking it under his
tunic away from prying eyes. The bag itself would not arouse suspicion
toward him; many in the Temple carried bags and packages. But as Judas
left through the Golden Gate, the money he clutched so tightly already had
death's stranglehold on him.

*[Judas] consented, and watched for an opportunity to hand Jesus
over to them when no crowd was present.*

LUKE 22:6, *NIV*

chapter sixty-nine

WASHING THEIR FEET

JOHN 13:1-8
LUKE 22:15-20

"Who gets the seat of honor next to Jesus?" James the Less asked as he
climbed the steps with the other apostles toward the narrow door that led
into the upper room of the house.

"Not you," Andrew said to the laughter of the others. "Anyone who aspires to the best seat doesn't deserve it!"

Peter and John busied themselves with final preparations for the Passover meal, working out the details with the master of the house. Until the group arrived this evening, only Peter and John had known the location of the meal. The day before, Jesus had sent the two of them into Jerusalem to prepare a place for this special occasion.

When they had asked Jesus whether he wanted to have the meal at an inn or a private residence, he said to them, "Go into the city, and you will meet a man carrying a pitcher of water. Follow him to his house and say to him, 'Our teacher says, "My appointed time is near. I am going to celebrate the Passover with my disciples at your house."' Then you shall ask him, 'Where is the guest room where we may eat the Passover meal?' Then he will show you a large, furnished upper room."

Peter and John were accustomed to the fact that Jesus had a way of knowing such things, so it did not come as much of a surprise to them when the young man, Mark, agreed to give them the use of his mother's home. "Make your preparations there," Jesus had told them, "but tell no one where we will be."

Peter and John had sacrificed the requisite lamb, which was prepared for the meal. The wine, cakes of unleavened bread and the ceremonial bitter herbs were also prepared.

When all had arrived, Philip announced, "The twelve are all here, Lord."

The apostles milled about, reluctant to take a place at the table. Although they had laughed about who would get the honored seat next to Jesus, there had in fact been a sharp discussion over who was greatest among the apostles. When Jesus asked them what they had been discussing, they had been too embarrassed to say anything.

Jesus had then told them, "Kings and rulers lord it over their subjects, and those who wield authority over them call themselves 'benefactors.' But you are not like that. Instead, the leaders among you will be like those who serve. He who desires to be first among you shall be last and the servant of all."

Now they were hesitant, unsure whether they should seek the spot near Jesus or the seat farthest from him. But Jesus settled the matter by seating himself and saying, "Judas, you sit to my left. John, you shall be at my right."

A broad smile broke through Judas' black beard, neatly trimmed for this evening's banquet. The apostles generally approved of the selection of Judas; he was respected among them for his ability to manage the money.

Young John, however, was a less than popular choice. His mother had recently asked Jesus to grant her two sons to sit at his right and his left in the coming kingdom. Her request, though denied, had perturbed the other apostles.

"Sit wherever you like," Jesus said to the others, and they quickly chose their seats.

"With great anticipation, I have desired to eat this Passover meal with you before I suffer," Jesus said to them. Then he took a cup and spoke thanksgiving over it, saying, "Blessed are you, Lord our God, who has created the fruit of the vine!"

Jesus rose to retrieve the pitcher and basin, then brought them to the table. He took off his outer coat and wrapped a towel around his waist. Jesus set the basin on the floor and poured water from the pitcher into the basin. The apostles glanced at one another, uncertain as to what they were supposed to do. They had expected to wash their *hands* at this point in the meal.

Jesus knelt before Judas Iscariot . . . and washed his feet in the basin. Then he dried them with the towel which was around his waist. From his knees, Jesus looked up into Judas' eyes, looking for repentance or even a tinge of regret for the act of betrayal to which Judas had committed himself. But all Jesus saw was the arrogance of a man who thought his sin was hidden and unknown.

When Jesus knelt where Simon Peter sat, the big fisherman leapt to his feet and shouted, "Lord, why are you going to wash my feet?"

"You do not realize now what I am doing," Jesus said to Peter, "but later you will understand."

"No! You will never wash my feet!" Peter blurted out, knowing himself to be unworthy of this act of utter humility from the Messiah himself.

"If I do not wash you," Jesus answered him, "you'll have no part with me."

Peter had not meant to defy Jesus. Nevertheless, he had once again spoken before thinking, protesting something he did not understand instead of obeying his master's direction. "Then, Lord," Peter tried to make amends, "do not wash only my feet, but my hands and my head as well!"

Jesus said to Peter, "A person who's had a bath needs only to wash his feet when coming in from the street. But you are clean." Jesus then glanced at Judas and said to them all, "Although one of you is *not* clean."

After Jesus washed the feet of each of the twelve, he put his robe on, then returned to his seat. The apostles sat unspeaking, stunned by their teacher's remarkable act of humility.

"Do you understand what I have done for you?" Jesus asked, breaking the silence. None looked him in the eye, nor would they look at each other. "You have called me 'teacher' and 'Lord,' and rightly so, for that is who I am. Since I am your teacher and have washed your feet, you ought to wash one another's feet. I have given you this example to follow.

"No servant is greater than his master, nor is a messenger greater than the one who sent him. Now that you know to do the things I have shown you, you will be blessed if you do them."

When he had finished washing their feet,
he put on his clothes and returned to his place.
JOHN 13:12, NIV

chapter seventy

"IS IT I?"

JOHN 13:13-30

"Though I have washed you, not all of you are clean," Jesus said to the twelve gathered in the upper room. "I know those I have chosen. But tonight will fulfill the scripture: 'He who shares my bread has lifted up his heel against me.'"

The apostles of Jesus had no inkling of the drama playing out before them that evening, but they were acutely aware that the festive occasion had suddenly taken on a dark and sinister tone. Jesus was clearly troubled by something they didn't know.

"I tell you the truth," he said to them, "one of you is going to betray me this night."

To a man the twelve braced their shoulders, shrinking back from the table. Several of them, including Judas, shook their heads in denial, babbling their protestations. Judas did not allow his expression to betray his intentions. Even after all he had seen in his travels with Jesus, he could not believe there was any way for the teacher to know of his meeting with the Sanhedrin. But to be sure, amid the hubbub he leaned over to his teacher to whisper innocently, "Teacher, is it I?" The sorry lie slipped easily off his tongue.

The apostles saw anguish in the face of Jesus. They nervously studied one another, looking for a sign that would brand one of them as a traitor. Peter motioned across the table for young John to ask Jesus for the identity of the betrayer. John, sitting on the right of Jesus, leaned back against his shoulder and whispered, "Lord, who is it?"

Jesus did not answer immediately. The other apostles turned their attention to him, all waiting for a clue, all wanting an answer to the question "Lord, is it I?" Jesus would not openly accuse Judas in front of these men who were fiercely loyal to him. Knowing this was the Father's will, Jesus would do nothing now to halt the chain of events that had been set into motion. Judas would be allowed to complete his mission.

So Jesus announced to the group, "The one who will betray me is the one to whom I will give the bread after I dip it in the stew."

Jesus broke the unleavened bread in two, putting aside half for use after the supper. Then Jesus placed the broken bread into a dish and held the dish aloft, saying, "This is the bread of misery which our Fathers ate in the land of Egypt. All that are hungry, come and eat. All that are needy, come, keep the Passover."

Sitting before him was a large bowl of lamb stew, the traditional meal of Passover. According to tradition, the master of the feast took the bread, broke it and dipped it into the lamb stew, then served first the guest of honor. Judas was in the place of honor to the left of Jesus. He would receive the bread first. So no one saw anything out of the ordinary when Jesus broke off a morsel of bread, formed a small cup in the bread, then dipped it into the lamb stew and handed it to Judas. None of them—except Judas—recognized the sign of which Jesus had spoken. Now Judas knew in his heart that Jesus knew he was the betrayer.

After Jesus served the guest of honor, he continued the process of serving the others. Judas instinctively reached down to touch the thirty pieces of silver tied to his sash; he could feel the sash tightening about him like a hangman's noose. Guilt and shame flooded his soul momentarily, but he shook off his guilt to smile tentatively and raised the bread to the other apostles in a toasting gesture. Judas hesitated, then with an air of defiance, he tore a chunk from the bread with his teeth, signaling the others to begin eating. At that moment, he surrendered his soul to Satan, and his heart turned black. If ever there were any flicker of light in the candle of Judas' life, it had been snuffed out once and for all. There was no retreat now.

Jesus whispered to him, "What you have to do—do quickly."

Judas arose, his face stone hard. Without looking back, he snatched the treasury bag of money that belonged to the apostles, clutching it tightly by the throat as one might squeeze the life out of a young bird. Then he slipped out the door, stopping only a moment in the doorway as if reconsidering his course of action.

Peter said to his brother Andrew, "Where is Judas going?"

Andrew said, "He had the money bag with him. Perhaps he has gone for more provisions for the feast. Or maybe he's gone to buy for the poor. It's almost time for *Chagigah*."

The great Temple gates were opened at midnight to begin early the offering of the Chagigah, a required festival sacrifice that accompanied Passover. Because many gave to charities at this offering, the poor thronged outside the Temple gates to receive their gifts.

As Judas hesitated in the doorway, he noted that the last trace of sunlight had fled from the sky and the moon had not yet risen. It was a sinblack night. Judas stepped out into the darkness.

As soon as Judas had taken the bread, he went out. And it was night.
JOHN 13:30, NIV

chapter seventy-one

A NEW SUPPER

MATTHEW 26:26-29
JOHN 13:36 – 14:27

Jesus had come to the Passover supper in the upper room with mixed emotions. Though this feast was the high point of the Jewish year, this would be his last supper, and he would spend it with those who meant the most to him.

After they had finished eating, Jesus stood and took the portion of unleavened bread he had set aside earlier. He blessed the bread and broke it, saying, "Take this and eat. This is my body which is broken for you. Do this in remembrance of me."

Jesus took the portion, passed it across the empty chair where Judas had sat. Andrew took it, broke off a part and ate. The bread was passed from man to man, each taking a portion and eating it.

The apostles were uncertain what Jesus meant when he said, "This is my body," but they knew and understood the symbolism of the unleavened bread. Leaven, or yeast, was a sign of sin. The Passover bread had no yeast because yeast did not have time to rise before the children of Israel departed from Egypt with haste when Pharaoh finally gave in to God's demands to "Let my people go."

According to the Jewish customs, the cup of blessing was filled at the close of the supper. Jesus took this cup, lifted it heavenward and gave thanks. Then he looked around at the men who followed him and said, "This cup is the new covenant in my blood, which is poured out for many for the forgiveness of sins. As often as you drink it, you will remember me."

Jesus handed the cup to Andrew on his left, and said, "Drink from it, all of you." And each apostle drank from the cup.

Then Jesus said to them, "As often as you eat this bread and drink this cup, you will testify of my death until I come again."

Then he taught them one last time before his death. "My children, I will be with you only a little longer, and then I must go away. And where I am going, you cannot come.

"A new commandment I give to you: Love one another as I have loved you. By this all men will know that you are my disciples."

Peter couldn't keep quiet any longer. He had heard enough of this talk about going away and about death. "Lord, where are you going?" he demanded to know.

"Where I am going, you cannot follow now, but you will follow later," Jesus said.

Peter boldly answered him, "Why can't I follow you now? I will lay down my life for you!" No one among the apostles doubted this was true; Peter was fiercely devoted to Jesus.

But Jesus didn't respond at once. He let Peter's words echo in the upper chamber, then said, "Will you really lay down your life for me? I tell you now, you will deny me three times this night before the rooster crows!"

Peter was shocked. "Even if I have to die with you, I will never disown you!" he declared, and the other apostles nodded their own resoluteness of commitment to their master.

Jesus shook his head, saying, "Peter, Satan would sift you like wheat. This very night you will fall away, but I have prayed for you, Peter, that your faith will not fail. And when you have turned back to me, you will strengthen your brothers."

"Do not let your hearts be troubled," Jesus said to the others. "You believe in God; believe also in me. In my Father's house are many mansions, and I am going there to prepare a place for you. Then I will come back to take you to be with me where I am. You know where I am going and you know the way."

Thomas asked, "Lord, we don't know where you are going, so how can we know the way?"

Jesus said, "I am the way, the truth and the life. No one comes to the Father except through me."

Philip spoke up. "Lord, show us the Father and that will keep us going while you are away."

Jesus answered, "Do you not know me, Philip, even after I've been with you such a long time? Anyone who has seen me has seen the Father. How can you say, 'Show us the Father'? I am in the Father, and he is in me. The words I speak to you do not come just from me, but also from the Father.

"Believe me when I say this, or at least believe the evidence from the miracles I have done. I tell you the truth, anyone who believes in me will do what I have done. And he will do even greater things than these. I will do whatever you ask in my name, so that the Son may bring glory to the Father. Ask me for anything in my name, and I will do it."

"I will not speak with you much longer, for the prince of this world is coming. He has no hold on me, but the world must learn that I love the Father and that I do exactly what my Father has commanded me. Come now; let us leave."

JOHN 14:30, *NIV*

chapter seventy-two

NO ONE PRAYED WITH HIM IN THE GARDEN

MATTHEW 26:36-46

The moon refused to show itself, shrouded by dark clouds looming in the east, though the sky over Jerusalem was clear. The apostles struggled to distinguish the garden path by starlight.

"If the master did not come here so often," Thomas said, "we would never find the garden in the darkness."

They knew the way because they came often with Jesus to pray in the Garden of Gethsemane. Now he strode toward the garden without a misstep, even as the apostles stumbled over stones and tree roots, unable to see the ground in front of them. Each was lost in his own thoughts, haunted by Jesus' dire predictions that each of them would forsake him before the night was through.

The city of Jerusalem slept silently behind them. Water gurgled in the creek of Kidron below them. The April rains had freshened the springs and the lapping brook was the only sound that broke the silence of the night.

Off to their right appeared the vague silhouettes of a grove of olive trees. Because their gnarled trunks made for excellent seats, Jesus directed the apostles, "Sit here," as they entered the garden. "I will go ahead to pray."

He took Peter, James and John with him, disappearing into the darkness. It was late in the evening and the apostles were tired and growing cold. They wrapped their tunics about them to ward off the damp chill. Soon they were sleeping propped against the olive trees.

Deeper in the garden, Jesus spoke to his three closest disciples, clearly in anguish. "I am overwhelmed with grief," he said, "crushed almost to the point of death."

Jesus instructed the three, "Stay here and keep watch with me as I pray." But even as Jesus walked away, the three men felt their eyes growing heavy and their shoulders sagging.

About a stone's throw away, Jesus fell to his knees to pray. Visions of the cross bore down on him; he knew the intense pain and agony that awaited him on the morrow. He cried out to his Father as the darkness pressed in on his Spirit from all sides. *My Father . . .*, the words poured from Jesus' heart like water from a pitcher, *. . . if it is possible, I don't want to drink this cup of suffering.*

Jesus' agony was so intense, he could no longer remain on his knees. He fell with his face to the ground . . . his fists clenched . . . his voice tightened. He repeated his plea. *Father, if you are willing, please take this cup from me.*

The garden usually talked to him at night. Jesus often heard the hoot of an owl . . . the coo of a dove . . . the unusual whistle of the night birds. But tonight silence surrounded him. There wasn't even a breeze to rustle the leaves. The garden seemed stillborn.

Then off in the distance came a low rumble. A spring storm moved down the Jordan Valley. Jesus did not see the lightning, but he heard the groan of heaven. One by one, the stars were extinguished by the fast-moving clouds. On his recent vigils in the garden, Jesus had enjoyed the light of the moon and stars, but tonight heaven seemed shut up.

Why? Jesus' heart cried out.

Disturbed by the distant thunder, Jesus rose and returned to where he had left Peter, James and John. There he found them sleeping soundly. He knew the weakness of being physically tired, but was disappointed that their professed love had not driven them to prayer. He shook Peter's shoulder to ask, "Could you men not stay awake and keep watch with me for even one hour?"

The three were embarrassed and could say nothing. Peter hung his head; John looked off into the distance.

"Keep alert," Jesus warned them. "Watch and pray or temptation will overcome you." The need to continue in prayer overwhelmed him and he turned to walk away. Looking back, he said to them, "Your spirit is willing, but the flesh is weak. Watch and pray."

Jesus returned once more to the spot where he had knelt and prayed, *My Father, if it's not possible for this cup of suffering to be taken away unless I first drink it . . . then may your will be done.*

He knew that in the morning there would be humiliation, pain, torture and finally death by the worst form of execution possible, yet he yielded to the Father's greater plan. There was no getting around it. He would have to go through the cross to get back to his home in heaven.

My Father, Jesus continued to pray, *my Father, why must I go through the cross?* Each time he came to the same conclusion: *Nevertheless, not my will, but yours be done.*

Jesus heard the sound of snoring and went again to his disciples, finding them sound asleep. "Why can't you keep your eyes open?" Jesus asked, but none of them moved.

Again, Jesus was overcome with anguish. He walked away from those whom he had called "friends." Lesser men had faced execution without a whimper, but lesser men did not wrestle for the souls of mankind. Lesser men did not understand what it meant to suffer the wrath of God.

Again, collapsing under the load of grief, Jesus fell to the ground. Clutching his fists and tightening his every muscle, Jesus struggled with fear. Drops of blood beaded on his forehead, running down into his beard. Perspiration dampened his whole body as he prayed with a ferocity unknown to any man before or since. His face appeared to have been bloodied by an opponent.

Satan his adversary gloated over the prostrate form of Jesus, certain that ultimate victory was at hand. Then an angel from heaven came to Jesus and renewed his strength, and Satan withdrew for the moment.

After a time, Jesus gathered himself and returned to his three most trusted disciples, the three who loved him most. They were asleep.

Then He came to His disciples and said to them, "Are you still sleeping and resting? Behold, the hour is at hand, and the Son of Man is being betrayed into the hands of sinners. Rise, let us be going. See, My betrayer is at hand."

MATTHEW 26:45,46

chapter seventy-three

ARRESTED

LUKE 22:47-53
JOHN 18:1-11

Jesus heard the distant voices of men coming down the road out of Jerusalem. A parade of torches and lanterns could be seen through the trees. But this was not a festive band on a pleasant evening excursion. These were hard men on a cruel mission. Jesus heard the low growl of men talking among themselves. Clearly they were intent on capturing him in the Garden of Gethsemane.

Jesus recognized the voice of Judas Iscariot amid the sound of talking and clamor. "The one I kiss is the man you want. Arrest him," came the unmistakable voice, and Jesus was again overcome with grief at Judas' betrayal.

"Why are you still sleeping?" Jesus awakened Peter, James and John. He announced, "Look, my hour is here, and the Son of Man is betrayed into the hands of sinners. Rise now, and let us go. Here comes my betrayer!"

Judas led an odd gathering of Roman soldiers, Temple guards, chief priests and Levites. He had assured them they could find Jesus praying in the Garden of Gethsemane. So the Temple guards and the Levites were issued torches and the troops made their way out of the city through the darkness to search the garden. As they passed beneath the olive trees, eerie shadows danced on the men's faces.

The soldiers discovered the eight sleeping apostles and awakened them, demanding to know Jesus' whereabouts. When the mob reached the clearing, they saw Jesus with Peter, James and John. Suddenly all voices were quieted; the soldiers' armor quit clanking as they stood transfixed by his presence. *Is this the man?* they thought. *Could he be so dangerous we were called out in the middle of the night to arrest him?* They looked beyond him to see three rugged fishermen, one of whom was carrying a sword, but Jesus was clearly in authority over them.

Then Judas gave them the prearranged signal. Stepping forward to embrace Jesus, he said, "Greetings, Rabbi!" his voice expressing mock surprise. Then he kissed Jesus on the cheek.

"A kiss, Judas?" Jesus looked beyond his eyes, into his conscience. "How can you betray the Son of Man with a kiss?"

The silence now broken, Peter stepped forward drawing his sword to ask, "Lord, should we fight?"

The Roman soldiers didn't move; they were not intimidated by this motley crew of fishermen and religious zealots. They had smelled the blood of battle and knew that an untrained swordsman couldn't stand against their shields and armor.

In one swift motion, Peter slashed at one of the servants of the high priest whose name was Malchus. In his rage, Peter was ready to kill, striking a blow at the head of Malchus. But Peter missed the center of his head, only cutting off his ear.

"Stop!" Jesus called, cutting off the screams of young Malchus. "No more of this!" Jesus commanded, and the soldiers who had stepped forward to retaliate halted their advance.

No one moved as Jesus picked up the bloody ear and replaced it to the head of the servant. When Jesus removed his hand, the ear was completely restored.

Then he rebuked Peter, saying, "Put your sword back in its place, for all who live by the sword shall die by the sword. Don't you know I can call on my Father, who will at once put at my disposal more than twelve legions of angels?"

Then Jesus turned to the priests to ask, "Do you think I am some dangerous criminal?" Jesus assessed the crowd. "Am I leading a rebellion, that you have come with swords and clubs to arrest me?"

There was no answer.

A priest turned and nodded at the soldiers and they stepped toward Jesus. As the soldiers made their move, the apostles inconspicuously melted into the crowd, slowly moving away from the light into the darkness. Jesus stepped forward to meet the soldiers, returning their steely glare with a look of love. He asked, "Who is it you want?"

"Jesus of Nazareth," the captain of the guard replied.

"I am he," came his simple response. And as he said this, the soldiers were driven backwards to the ground, as if they had been standing on a chariot when the horse bolted into a run, throwing them backwards.

"Who are you looking for?" Jesus repeated his question, as the soldiers righted themselves to regain their defiant position.

"I told you that I am he," Jesus said. "If you are looking for me, then let the men who are with me go."

The captain looked to the chief priest, who answered, "We have no interest in them . . . at this time."

Then one by one, the apostles of Jesus slipped away into the darkness, through the olive trees of Gethsemane. When they were out of sight and sound, they began running.

Then the detachment of soldiers with its commander and the Jewish officials arrested Jesus. They bound him and brought him first to Annas, who was the father-in-law of Caiaphas, the high priest that year.

JOHN 18:12,13, NIV

chapter seventy-four

INTERROGATION

JOHN 18:12-27

The tramp of Roman troops echoed through the narrow cobblestone streets of Jerusalem in the early morning hours of Friday, just after midnight. A few light sleepers watched from their windows as the soldiers led their prisoner toward the upper city and the luxurious palace of Annas. The prisoner was lean and strong but offered no resistance. He was bound with leather straps. Levitical guards from the Temple followed after the hardened Roman soldiers like little dogs chasing a wagon. *Who is this criminal?* the onlookers wondered.

What is his crime?

Annas was the power behind the office of the high priest, even though Rome had removed him from office because he would not fully cooperate with them. In Annas' place, Rome had appointed his son-in-law, Caiaphas. But the Jews still considered Annas to be God's chosen instrument for the office. To them, Annas was ordained for life and few recognized Caiaphas as long as Annas was alive.

The silver-haired Annas had cold, calculating serpent's eyes that seemed never to blink or vacillate. Annas made decisions, and Caiaphas carried them out. Annas had acquired his immense wealth from the Temple booths, which Jesus had twice cleared from the Temple, much to his consternation. Although a Levite by birth, Annas had aligned himself with the Sadducees, who denied the existence of miracles. Jesus would certainly be found a charlatan as well as a troublemaker under the scrutiny of Annas' unwavering eyes.

Jesus stood bound before Annas. The deposed high priest didn't offer to untie the prisoner—something that should have been done in a religious hearing. But they had not come together to discuss what was right under the Law of Moses, nor were they concerned about the alleged crimes that Jesus had committed against the state. They were there to plot his execution.

Annas whispered to his attaché, "Dismiss the soldiers as quickly as possible." This was done, and the Roman soldiers returned to their quarters.

Dawn was coming, and Annas and the priests needed to agree on a criminal charge that would be lodged against Jesus when brought before a Roman court. Because the Romans did not allow the Jewish officials to exercise capital punishment, only the Romans could execute Jesus. Therefore, the charge must be one that would be worthy of swift execution, especially because the Sabbath was fast approaching. But when Annas interrogated Jesus regarding his teachings, Jesus would not answer his questions.

"I have spoken openly to the world," Jesus replied. "I taught in synagogues and at the Temple, where all the Jews come together. I said nothing in secret. So why question me? Ask those who heard me. Surely they know what I said."

When Jesus said this, one of the Temple guards nearby struck him in the face. "Is this the way you answer a high priest?" he demanded.

"If I have said something evil," Jesus said, "then tell me what evil I have spoken. But if I spoke the truth, then why do you strike me?"

Annas had heard enough. Any official charges would have to be made by his son-in-law Caiaphas and the Sanhedrin anyway, so Annas sent Jesus to Caiaphas' palace down the hill and summoned the Sanhedrin.

As the Temple guard led Jesus, bound, toward Caiaphas' quarters, Simon Peter and the youngest apostle John fell in behind the procession through the darkened streets. John was known to the servants of the high priest and would be able to talk his way into the house to keep watch on the proceedings, but he didn't know about Peter. At Caiaphas' house, the Temple guard entered with Jesus, but the young woman at the door kept the others out.

John recognized the girl and approached her, saying, "You know me." John put his face to the lanterns. "My father is Zebedee who sells fish to Caiaphas." She allowed John to enter the house. She would later allow Peter to wait in the courtyard.

Jesus was led up the stairs into Caiaphas' second-floor chamber. The younger Caiaphas bore little resemblance to his father-in-law in stature or demeanor. Caiaphas was jittery, high-strung and explosive. Rome had placed him in office because he was not decisive; Caiaphas could be manipulated, whereas Annas could not. As Jesus was brought into the room, the high priest babbled, "I have you now, Galilean! Your fate is now in my hands."

Jubilantly, Caiaphas bragged to the Temple guards about the capture of Jesus as though he had done it single-handedly, while Jesus stood motionless before them. He wanted to summarily order an execution, but Rome had taken the death penalty from the Jews. He could excommunicate Jesus from the religious community, but what good was that? He would gladly kill Jesus with his bare hands, but his position wouldn't allow him. Caiaphas stood perplexed, his regal high-priest garments woven with gold glistening in the candlelight. He had all the symbols of office, but Caiaphas was only a hollow bureaucrat. Caiaphas felt essentially powerless against Jesus of Nazareth.

Upon entering the courtyard, Peter gravitated toward the red glow of a char-coal fire and its blue flame that threw shadows against the courtyard walls. Several bearded men—servants, guards and lesser officials—huddled around the fire to warm their faces. Peter hunkered in between two men, holding out his chilled hands to the flame. The coals sizzled and the flame flickered, driving away a bit of the damp spring night. Peter looked up to the inner chamber on the second floor. He knew Jesus was up there, but what could he do for him?

The young woman at the gate was busy; members of the Sanhedrin kept arriving in twos and threes in answer to Annas' summons. Walking quickly, they mounted the stairs to the upper chamber.

The cold in Peter's body ran much deeper than his flesh; his soul was chilled to the core. Peter attempted to blend in with the other men at the fire, appearing to be indifferent to what was going on. Then he was spotted by the young woman at the door as she admitted the last of the Sanhedrin to arrive. She said to him, "You were with Jesus of Nazareth, the man they have on trial upstairs."

"Not me . . . ," Peter protested. "I don't know him."

But she continued to stare at him.

Flustered, Peter shouted at her, "I don't understand why you are saying this!"

The men around the fire paid no attention to the woman or to her accusation. Also, they paid little attention to Peter's passionate denial. They didn't care. They sat stoic, their faces to the fire. Peter looked away from the woman and back into the fire.

Now the chief priests, the elders, and all the council sought
false testimony against Jesus to put Him to death.
MATTHEW 26:59

chapter seventy-five

PETER DENIES JESUS
MATTHEW 26:57-75

Confusion reigned upstairs in the palace of Caiaphas. Dawn was rapidly approaching. The chill of the evening would soon give way to the warmth of the spring morning, and those gathered in the second-floor chamber couldn't agree on a criminal charge to bring against Jesus of Nazareth.

This was not a formal gathering of the Sanhedrin. A quorum was present, allowing them to conduct business, but the Sanhedrin had no desire to go on record that night. They didn't want the followers of this man Jesus to trace responsibility for his death back to them. Let the Romans take the blame for what happens to him, they agreed.

But proof was needed to back up any charge against Jesus if the charges were to hold water with the Roman governor, Pontius Pilate. Many council members knew someone who could bring charges against Jesus, some of whom would accept payment to make false accusations against him. Quickly, servants were dispatched to find those witnesses, arouse them and use force if necessary to persuade them to come immediately to testify against Jesus.

Members of the Sanhedrin stepped into the shadows to coerce their servants to give testimony in which they would lie about Jesus. But it didn't work. First one man would speak out against Jesus, then another would contradict his story. The false witnesses compounded the confusion of the council; rather than bringing them nearer to a legal charge against Jesus, the council broke into quarreling factions.

Jesus stood in silence before the scheming council. Caiaphas impatiently fidgeted in his seat, constantly springing to action to question the witnesses, only to fall emotionally defeated back into his chair.

Since the servants and false witnesses could not get their stories straight, some of the members of the Sanhedrin brought charges against Jesus. One of the council members stepped forward, charging, "This fellow said that he was able to destroy the Temple and build it again within three days."

Nervous laughter filled the room. They all had heard about this claim made by Jesus.

"His violent hands have been raised against the Temple of God!" the council member continued in derision. "And by some magical pretense, Jesus of Nazareth claims he can build the Temple in three days. We all know that can never happen."

Caiaphas seized the opportunity to cross-examine Jesus. "What do you say to this charge?"

When Jesus did not answer, Caiaphas lashed out at Jesus, demanding,

"Tell me who you are!"

Jesus answered, "Why do you ask me who I am? Ask your witnesses. They know what I said."

Caiaphas jumped to his feet, waving frantically at Jesus, and yelled, "I demand by the Living God: Tell us whether you are the Christ, the Son of God!" Caiaphas' words echoed in the chamber hall. No one dared speak.

As the echoes died, Jesus waited to respond.

"Yes, it is as you say." There was a collective gasp. "But I say to all of you, one day you will see the Son of Man sitting at the right hand of the Mighty One and coming on the clouds of heaven."

The majestic calm of Jesus further contributed to the emotional upheaval of Caiaphas. "Blasphemy!" the high priest cried, ripping at his gold-laced robe. "This is blasphemy!"

An attendant rushed to Caiaphas, pleading in hushed tones, "Don't rip your robe. That will disqualify you to judge the prisoner."

The Sanhedrin knew the law, that if one were pronounced guilty he could be tried on the same day that he was charged, but he could not be punished on that same day. However, in the case of blasphemy or profaning the divine name, the offender could be judged immediately. That's what they had been hoping for—immediate execution.

"Put him to death!" the high priest screamed at the top of his voice. "We don't need any further witnesses. We have heard his blasphemy! We'll charge him with blasphemy before Pilate."

The crowd muttered their agreement.

Caiaphas then brought the matter to a conclusion as required by the Sanhedrin. He asked, "What think you, gentlemen?"

All the men knew the next question Caiaphas would ask. It was the question required by law.

"For life?"

Silence.

"For death?"

"For death!" they cried.

"Then we shall recommend this sentence to our friend Pilate," smiled Caiaphas, and the members of the Sanhedrin swiftly left the chamber and disappeared into the streets of Jerusalem.

After the Sanhedrin departed, Jesus was exposed to the insults and brutality of the guards and servants at the behest of Caiaphas. They mocked Jesus, kicked him and spat on him. They covered his eyes and slapped him in the face.

"Prophesy to us, Christ," they laughed. "Who hit you?"

They then beat his face with their fists. Blood and mucus ran down his beard and onto the floor. After the dignitaries representing civilization had gone, these brutal people vented their savage nature on their defenseless victim.

Peter sat by the wall, despairing, knowing he could do nothing to stop what was happening. He had heard the cry "For death!" from the upper chamber and knew what it meant for Jesus.

Then out of the darkness stepped a Temple guard, a cousin to Malchus, the young priest whose ear Peter had cut off. This man had been in the garden and had seen Peter with Jesus. He challenged Peter, pointing to Jesus. "Didn't I see you with this man in the olive grove?"

"You are mistaken, sir," Peter said nervously. "I do not know the man."

Within the same hour, another guard stood with Peter by the fire, saying to one of his comrades, "Certainly this fellow was with him, for he is a Galilean." Then he said to Peter, "You *are* a Galilean. Your accent gives you away!"

"I tell you, I do not know the man!" Peter blurted out, but knew the guard didn't believe him. So Peter began to curse and vowed an oath to God that he did not know Jesus of Nazareth.

At that moment, Jesus was led down the stairs and into the courtyard. Jesus glanced over at Peter, and their eyes met.

Even before the tears came to Peter's eyes, a heaving sob welled up within him. He opened his mouth, but no sound came out. He immediately rushed out the front gate and into the darkness.

In the distance, a rooster crowed.

And the Lord turned and looked at Peter. And Peter remembered the word of the Lord, how He had said to him, "Before the rooster crows, you will deny Me three times." So Peter went out and wept bitterly.

LUKE 22:61, 62

chapter seventy-six

BEFORE PILATE

JOHN 18:28-40

In the early morning light, just before the sun broke over the mountains east of Jerusalem, a parade marched from the palace of Caiaphas to the fortified barracks of Antonia. Jesus of Nazareth was dragged relentlessly through the streets, his captors jerking at the leather thongs that bound his hands, pulling him to the ground each time he tried to stand. The leather straps binding his wrists ripped at his raw, burning skin, while the stone streets scraped the flesh from his ankles and knees.

Antonia was an overgrown, ugly structure that looked out of place next to the majestic, ornate beauty of the Temple. The mere sight of the fortress frightened the citizens of Jerusalem, for in its bowels Jews were interrogated, some tortured to death. No Jews voluntarily ventured within; they only entered out of compulsion. Jesus was taken inside and made to stand in the judgment hall.

The few members of the Sanhedrin who accompanied the procession refused to enter the doors of Antonia. Their entrance into any heathen dwelling made them Levitically "unclean" for one day, and there were Passover sacrifices to be made later that day in the Temple. Although they had few qualms about sentencing an innocent man to death, their religious scruples prevented them from deliberate defilement under the Law. Instead they sent word to Pontius Pilate, the Roman governor over Judea, to meet them on the large porch at the front of the fortress.

"What is the charge against this man?" Pilate demanded when he stepped out onto the porch. The Jewish leaders had interrupted his breakfast; he wanted to get down to business and get the Jews out of his hair.

Despite his bluster this early spring morning, Pilate was a consummate politician skilled in the art of pleasing everyone, as suited his needs. His superiors in Rome continually received glowing letters commending his accomplishments in Judea—written by Pilate, of course. He made deals with Jewish leaders which enabled him to rule them. Unlike the iron Roman laws he enforced, Pilate's ego allowed him to be swayed by public opinion. And only a few days earlier, public opinion seemed to favor the unusual teacher from Galilee.

When the Jewish leaders did not answer him immediately, Pilate bellowed, "What charges are you bringing against this man? I presume he has committed some crime."

"If he were not a criminal, we would not have brought him to you," a chief priest said, evading the question.

Being a political animal himself, Pilate was not surprised by the Sanhedrin's reluctance to bring a direct accusation against Jesus of Nazareth. He was familiar with this game. Pilate knew the Sanhedrin had religious differences with this man and they were hoping to force the Roman court to do their dirty work for them. Pilate would have none of it.

"Take him and judge him according to your Jewish laws," he said to them. Pilate wanted to get back to his breakfast. He had an agenda of other cases, plus he had soldiers he needed to interview before returning to his home in Caesarea. Pilate didn't want to deal with Jesus; it was simply a night court docket case that he wanted to avoid. But the priests were persistent.

"He has committed a capital offense, and it is not lawful for us to put any man to death," they reminded Pilate. They stood on the steps shouting up to the governor, who stood above them on the large porch at the front of Antonia.

"What has Rome to do with this man?" Pilate shot back. "We have no quarrel with him."

The priests were dumbfounded by Pilate's pleas of ignorance. "You assigned to us soldiers from your garrison for the arrest Jesus of Nazareth just last night. Surely you know that this man has claimed to be the king of the Jews. He has claimed to be the Christ, whom the people believe will lead a rebellion against Rome, so we have found him guilty of blasphemy."

"Huh!" Pilate snorted. Then he turned sharply and marched into Antonia's judgment hall. There Pilate faced Jesus, the bruised and battered teacher, whose hands were still bound tightly in front of him.

"Are you the king of the Jews?" Pilate sneered. He rather enjoyed asking the question for he knew that Herod Antipas, his rival and tetrarch over Galilee, considered himself to be king of the Jews. Pilate had no love for Herod and he had no love for the Jews.

Jesus looked up at Pilate and asked, "Did you think of this question, or did someone talk to you about me?"

"How would I know about these things? Am I a Jew? Your own people handed you over to me. Your chief priests had you arrested."

Pilate sat down awkwardly, staring intermittently at Jesus. He looked to his aides for help, but none was forthcoming. Finally, Pilate asked, "What is it you have done?"

"My kingdom is not of this world," Jesus answered. "If my kingdom were of this world, then my followers would fight to prevent my arrest by the Jews. If my kingdom were of this world, my subjects would deliver me."

"You are a king, then!" Pilate perked up at this. Perhaps there was something to this charge . . . .

"You are right in saying I am a king," Jesus said. "I was born to be a king. This is the reason I came into the world, to bear witness of the truth. Everyone who sides with the truth will hear me."

Weary of the political games his position demanded he play with his own superiors and with the Jewish leaders, Pilate snorted and said, "What *is* truth?"

Rising from his judgment seat, Pilate walked out to the porch where Jesus' accusers waited below. A large crowd had gathered there, presumably to hear his verdict. Pilate announced, "I find no fault in this man. I have found no basis for a charge against him."

An angry murmur went up from the crowd. Pilate quickly reassessed his decision and decided perhaps the winds of public opinion had shifted against this man Jesus. Then he hit upon a clever idea. It was the custom at the Passover feast for the governor to grant amnesty to one prisoner being held in the Roman prison—a prisoner of the people's choosing. Usually this was someone who had been unjustly imprisoned or perhaps a champion of the people. He wanted nothing to do with Jesus of Nazareth, so he would let the choice belong to the people.

There was in prison a man called Barabbas, the most reviled criminal in Jerusalem. Barabbas, who had once taken part in a planned rebellion, had become a thief, stealing from the Temple and ruthlessly beating helpless victims in the streets. Whatever the people might think of Jesus, everyone hated Barabbas. Pilate knew they might agonize over the choice, but he enjoyed seeing the Jews squirm. He felt certain, however, that the people would release the religious fanatic Jesus.

He said to the crowd, "It is your custom for me to release to you one prisoner at the time of the Passover. Which do you want me to release to you: Barabbas, or Jesus who calls himself your Messiah?"

There was a moment of stunned silence, for the crowd had not expected to be presented with this choice. They had been recruited by the chief priests and Pharisees merely to shout down anyone who would voice their support for the Nazarene teacher.

"Well, shall I release the 'king of the Jews'?" Pilate asked again.

"No!" one of the chief priests shouted, regaining his composure. They couldn't pass up this opportunity to rid themselves of Jesus. "Not Jesus! Give us Barabbas!"

And the crowd took their cue from the priest, shouting out. "Barabbas! Barabbas!"

"Barabbas! Barabbas!" the religious leaders cupped their hands and yelled in cadence. Quickly the crowd picked up the chant.

"What shall I do, then, with Jesus your Messiah?" Pilate asked the crowds.

"Crucify him!" the priests shouted.

"Why? What crime has he committed?" Pilate demanded.

But the priests goaded the crowd into shouting all the louder, "Crucify him!"

When Pilate saw that he was getting nowhere, but instead an uproar was starting, he called for a bowl of water and washed his hands in front of the crowd. "I am hereby innocent of this man's blood," he shouted. "This is your doing!"

And the people cheered.

Turning to the guards, he said angrily, "Release Barabbas!"

Furious that his ploy had not worked, the Roman governor stalked back into the judgment hall and took out his anger on the only one there who couldn't protect himself. Without looking away from the already bloodied form of the man they called Jesus, Pilate said to his soldiers, "Flog him."

Then he released Barabbas to them. But he had Jesus flogged,
and handed him over to be crucified.
MATTHEW 27:26, NIV

SCOURGING

JOHN 19:1-16

Jesus was dragged into the belly of Antonia. Pushed and pulled down several flights of stairs, Jesus' tired limbs were hammered by each cold stone step.

The stairs finally emptied through a heavy door into a dank dungeon, where a charcoal fire in the corner of the room was intended to chase away some of the dampness. Its tiny flame and a single shaft of light from a small window high above threw bizarre shadows on the walls, intensifying any fears new prisoners might bring with them. When the massive door slammed shut behind them, the terrifying sound echoed off the stone walls like a final, sickening verdict.

The Roman guards hooked the leather thongs binding Jesus' wrists to a beating post, extending his arms above his head where he hung from a simple metal hook. They ripped his tunic to the waist, and the perfect olive skin of his back was revealed. For a few moments the coolness of the dungeon brought some small measure of relief to Jesus, but it could not lessen his anticipation of what was to come.

A soldier took hold of a cat-o'-nine-tails, a short leather whip of nine thongs. At the end of each thong was a small knot tied around a bead of metal. The thongs had been dipped in water to stretch the leather around the metal, then tied tightly. When dried, it formed a vicious weapon. The whip had been dampened many times with the blood of prisoners, as it ripped the flesh on the outstretched backs of its victims.

"ONE!" a centurion yelled out as the guard laid the first stripes on Jesus' back. The voice echoed down in the prison chamber, but there was no sound from Jesus.

"TWO!" came the second command, the second set of stripes and the horrific echo.

No sound from Jesus.

"THREE!" the centurion ordered.

Still no sound from Jesus.

The lashes reached thirty-nine. Forty was the number of judgment, but they never administered forty, lest the prisoner die under the scourging whip. And if the prisoner died before forty lashes were administered, there was no guilt assigned to the executioner because he had not administered the whole judgment.

"If he dies with thirty-nine stripes," was the common refrain, "then it proves he was guilty." But the scourging didn't kill Jesus. It merely humiliated and tortured him, spilling his innocent blood.

The soldiers loosed the knot in the straps about his wrists, and Jesus crumbled in a heap on the floor. The centurion jested, saying to the soldiers, "This man is royalty, gentlemen. Where is his finery?"

One of the soldiers draped a scarlet robe across his swollen back. Then they twisted together a crown of thorns and set it on his head, pressing it down until the sharp thorns pierced his skin. They placed a reed in his right hand, pretending it was a royal scepter.

Then, bowing before him in mockery, one of the soldiers said, "Hail, king of the Jews," and the others laughed aloud at this sport.

Then a soldier spat in his face, and the one who bowed to Jesus snatched the reed from his hand to beat Jesus about the head and face. Each blow rammed the thorns farther into his flesh. Again blood ran down his face into his beard. The night before in the garden, sweat and blood had run down his face because of his intense intercession for the souls of mankind. Now those for whom Jesus had prayed caused his blood to run once more.

Dragging Jesus up the stairs into the judgment hall where the morning sunlight poured through the windows, the soldiers threw him onto the floor before Pilate. Rising from taking refreshment in his seat, Pilate walked around Jesus, hovering over the prisoner like a scavenger ready to feed. Jesus was a pitiful sight; his face was bruised, swollen and torn beneath the thorns. But Pilate was hardened; he had seen this sight many times. He encouraged his soldiers to find pleasure in their work punishing the prisoners. Pilate inspected the crown of thorns, thinking it was a clever addition. Pilate especially liked the scarlet robe; it covered the gruesome welts and gashes and was an ingenious way to mock a would-be king.

Perhaps, he thought, the humiliation, pain and indignities this man had suffered would appease the Jewish leaders. So he took Jesus by the arm and half-carried him to the porch, where Pilate presented him in his mock regalia to the assembled crowd.

"Behold the man," Pilate called for all in the courtyard to hear. "I have brought him out to show you what you have done and to let you know once more that I find no basis for a charge against him."

And the chief priests and Pharisees took up the shout once more: "Crucify him! Nail him to the cross!"

Pilate said to them, "*You* take him and crucify him! As for me, I find no fault in him."

The Jewish leaders had not expected the Roman governor to be so squeamish. Frustrated in their inability to convince Pilate to execute Jesus, the priests announced, "We have a law, and according to that law he must die, because he claimed to be the Son of God."

But this did not move Pilate. Violation of Jewish law was not enough to execute a man in the Roman Empire. Jesus had not broken any Roman law, only their Jewish traditions. Pilate didn't care whether Jesus called himself the Son of God, but there was something about this man and his claims that frightened him deep within his soul. Pilate pondered his dilemma.

Then he took Jesus inside and demanded of him, "Where do you come from?" But Jesus said nothing. "Do you refuse to speak to me?" Pilate said, his voice rising. "Don't you realize I have the power either to free you or to crucify you?"

Then Jesus answered him, saying, "No one takes my life from me, but I lay it down of my own accord. You would have no power over me if it were not given to you from above."

Outside the Jewish leaders discussed among themselves how they might sway Pilate once and for all. They agreed the accusation against Jesus must be changed if they were to convince Pilate to execute Jesus.

When Pilate returned to the porch, the spokesman for the chief priests stood and shouted for all to hear, "If you let this man go, you are no friend of Caesar. Anyone who claims to be a king opposes Caesar. Jesus of Nazareth has set himself to be king, and that is treason!"

Pilate's face went pale. He could not ignore this line of reasoning. If such an accusation were to get back to Rome, Pilate could very well lose his position—perhaps even his life.

"Shall I then crucify your king?" Pilate cried out to the religious leaders. "We have no king but Caesar," they answered.

Pilate knew the Jews' long-standing hatred of Roman rule over their land. But apparently, he thought, their hatred for this Galilean must run even deeper for them to openly acknowledge Caesar as their king. *We have no king but Caesar.* When he rose that morning, Pilate would gladly have wagered with his men that he would not hear those words from the lips of the Jews that day.

> *Finally Pilate handed him over to them to be crucified.*
> *So the soldiers took charge of Jesus.*
> JOHN 19:16, NIV

chapter seventy-eight

THE VIA DOLOROSA

JOHN 19:16-22

The scarlet robe was torn off the dried wounds of Jesus' body, causing his stripes to bleed afresh. His own torn, bloodstained garments were placed on him. After only a few hours of legal maneuverings, cross-examinations and a mock trial, Jesus of Nazareth was led out of the fortress toward the hill called Golgotha—Calvary in Greek—which means the Place of the Skull.

A centurion led a detachment of four men, with a hammer swinging menacingly from his belt, the nails stuffed in his pouch. The four soldiers made sure the victim carried his own instrument of execution—the cross beam of a wooden cross—to the place of death. But after the beatings and the scourging, Jesus was too weakened to carry his load unassisted. He continually fell, raising the ire of the Roman soldiers. "Up!" one of the soldiers cried again and again, each time beating Jesus with a rope.

Behind Jesus came two convicted thieves, each carrying his own cross. Each thief was led by a centurion and each had his own personal guard of four soldiers who beat him every step of the way.

Following close behind the death squads was John, the only one of the apostles who hadn't run away. Young John had been among the first to leave everything to follow Jesus; now John would follow Jesus to the cross.

Word of these happenings had reached many who had heard and believed Jesus' teaching in the Temple. Hundreds of weeping men and women now lined the street in shocked disbelief, mingling with his detractors and mockers and curious onlookers as the grisly procession made its way by the traditional route—which has since become known as the Via Dolorosa, or the Way of Sorrows—toward the site of crucifixion.

A wooden shingle was placed around Jesus' neck to announce his crime; later it would be nailed to the top of the cross so that all might know why he was being executed. On the shingle Pilate had written in Aramaic, Latin and Greek, "JESUS OF NAZARETH, THE KING OF THE JEWS."

When they heard he had written this, the chief priests had gone in protest to Pilate. "Do not write 'The King of the Jews,'" they pleaded. "Write that this man *claimed* to be king of the Jews."

Pilate had had enough of the entire sordid business. He denied their request. "What I have written, I have written," he said and walked away from them.

After Jesus had fallen several times along the route, the Roman soldiers didn't waste time beating him again. Clearly, this man was unable to carry the cross any further.

"You!" the centurion yelled to a man standing among the crowds.

Simon, a pilgrim from the land of Cyrene, was dressed differently; his exotic dark-green robe and red tunic stood out in the crowd of mostly white and brown tunics. He was easily singled out, so the centurion pointed to the cross and said, "Pick up that cross and follow us."

So Simon the Cyrenian hefted the cross onto his shoulder and carried it for Jesus to the place called Golgotha.

The place of the skull was appropriately named, for the barren white limestone hill resembled nothing more than a human skull. Two dark, foreboding caves at the front of Golgotha were like two darkened eye sockets; a hollow depression beneath the eyes resembled a jaw frozen open in a pained grimace. Golgotha was a place of death.

Crucifixion was not an approved Jewish form of execution. According to their Law, the Jewish people usually strangled, beheaded or stoned those who had committed capital crimes. The cross was a Phoenician instrument, adopted and improved upon by the Romans. Because of its extreme cruelty, crucifixion had become widespread under Caesar, frightening the subjects of the Empire into submission.

The heavy timbers made a cracking sound as Simon the Cyrenian dropped the cross beam at the top of the limestone hill. Calloused hands assembled the cross, then stripped the sandals, cloak and tunic from Jesus and stretched him out on the timbers. The executioners were efficient at their task; they had done it many times before. Ropes tied his hands and feet to the cross to prevent struggling, but the Son of Man offered no resistance. Then a greasy, less-than-tidy-for-a-Roman soldier, swinging a large wooden mallet, approached Jesus. This hairy, muscular man took a black iron spike, placed it in the palm of Jesus' right hand and then with a mighty swing of his hammer, began driving the spike into the timber.

THWAPPP . . . , the sound rang out.

THWAPPP . . . .

THWAPPP . . . .

The other soldiers didn't pay any attention—they had heard the sound may times—but went about preparing the day's other two victims.

Next, the executioner turned to Jesus' other hand, repeating the process. He lifted the hammer.

THWAPPP . . . .

THWAPPP . . . .

THWAPPP . . . .

He did the same to the feet of Jesus.

A hole almost two feet deep had been chiseled out of the limestone. The same hole had been used to mount countless other crosses before this one. With Jesus nailed to the cross, the soldiers put their huge shoulders to the weight while others pulled with ropes to erect the cross. Slowly they lifted the cross skyward. The weight of Jesus' body caused the nails in his hands and feet to rip at his flesh. His body screamed in agony, but he said nothing. The soldiers raised the cross ever higher until it was nearly upright. Through swollen eyes filled with blood and sweat, Jesus looked down upon those who were crucifying him, but he said nothing. Then the executioner walked over to the cross, and viciously kicked it so that the base of the cross dropped into the hole.

THUMP.

Jesus shut his eyes as his body shook with pain, but he said nothing for a moment. Then he lifted his eyes to heaven in prayer for his executioners, "Father, forgive them, for they know not what they do."

It was nine o'clock in the morning.

When a person is suspended by his two outstretched hands, the blood sinks rapidly to the lower extremities in his body, his blood pressure dropping while the rate of his pulse doubles. The heart pumps harder and faster, even as the person tries to pull himself up to lessen the strain on his body and the constriction of his chest. When the heart can't pull the blood up from the lower extremities, the victim repeatedly faints and collapses on the cross. But then the excruciating pain awakens him, and the victim lapses in and out of consciousness. Usually the victim dies of heart failure, suffocation, traumatic fever or dehydration.

Jesus would die of a broken heart.

And when they had come to the place called Calvary, there they crucified Him, and the criminals, one on the right hand and the other on the left.

LUKE 23:33

chapter seventy—nine

BLOOD MONEY

MATTHEW 27:3-10
ACTS 1:16-19

The well-dressed man was frantic. He desperately pushed his way through the crowd of humanity that was streaming against him out of the Temple. Judas Iscariot elbowed his way between the people, but made only slow progress toward his destination inside. The thirty pieces of silver he had tied to his sash now hung like a huge weight that slowed his journey.

"I have sinned . . . ," he panted in a low voice. "Get out of my way!"

As the crowd flooded out the exits of the Temple, Judas found himself being forced backward. *But I have sinned!* he thought. *I have betrayed innocent blood. I must see the priests now!*

One of the priests standing nearby recognized Judas and opened a small solitary side door to him. Judas fought his way into the door and ran headlong past the columns of Solomon's Porch toward the caucus room, where he had made his deal with the enemies of Jesus. Before they had been a dour bunch, but this time Judas came face to face with a knot of laughing priests.

"You must stop this execution!" Judas demanded.

But they laughed all the harder, ridiculing him. "You have your money," they spat out the words. Judas was intruding on their celebration. "Take your silver and go."

But Judas had to cleanse his soul. "I will be heard!" Judas raised his voice to a shout. He expected his protests to put his burden of guilt on them. He had borne this weight for but one day, but it was one day too long. With a hoarse cry, he sobbed, "I have sinned . . . I have betrayed innocent blood. I am doomed to hell!"

The priests again laughed. They had no words of mercy for Judas. "What is that to us? We don't care about your sin or your fate. That's your responsibility."

For a few moments, Judas glared wildly at them, his chest heaving with anger and sorrow. Then he untied the bag holding the thirty pieces of silver, removed a coin and turned it over in his hand. Turning, he ran out the door toward the sanctuary of the Temple.

"Wait!" the priests shouted after him. They could not allow him to do what it appeared he might do.

Judas ran wildly toward the Court of Israel. It was there that penitent worshipers patiently would wait while the priests offered sacrifice of forgiveness for them; it was a place where Judas had felt forgiveness. With a mad cry, he hurled the thirty pieces of silver onto the marble pavement of the place of forgiveness, yelling, "I have sinned! I betrayed innocent blood! I need forgiveness!"

Before the rushing priests could reach him, Judas fled the Temple and the city and ran down into the valley to where the Brook of Kidron bounced innocently along. There Judas dashed to his right, and beneath the shadow of the Temple, headed toward the Valley of Hinnom, a terrible place where the garbage of the city was burned, a place of stench and decay. As Judas walked among the garbage, he had a ghastly, foreboding feeling that he was already in hell.

Judas crossed the valley, frantically climbing up the steep ascent with his hands to the plateau above him, the place called Potter's Field. Jeremiah the prophet had preached in the clay soil of this field, surrounded by rocks and scattered olive trees. Around the edge of the plateau were cliffs that dropped off into the valley. The cliffs were lined with jagged rocks, and those who fell on them died quickly.

Judas Iscariot was heading to the place purchased with his stolen money. He was heading specifically to a gnarled tree that grew in the field—a tree that extended from the cliff out over the valley below. There Judas knelt to untie his sash, the long flowing gold sash where he had tied the thirty pieces of silver. His ego had seen to it that his was a sash longer than any worn by the other men who followed Jesus.

For the past day, his mind had been in a storm as threatening as the rocks about him. Now he grew quite calm and collected. He had returned the silver and had asked for forgiveness. He couldn't believe it was forthcoming, however, and now he knew what he must do.

Judas first tied one end of the sash around his neck. Then he climbed the gnarled trunk of the tree, leaning out over the precipice to attach the sash to the tree limb from which he would be hanged. The tree was visible across the Hinnom Valley, so those in the city would be able to see what he was about to do. Judas wanted his death to send a message to Jerusalem.

As he leaned, he slipped and almost fell, but instinctively Judas grabbed a limb to keep from falling. He didn't want to die by accident; he wanted his death to be intentional and deliberate. He wanted his death to be done right.

Returning to the ground, Judas was ready. He stood at the edge of the cliff, not looking down at the jagged rocks, but looking across the valley to Jerusalem. He thought he should make his peace with God before he died. He thought he should pray, but the only prayer that came to his lips was the prayer he had breathed throughout the evening: "I have sinned. I have betrayed innocent blood."

With those words, Judas jumped out over the precipice. He swung there for a moment, but before he passed into unconsciousness, the knot in his sash loosened under the weight of his body. Judas fell awkwardly onto the jagged rocks far beneath him, his stomach pierced by the sharpest of all rocks. His intestines spilled out as the body bounced from one rock to another to the bottom of the gorge.

Even as Judas' body was still warm, the priests in the Temple were still arguing over what should be done with the thirty pieces of silver. They were men of the Law, and they all knew it was unlawful to take blood money into the Temple treasury. This money had been unlawfully gained, and money that was made by an evil act must be returned. They would not try to forcibly return it to Judas, for he might tell everyone of their hand in the conspiracy to crucify Jesus of Nazareth.

"We must do something!" the oldest priest said to the others, the thirty coins stacked before them on a table. No one wanted to touch the coins.

Shortly, a Levitical guard burst into the room to report that Judas Iscariot had died in a fall from Potter's Field, probably in a botched suicide attempt.

"Potter's Field is not good for anything," the old priest said with a twinkle in his eye, a plan forming in his mind. He turned to the others and announced, "The Law provides that if a donor will not take his money back, we should spend it for public good."

With the approval of the Sanhedrin, Potter's Field was later purchased by the Temple for thirty pieces of silver, and the land was used for charitable purposes—to bury strangers and the poor of the city. And although the graveyard was still called Potter's Field, among those who knew what had happened there the place became known as the Field of Blood.

Then was fulfilled what was spoken by Jeremiah the prophet, saying, "And they took the thirty pieces of silver, the value of Him who was priced, whom they of the children of Israel priced, and gave them for the potter's field."
MATTHEW 27:9,10

ONSET OF AGONY

LUKE 23:32-43

The soldiers hovered like vultures over the clothing of Jesus, which had been left in a crumpled heap beneath him. They knew the rules of the game: They divided the clothing into four piles, each of the four soldiers taking a share, determined by casting lots. They would then keep the best pieces for themselves and sell the others in the bazaar.

As they divided the clothing, they came across a finely woven, seamless inner garment, by far the most valuable of all Jesus' possessions. "It is too valuable for just one of us to take. Let's rip it into four sections," one of the younger, more impetuous of the soldiers suggested.

"No!" the eldest soldier stopped him, scowling through his unshaven whiskers. "This robe is worth more than all the rest put together." Then he smiled. "It would be worthless if torn into four parts. Let's gamble for it, same as the rest."

The young man glared at his elder's rebuke, then said coolly, "Cast the dice."

Another soldier stooped and rattled primitive dice in a cup, while the old soldier leaned over his shoulder and demanded, "I'll take the lowest number."

From the cross flanking Jesus to his left, the convicted thief looked down upon these sordid proceedings with unbridled hatred for the Roman soldiers. In fact, hate was the only sensation or thought the man could summon from beneath the throbbing pain that engulfed his head. He hated Pilate for condemning him. He hated God in heaven for allowing him to be born. The thief screamed as he used the nails that held him on the cross to pull himself up where he could take a deep breath, then he slumped down again as he lost consciousness. But from within the blackness, he heard the soldiers mocking Jesus.

"If you are the king of the Jews," the soldier who had Jesus' robe draped over his shoulder said, pointing to the accusatory shingle on the cross, "come down from there and save yourself."

The soldiers laughed heartily.

Returning to consciousness, the thief at Jesus' left hand turned his sweat-blinded eyes to the center cross. "You're no king," he said to Jesus, heaving for more breath to finish his words. "If you were the savior, then you could save yourself and us."

But the thief at the other hand of Jesus had seen him teach in the Temple. He had heard the Antonia guards talking about how Pilate had found no fault in the man. He had seen the shingle that identified him as JESUS OF NAZARETH, THE KING OF THE JEWS, and he believed the writing there. He heard much about this man—his love for children, how he made the blind see and the lame walk, how he cared for tax collectors and sinners. He had heard Jesus say on the cross, "Father, forgive them, for they know not what they do," and the thief was amazed.

"Don't you fear God?" he gasped to his fellow thief. "We're going to die."

"We're thieves," his hardened cohort answered, "we deserve to die. Take it like a man . . . ."

"But this man does not deserve to die," the repentant thief protested. "He has done nothing wrong."

"Hah! If he's done nothing wrong, then why is he here with us?"

But the repentant thief only shook his head. If Jesus had forgiven the Roman soldier who nailed him to a cross, perhaps Jesus might forgive him, too. He could not know that one day millions would be drawn to God by the cross, but this thief was the first to respond. He looked toward Jesus, searching for forgiveness. The thief beseeched him, "Remember me when you come into your kingdom."

In hours of extremity, some deceive themselves with faulty reason. Others in times of trial take giant leaps so that in a few moments they learn what others take years to master. The repentant thief learned in his hour of suffering what Jesus had been teaching for three years.

Jesus smiled weakly and promised, "Today you will be with me in Paradise."

Often the victims of crucifixion would hang on to life for two or three days; some strong of body and stubborn of spirit refused to die, lasting as long as seven days or more. John, the young apostle who had watched in horror as they crucified Jesus, did not think his master was going to last out the day. So he left Golgotha to retrieve Mary, the mother of Jesus. John knew she would want to see her son one last time, even in this condition.

The beloved apostle led Mary to the foot of the cross. With them came three other women—Mary's sister Salome, Mary the mother of James the Less and Mary of Magdala—who came to the cross to bid a mournful farewell to Jesus, the one in whom they had placed all their hope.

Without thought for himself, Jesus looked upon his mother as she stood in the shadow of his cross. No one in the crowd knew who she was or why she was there.

Jesus said to his mother, "Woman . . . ." He did not call her mother, lest she be laughed at and reviled by the crowd. "Woman, here is your son," Jesus said, nodding at John.

Through blood-filled eyes, he then gave John a final command: "Here is your mother."

Jesus was entrusting the care of his mother to the faithful apostle, the only one who had not run away. John understood. He owned a house in the city, inherited from his father and located on Mount Zion. It was a place where Mary could find solitude after the oppressive sight of seeing her eldest son dying upon a cross for crimes he had not committed. John left Golgotha that day with his arm around Mary, and they went to his home in Jerusalem.

From that time on, this disciple took her into his home.

JOHN, 19:27, NIV

chapter eighty-one

IT IS FINISHED

MATTHEW 27:45-53

About the noon hour, the sun slipped behind a curtain of clouds in the sky, and a shadow fell across Golgotha. A brisk gust whipped across the hilltop, stirring up dust, as tunics flapped about legs in the crowd. The festive Passover banners on the north wall in Jerusalem fluttered wildly as the wind picked up intensity. The sun plunged deeper into the gathering clouds, and the sky began to grow dark, thrusting Jerusalem—indeed, the entire region— into deepening shadows.

At Golgotha, a worried and frightened multitude watched as Jesus of Nazareth suffered, his body contorted in excruciating pain, the likes of which no one had ever seen. This pain was clearly more than physical sensation; this was deep spiritual agony, as his soul was being made an offering for the sins of mankind.

The soul of Jesus groaned and, it seemed to the observers, all of creation groaned with him.

Jesus lifted his head slightly and tried to open his eyes. Then arching his neck toward heaven, he cried out, "My God, my God, why have you forsaken me?" He did not call him "Father," for never had Jesus felt more detached from God in heaven than as he hung on the cross, bearing the weight of the sins of the world.

Within minutes the land was shrouded in darkness, as though it were the dead of night, although no stars or moon could be seen. The minutes passed into an hour; then two hours; then three.

A voice from the crowd gathered at Golgotha cried out, "It's the end of the world!"

"God has shut off the sun because we have crucified an innocent man!" wailed another.

"No," said another, in nervous defiance. "It's only a storm . . . a terrible storm."

In the third hour of darkness, Jesus said from the cross, "I thirst . . . ." A subdued Jesus felt his physical strength ebbing.

One of the soldiers, moved with pity, stood up and went to fetch something to relieve the intense thirst of Jesus. The soldier fastened a sponge to a three-foot reed, then dipped the sponge in some sour wine. He then lifted the sponge to the mouth of the dying man, and Jesus drank.

Red drops dripped from his lips as the sponge was removed.

From a distance, Mary Magdalene sobbed and said to Salome, "He has tasted death for every man."

With renewed vigor, Jesus tugged at the nails holding him to the cross, pulling himself up to look to heaven. Then he cried aloud, "It is finished!"

His work on earth—and his sufferings—were over. The price had been paid. No longer would his people be asked to bring a blood sacrifice to the Temple to receive forgiveness for their sins. The Son of God had taken the full punishment for the sins of the world. It was about three o'clock in the afternoon.

Finally, Jesus called out in a loud voice, "Father, into your hands I commit my spirit!"

The low grumblings of the crowd ceased. Every eye turned to stare at him, hanging on to the words of a dying man.

There was silence.

Then Jesus of Nazareth bowed his head—it did not drop out of exhaustion, nor did death take his strength from him. In an act of triumphant willpower, he bowed his head and gave up his spirit.

At that moment, a shudder arose beneath the feet of those watching at Golgotha, and the city of Jerusalem began to shake. For what seemed an eternity to most of its residents, an earthquake rumbled through the city and in the Temple, shaking its structural and spiritual foundations.

The veil of the Temple, the massive curtain that separated the Jewish people from the Holy of Holies—the dwelling place of God—was torn in half from top to bottom by the hand of God. On this momentous day, the Holy of Holies was opened for all to enter. People would no longer come to God through a human priest in the Temple; they would come to God through his beloved Son. The earthquake rumbled on.

The Temple gates swung open of their own accord, and for years afterward, rabbis would speak of the supernatural opening of the Temple during the quake, saying it foretold the coming destruction of the Temple.

"The earthquake has torn the veil!" shouted a young Levite as he came running from where he had been posted near the Holy of Holies. Planning to replace it quickly with the veil from the previous year, he burst into the living quarters, where he gathered a number of young Levites. One man could not lift the veil alone—the veil was sixty feet long and thirty feet wide and thick as the palm of a hand.

"Get everyone!" the young Levite yelled as he ran through the Temple. Eventually, three hundred priests answered the call, and together they lifted the replacement veil into place just as the shaking subsided and the darkness over the land lifted.

> *And, behold, the veil of the temple was rent in twain from the top to the bottom; and the earth did quake, and the rocks rent; and the graves were opened; and many bodies of the saints which slept arose.*
>
> MATTHEW 27:51,52, KJV

chapter eighty-two

FROM THE CROSS TO THE GRAVE

JOHN 19:31-42

He had in his twenty-two years serving in the Roman legions witnessed some horrible deaths and he had seen any number of atrocities in battle. But today, as a centurion of the Praetorian Guard, he was sickened, for he had presided over the execution of an innocent man.

He had heard Pontius Pilate declare this man Jesus to be innocent. He had seen the wicked intent of the Jewish leaders, who had been bent on having him crucified for imagined crimes. He himself had observed the gentle spirit of the man, even as Jesus was being lifted up on the cross.

Then there was the terrifying darkness that had enshrouded the land at midday and, at the very moment of the man's death, the seemingly interminable earthquake.

The centurion read again the shingle mounted at the top of the cross. JESUS OF NAZARETH, THE KING OF THE JEWS. The centurion took a step from honest opinion to faith; he was convinced. *This man was no criminal,* he thought.

He removed his helmet, looked into the lifeless face of Jesus and confessed aloud, "Truly this was the Son of God."

The shadow of the cross stretched out over the crowd. Within a few hours the sun would set, beginning the Sabbath celebration. Then nothing could be done about the corpse which hung on the cross, and it would remain there until the Sabbath had passed. Meanwhile, scavengers—ravens, buzzards, vultures—would swoop in to peck away at the flesh, thereby desecrating the body.

The Law of Moses demanded that the body of a criminal should not be left unburied overnight, particularly during a Sabbath. To make matters worse, this was a high Sabbath of the Passover. So it was that the chief priests went to Pilate and petitioned him to hasten the deaths of those being crucified that their bodies might be buried before sundown.

So Pilate commanded that the *crurifragium* be administered—that the bones of the crucified's legs be broken with a club or hammer, followed by a swift stroke from a sword or lance to put an end to what remained of life. Breaking the kneecaps and legs was not meant to kill the victim; it was merely Rome's way of increasing the suffering momentarily to compensate for the merciful end which followed.

When word reached Golgotha, the centurion ordered one of his men to take the hammer—the one that drove the nails through the hands and feet of Jesus—and smash the kneecaps of the thief to the left of Jesus. Screams of anguish pierced the silence. The same was done to the malefactor to the right of the Nazarene.

But when the soldier stepped toward Jesus, the centurion restrained him. "Jesus is dead," he said to the soldier, who seemed to be relishing his task.

"Are you certain?" the soldier asked, then shrunk back under a withering look from his commanding officer. Certainly the centurion knew when a man was dead, for he was an experienced and efficient executioner.

The centurion was enraged at first that his judgment should be questioned, but he regained his composure and confirmed quietly, "He is dead."

The soldier shrugged and picked up his lance. He scraped the spearhead two or three times on a stone to ensure it was sharp, then ran his fingertip down the edge of the blade to remove all doubt. Then placing the lance against the exposed side of Jesus, he put his weight against the spear, thrusting it straight up into the heart of the dead man. To the astonishment of the onlookers, a sudden gush of blood and water poured out of the body.

At the fortress Antonia, Pilate granted an audience to Joseph of Arimathea, a member of the Sanhedrin and secretly a disciple of Jesus of Nazareth. Joseph had known of the plot to destroy Jesus, but he had not been informed about the early morning meeting in which Jesus was summarily tried and convicted— probably because he had dared to express some modicum of sympathy for the teacher in a recent council meeting.

When word reached Joseph of the death of Jesus, he went to Pilate and, using the full influence of his office, demanded the body be turned over to him.

"Why do you want the body of the Galilean?"

Joseph explained his secret devotion to Jesus and his teachings. "Now that he is dead, I want to pay my respects for my master," he said.

Pilate considered this for a moment, then a strange smile crept over his face. "It pleases me to offer assistance to one who would risk exposure to defy that bunch of snakes you call the Sanhedrin," he said. "Take the body and go. I give it to you." Then Pilate instructed his secretary to write a letter giving Joseph of Arimathea authority to receive the body of Jesus from the soldiers at Golgotha.

Because of his own advanced age, Joseph knew death would visit him soon. He had a few years earlier purchased a garden in an exquisite setting and ordered a new tomb be hewed from the rock there in preparation for his burial. It was the tomb of a wealthy man; but on this day he would lay there the body of a poor carpenter-turned-teacher from Nazareth. *Nothing is too good for the Son of God*, Joseph thought.

Accompanied by his servants, Joseph went immediately to the centurion with his letter of permission to receive the body of Jesus. The cross was lowered and laid on the ground. The ropes were loosened and the cruel nails drawn out one by one. Joseph and his servants washed the dried blood, sweat and spittle from the face and body of Jesus. Then they wrapped his body in a linen cloth and carried it quickly to the garden, which was close by.

It was after five o'clock when they entered the tomb. Inside the rock was an inner court approximately nine feet square where the body was laid. Nicodemus, the teacher of the Law who had met Jesus by night and had since also become a follower in secret, met the burial party there with expensive lotions of myrrh and aloe to anoint the body for the tomb. Those closest to Jesus—his apostles—were not there, for they had gone into hiding. Jesus was instead buried by two members of the very group that had condemned him to death.

In haste, Joseph and Nicodemus wrapped the torso and each limb in long strips of linen in accordance with Jewish burial customs. A layer of myrrh and aloe was generously applied on the cloths, then another layer of cloths was applied over the lotion. Finally, the head was gently wrapped in a napkin.

Joseph of Arimathea and Nicodemus then exited the tomb, instructing their servants to seal the tomb by rolling a flat carved stone, some four feet in diameter, down a designed trench until it covered the entry completely. Then a smaller stone was squeezed into the crack to lodge the larger stone into place.

Three women stood far off on a small hill overlooking the garden where the tomb was located. Mary Magdalene, Salome and Mary the mother of James the Less had followed the burial party to this place to see where Jesus was laid. They wanted with all their hearts to run into the garden to help anoint the body of him whom they loved, but they could not violate Jewish customs by mingling with the men, two of whom they knew to be prominent leaders. Could these men be trusted, they wondered, to give him a proper burial?

"We'll come back after the Sabbath . . . ." Mary Magdalene let the words trail off wistfully. Then, gathering herself, she said resolutely, "We'll come back after the Sabbath to anoint his body. Come, we must prepare for the Sabbath."

A delegation from the chief priests and Pharisees went to see Pilate. "Sir," they said, "we remember that while he was alive the deceiver, Jesus of Nazareth, claimed repeatedly, 'After three days I shall rise again.'

"We now have reason to believe that his disciples are planning to steal the body so that they may tell the people he has been raised from the dead.

This final deception will be far worse than the first he perpetrated. So we ask that you give the order for the tomb to be placed under constant guard until the third day has passed."

Pilate despised the Jewish leaders and their elaborate rituals and pretenses, but he found the machinations and claims surrounding this Jesus intriguing. He considered their request for a moment, then said, "Take a guard." Pilate smiled. "Go, make the tomb as secure as you know how."

So the chief priests and Pharisees went and made the tomb secure by putting a seal on the stone and posting a guard of six Roman soldiers.

> *So they went, and made the sepulchre sure, sealing the stone,*
> *and setting a watch.*
> MATTHEW 27:66, KJV

chapter eighty-three
A SATURDAY EVENING FESTIVAL
LEVITICUS 23:9-14

After the setting of the Sabbath sun, a noisy throng made its way through the Golden Gate, out of the city of Jerusalem, across the brook Kidron, toward the sheltered Asher Valley. Hundreds of rejoicing pilgrims followed a delegation from the Sanhedrin to a predetermined location for the ceremonial cutting of the Passover sheaths.

The previous morning, Friday, Levites had been sent out to a field of barley in the Asher Valley to select and mark the pilgrims' destination. The Levites had inspected the field and found a patch of grain that was "first ripe"—some call it prematurely ripe—and they had tied the grain together in bundles while it was still standing in the field. This was the grain to be harvested in the Saturday evening ceremony, then waved before the Lord early on Sunday morning in the Temple as the "firstfruits" wave offering.

As the people marched in celebration toward the field, a tired little boy in the congregation dragged his feet and asked his mother, "Why did we wait so late to come out here?"

"We must observe the Sabbath day and keep it holy," his mother answered without going into a long explanation, raising her voice to be heard amid the hubbub. "We had to wait until the Sabbath was over before harvesting the grain."

"Are we going to eat it?"

"No. The priest will take the grain into the Temple to wave it before the Lord."

"Why?" the boy persisted.

"The wave offering is our promise to God that we will give him some of our grain when it is harvested." She wondered how much of this a small child could understand.

A beautiful spring day was coming to an end, and somewhere a meadowlark chirped. Though it was not yet dark, the sun had fallen behind the hills, leaving a long, red streak across the horizon. Several stars had already made their appearance in the eastern sky by the time the festive crowd arrived at the field.

Three men, each with a sickle and a basket, waded into the barley like fishermen wading into the sea. Then the first turned to the crowd and called loud enough for all to hear, "With this sickle I will cut down the firstfruits that God has given us." He held the sickle high for all to see. "Into this basket I will place the firstfruits." He lifted a large basket over his head.

Then he asked the questions they had all come to hear. "Has the sun gone down?"

"Yes!" the crowd responded.

"With this sickle?"

"Yes!"

"Into this basket?"

"Yes!"

"On this Passover day?"

"Yes!"

"Shall I reap?"

"YES!" the people affirmed loudly.

When the bundles of barley had been cut down and placed into the baskets, the crowd clapped and cheered.

The followers of Jesus were not in a festive mood. Most of his closest disciples had run away, many of them hiding, cowering, hoping to escape the fate of their master. Peter and John and the women who gathered at the home of John did not say much among themselves. The one in whom they had placed their hopes to restore the glory of Israel was dead.

They did not recognize the significance of the firstfruits festival taking place that evening in the fields, nor did they care about attending the celebration the next morning when the high priest would wave the symbolic grain before God—a symbol of life from the earth. They did not understand that the man whose death they mourned would soon become the firstfruits that would be raised up and offered to God for all time on the third day of reckoning.

The grief-stricken gathering could not see past their pain to see the plan of God.

The garden where Jesus had been buried was silent. Two stolid soldiers stood their post before the large stone, protecting the rock-hewed tomb from robbers and ensuring the seal remained unbroken. Their fellow soldiers lounged nearby on the grass, ready for sleep, deep in their own thoughts.

> *And if Christ is not risen, your faith is futile; you are still in your sins! Then also those who have fallen asleep in Christ have perished. If in this life only we have hope in Christ, we are of all men the most pitiable.*
>
> 1 CORINTHIANS 15:17-19

chapter eighty-four

"THEY STOLE THE BODY"

MATTHEW 28:2-4, 11-15

First light came to Golgotha on Sunday morning, but nothing stirred there. Trash was scattered over Calvary—a broken ladder, a few pieces of rope, some rotten, bloodied clothes. Golgotha had never been a pretty sight and on this morning it was still ugly, though the dawn promised to wash away memories of days past. This was the beginning of a new day, the beginning of a new week and unknown to the few awake and walking the streets of Jerusalem, it was the beginning of a new era—the Age of Grace.

Light had not yet pierced the deep shadows of the nearby garden where Jesus had been entombed. Darkness crouched beneath trees and bushes. The eyes of those guarding the tomb had become acclimated to the darkness, but a new arrival would have needed a torch to find his way about the garden.

It came slowly. The Roman soldiers watching in the garden did not feel it at first. Leaves on the trees began shimmering, then bushes began shaking. Then came the low moan of dirt and rock being awakened from their bed. A gentle earthquake rumbled through the garden, dislodging the small stone holding the larger stone in its place covering the opening of the tomb. The Roman seal, stamped in a handful of cement that held the stones together, cracked and splintered into small pieces.

Out of the darkness—out of nowhere—stepped an angel. The brilliant light emanating from the angel's garment flashed through the garden, and the darkness hiding under the bushes scampered away. The two soldiers standing guard at the entrance to the tomb trembled at the sight and immediately fell over as if dead. Before the others nearby could even detect the source of the dazzling light shining about them, the angel put his shoulder to the stone and with one mighty shove, rolled the stone away from the tomb. The angel then sat upon the stone and smiled as if to say, *This stone cannot keep the Lord in, and it cannot keep me out.*

The four remaining Roman soldiers, who had stood shoulder to shoulder in battle, did not fear death, but they were shaken by the brilliance of the angelic being and intimidated by the heavenly power he had displayed. With a whimper, these courageous soldiers—seized with mortal terror—began to run.

"Quick! To Antonia! We must get reinforcements!" one shouted as they stumbled into the city.

"No, wait!" another called, suddenly stopping. The others pulled up and turned to hear him. "If it is known we ran away from this man," he cautioned, "we will be put to death."

The dew of the morning had settled on the trees, and Jerusalem still lay silent. Indeed if they reported that one warrior had driven them away, they would at the very least become laughingstocks. Certainly they would be beaten and imprisoned. They could even be executed, depending upon the mood of Pilate.

"Let's go to the Jewish leaders," one of the guards reasoned.

"Yes!" another of the soldiers liked this idea. "Technically, we were at the tomb under their authority, though they have no power over us. And it is said they know of the supernatural."

With that, they headed toward the Temple living quarters. They aroused the Levites residing in the Temple, who in turn quickly summoned the chief priests and members of the Sanhedrin.

The sun still had not risen when a handful of religious officials walked toward the Temple. Dressed casually—not in their official robes—they brushed sleep from their eyes as they quickly assembled. This was an emergency.

With skeptical hearts, they listened to the soldiers tell about the earthquake and the heavenly being who rolled the stone away from the cave. They all doubted the earthquake for they had not felt it. The Sadducees among them did not believe the soldiers, for they doubted the supernatural. The Pharisees believed in miracles, but their hearts told them God would not come to the rescue of a man convicted of blasphemy.

Finally, a leader of the Sanhedrin stood and waved his hands in a gesture calling for silence. "This second evil is worse than the first," he said, for he considered the crucifixion of Jesus to be a necessary evil. He explained that although the death of the Nazarene was meant to crush the movement that had sprung up around him, such wild, unsubstantiated stories about his resurrection would only bolster his fanatical followers and lead more people to believe in his teachings.

The leader turned to the Roman soldiers and asked, "Did you actually see this 'person' roll away the stone?"

"Yes," they answered.

"Did you actually see Jesus of Nazareth walk out of the tomb?"

"No."

"Well, then. There is your answer!" the leader said to the Sanhedrin. "He did not rise from the dead. No one saw him come out of the tomb." Then he smiled at the gathering. "The body of Jesus was stolen by his disciples while the guards lay sleeping."

"But . . . ," the soldier protested.

However, before the soldiers could get the words out, they were cut off by a loud CLUNK. A bag full of coins had appeared on the table before them.

"We understand that hardworking soldiers have certain needs," the leader of the Sanhedrin said benignly. This was clearly more money than the soldiers had seen in a long time.

No one in the room dared say what they all were thinking, for it was a serious offense to bribe a Roman official. It was also against Jewish law to offer a bribe. So the word "bribe" was never mentioned.

A chief priest finally broke the silence. "This money is simply a token of our appreciation for your diligence. Consider it a reward for information that will lead to the destruction of a criminal conspiracy."

"But . . . we will be punished for sleeping on our watch," a soldier protested.

"Pilate is our friend," the leader of the Sanhedrin said, dismissing his concerns. "If this report gets to the governor, we will talk to Pilate and keep you out of trouble. You will not be punished."

Once the ruling council reached agreement on their fictitious account of the disappearance of the body of Jesus, they quickly spread word throughout Jerusalem that his disciples had robbed the sepulchre during the night and had stolen the body of Jesus.

Those who had rejected Jesus in the Temple were quick to believe the lie, but others were not so sure.

So the soldiers took the money and did as they were instructed. And this story has been widely circulated among the Jews to this very day.

MATTHEW 28:15

chapter eighty—five

THOSE FIRST TO THE TOMB

LUKE 24:1-8
JOHN 20:1-18

A red glare made dark shadows of the eastern hills as a group of women made their lonely way toward the rock-hewed tomb in the garden. They had rested on the Sabbath day according to Jewish Law, and now it was the third day since the burial according to Jewish reckoning, and they carried oils and spices to the tomb of Jesus. The sun had not yet risen.

"Wait here," Mary Magdalene said to the other women in the waning darkness. "The soldiers are just ahead."

Joanna and Mary the mother of James the Less did not argue, for they knew the dangers of encountering Roman soldiers alone, especially in a secluded place like the one where they were headed.

But Mary Magdalene was a woman of the world. Jesus had cast seven demons out of her and she understood that evil was a hard taskmaster. The soldiers could do little to her that had not been done previously.

Stealthily approaching the place where the Roman soldiers were said to be guarding the tomb, she parted the leaves to spy out the garden.

Nothing! she thought.

She saw no soldiers, no fire, no signs of life anywhere. The great stone that had covered the tomb was rolled back. The tomb was open. *Where would the soldiers have gone?* Mary Magdalene's mind was reeling. *Why would the tomb be open?*

Quickly she surveyed the scene and hastily concluded that the body of Jesus had been taken away. Without further hesitation, she began running furiously. She ran for those who could help her. She ran for Peter and John.

Mary Magdalene took another path back into the city, leaving the other women behind. They remained in hiding until they were certain something must have happened to their friend. Fearing the worst, they made their way toward the garden tomb, trying not to be seen. They too were perplexed by the absence of the soldiers and by the open tomb, but it was concern for their friend that forced them to walk into the clearing.

Joanna and Mary entered the tomb, frightened by the unknown but driven by love; they would not run away. Scarcely conscious of anything but the missing body of their Lord, the women were greeted heartily by two gleaming angels who were waiting there. One sat at the head of the place where Jesus' body had been laid, the other at the feet.

"Do not be afraid," the first spoke to the women. "I know that you are looking for Jesus, who was crucified."

Petrified, the women fell to their knees with their faces to the ground.

"He is not here," the angel said. "He has risen from the dead, just as he said he would." He beckoned the ladies to look carefully. "Come in, see the place where he lay."

The women slowly stood and looked about them at the empty tomb. Jesus was not there, just as the luminous stranger had said.

The other angel spoke. "Why do you look for the living among the dead?" he asked. "He is not here; he has risen! Remember how he said to you that the Son of Man must be delivered into the hands of sinful men to be crucified, but on the third day he would be raised again?"

The women nodded, but the emotions of the hour brought only hazy recollections back to them.

Then the first angel said to them, "Go quickly and tell his disciples that Jesus is risen from the dead. Say to them, 'He will go ahead of you into Galilee. There you will see him.'"

The women quickly left the tomb, still not knowing quite what to think. While it was jumbled in their minds, they nevertheless bubbled with joy. Without looking back, without further conversation, the women began running toward the city to do what the angel had instructed them.

Even before Mary and Joanna had emerged from their hiding place, Mary Magdalene ran shouting into the home of John the disciple, where Peter and John were still sleeping.

"Peter!" she yelled "They've taken his body!"

"Wha-a-at?" Peter muttered as he stirred from a heavy slumber.

"What is the matter, woman?" asked John.

Mary of Magdala paused to catch her breath, then said calmly but with a sense of urgency, "They have taken the Lord out of the tomb, and I don't know where they've put him."

Peter and John grabbed their tunics and ran out the door without further discussion. Peter was first out the door, although the younger John easily out-ran him to the garden tomb.

But when John reached the deserted garden, he stopped outside the open tomb. He hesitated there, the unknown rendering him captive to his apprehensions. John did not enter but only stooped to look into the tomb. By now the rising sun was peeking over the eastern hills, and John could see the linen swaths lying in the tomb. However, the body was not there. The tomb was empty.

Within moments, Peter came trudging through the remains of the Roman encampment and into the garden. Without stopping he plunged into the tomb to examine its contents. Peter carefully looked from one end of the tomb to the other. He examined the burial cloths still wrapped together, layers of linen held together by lotion. Then Peter saw the napkin that would have been placed about the head of the deceased; it had been folded and placed at the other end of the tomb.

Following Peter's lead, John entered the tomb cautiously. He reached out to touch the burial cloths, rubbing his fingers over the smooth lotion; it was not yet caked or dried.

Peter said, "What does this mean?"

Without speaking, John thought, *Jesus is alive!* John knew what had happened and believed. He closed his eyes in grateful tears. *My Lord is not dead. My Lord is alive! He has risen from the dead as he promised.*

Back in the city, Mary Magdalene sat weeping on a bench; she was still winded. Her legs trembled with exhaustion after running from the tomb to John's house. After several minutes of rest and fanning herself, Mary slowly rose and stumbled haltingly into the street. She didn't know what to do or where to go.

Shopkeepers were busy opening their stores for business. Subdued whispers turned to boisterous talk in the streets. Here and there were small fires for boiling water and cooking breakfasts. But Mary was not interested in breakfast. She was lost in her thoughts, saying to herself, *What have they done with my Lord?*

She found herself inexplicably drawn to the tomb, not knowing why she was returning there. She had forgotten that she left her friends there, and she didn't know where Peter and John might be. Wandering aimlessly through the city, she missed the women returning from the tomb with the good news proclaimed by the angels. Mary's discouragement was wrapped up in her ignorance, and she didn't know what to do but return to the tomb.

When she arrived at the garden, she looked into the tomb through her tears and saw two men dressed in white sitting in the tomb where the body of Jesus had been laid.

"Why are you crying?" one of the men inquired.

Mary didn't know who these men were, but found it strange that she did not feel threatened by their presence. So she answered them, saying, "They have taken my Lord away." Then through her sobs, she added, "And I don't know where they have put him."

Instinctively, Mary became aware that someone was behind her. She turned to see a man standing there with a kind face and smiling eyes, but through her tears she did not recognize him. She assumed he was the gardener.

The man spoke. "Woman, why are you crying? Who are you looking for?"

"They have taken away the body of my Lord," she said. "Oh, sir, if you have carried him away, please tell me where you have put him, and I will go and get him." At the thought of his stolen body, Mary wept uncontrollably, her face in her hands.

Then the stranger said, "Mary."

She heard her name spoken. *How could the gardener know my name?* she thought. Then she thought she recognized his voice, and despair began to melt away and hope swelled within her. *Can it be?* Lifting her tear-stained face from her hands, Mary Magdalene looked directly into the eyes of Jesus, the same loving eyes that had first looked into her soul when he delivered her from the seven demons.

"Rabboni . . . ?" she whispered, using the name which she alone called Jesus, the affectionate Aramaic word for "teacher." A smile slowly spread across her face and her eyes widened. Then she cried out in joy, "Rabboni!" and instinctively fell at his feet, clutching them frantically. He was alive! Jesus was here, and she would not let him go.

"Do not hold on to me," Jesus said to Mary, "for I have not yet returned to the Father. Soon I will return to my Father and your Father, to my God and your God. Now go and tell my brothers what you have seen."

As Mary stood, wiping away her tears, Jesus smiled and said again, "Go."

She turned to run back into the city to tell of her risen Lord. She couldn't wait to tell his disciples that she had seen her Rabboni.

She went and told those who had been with Him, as they mourned and wept.

MARK 16:10

chapter eighty~six

HEARTS BURNING AT EMMAUS

LUKE 24:13-35

The early afternoon sun began to descend from its zenith on this spring day. The midday meal past, Cleopas and his wife departed the house of John, leaving Jerusalem to return to their home in Emmaus, a small village a few hours away by foot. As followers of Jesus, whom they called Christ, they were bewildered concerning the events of the day.

Jesus had been murdered and his disciples scattered. Only a handful of his followers had shown up that morning at John's home following the Sabbath. Some women had arrived there claiming to have seen Jesus that very day. Cleopas had not been an eyewitness to what had happened at the garden tomb and only knew what he was told. His love for Jesus was unshaken, but he had difficulty believing the reports from the women, who were understandably distraught. Cleopas believed nothing could be done, so he was returning home.

He and his wife exited the western gate, leaving behind them the blood-stained city where their Lord had died. For about half an hour, they walked up a narrow trail into the small hills until they reached a paved Roman road, the fresh scent of the mountain air invigorating them. On both sides of the road were country houses and farms, each one tidy according to Jewish expectation. At the fork in the road—where they would leave the paved highway to walk up a lovely valley in a northwesterly direction toward Emmaus—was an oasis where travelers could refresh themselves. A bridge over a gentle stream amid aromatic orange and lemon trees provided a pleasant respite for the weary traveler.

A festive mood filled the oasis, where a number of pilgrims had stopped on their way home from Jerusalem to Emmaus and other villages in the high-lands. Like Cleopas and his wife, they had spent eight days in Jerusalem as prescribed by the Law. Many had witnessed the triumphal entry of Jesus into Jerusalem on the first day of the week, and all had celebrated the Feast of the Passover on Friday. Earlier this same morning—Sunday morning—they had gathered at the Temple to see the priests wave the ceremonial offering of firstfruits before God.

Yet as Cleopas and his wife rested in the midst of the revelers, their long faces bore the marks of confusion. Their hearts were heavy as they left the oasis, talking of things that might have been. They spoke about great hope and dreams that had been trampled in death.

"Why are you so discouraged?" a stranger asked; he had walked up behind them unnoticed. "Tell me, what are you discussing?" he asked, smiling.

"Are you the only one in Jerusalem who hasn't heard?" Cleopas exclaimed incredulously. "Haven't you heard about the things that have happened in Jerusalem these last few days?"

"Tell me about them," the stranger replied, as they resumed their journey to Emmaus.

"Much has happened concerning Jesus of Nazareth," Cleopas began to tell his story. "Jesus was a prophet, powerful in word and deed before God and all the people." Cleopas told how the chief priests and rulers hated Jesus, condemned him to death and crucified him. Then Cleopas added his own sad outlook. "We had hoped that Jesus was the one who was going to redeem Israel and deliver us from Rome."

Then pausing a moment to gather his thoughts, Cleopas said with some measure of perplexity, "Today is the third day since all this took place. Certain women who followed Jesus went to his tomb early this morning, but his body was gone. They came to tell us they had seen a vision of angels, who said he was alive. Some of our companions went to the tomb and found it just as the women had said, but they did not see the angels, nor did they see Jesus."

The stranger listened to the litany of doubt from Cleopas, then said, "How foolish you are! Why are you slow to believe all that is written about Jesus by the prophets?" Now the stranger had their attention. "The Scriptures tell that the Messiah would have to suffer these things before entering into his glory."

Then the stranger began to explain to them from the books of Moses, the prophets and the Psalms all the prophecies concerning the Messiah—that he would be born, that he would offer himself as the redeemer of Israel, only to be rejected and subjected to a cruel death, but would be raised from the dead.

Cleopas and his wife were engrossed in the teaching of the stranger as they walked past several cottages entering Emmaus. Then Cleopas stopped and said, "This is our home." He pointed to the small, white-stoned house beside the road, but the stranger made as though he were going to continue walking.

"Wait!" Cleopas called after the stranger. "Please, stay with us, for it is nearly evening, and the day is almost over."

The stranger agreed and entered their home. And as they sat around the table, the stranger took a loaf of bread, gave thanks and then broke it and began to give it to them . . . just as he had with his disciples only three days earlier. At that moment, their eyes were opened, for they had been spiritually blinded. Cleopas and his wife recognized that the man they had walked and talked with that day was Jesus. They had been in the company of Jesus of Nazareth, but had not known it.

Jesus then vanished from their sight.

As they discussed this strange happening, Cleopas said to his wife, "Didn't our hearts burn within us while he talked with us on the road and opened the Scriptures to us?"

No longer hungry or tired from their long walk, they left the food on the table and hurried back to Jerusalem to tell the disciples what had happened. There they found the disciples, telling them, "It is true! The Lord is risen indeed and has appeared to us!"

> Then the two told what had happened on the way, and how Jesus was
> recognized by them when he broke the bread.
>
> LUKE 24:35, NIV

chapter eighty-seven

AN EVENING MEAL

JOHN 20:19-25

Throughout the afternoon that Sunday, the remaining apostles came out of hiding to make their way into the upper room. One by one they emerged because they heard rumors in the marketplace that the body of Jesus had been stolen; others had heard wild tales that the women had seen angels at the empty tomb. Some had heard that Mary of Magdala had actually seen Jesus and touched him.

Believing they may be in danger from the Sanhedrin, who were spreading the rumor that the disciples themselves had stolen the body, Peter had decided the house of John may not be safe, so he had left word there for the disciples to congregate in the upper room, where they had shared their last supper with Jesus. There, Peter and John waited for the others behind a locked door.

The evening had set in when an anxious knock sounded at the door. "Who is it?" demanded Philip, who was watching the door.

"Matthew," came the response. They all recognized the cultured voice of the former tax collector.

"Let him in," Peter said.

Philip counted heads. Ten were there, two were missing. Thomas was nowhere to be found. Some of them had hidden in the homes of relatives, others had gone to familiar places. But Thomas was a loner and no one knew where he was.

"Have you heard about Judas?" Philip asked the others. All eyes turned to Philip as he told them what he had been able to piece together from various rumors. Judas was dead, he explained, having hanged himself or jumped off a cliff. Apparently, he said, Judas had betrayed Jesus for thirty pieces of silver, then tried to return the money to the Temple as Jesus was hanging on the cross.

Philip rattled the door again to make sure it was locked. He didn't want any more surprises. A loaf of bread and some fish were set on the table with a flask of wine. The ten men gathered around the table to eat, each sitting at the place where he had been sitting during the Last Supper. But no one took the place where Jesus had sat. Whether they were aware of it or not, the place in the center was vacant, even though Jesus was at the center of their thoughts.

Again, they discussed the events of the day and the lies that had been spread by the Sanhedrin. As they ate, they talked about the report from Mary Magdalene, who claimed to have seen Jesus. Peter and John told everyone how the burial clothes were lying in their place and the cloth that was over his head was folded in another place.

It was at this time that Cleopas and his wife came to the door. After they told the amazing story of all they had seen and heard at Emmaus, John sent them back to his home and bade them spend the night there as his guest.

The disciples discussed this new development. If Jesus had appeared, they didn't understand why he did not come to them and talk with them. Some doubted whether Jesus had actually appeared in the flesh; they thought perhaps he might have manifested himself in his spirit. Still others thought these may be only dreams or visions.

Then, suddenly, Jesus was in their midst, standing at the central place at the table. "Peace be with you," he blessed them, lifting his hands.

Some of the men were startled, others terrified, but none could do anything but stare at him. They didn't know what to say.

Jesus said, "Why are you troubled? Why do you have doubts?" He held out his nail-pierced hands to them. "See for yourself. Look at my hands and my feet!" The disciples all craned to see the wounds where the nails had been driven into his flesh. "See? It is me!"

Young John reached out tentatively toward Jesus. "Touch me and see, a ghost does not have flesh and bones, as you can see I have."

John examined the wounds then looked into the eyes of Jesus. "Rabbi," he said, "it *is* you!"

The apostles were amazed and overjoyed, yet they dared not shout lest they be heard. Then Jesus asked, "Do you have anything here to eat?"

Left on the table was some broiled fish and sweet honeycomb. Jesus ate the fish then the honeycomb as the apostles watched. Clearly this was no spirit; they all knew it was Jesus in the flesh.

After he ate, Jesus taught these ten frightened men from the Scriptures concerning his purpose. "As my Father has sent me into the world, now I am sending you."

And he gave them their commission. "When people believe the message you preach concerning me, their sins will be forgiven them. Where your message is not received, the sins of the people will remain with them." Then Jesus breathed on them and said, "Receive the Holy Spirit."

Immediately, the Scriptures and the teachings of Jesus became clear to them, and they were bolstered with an inner strength they would need to carry them through the next few weeks.

Then Jesus disappeared from their sight.

Two days later, the apostles were huddled in the front room of John's home, still talking excitedly about the visitation from Jesus on Sunday evening. They had all seen him, but even now some of them were having second thoughts.

"Was that a knock at the door?" Philip heard a fearful, timid knock. He peeked through a crack in the door to see Thomas standing outside. Philip threw open the door to ask, "Where have you been?"

"Out of town," he sheepishly answered. "I knew the Roman soldiers could never find me out in the hills."

"We've seen the Lord," Philip blurted out the words as he ushered Thomas into the house. "Jesus is not dead. He is alive! The women saw him and we ate with him Sunday evening."

Thomas reacted with skepticism—this news was too much to believe. Thomas always had trouble believing what people told him unless he could see it with his own eyes. *If only Jesus were here*, he thought, *this would be wonderful news indeed*, but Thomas only shook his head from side to side in disbelief.

"But I touched him," John said. "I saw the wounds in his hands."

"It was him," Matthew piped up. "He was as real as anyone in this room." Then Matthew wrinkled his forehead. "But . . . ."

"But what?" Thomas demanded.

Matthew explained how the door had been locked and the windows secured, yet Jesus had appeared right in the middle of them. "We don't know how he got there . . . or how he vanished from our sight."

Thomas listened carefully to all the accounts, all the stories about the resurrected Jesus. He heard how Jesus had breathed the Holy Spirit into them, giving them spiritual understanding.

Thomas paused, because he had no desire to injure or slander his friends, but he would hear no more. "Unless I see the nail marks in his hands and put my finger into the print of the nails, unless I put my hand into his side where the spear pierced him, I will . . . not . . . believe it!"

Thomas apologized for his stubbornness, but he needed more than hearing stories. He spoke out of utter frustration. "I really want to believe . . . but it is difficult."

Thomas didn't listen to any more of their arguments, nor did he change his mind. He was more certain of his doubts than the apostles were of their experiences.

The other disciples therefore said to him, "We have seen the Lord." So he said to them, "Unless I see in His hands the print of the nails, and put my finger into the print of the nails, and put my hand into His side, I will not believe."

JOHN 20:25

chapter eighty-eight

JESUS AND THOMAS

JOHN 20:26-31

The week was filled with tension. The eleven were unsure where to go or what to do. Some wanted to return to Galilee, where Jesus had said he would appear to them, but most thought it best to stay in Jerusalem where they had last seen Jesus. They quarreled among themselves, even as they were ridiculed publicly by the ruling council. Despite their announcements to all that they had seen Jesus alive, rumors persisted that the disciples had stolen his body to make it appear he had returned from the dead.

Peter and the others were ridiculed in the marketplace and in the streets of Jerusalem with cries of "Thief!" and "Liar!" Thus far, they had not been physically assaulted, but the potential for violence was there and all the eleven felt it. So they made every effort not to be seen together in public and went out of their way to avoid the religious and Roman authorities.

They decided to come together again on Sunday to celebrate the day he had risen from the dead and appeared to them. One by one, they arrived at the upper room, knocking quietly on the door and identifying themselves.

When they were all together, Philip locked the door and went around to each window, making sure it was bolted shut. "We can't be too careful," Philip reasoned. "If the authorities know where to find us together, they could make trouble for us." The others nodded their heads in agreement.

Without Jesus to lead them, they didn't know who to turn to, who should give directions. Matthew, being the oldest of the eleven, finally spoke up. "Jesus has not appeared to us in seven days," he remarked. "We don't know where he is or what we are to do. Does anyone have a suggestion?"

Some suggested reading the Scriptures as they did in the synagogue, while others suggested prayers that were voiced in the Temple.

Without warning Jesus was standing in their midst once again. "Peace be with you!" he blessed them, smiling broadly.

The disciples rejoiced and praised God, their fears instantly erupting into smiles and heartfelt laughter. Jesus talked with them, as they excitedly gathered around him.

Then he turned to Thomas, who was standing alone, and instructed him, "Thomas, put your finger into the print of the nails in my hands." He opened his hands for all to see. There in the palm of his hands were the wounds left by the Roman nails.

"Reach out your hand and put it into my side," Jesus held back his tunic to reveal the wound caused by the spear.

The men in the room, embarrassed by their own unbelief, drew back. They glanced nervously at one another, trying not to look at the wounds.

Jesus said, "Thomas, can you believe in me without feeling my wounds?"

Thomas hesitated.

Jesus smiled and with love in his voice encouraged him, "Stop doubting and *believe*."

As Jesus stood there with hands held out exposing his wounds, Thomas dropped to his knees with tears in his eyes. "My Lord and my God!" he exclaimed.

Jesus accepted the faith of his doubting disciple. Then, placing his hands on Thomas' head, he said, "Because you have seen me and my wounds, you have believed. Many others will not see my wounds, and yet they will believe in me. Blessed are those who will not see and yet will believe."

Then as they enjoyed fellowship around the table—the same table where he first told them of his betrayal and death—Jesus again told them of the commission, saying, "Go into all the world and preach the gospel to every person."

He told them they were to take the message of Christ and his kingdom to every person. In his name, they would cast demons out of those who were possessed, they would heal the sick as he had done and they would speak with new tongues.

"And these signs will follow those who believe," he said.

Jesus did many other miraculous signs in the presence of his disciples, which are not recorded in this book. But these are written that you may believe that Jesus is the Christ, the Son of God, and that by believing you may have life in his name.

JOHN 20:30,31, *NIV*

chapter eighty-nine

ON A BEACH IN GALILEE

JOHN 21:1-25

Simon Peter stood alone in the courtyard of his home in Capernaum, staring wistfully at the small guest house where Jesus had often slept. Where was Jesus now? Jesus had disappeared from the upper room, leaving his inexperienced disciples with little more than a daunting task for which they all felt ill-equipped and ill-prepared. How were they supposed to teach an entire world, and what were they supposed to tell people?

They had no money to pay for the expenses of such an undertaking, since Judas Iscariot had pilfered all their money. Now the eleven were without money, without jobs and without courage. They knew they were to teach everyone about Jesus, but they had no idea how to go about it or where to begin.

In recent days, Peter had often found himself walking the streets of Capernaum, not knowing whether to turn left or right. He wanted to do *something* but felt helpless.

The evening of the Sabbath, Peter sat on an outcropping of rocks near the dock, looking south toward the beach where Jesus had first called him to be a fisher of men. The sun had already set, but it was not yet dark. Peter remembered the morning after he and Andrew had fished all night and caught nothing, when Jesus had come to them announcing, "Launch out into the deep and let down your nets for a catch."

Peter remembered his great laughter at the tremendous catch of fish that nearly burst their nets, then his stark terror at the realization that a worker of miracles was a passenger in his boat.

Before he met Jesus, Peter had never known greater satisfaction than when he was fishing. Suddenly, he knew what he would do. He rushed up the road and ran into his house, where Andrew, John, James, Nathanael, Philip and Thomas were sitting around the table talking.

"I am going fishing," Peter announced. He looked around the room to ask, "Who's going with me?"

The clouds hung low over the Sea of Galilee that evening. There was no moon, no stars—a perfect night for fishing. On dark nights the fish came closer to the surface to feed.

"We'll fill our nets tonight!" Peter declared as they prepared their nets and sails for their first time fishing in almost three years. Philip, Nathanael and Thomas, while not practiced fishermen, had lived near the sea all their lives and knew their way around a boat.

Peter and James put their strong shoulders to the boat to push away from the shore. The sand crunched beneath them until the boat floated free, then the sail caught the stiff wind and they were off.

That night, they let their nets down shallow and deep, near the shore and in the middle of the lake. But they caught nothing.

In desperation, they threw their nets among the reeds along the shore; still they caught nothing.

Not one fish.

It was as though all the fish had fled the Sea of Galilee for fresher waters.

When the stars in the eastern sky began to fade, the fishermen looked at one another in resignation. Dawn was coming soon, and they certainly wouldn't catch anything after that, so they headed for shore.

But as they drew near to Capernaum, they heard a shout from the beach about a hundred yards away. "Have you caught anything?" A stranger was standing on the beach calling to them.

Peter wanted to ignore him, not wanting to admit failure. But his more affable brother Andrew yelled back, "Nothing!"

"Throw your net down on the right side of the boat," the voice came back clearly in the still morning air.

The moment was familiar, and Peter felt his heart stir. He then snapped at the others, "Quick, pull the net out of the water!" The men went to work feverishly. "Throw it over the other side!" Peter urged them.

Even before the net was fully submerged, a school of fish churned in the mesh.

"Pull!" Peter barked his orders. "Pull . . . put your back into it!"

But there were so many fish already in the net that seven strong men, straining with all their might, could not get the net into the boat.

John looked at Peter and shouted, "It's the Lord! That's Jesus on the shore!"

Without thinking, Peter reached for his tunic and slipped it on. Then in one swift motion, he dove into the water and with long, powerful strokes began swimming toward the shore. Peter had to get to Jesus. *I will not fail the Lord again!* he thought.

Back at the boat, Andrew and James manned the oars, pulling the boat through the water, while the others held the net taut, towing the massive catch to shore.

Peter splashed onto the beach to where Jesus sat by a small charcoal fire, warming himself. Jesus had some bread and one small fish cooking on the fire.

"Help us!" young John called to Peter from the water.

Jesus said to Peter, "Bring some of the fish you have just caught. Add them to mine, and we'll have breakfast together."

So Peter waded out into the shallow water. In his exuberance, he grabbed a rope holding the net and, with his mighty shoulders and legs, dragged the net full of fish through the shallow water onto the shore.

As his disciples disembarked, Jesus called to them, "Come and have breakfast!"

Their doubts, their questions faded away as Jesus took the bread, broke it and handed it to each of them. Then he removed the fish from the fire and passed the baked fish to each man, and together they had breakfast.

After the meal, the disciples expected their master would teach them again. During the three years they had spent with Jesus, it had been his custom to instruct them in his kingdom as they sat digesting their food. After meals was usually a time when they asked many questions.

But this time, Jesus asked a question. He turned to Simon Peter to ask, "Simon, do you love me?"

In the question, Jesus used the word for a deep, abiding love like a mother has for her children. Despite his exuberance at seeing Jesus again, Peter knew his own weakness. He had denied even knowing Jesus only hours after he had boasted that he was willing to die for his master. So Peter answered Jesus using the term of affection as one friend might have for another.

"Yes, Lord, you know I am fond of you."

"Feed my lambs," Jesus said to him.

Then Jesus asked a second time, "Simon, do you truly love me?"

Peter was grieved that the Lord had to ask him a second time. Still Peter knew in his heart how superficial was his love. So Peter again answered, "Lord, you know that I care for you."

"Take care of my sheep," said Jesus.

The others did not get involved in the conversation; their eyes stared at the small flames of the fire. No one looked at Peter, and no one looked at the Lord lest he challenge them with the same question.

Then Jesus asked the same question of Peter, this time using the same term of affection that Peter had used. "Simon, do you care for me?"

Peter was hurt, because Jesus had asked him three times, just as he had denied the Lord three times. But truth, like a light, cannot be hid under a bushel, and Peter could not keep sin in his heart. He answered, "Lord, you know all things. You know I love you, but . . . ."

"Feed my sheep," Jesus said, putting his hand on Peter's shoulder. There was forgiveness in his smile and resoluteness in his eyes. Jesus had named the man Peter, and on this rock he *would* build his church.

"When you were younger," Jesus said, "you dressed yourself and went wherever you wanted to go. But when you grow old, you will stretch out your hands and someone else will dress you, and they will lead you where you do not want to go. Things will change."

Peter looked into the eyes of his master as Jesus said, "By this I mean they will nail you to a cross, and that is how you will die. And by your death you will glorify God."

Peter heard these sobering words, but he would stand firm in his faith. Jesus was giving him a second chance and Peter knew this time he was willing to die for the Lord.

Jesus saw the fire of commitment in Peter's eyes. He smiled again at Peter, reminding him, "Follow me!"

After his suffering, [Jesus] showed himself to these men and gave many
convincing proofs that he was alive. He appeared to them over a period
of forty days and spoke about the kingdom of God.

ACTS 1:3, NIV

chapter ninety

WHEN HE SHALL COME

MATTHEW 28:16-20
ACTS 1:4-11

A gentle breeze tousled the grass where the eleven sat waiting atop the hill overlooking the Sea of Galilee. From here they could see Tiberias directly to the south and Capernaum off to the north. Behind them lay the large white limestone rock from which Jesus had preached what would become known as the Sermon on the Mount.

"Greetings!" Jesus hailed his disciples from where he sat on the rock. No longer startled by his sudden appearances—Jesus had told the disciples he would see them here—the eleven smiled and gathered around Jesus to hear him teach. In the distance, the city of Tiberias bustled with afternoon commerce on this first day of the week. Only a few clouds hung in the deep blue sky. It had been a week since the disciples breakfasted with Jesus on the beach in Galilee.

Jesus said to them, "All authority has been given to me in heaven and on earth, and now I give you authority to teach in my name. Therefore, go and make disciples of all nations, baptizing them in the name of the Father and of the Son and of the Holy Spirit, teaching them to obey everything I have commanded you."

The eleven looked at one another. They had been comfortable teaching about the Messiah and his kingdom in Jewish communities, but they had now been told to go out among the Gentiles with this message.

But Jesus knew their doubts and said, "Go to every part of the world, to every tribe and people, preaching the gospel to men and women of every color and every tongue. Teach them of repentance and the forgiveness of sins."

"How can we teach an entire world?" Nathanael asked, daunted by this formidable assignment. "Will you not be with us?"

"I will not be present in the flesh," Jesus told them. "Nevertheless, I will be with you in Spirit . . . always . . . even to the ends of the earth."

Two weeks later, the eleven gathered at Jerusalem in the upper room, now a convenient place for them to assemble. The warm spring morning encouraged them as they prepared to sit down for a midday meal.

"I look forward to seeing Jesus again," Thomas told the others.

"Do you think he will appear today?" John asked with anticipation.

Then Jesus was standing there. "Peace be with you, my friends," he blessed them, then sat down to eat with them. When they finished the meal, Jesus gave his disciples a new command.

"Do not leave Jerusalem," he said. "For I am going to send you the gift of the Holy Spirit. Then I will send you out into the world to preach the truth. But stay in the city until you have been clothed with power from on high. For John baptized with water, but in a few days you will be baptized with the Holy Spirit."

Then, once again, Jesus gave them a commission to go everywhere to persuade people of the world to follow him and to enter the kingdom of God.

"But what shall we preach?" Nathanael asked. "What shall we tell the people that will persuade them to follow you?"

"Tell them the Son of Man came to suffer for the forgiveness of their sins, but that he arose on the third day to give them new life," Jesus said. "Teach them the repentance and forgiveness of sins. Tell them to turn from their sins and believe in me, and they will experience life more abundantly."

It was late afternoon when they left the upper room. Jesus walked with them from Jerusalem toward Bethany and the Mount of Olives.

"Lord, will you restore Israel and establish your kingdom on earth at this time?" Andrew asked. After all, Jerusalem was still patrolled by Roman soldiers and the Jews still paid taxes to Rome. The people of Jehovah still did not rule the Promised Land.

Jesus didn't answer immediately but continued walking, passing over the spring flood runoff of the Brook of Kidron and beginning the climb up Olivet. Near the summit, he turned to look on the city he loved—Jerusalem. Finally, Jesus answered, "It is not for you to know the time or seasons under God's authority or when he will return the kingdom of David to this land."

"What will happen to us?" Philip asked.

"As I said, you will receive power to go into all the world to preach the gospel," Jesus said. "You will be my witnesses in Jerusalem, then in all Judea and Samaria and to the ends of the earth."

At last, John felt he understood. Their mission was not to drive the Romans from Palestine or to reestablish the throne of David; they were to conquer hearts with the message of the Lord's death, burial and resurrection. They were to preach the message of everlasting life: that at death, believers would enter heaven.

Then Jesus lifted his hands to bless his disciples. Then slowly he began to lift off the ground, higher and higher, ascending to heaven.

Jesus did not vanish like the other times, John thought. *This time he is returning to the Father. We will not see him again until his return to earth.*

Jesus ascended slowly, his hands still raised in blessing. John wanted to say good-bye, but the moment demanded silence. No one spoke; no one took their eyes off Jesus.

Finally, a cloud blocked their vision, and John could no longer see him, yet he thought he knew what was happening at this moment. While the other apostles searched the sky for Jesus, young John looked into his heart to watch Jesus' triumphal return to heaven. He knew that the angels were greeting him with shouts of "Hallelujah!" and that the Father would arise from his throne to meet his beloved Son. John could almost hear God say, "Sit at my right hand, while I make your enemies your footstool."

The apostles stood a long time, staring up into the sky, watching and wondering. Then their thoughts were interrupted by two men in white who appeared beside them saying, "Men of Galilee, why do you stand gazing up at the sky? Has he not given you your commission?" The heavenly messenger then commanded, "Return to Jerusalem. Tarry in prayer. The Holy Spirit will come on you, then preach with power the message of Jesus."

The apostles knew in their hearts this was the end of their time on earth in the presence of Jesus. Their time of instruction was over, and soon they must go to work. Soon they would go into all the world to preach the gospel with joy.

The heavenly messenger smiled on them and promised, "This same Jesus, who has been taken from you into heaven, will come again. In the same way you have seen him ascend into heaven, he shall return."

Even so, come, Lord Jesus!
REVELATION 22:20

Epilogue

THAT WHICH WAS FROM THE BEGINNING, WHICH

WE HAVE HEARD, WHICH WE HAVE SEEN WITH OUR

EYES...THESE THINGS WE WRITE TO YOU THAT

YOUR JOY MAY BE FULL.

1 JOHN 1:1,4

You have just read the story of Jesus of Nazareth—not a history of Jesus, but a Jesus story that, like a film, portrays many significant events from a life to tell the story. *The Son* is one story made up of many stories, just as many threads are woven to make a rope—in this case, a rope of salvation that stretches from heaven to reach the lost souls of this world.

Within these pages, I have not said everything about Jesus that could be said. I have left out many of the events recorded in the gospels. Some of the long sermons are not included, and some of the many parables are missing. A number of people to whom Jesus talked were also not included. Yet everything that Jesus did while on earth was important and nothing can be omitted from a complete history of Jesus.

However, this is a story—the Jesus story. I tried to include everything you need to know to love Jesus . . . to believe Jesus . . . to begin to follow Jesus. I tried to write a story that will help you feel the life of Jesus, see the world as He saw it and experience His life and death and resurrection.

As you read *The Son*, you may have noticed that I have in fact added a few people who might have talked with Jesus and I have imagined some conversations they may have shared. None of these additions is contrary to what is found in the Bible, nor do they deny or take away from Scripture, but rather are included like props on a stage to focus attention on the actors and the story that's being acted out on the stage.

I have tried to be accurate in portraying the facts as provided in the Bible and in no place has the Bible been intentionally changed. Many of the customs and religious traditions of the Jewish people are included for those who may not be familiar with the culture in which Jesus lived and taught. My primary source for details of these customs was a most wonderful book, *The Life and Times of Jesus the Messiah* by Alfred Edersheim. Born in Vienna in 1825 to Jewish parents, Edersheim was converted to Christianity as a young man and became one of the leading authorities of his time regarding the historic doctrines and practices of Judaism. I have relied on his insights to color in the background of the story to help you see the hue and texture of these events.

I began teaching on the life of Christ in 1958 and have spent a lifetime researching the books of the New Testament. I don't know that I am always correct in my interpretation of Jesus, but I've tried to be as accurate as my research and reading allow. I do not know that Edersheim was always right in his interpretations, nor do I know that you will be correct in your interpretations. But I must write the truth as accurately as I know it.

The events in *The Son* are taken from the four Gospels: Matthew, Mark, Luke and John. Each Gospel writer has given us a somewhat different rendering of Jesus as told from his point of view. None of the four books contains everything there is to know about Jesus, just as my story does not. While the events of His life are not always conveyed by the Gospel writers in a clear, specific chronological order, I believe the four Gospels do not contradict one another and are always accurate. Why then have we been given four versions of essentially the same story? Why couldn't one author capture for us all we needed to know about Christ? Because the Gospels enhance one another, just as four children in a family will tell a different story about the new baby that's just been born into the family. You must read all four to piece together a complete picture of Jesus.

As for the chronological placement of the events of the life of Christ, I have generally followed the storyline of Jesus that is presented by Edersheim in the aforementioned *Life and Times of Jesus the Messiah*, and I have also relied on A. T. Robertson's *A Harmony of the Gospels*. These two authorities lived more than one hundred years apart, yet their versions of events in the life of Jesus follow a very similar sequence.

The most important thing about the story of Jesus is not the details, nor is it what the people said or the exact sequence of events. The most important thing is Jesus Himself. The apostle John tells us, "He who has the Son has life" (1 John 5:12). My prayer is that you meet Jesus in *The Son*. Remember, on the last day He taught in the Temple, some Greeks came seeking Jesus. Their petition was: "We would see Jesus." May this also be your desire, and I hope my petition was answered in your life as you read this humble work.

May you have seen Jesus.

And there are also many other things that Jesus did, which if they were written one by one, I suppose that even the world itself could not contain the books that would be written. Amen.

JOHN 21:25

ABOUT THE AUTHOR

E. L. Towns is dean of the School of Religion at Liberty University in
Lynchburg, Virginia, where he teaches the 2,000-member Pastor's Sunday
School class at Thomas Road Baptist Church. He is a Gold Medallion
Award-winning author whose books include *Fasting for Spiritual
Breakthrough* and *My Father's Names*. E. L. Towns and his wife, Ruth,
have three grown children.

etowns@elmertowns.com

ALSO BY

E. L. Towns

THE NAMES OF JESUS

MY FATHER'S NAMES

THE NAMES OF THE HOLY SPIRIT

FASTING FOR SPIRITUAL BREAKTHROUGH

PRAYING THE LORD'S PRAYER FOR
SPIRITUAL BREAKTHROUGH

MY ANGEL NAMED HERMAN